For the ones who share my home and my heart — your love, your laughter, your questions, and your chaos made this book possible.

With deep gratitude to DMJK for your constant encouragement. And to all the friends who helped shape this book, thank you.

The Last Good Queen of These United States

Adam Owenby

Moosebane Press

— First Paperback Edition —

Published by

MOOSEBANE PRESS

Printed in the United States of America

10 9 8 7 6 5 4 3 2 1
First Printing

Library of Congress Cataloging-in-Publication Data
Owenby, Adam. *The Last Good Queen of These United States* / Adam Owenby.
— First edition. South Windsor, CT : Moosebane Press™, 2025.
www.moosebanepress.com
Cover art by Billy Design.
ISBN 979-8-9987035-0-8 (paperback) | ISBN 979-8-9987035-1-5 (hardback)
    1.   United States—Fiction. 2. Revolution—Fiction. 3. Alternate
            history—Fiction. 4. Empires—Fiction. 5. Dystopias—Fiction. 6.
            Science fiction. I. Title.
PS3615.O94 L37 2025
813'.6—dc23
Library of Congress Control Number: 2025908026

CHAPTER ONE

*The authors and promoters of this desperate conspiracy
have laboured to inflame my people in America... It is now
become the part of wisdom and in its effect of clemency, to
put a speedy end to these disorders by decisive exertions.*
King George III, Speech to Parliament —Fall 1775

New York, Capital of the British Empire —Fall 2052

S HE SLAMMED THE DOOR SO hard that the glass cracked across
the frame. The noise startled her, and for half a breath, she was
distracted from the anger that had led her to Carl's office.

"What the hell, Alex?" Carl barked.

Alexandra Baker hated crying, but tears welled in her eyes, her
jaw clenching. Crying was just one of those things that couldn't be
helped. Despite all her years of training, her discipline, and the
instincts drilled into her, it was harder to suppress than pain or
exhaustion.

She turned her face slightly and took in the pale, sad, gray office
with no art on the walls, no knickknacks, nothing to show that Carl

had worked there for eleven years. It reminded her of briefing rooms she'd once sat in, stark and cold, designed to strip away distractions. The midday sun streamed in through the cracks in the blinds and reflected off the glistening on her cheeks. You can't hate your tears enough to stop them, she thought.

Alex wiped her eyes with the back of her sleeve and turned back toward her boss, who alternated between staring awkwardly down at his desk, past her to the broken door, and then back again, always avoiding eye contact.

"Screw you," she said through clenched teeth. "I'm not giving up on this story!"

She had known that writing such an article would be controversial. She had even expected resistance from her editor, Carl. But he was uncharacteristically mean. She'd come back now, ready to fight. But his earlier meanness felt brittle, forced. She saw the flicker in his eyes when he glanced at the door—he was scared.

"Listen, Alex," Carl said, his tone softer now. He realized he'd gone too far earlier. "It's just not going to happen. You know the sedition laws as well as I do, and I'm not going to jail over something like this. Hell, I'm not letting you go back to jail. You're not going to put me, or the paper, in this kind of jeopardy again."

Carl swiveled his chair sideways as if to say the conversation was over. Alex stood for a moment, glaring at him, eyes still brimming, jaw still clenched. She paused for a minute, thinking about what to do next. Abruptly, she gathered her materials, turned, and slammed the door one more time for good measure. Glass crackled onto the floor as she walked away.

The newsroom was loud, but Carl's voice still managed to cut through it. Alex grabbed her bag and kept her head down. No use staying within range—of his shouting or his excuses. She didn't slam the drawer shut, didn't say goodbye. Just walked.

She was halfway to the elevator when Ben caught up, a crease between his brows.

"That bad, huh?" he asked.

She didn't slow. "I don't want to talk about it."

He matched her pace, weaving through desks and cables without another word. His silence followed her into the hallway, then into the elevator. Only once the doors closed did he put an arm around her and kiss her temple, gently, as if she might break.

Her throat tightened. She leaned into his shoulder, eyes shut, riding the thirty-nine floors down in silence.

The words of her article ran through her mind like a headline she couldn't unsee. Corruption in the palace. Rerouted funds. Supplies disappearing under the noses of the Crown's most loyal commanders. Her sources had been clear—and scared. Low-level accountants in the Exchequer's office who'd shown her the numbers, circled them in red.

She had written it clean. Tightly sourced. Classic work.

And Carl had buried it.

Embarrassing the Crown wasn't a charge, exactly. Just a mistake you weren't supposed to make. And he hadn't even tried to pretend otherwise. She might not be in jail this time, but the message had landed.

When the elevator doors opened, her face was calm again.

"Let's go get some lunch," Ben said, tone light, his hand a little firmer than usual on her elbow.

She let him steer her through the lobby and out into the gray. A wind cut down the avenue like a blade. The sky hung low, the color of wet cement.

On the corner, three of the King's officers stood around a brazier, warming their hands. Their rifles hung loose on their shoulders. Alex recognized one instantly—Marby.

Uniform or not, he always looked like someone playing a part. The smirk, the weightless posture, the sense that the sidewalk itself should salute him.

He cracked a joke. The other two laughed, low and mean. The youngest muttered something and they laughed again, louder.

Beside her, Ben tensed. His gait faltered. Just slightly—but enough.

Alex kept walking.

That was the difference. He feared them.

She didn't.

"Oh, my. Now look who it is."

Marby's voice oiled its way across the street, loud enough to make people look.

She didn't flinch. Not until he stepped forward and took off his hat with a bow that dripped sarcasm.

"Our Lord's favorite little intrepid slanderer."

More laughter. Another private remark. Jackals, the lot of them.

Ben's grip tightened on her hand.

Marby turned theatrically, playing to the street. "Gentlemen, may I present Ms. Alexandra Baker of the *Courier and Post*, and more recently, Prisoner 78261 of the Staten Island Jail."

A woman crossing with her child turned away sharply. No one stopped. No one ever did.

Marby watched their reaction with delight.

He turned back to her, smile like a knife. "It seems lockup has done much for your attitude, Ms. Baker. I've heard no rejoinder, no malapert remark. A rarity for a woman..."

He paused, savoring the setup.

"...of your particular temperament."

Her fists clenched.

He wanted her to snap. He wanted a reaction. A mistake. And for half a second, she almost gave it to him.

But Ben tugged her forward.

"Not worth it," he muttered, voice tight.

They crossed on the green. Behind them, Marby barked out a laugh.

"Oh, come now, Ms. Baker. No parting words? No brilliant exposé for tomorrow's paper?"

Ben pulled faster. She let him.

She didn't look back until they reached the curb.

Marby was still there. Hat still in hand. Still grinning.

And then he raised one hand and pantomimed writing something down.

She stopped. For a moment, the wind didn't seem so cold.

He knew.

About the article. About the story Carl had buried. About the sources. About the threat it posed.

That gesture—so quiet, so mocking—said everything:

We see you. We know what you're doing. And we'll be waiting.

Alex turned away, jaw tight.

She didn't look back again.

At the *Hop and Pig*—their sometimes-bar, not too loud, never too empty—Alex sat hunched over the table, arms crossed. Her shoulders were stiff, her mouth tight, and she barely looked up until the food arrived. She took a few bites in silence. Gradually, color returned to her voice.

Within the hour, she was leaning across the table, recounting how her old college roommate had just had a baby. "I can't remember what they named him—something absurd, probably," she said with a small laugh. "Back at Oxford, Libby swore she'd never have children. She said she'd rather raise cats and cocktails."

Ben smiled faintly, stirring his drink more than sipping it. He was half-listening, watching her carefully. Relief crept into his features as her voice grew animated again.

Then he froze.

At first, Alex didn't notice. She kept talking. But the pub had gone unnervingly quiet, and her voice sounded too loud in the hush. She trailed off, turned—and saw Ben's expression.

Wide-eyed. Locked on something behind her.

"All rise for His Majesty, King Frederick!"

The voice cracked like a whip. Chairs scraped, sharp and frantic. Glasses rattled. Dozens of people shot to their feet at once, hats torn off and clutched to chests like talismans.

Alex didn't move.

Ben was already standing, but his hand shot down to her wrist, gripping hard. His fingers were ice. "Alex," he said under his breath, strained and urgent.

She stared straight ahead.

Someone nearby cleared their throat—a warning disguised as politeness. She could feel the tension radiating from the man next to her, his knuckles white around his pint. He wasn't looking at her. He was looking at the guards.

She speared another bite of salad and chewed, slow and deliberate.

The door slammed open. Wood on wood, hollow and violent. Two of the King's guards stepped inside, rifles slung but ready, faces carved from stone. Three attendants followed, their coats gleaming gold in the fake candlelight, every thread declaring importance.

And then, King Frederick.

He moved like gravity bent around him, tall and broad in his fur-lined coat, a feathered hat crowning his presence. The warmth in the room seemed to recoil. Conversations died mid-sentence. The space shrank.

The announcer stood stiffly, drawing a thin padfolio from his pouch like it contained scripture. He bowed and presented it with both hands. The King accepted it without ceremony, pushing up his gold-rimmed spectacles to scan the room.

His gaze settled on the barkeep.

"It is my wish," he said, his tone deliberate and theatrical, "to meet with interesting meals in novel places. And whilst I am not oft able to take time from my duties to the realm, even I must away, from time to time."

He didn't blink. "Are you John Norcamp?"

The barkeep bowed deeply, staring at his shoes. "Yes, Your Majesty."

"Wonderful!" the King said, his grin wide but empty. "I have come for a roast pork meal and a stout."

"We'd be honored, Your Majesty," Norcamp stammered.

No tables were open. Alex had noticed.

So had the King.

Two businessmen in the corner moved without being asked, scooping up their plates and vanishing like smoke.

One man didn't move fast enough.

The older regular near the door struggled to rise. His cane caught. His knee buckled. Too slow.

One of the guards stepped forward.

The crack of the rifle butt into the man's gut echoed like a breaking bone.

He collapsed with a wheeze, pint glass shattering beside him. His mouth opened, but no sound came out. He clutched his ribs, kneeling, face pale.

The guard returned to his place, unbothered.

Silence.

Ben stood trembling. He hadn't let go of Alex's wrist.

She kept chewing.

Then, slowly, she stood.

She did not bow.

She did not avert her eyes.

Frederick's gaze found her and lingered. He didn't move. He didn't speak. But something behind his stare shifted—something cold, clinical. He studied her like a pinned insect, unmoving and unamused.

And then, with a flick of disinterest, he turned.

The announcer crossed to the vacated table and began to set it formally, laying silverware with reverent care.

The spell broke. Chairs creaked. Conversations restarted, low and uneasy. Some patrons whispered excitedly, delighted by proximity to royalty. Most simply ate faster and disappeared.

Alex didn't speak. Her hands itched for a pen, a pad, anything to trap the moment in words.

But she wouldn't need it.

She would remember all of it. Every single detail.

On the sidewalk, a small crowd was gawking at the line of limousines hovering in front of the pub. A few were capturing holos of themselves while guards glared openly at them. No one got too close. Alex looked disparagingly at the crowd. *Idiots*, she thought to herself. Ben knew what she was thinking and suggested they move on.

Alex had decided to work from home the rest of the afternoon. She and Ben started walking the nine blocks to her apartment. The clouds were rolling in thickly, and the wind had suddenly picked up, biting at her ears and the tip of her nose. She wrapped a scarf around her neck and ears and moved closer to Ben, who seemed oblivious to the cold. Cars and buses rolled slowly by, with a traffic jam building due to the lanes blocked by the King's convoy.

"I wish I had said something to him," said Alex. "He's vile, and no one speaks truth to him."

Ben glanced around cautiously. "Are you trying to get locked up again? Or worse?" he whispered to her.

She sighed, "I know, but something has to change. People have to wake up to this."

"We both know they already have… five times already. I mean, look what happened in Texas."

Texas, she thought. That could have been the start of something great. Just a decade ago, Texas had become the latest of the colonies to declare independence. They had the backing of the Spanish and the French, with troops already stationed there, before declaring. This was something none of the other rebellions had achieved. People had flocked from all over the Empire to support the effort. Alex had been there. An accomplished officer in the British military, she knew how to lead and how to shoot. With the rebels, she rose in the ranks quickly and was a colonel at age thirty-five. Though she lived in a completely different world now, she still had the hard edges that her years of military experience had provided.

Initially, the Empire had sent troops to quell the rebellion. But the Spanish and French reinforcements were able to force a protracted stalemate. Eventually, the crown began blockading the highways and ports and arresting people trying to make their way across the border. Some of them were merely trying to get home and didn't have a rebellious bone in their body. But they were hanged, the same as the other "traitors." Gallows hAad been erected roadside all along the highways and the bodies left there for the duration of the war as a warning to those who might think about making their way to the Republic of Texas.

The war had started, they now knew, before the Spaniards had even arrived in Galveston. King Frederick had easily tracked their journey across the Atlantic and didn't fall for their fleet feigning diplomatic and humanitarian interest in Brazil. The King had thought better of it and had quietly tripled his garrisons in Houston, months before the declaration had been finalized. Delays caused by infighting between the Texans and the French over post-independence terms had given the King even more time to make preparations and be better informed by his spies. By the time the campaign had begun in earnest, the rebels were hopelessly outnumbered eight to one. That led to desperation.

During the long stalemate, the rebels began to lose numbers to attrition and fatigue. As a last-ditch effort, they detonated a nuclear bomb at the fort at Brownwood, in a bid to make the cost of war too high for the King. But the King did not relent. Survivors said Dallas was bombed beyond recognition in retaliation. Millions fled their homes. Many took up arms knowing that fighting was their only hope.

But the crackdown was brutal and absolute. And after losing twenty-one thousand men in eight months, the Spanish had had enough and, being threatened by the 9th British Fleet at home, withdrew their support. The logistics and supplies the French had been providing was being successfully blockaded by the 3rd Fleet. Soon, starved of supplies, allies, and soldiers, the Texan government agreed to a summit with the King's envoy to discuss terms. Though they had been permitted to travel under diplomatic cover, upon arriving in Wichita, many were shot on sight. Norcross Garland, the first President of the Independent Republic of Texas, was assassinated by British snipers the moment he stepped from his car. His Secretary of State, Leland Anderson, was seized and dragged to New York to personally stand before the enraged King. To his credit, Secretary Anderson remained loyal to the cause, and before being shot in the head, he had reportedly begun to recite the *Nine Grievances*. He had been dragged out to the palace balcony by a guard, still reciting. He made it to number four when the King himself shot Anderson. His body fell over the balcony's edge. This dramatic anecdote was retold time and again in dissident circles and was captured in a plea letter sent to embassies around the world by the famous anonymous writer using the pen name, "*Captain Lessmore*," an old joke from the Texan navy, who did more with less. Enraged at the breach of international law, the Generals in Texas tried to rally support from allies and the international community, but hopelessly so. The appetite for total war with the Empire had waned.

The decapitation of leadership was devastating. Attrition in the volunteer army became unsustainable as tens of thousands of Texans realized the end was at hand and decided that to live and fight another day was better than dying uselessly in a failed bid. But another day never came. The permanent presence of British regulars, even now, was greater than in the capital. The guns of the people had been confiscated, holdouts were hanged or, terrifyingly, quartered alive in public. The King had decreed new laws concerning "rebellious thought," which had, in practice, been a blank check for summary execution of troublemakers, real and perceived, by the new Texas Governor.

Alex shook her head and sighed, "We have to keep fighting. There has to be a way."

They walked past the *Elios Church of England Cathedral*, the largest church in New York, just as it tolled the hour. The loudspeakers began the daily message. People on the street stopped and stood in place. Many, though not all, removed their hats despite the fact that snow was falling steadily now. Alex kept walking, Ben hesitating before going with her. The King's prerecorded voice bellowed in the square:

"The surest way to happiness is in obedience to God and His Earthly emissary, our King." The bell chimed the melody to '*God Save the King,*' and then people continued on their way.

Suddenly, they heard a loud explosion from near the pub they'd left only moments earlier. They were too far away to see anything other than the thick plume of smoke billowing up from the street. Sirens called out and sentry drones buzzed by at alarming speeds. Alex began running toward the commotion.

Ben called out for her to stop, but she shouted back, "I'm a journalist, dammit!"

The carnage was overwhelming. The acrid stench of burned flesh and explosives clung to the air, thick and suffocating. Dozens of wounded staggered aimlessly, their faces frozen in shock, eyes unfocused. Blood pooled in a massive crater at the center of the street, dark and glistening under the gaslights. Limbs—some small, some large—were strewn haphazardly across the pavement like discarded dolls. The King's limousines were gone, vanishing like specters in the chaos, and yet, somehow, the *Hop and Pig* remained untouched.

Alex moved forward, her boots sticking slightly to the pavement where the blood had begun to congeal. She reached the nearest person, a woman clutching her arm, trembling violently.

"What the hell happened?" Alex demanded.

The woman turned, her face pale and smeared with soot. Her lips quivered. "It was a suicide bomber. He got close before they shot him, but..." She hesitated, swallowing hard. "*Unfortunately*, he didn't get the King."

Alex arched a brow. The woman's eyes widened in horror, realizing what she had just said. "I, I mean, *fortunately*. Of course."

She was shuddering uncontrollably now, her breath coming in short, sharp gasps. Alex took a step closer and that's when she saw it: the woman's right hand was gone.

"You're hurt!" Alex crouched beside her, pressing down on the raw, mangled stump where her wrist had once been. Blood leaked between the woman's trembling fingers, dripping onto the sidewalk.

The woman whimpered, her body sagging. She was losing too much blood.

Alex yanked off her belt and fastened it above the wound, pulling tight. The woman gasped in pain, her knees buckling, but Alex held her steady. Their eyes met—two strangers caught in the same nightmare, fear reflected in both their gazes.

Alex worked quickly. This wasn't the first severed limb she'd treated in the field.

As she secured the tourniquet, a medical droid whirred to life beside them, its artificial voice calm and sterile: "Emergency response initiated. Please step back."

Alex exhaled, blood and ash smeared across her arms, her sweat-dampened hair clinging to her face. She pushed to her feet, her legs aching, and pulled out her pad. She needed to capture this. The world had to see.

She lifted the camera, her hands steady despite the horror unfolding around her. The redcoats had arrived, forming a perimeter, shouting orders as they began to clear the square.

Ben finally caught up with her, breathless, eyes darting between her blood-covered hands and the devastation around them.

"Alex," he murmured, barely above a whisper.

She ignored him.

She kept filming.

Back at their apartment, Alex began scanning the latest releases from the official news service, navigated to her own paper's page, and then opened several others, pulling up multiple projections at once. As usual, there were few differences in the reporting between the official news service and the so-called "free press reports." Usually, the only differences consisted of more entertainment news and gossip pieces. On a typical day, it would be the coverage of Parliament's debates on some meaningless pieces of legislation, which received only cursory mention and a little pro-monarchy analysis.

But now, all the coverage was about the attempted assassination of the King. Most of the services were incorrectly reporting details as simple as the location. But all had noted that the King had escaped, though three guards had died at the scene. Alex had submitted her own eyewitness report back to her paper, but it had been drowned out in the other coverage.

She began skimming to see what the other news was, prior to the bombing. As usual, it was all pro-monarchy commentary. Criticism—if you could call it that—was a single article which had been posted the night before, and it was only critical because it quoted, in part, what Alex had said to get her locked up the previous week. It was in a rival publication, the unintentionally ironically named *Independent*:

"*Courier and Post* reporter Alex Baker was jailed under a magistrate's order on Friday. She was jailed under charges of contempt for the crown after her outburst at a local checkpoint in which she yelled profanity at a sentry and was overheard saying, "When will we say enough is enough? The King does not own us. We are not chattel. Freedom to move about should be the minimum! Damn you and damn King Frederick." Baker was stopped under suspicion of having attended an underground meeting of dissidents in the neighborhood. When she refused to explain her presence in the area, she was detained and then arrested after her outburst. Our attempts to contact her employer concerning her alleged associations with provocateurs were not returned..."

It went on like that, talking about the rebukes against the *Courier and Post* and the publishing license suspension it received several years ago when it refused to fire another reporter who had published an interview with a French veteran of the Texas War living in hiding under an assumed name. That had been that line in the sand that had drawn her to the paper in the first place. But in her years there, Carl had become the managing editor, and the fearless reporting she had hoped to accomplish had instead become a daily battle with him to get the truth out.

Ben was dispensing afternoon tea from the automatic wall amphora and poured each of them a cup. Alex absentmindedly stirred sugar while thinking about the article. It was true. She had been at an underground meeting. But *dissidents* was a strong word. She had gone to learn more about the group and had spent months building a network of contacts and gaining their trust so she could find out the location of the meeting. It had turned out to be a hodgepodge of frustrated people who spent as much time arguing about the cost of electricity as they did even discussing the abuses of the royal family. She had hoped it would be more.

She mentally wrote her article about the meeting while sitting in the county lockup and as soon as she'd been released on Monday, she went straight to work. But that morning's meeting had tamped down her initial enthusiasm. Carl was convinced that publishing the article would amount to an admission that she had attended—and would end up getting her and the paper into serious trouble with the authorities. Alex had thought of that and had come up with a plausible explanation: that after she was released from jail, someone, having read about her troubles, had come to her saying they had been at the meeting. But Carl saw the lie in her eyes and flatly refused.

Just as they were finishing their tea, a soft knock echoed at the door. Ben checked the visor and saw Mrs. Sadakis, their widowed, pensioner neighbor, standing in the hall holding something. When he opened the door, she smiled kindly, shifting the weight of a casserole dish in her hands.

"I heard about dear Alex's troubles," she said. "I brought this for you."

Ben took the dish, ushering her inside. "Come in, Mrs. Sadakis. That's very thoughtful of you."

She moved carefully to the living room, settling into her usual chair. Ben poured her a cup of tea, adding two lumps and a splash of cream without asking. She smiled at the gesture, accepting it with a nod.

The conversation drifted toward the weather, the early snowfall dusting the streets, and the price of heating oil. It was polite—almost too polite. Mrs. Sadakis rarely stopped by without reason. After a lull, Alex mentioned the pub.

"...yes, right there in the pub where we were trying to eat. He came in like he owned the place." She gave a dry chuckle. "I suppose that's the point, isn't it?"

Mrs. Sadakis stirred her tea slowly. "I know it's not seemly to say such things, but I liked his father more. He was harsh at times, too, but King Harold had a greater sense of justice."

Alex leaned forward. "Didn't your husband serve under him?"

"Oh, yes. Samuel was a Captain in the 3rd Cavalry. He was at King's Cross, you know. Earned a medal for bravery." She smiled faintly, but it didn't reach her eyes. "He was a hero under Harold, and labeled a villain under this king."

Something about the way she said it made the air in the room shift. A weighted silence settled between them.

Alex hesitated. "Mrs. Sadakis... what happened to your husband?"

The older woman took a deep breath, closing her eyes for a long moment. When she opened them, her gaze locked onto Alex's—sharp, unreadable.

"Did you meet with the dissidents?" she asked, her voice quiet but firm.

Alex's breath caught. The directness of the question threw her off. She glanced at Ben, who gave a barely perceptible nod.

"Yes," Alex said.

Mrs. Sadakis didn't react right away. Instead, she took a slow sip of tea, as though she had expected the answer all along. When she finally spoke, her voice carried a weight Alex hadn't heard before.

"Then you need to hear this."

She set her cup down carefully, lacing her fingers together in her lap. "Samuel was a good man. Loyal, to me, to God, to the Crown. He worked hard, and he believed in his duty. When the war started, they sent him to Paris, told him he had an important mission. But when he got there…" She paused, staring down at her hands. "*Something changed.*"

Alex didn't dare interrupt.

Mrs. Sadakis looked up, eyes glistening with something unreadable. "It's not what they tell you. France… democracy… it isn't what they say it is."

Alex leaned in, heart pounding. "What do you mean?"

The old woman exhaled, the lines of her face deepening as she prepared to tell them the truth.

"He worked hard in the Army. He volunteered, you know; he wasn't drafted. He had a knack for fixing things, so they sent him to school to learn engineering. But they also figured out he was good at solving other problems. And so, they taught him to be an intelligence officer." She took a sip of tea and smiled, "Just like I like it. Thank you, Ben."

"Samuel liked the work he was doing at first. It was mostly reports and analysis. But eventually they wanted him in the field. The French had infiltrated the security branch of the Army back in the '20s, you know, and had done considerable damage. They say that's why they were so bold in Texas, because they thought they knew everything. Anyway, Samuel had been ordered to approach France as a defector, to feed them disinformation and learn what he could. It was a terrible time for us. He was sent off to Paris, I was left here alone. I couldn't tell anyone what was going on, of course. Not even my sister in Richmond.

"When he got to Paris, things did not go as planned. The French didn't believe he was defecting. They thought he was a spy and they locked him away. But eventually a Major met with Samuel and took him to be debriefed," Mrs. Sadakis paused. A pained look showed on her face.

Alex reached out and grabbed her hand. "Go on," she whispered.

"Something strange happened while he was there." Mrs. Sadakis looked as though she were reliving it in her mind and the sadness now washed over her.

"It's not what it looks like on the holos, you know. France is not some backwards, evil regime. Their democracy doesn't threaten God's order. It reveals it."

"What do you mean?" asked Alex.

"It all started after the first rebellion," said Mrs. Sadakis. "They don't teach these things to the kids now, but when I was a little girl, things weren't so censored. That was before the London bombing—and Texas, of course. Before everyone who believed in a different form of government was a terrorist. When I was young, they told us about Washington, and Adams, and Jefferson. They were traitors, of course, but we learned about their ideas and how dangerous they were to the order of things. Do you know what happened to Jefferson?" she asked.

"He went mad in Paris and died in disgrace at an asylum," Alex said.

"No," said Mrs. Sadakis, "he did wonderful things. He *freed a nation.*"

Over the next hour, Mrs. Sadakis drank her tea and ate some biscuits. She also recounted the forgotten history of how France became a republic. She told of the triumphs and tragedies of their people. And, in the end, she told how Mr. Sadakis had become enamored with the freedom—the ideology—of the French people, and how it had changed their lives forever.

After the door had closed, Alex turned to Ben wide-eyed. They had a lot to talk about.

Chapter Two

THE BASEMENT SMELLED OF OLD paper and damp stone. A single lantern flickered in the center of the room, its glow barely reaching the curved brick walls.

Around the table, a dozen figures sat in tense silence, their backs hunched over as if bracing for the weight of the past.

"Close the door," a voice rasped.

A young boy, no more than fifteen, hurried to obey, sliding the iron latch into place. The tension in the room eased slightly, but the flickering lamplight still cast uneasy shadows.

At the head of the table, an old man with deep lines in his face set down a heavy, leather-bound book. The title had been burned off long ago, but every rebel in the room knew what it contained.

"Do you know why we are here?" the old man asked. His voice was hoarse, worn from years of whispering forbidden truths.

A woman shifted in her chair. "To learn," she said.

The old man nodded. "To learn," he repeated. "Because they have stolen our history. And when they steal your past, they steal your future."

With slow, deliberate hands, he opened the book. Inside, the yellowed pages were filled with cramped, handwritten text, fragments of stories that had been erased from every archive, burned from every library.

He turned the page and pointed to an inked sketch of a great ship cutting across a vast ocean.

"This is where it began," he murmured.

The rebels leaned in closer as he continued.

"By May 1607, the drought had entered its second year."

The young warrior Opitchapam was hunting in the lowlands when he saw the great beast on the water.

He froze.

It had pale, billowing sails that caught the wind, carrying it across the bay like nothing he had ever seen before. The *Paspahegh* people had lived on this land for generations, but this creature was something new, something unnatural.

He ran.

His brother met him at the clearing, breathless. Together, they crouched in the underbrush, watching as the three massive ships drew closer. They could see the men now, figures as pale as bone, dressed in strange cloth, their faces sharp with hunger.

It landed on the shores of the *Paspahegh* lands. Nothing would be the same for Opitchapam or his tribe again.

The old man turned the page. "From this point onward, the North American continent had a steady and ever-increasing number of Englishmen settling here. Despite wars with the indigenous people, conflicts with other colonies, and the hardships of weather and food, the English continued to come. By 1770, nearly three million English subjects lived in the New World, which they claimed as their own."

He looked up at the rebels gathered around him. "In the process, they pushed out or exterminated those who had lived here for millennia. To the English, the New World was theirs, a place they should rule by divine right."

He turned another page, revealing a drawing of redcoats marching in line, muskets raised. "Over time, the settlers became a people of America, with a distinct culture and accent, and they bristled at the weight of the monarchy across the sea on their backs. The wild and wonderful continent, rich with bounty and tradition, has since fought five times to throw off the shackles of oppression from the Crown. But after each attempt, the spirit was broken a little more."

"In 1776, the first rebels—Jefferson, Paine, Washington, Madison, Adams, and many others, went against incredible odds, sacrificing everything in pursuit of liberty. It was close, but in the end, they failed."

He let the silence settle.

"But a people who dream of freedom do not let its flame die easily. They tried again and again: 1812, 1860, 1955, 2042."

He paused, his fingers lingering on the edge of the next page. "Other heroes died for the cause—Scott, Hull, and Jackson. Grant and Lee. Eisenhower and MacArthur. Garland and Anderson. These men, and so many more, sacrificed in the name of an idea."

A heavy silence filled the room.

He turned the page again, revealing a map of Texas, with a black *X* slashed across it. The old man's voice grew quieter.

"The last rebellion. The one that nearly changed everything."

"The Republic of Texas declared its independence in 2042. It was the first rebellion to have foreign support. Spain and France stood behind them. Thousands of volunteers came from around the world. It was the best chance we ever had."

"And then?" a voice asked.

The old man exhaled sharply. "And then the King did what he always does. He blockaded the highways. He built the gallows before the war even began. The highways leading into Texas became execution sites, bodies hung as warnings. *Dallas... Dallas was bombed into nothing.*"

The weight of those words hung over them.

The old man turned another page, revealing a vast, intricate map of the Empire.

"The British monarchs of the early period had been constrained by Parliament. Many were faithful to the ideas of the rule of law, the end of slavery, the protection of rights. These ideas defined the just wars of the Empire's early expansion."

"But after every rebellion, the Crown used it as an excuse to increase its power."

His finger traced the map, pointing out key territories. "What had started as a mere colony in Virginia now stretches from the Bahamas to the Arctic, from the Indian subcontinent to Palestine, Australia, and the Pacific Islands. Britain's wealth, reach, and power became larger than any other empire in history."

He turned the page, revealing a ruined skyline, an abandoned city lost to time.

"London is gone," he murmured. "A nuclear wasteland. A war, started by the rebels, finished by the French. The King fled. And the seat of the Empire shifted to New York."

A younger rebel frowned. "But Parliament..."

"Is *nothing*," the old man cut in. "They meet, they pretend to debate the King's policies, but they rubber-stamp every decision. The monarchy is absolute. It has no equal. The brutality is unchecked."

He turned one final page, revealing portraits of the ruling family, each more severe than the last.

"The royal family governs every part of the world," he continued. "King Frederick's brother, Charles, rules India. His nephew, Frederick, controls Australia and the Pacific. His wife's brother, Craig, governs Africa and the Middle East. His nephew, Edward, holds Canada and the Pacific Northwest."

"Even now," the old man said, closing the book, "the King consolidates more power. To speak of the past—to even hint at rebellion—is to invite execution. The world is ruled through terror, and history is rewritten to serve the throne."

The room was silent.

Then, from outside, the sound of boots on cobblestones sent a chill through the room. The boy by the door blew out the lantern.

And in the darkness, *history lived on.*

The Royal Palace, New York

King Frederick looked up from the screen as his butler came in holding a Pomeranian. The dog began squirming in the butler's arms as he crossed the great room.

"Sussy, come," shouted the King, and at the invitation, the dog wriggled loose from the butler's hands and ungracefully fell to the floor, landing mostly on its chin. Undeterred, it scurried toward the King yapping excitedly. Markson, the King's private butler, sighed quietly and asked if there would be anything else. After waiting a moment for the king's reply—and, as usual, receiving none—he turned and walked the length of the room, closing the double doors softly as he left. The King returned to his call.

"I know, Charles, but I do not think it is wise to visit until we..." He paused. "Until we know more."

His brother was on video from India. "I think now is the perfect time. By either having you travel here or me coming there, it signals we are not concerned by these mere rabble-rousers," said Charles.

"What news from Bombay?" asked the King.

"We've had reports this morning from the Adjutant General that the recruiting base there is back up and running. They've brought in more security, but the suspects have been caught and appear to have been working alone." Charles looked at a piece of paper and then back at his brother on the screen, "I believe they are holding them in *Senstal Prison.*"

The King petted the dog in his lap and thought about the attack that had left nine soldiers dead, including a colonel that had once served as his personal aide. He had been a good friend, and his death had angered the King greatly. Time had done nothing to make him less angry.

"I want them hanged. Tomorrow. In front of the recruiting base in Bombay," he said.

"But Sire, we've not finished interrogating them and a trial hasn't even been scheduled yet," protested Charles.

"Did they confess?" asked the King.

"Tacitly, but not expressly."

"Hang them. Publicly." The King left little room for more argument and his brother knew better than to try.

Before he could say anything more, the King disconnected the call. Charles sighed and stared a minute at his own image on the screen. He turned off the camera and stretched. It was *1:00 a.m.* He had stayed up to talk to his brother about some kind of visit. But predictably, the conversation had not gone as he had planned. He pushed away from the chair and looked at a map on the wall. His brother's Empire was in red. It touched all corners of the globe. After the death of the King's son, Charles was next in line to the throne. He wondered if he would live to govern—or if Frederick would change the rules of succession and prevent him from ascending. *Would he ever be king?* With that recurrent thought on his mind, he turned for bed.

In New York, the King also thought about his brother. Charles was a good man, even though he was too lenient.

That was why he was having all these problems.

Trials.

Traitors don't need trials. It just gives them a platform for spreading their seditious hate against the royal family. It was bad enough the foreign press kept publishing lies about the kingdom, and the rumors that spread across the open net, he didn't have to tolerate it in his own Empire. He knew that the media filtered through the blocks. Even though the *ISS* had assured him that less than five percent of the people were sophisticated enough to bypass the censors, he knew that the net was where most of this discontent was festering. For years, he had toyed with the idea of blocking it altogether but his economic advisors told him that it was just too ingrained now. Restricting the net now would collapse the economy.

Frederick glanced at his schedule. He was supposed to meet with the Earl of Philadelphia and the Earl of Dover to settle some business disputes. While he could technically delegate such a task to the High Chancellor, he felt that these regular meetings with the peerage gave him a chance to gauge attitudes and press his authority. He kept extensive notes of breaches of protocol, perceived slights, and his impression of the men in the ranks of the monarchy. He pushed a button on his desk.

Markson, the butler, returned holding a pint of beer and a bowl of chocolate covered pretzels, one of the King's favorite snacks. Sussy immediately began jumping at Markson's legs and waist, yapping. Trying not to spill the beer or step on the dog, the butler made his way across the room. He hated that dog.

"Take Sussy with you," said the King. "And tell me when the Earls arrive."

"Yes, Your Grace." Markson scooped up the dog.

The King turned his chair to the video wall projected in front of him and un-muted the sound. The domestic news was on, talking about the affairs of the Empire. The news was the usual mix of celebrity gossip and cursory reports on actual matters of state. The international channels—*not available to most citizens*—spent most of their time on internal politics of their host nations. Periodically, they would discuss the Empire, and the King liked to be aware of such reports. Even though media monitors wrote reports for him, he liked to see for himself.

On one of the screens, something caught his eye. He enlarged the feed to full-screen and enabled the source audio. An Indian reporter was standing outside the Kremlin.

> *Russia has agreed to meet with the Indian rebels'*
> *delegation for the first time in more than thirty years amid*
> *news of growing discontent around the British Empire*
> *concerning the, and I'm quoting here, 'increasing totalitarian*
> *nature of King Frederick's regime.' While billed as merely a*
> *fact-finding opportunity by the Russian foreign minister,*

Anton Breshkev, some observers are reading into the meeting as a significant milestone in the rebels' ongoing efforts to gain support for their separatist movement...

The King muted the vid and dialed a number on his desk pad. "Get Wallstater, Trundle, and Charles on the line. Now." His secretary nodded and disconnected. A few minutes later, the King's Defence Minister, Foreign Minister, and his brother were on the screens in front of him.

"What is this news of Breshkev meeting with the rebels?" his question was directed at Charles, who was now in his pajamas and looked clearly unprepared.

"I'm not sure what you're talking about," Charles hesitated.

"We're just learning of this now," said Wallstater. Behind him, a flurry of activity was taking place in a large conference room at the Ministry of Defence. A young officer handed him a sheet of paper, and looking over it, he said, "We have the list of attendees. It appears to be..."

The King cut him off, "How did they get out of the country?"

The minister of the Home Department joined the call. "Your Grace, I may have the answer to that last question," she said. "*ISS* tracked the rebel leaders leaving Delhi yesterday but lost them when they neared the border with Tibet. A large explosion at a petrol station at the border checkpoint diverted resources for approximately an hour. We believe that it was there they crossed into Tibet and secured air travel aboard a chartered Russian flight to Moscow."

CHAPTER THREE

Moscow, Russian Federation —Early Winter 2052

I N MOSCOW, COLONEL VIHAAN CHADRA was preparing for the most important meeting of his life. Vihaan never aspired to a life of politics. Despite coming from a prominent political family in Bombay, he had wanted to be an artist. His father, Rajan, had been a Councillor of the Bombay Municipal Corporation (the governing body of the city) for most of Vihaan's childhood.

Rajan had kept his position by being loyal to the Crown, a point which Vihaan had no strong feelings about either way, at the time. Everything changed when Vihaan turned eighteen. He was drafted into the continental army. He would not be heading to art school as he had hoped. Despite his disappointment, he reported for duty. His first six months were largely uneventful, but in the seventh month, he received a letter from his mother. His father was under investigation for comments he had made against the governing authority's plans to store nuclear arms in the Bombay harbor. He had been strong in his condemnation, but not treasonous. The authorities were coming down hard on him, Vihaan's mother warned, and the Army could try to take it out on him as well.

His mother's warning proved to be true. A few days after getting her letter, Vihaan was told to pack up and catch a transport. He wasn't told where he was going but was shuttled to the air base, then to a transport plane. He fell asleep on the ride and when he woke up, he was at another air base, being told that the plane was refueling. Several other men got on board, but they were not Indian. Then the plane took off again. The next time it landed, Vihaan learned that he was now in the Solomon Islands, the location of the Empire's largest stockpile of nuclear weapons. It was here he was to remain for the next year. Isolated. Afraid.

His job was in the fuel containment unit. One of the most dangerous jobs in the Army, primarily because of the radiation exposure. It was a cruel twist of the knife by the government to which his father had been so loyal. But it was not the last, nor the worst.

After hearing about his son's transfer, Rajan became even more vocal. He held community meetings. He spent his time at the dais railing against the Lt. General in charge of the storage plan, much to the fear and consternation of his fellow councillors. He was sent a warning letter by the head of his party. Then he was arrested. He had been charged with subversion of order and sedition against the crown. He was interrogated for hours. The prosecutor tried to force him to sign a confession. But he would not. Then, that evening, while he awaited a judicial hearing set for the morning, something happened in his cell. The details were never quite clear. But Vihaan had seen the photos. The word *traitor* was scrawled on his forehead and he was found hanging from the ceiling.

Despite this setback, after his father's death, Vihaan was in the strange position of being promoted early and consistently. He was given increasing authority and moved less often. It was a strange juxtaposition. He held his resentment close to his chest. But he did not forget. He learned and watched and gathered valuable intelligence. He studied methods and strategy and became intimate with the ways and philosophies of the Empire's military—until he betrayed them.

Vihaan now sat in the long hall of the Russian Ministry of Foreign Affairs. It was very cold here. His mind was wandering, thinking back to his father—to all the things that led to where he was today. He was waiting on a meeting with Anton Breshkev, the Foreign Minister. He was hoping to discuss the simmering Indian rebel movement. From a door down the hall, a group of men emerged. Vihaan stood as they approached. As they drew near, Vihaan recognized someone he didn't expect to see. He quickly came to attention.

"Hello," the man spoke English with a heavy Russian accent, "I am Boris Aslanov. I know you were waiting for the Foreign Minister, but I thought I might like to meet you myself."

"Vihaan Chadra, it is a pleasure to meet you Mr. President."

"Come Colonel, let us speak," said the president.

The group walked further down the hall into an ornately decorated meeting room. At the far end was a large fireplace with a roaring fire. On the table, there were sandwiches and drinks. Vihaan wasn't sure where to sit, but a young woman motioned for him at one of the chairs near the middle of the table. Others were filing in and talking with the president in anxious tones.

Once they were all seated, the young woman went to the head of the table and opened a flip panel. She pressed a button which made a huge screen appear over the fireplace. On it was the face of someone Vihaan immediately recognized.

Before he could stop himself, he stood.

Aslanov laughed good-naturedly.

Slightly embarrassed, Vihaan took his seat again.

Breshkev entered from a side door silently, taking a seat next to his president.

"Mr. Greg, thank you for joining us on such short notice," said Aslanov.

"Thank you for inviting me, Mr. President," the man replied with a thick Texas drawl.

Andrew Greg was a familiar face to anyone in the rebellion. He was the leader of the American exiles in France. After the war of '32, many Americans had fled to France to assist in the efforts there. After the armistice, they remained—largely in hiding. The movement lived on and many leaders were still wanted by the British government.

Many, like Greg, had been convicted in absentia and had sizable bounties on their heads.

"I would like to introduce someone to you, Mr. Greg," said Aslanov, "this is Vihaan Chadra of the Indian People's Movement."

Greg smiled warmly at Vihaan. "It is nice to put a face to the name," he said.

It was the first time the two men had met, though each knew the other by reputation. Greg was a venerable veteran of the Texas conflict and the land war in France. He was as well regarded among Texans as he was among the French—not an easy task.

The Brits had been searching for him since the armistice in France. They first threatened Belgium, where he was believed to be (he was in Norway). As the years went by, he went silent. Unlike a few of the other former rebel leaders, he did not post on the net. He did not release inflammatory videos. He, in fact, fueled rumors of his own death. He assumed a new identity and worked as a butcher in a meat processing plant outside Skien.

Vihaan looked at the legend on the screen in front of him and then turned to see Aslanov's face, "I'm very honored to be here."

"There's more to this meeting than was originally discussed, obviously. Though I suspect, you've figured that much out already," said Aslanov.

As he spoke, the large screen split in half with the right side now displaying a world map. "Mr. Greg, are you able to see our graphics?"

"Looks good here," said Greg.

"Gentlemen, this is the reach of the British Empire," Aslanov tapped a button causing the map turn predominantly red. "General, would you mind?"

At that, a highly decorated general stood and began speaking in Russian as he pointed to areas on the map. At first Vihaan was bewildered, but the female aid motioned to a cord sticking up from an alcove in the middle of the table. He placed it in his ear, and now heard a translation—to his surprise—in Hindi.

"...now we know that the progression of the Empire into Asia and the Pacific was not a temporary protective measure as the King had implied, but rather another expansion of his territory under guise of preemptive security. The Empire surrounds Russia on the west, southwest, and east. Only mainland China, excluding Hong Kong, remains a buffer..."

At the mention of China, Aslanov interrupted. "I invited the Chinese to this meeting, but they declined. Premier Jun Wiaping has decided to wait until the first volley of hostilities to determine whether or not to enter the war."

Vihaan's ears perked up at the word *war*. What did Aslanov mean exactly? Was there about to be a war—or had it already started?

Breshkev finally broke his silence. "You have asked for this meeting. You have my attention. Tell me why Russia should care."

Vihaan straightened, choosing his words carefully. "Your government has long opposed British expansionism. The Empire is weak, fractured by internal dissent. This is an opportunity to strike at its core."

Breshkev folded his hands on the table. "An opportunity, you say."

"Your Excellency, the resistance is gaining momentum," Greg added. "We have cells operating in Texas, India, parts of Africa, and the Caribbean territories. We don't need soldiers—we need supplies, funding. Safe harbors for defectors. With your help, we can dismantle the Crown's grip."

Vihaan saw Aslanov shift, then lean forward.

"You *overestimate* your position," the old diplomat said, his voice heavy with skepticism. "You speak of momentum, yet the last five revolts have ended in massacres. Why would this one be different?"

Vihaan held his gaze. "Because this time, we have the ability to coordinate. We have contacts within the Imperial military, access to intelligence. *The cracks are showing*. If we move carefully, we can break them apart."

Aslanov scoffed, shaking his head. "You ask us to supply weapons and support a war against the most powerful empire in history. Do you know how many times your people have 'almost won'? How many rebels have promised that *this* time would be different?" He exhaled through his nose. "And each time, the empire is still standing."

Breshkev remained silent, watching.

Vihaan steadied himself. He had prepared for this. "The British have overextended themselves," he said. "Their economy is stretched thin from colonial uprisings. India alone costs them billions to maintain control. The same goes for Texas, the Caribbean, the African protectorates. The Empire is bleeding. You don't have to strike them directly. Just let them continue to rot from within."

Breshkev finally spoke again. "And what would Russia gain from this?"

Vihaan exchanged a glance with Greg.

"The same thing you've always wanted," Greg said plainly. "A weakened Britain. A Britain too consumed with internal collapse to challenge your interests."

Breshkev allowed a thin smile. "And yet, your rebellion has no guarantee of success."

"Which is why we ask only for discreet support," Vihaan said. "Arms shipments. Smuggling channels. Assistance in intelligence-gathering. *Low risk, high reward.* If we fail, you lose nothing. If we win, Britain's dominance is broken, and Russia is in a position of strength."

Aslanov exhaled slowly, rubbing his chin. "And yet, a wounded animal is most dangerous when cornered. If Britain senses true collapse, what makes you think they won't lash out? You have seen what happened to Paris."

Vihaan tensed. "We are aware of the risks."

"The risks are not yours alone," Breshkev countered. He exchanged a look with Aslanov, then tapped his fingers against the polished wood of the table.

"This discussion will continue," the Foreign Minister said, rising from his seat. "We will deliberate on your request and give you an answer soon."

That was as much as they were going to get today.

Vihaan stood and extended his hand first, and Breshkev shook it with a measured grip.

The message was clear.

Russia wasn't convinced yet.

As Vihaan was led from the room, he clenched his jaw. He had made his case. Now, all he could do was wait.

CHAPTER FOUR

New York — Winter 2053

THE MORNING BROKE WITH DARK skies and thunder rumbling between the buildings of the city. It had been two months since her encounter with the King. As fog rolled in, Alex stretched and yawned. She was not a morning person. She got up and headed for the gym in the basement of her building, feeling groggy and cranky. By the time she got back, Ben had made breakfast. He kissed her on the cheek, and they sat down at the small table that served as a dining table in their cramped apartment. Eggs, sausage, a rasher of bacon, beans, tomato, blood pudding, and tea were spread before them. Ben noticed Alex's bemusement at the full English breakfast.

"I was feeling traditional this morning," said Ben with a smile.

"I saw that man in the gym again," said Alex.

"We really ought to tell someone."

"I stopped at the desk on the way up. They said he's new in the building," said Alex, "But it's still weird. Who just sits and reads the news in the gym every morning? It's super creepy." Alex gave a shudder and picked up her tablet.

As she sipped her tea, she read the news on the web, seeing no irony in her last statement. "Hmm," she said.

"It says here that some rebels in Italy have begun to openly ask for international aid."

"You are a woman obsessed," laughed Ben. "Rebellion this, dissident that—it's likely to get us in hot water."

"Yeah, yeah," mumbled Alex.

As she and Ben walked to work, Alex thought about the meetings that were happening halfway around the world. She wished she could be involved somehow. She felt that her mission was to end the tyranny of the throne. But she felt so small, so weak, in comparison to the sheer size of the forces against her. She decided right then that she was going back to the dissidents' meeting that night.

At work, she was distracted. Ben was busy putting together an article about some of the places the King had recently eaten, inspired by their encounter at the pub. He hummed to himself as he happily wrote. Alex loved the way he did that. He always seemed to be in a good mood—not a care in the world. She wished she could do that.

She walked over and put her hand on his shoulder, "How's the article coming?" she asked.

"Not too bad, I think," he said. "I think I'm going to go back and talk to the pub owner at lunch today. Wanna come?"

"Sure, why not?"

At the *Hop and Pig*, John Norcamp was not manning the bar. In fact, he was many feet below the pub in what had once been a storeroom cellar. He looked at the piles of rifles around him, making notations on a clipboard. The far back wall had a small door which was too low to walk through while standing.

John slid the key into the lock and opened the door. Crouching, he went into the small munitions locker and sat at a bench. He began the dangerous and tiring work of producing more of the small bombs he had been making for months now. He thought of the King eating at his pub and smiled at the thought of what he had done. The monarchy had brought such pain to his family. But victory would be his in the end.

John was the latest in a long line of rebel fighters in his family. He was a member of the group known as *Fidelis*—the Faithful. Unlike many of the resistance's more impulsive factions, Fidelis operated under a strict code: no civilian casualties, no collateral targets, no glorified vengeance. John, as their munitions leader, personally signed off on every device the group used. He insisted on knowing where and how each bomb would be deployed. Every operation had to serve a tactical purpose and align with their principles. They weren't just fighting to tear something down—they were fighting to build something better.

But not all resistance groups shared that restraint.

The car bombing outside his pub earlier that week had troubled John deeply. The authorities hadn't named a suspect, but the underground networks were already whispering. It hadn't been a Fidelis bomb. The device had been cruder, louder—meant to send a message, not win a war. A warning wrapped in fire.

The *Second Sons of Liberty*, most likely. A splinter faction born from disillusionment with the mainline resistance. They claimed to descend—ideologically, at least—from the original Sons of Liberty of 1776. But if Fidelis saw itself as a scalpel, the Second Sons were a hammer. To them, the Empire had already crossed every line, and so the rules of engagement were obsolete. They didn't differentiate between soldiers and collaborators, between soft targets and hard. Every explosion was a declaration. Every death, a price of freedom

John didn't need confirmation. He knew the signs. The placement of the car, the lack of evacuation, the timing. It was deliberate. A shot across two bows: one aimed at the Crown, the other at him.

The message was clear.

After finishing three more bombs, John locked up and headed back upstairs.

It was nearly lunch and customers were starting to trickle in. He smiled and welcomed regulars and newcomers alike.

As he was pouring, he heard a familiar voice boom, "John, my man!" He knew instantly it was Bear.

Celsus Berning, who friends (and enemies) called "Bear," lived up to his nickname. He stood six foot four and weighed more than twenty stone. He had quick eyes and a big grin. His ginger hair and beard made him seem at once menacing and friendly.

"Bear! How are you, you old dog?"

"I'll be better with a pint in m'hand," said Bear.

As John pulled, Bear leaned in and whispered, "There's a dance Thursday in the old clock at ten."

John nodded.

To those in the know, that meant there would be a meeting of the rebels at the garage tonight (it was Tuesday) at eight o'clock (not ten). John and Bear had known each other for a very long time. Bear had been in the war in the King's army. He had won the Military Cross in the battle of El Paso. He'd almost lost his arm there, but the man refused to let them amputate. After years of work, he still had his arm and though it was sore when it rained, he was as strong as ever.

Bear's road to rebellion was less philosophical than others. The army wouldn't let him serve anymore because of his injury. They also no longer would have given him free rein in his interactions with the "enemy." He was ruthless to his enemies.

When he almost lost his arm, it was to a Texan with a shotgun. Bear had kicked in the man's door to search the house. The man was waiting and shot as soon as he saw daylight. With his left arm in shreds, dangling in a bloody pulp, Bear ran through the door and grabbed the man with his good hand and crushed the man's skull.

Bear sought action. He had always craved it, wherever it took him and for whoever could pay. He had never cared much about causes or politics. War was its own reason. But after the Crown dismissed him, cast him aside like a broken tool, something in him began to change. Restless and untethered, he found himself drawn to the rebellion. At first, it wasn't the ideals that called to him. It was the fight. The movement gave him something to do, somewhere to go, someone to stand beside.

He didn't believe at first. He scoffed at the rhetoric, ignored the speeches, rolled his eyes at talk of freedom. But the people around him were different. They weren't in it for glory. They believed in something greater than themselves. They fought because they had to, because they refused to live on their knees. And over time, Bear saw it. He listened more closely. He stayed behind after meetings and asked questions, not just about tactics but about purpose. He began to understand.

The change didn't happen all at once. It came slowly, in shared meals, long nights, and the quiet courage of the people who refused to quit. The cause became real to him, not in slogans, but in the faces of his comrades. They had become his family. In them, he found a loyalty stronger than any he'd known in the army. His devotion was no longer paid for. It was earned, built in blood and trust and the knowledge that he would kill for these people, and die for them if it came to it.

Back in the pub, Alex and Ben walked in chatting softly. They took their regular table as a waitress came by to greet them.

"Damn, look at the size of him," whispered Ben.

"Shh," mouthed Alex.

Ben stared at the man and noticed he had a tattoo on his neck of a snake eating a rat. It was small, faded, and partially hidden behind his collar. But as Ben looked, he remembered something.

"Hey," he whispered again, "see that tattoo? He was in Texas."

Alex glanced at the towering man at the bar and immediately recognized him from the dissidents' meeting she had been to. He and the bartender seemed to be close friends and were having an animated conversation, though in hushed tones.

After they finished lunch, Alex told Ben she wanted to run some errands and would meet him back at the paper. Instead, she decided to double back to the pub. By now, John wasn't behind the bar. The midday crowd had left. She asked the pretty blonde behind the bar if John was still around. She showed the barmaid her press pass and said she wanted to interview him about the King's earlier visit.

"Oh, that *was* exciting," said the barmaid. "I'd never seen the King in person before. Can you believe how fat he was?" she whispered as she giggled.

Alex said, "People never look in person like they do on the holos. They say the vids add ten pounds... but if that's true, he must've eaten the other twenty in person."

The barmaid laughed. "I'll let John know you'd like to talk."

"Thanks," said Alex.

The barmaid walked over to a pad on the wall and pressed a comm receiver. Coming back to Alex a few moments later she said, "He'll be over in a few minutes. Can I pour you another drink while you wait—on the house?"

"Sure," said Alex.

As the barmaid poured a pint, Alex checked her pad. A news report mentioned that the Indian rebels had launched an offensive. Apparently they had hijacked an armored bank car, killing several police officers before escaping. Alex thought about that for a minute. Decades of violence, and nothing had changed. Maybe there was a better way. Maybe not.

After the lunch rush, John and Bear had gone to the cellar and were now sitting at the long bench that served as John's assembly station for munitions. Bear was absentmindedly loading 9 mm bullets into magazine after magazine from a large box while John measured gunpowder.

"I don't understand, mate. You had him in your damn pub. Why didn't you just shoot him?" Bear asked.

"Because I didn't want to get shot myself… but I left him a surprise," said John.

"Oh?"

John pointed to a small, heavy container on the shelf behind Bear. The metal canister was lead-lined and sealed tight, and a warning symbol had been etched into its side. Bear reached for it, but John's voice was sharp.

"Careful. Don't open it."

Bear whistled as he inspected the heavy case. "What the hell is this?"

"Polonium-210," John said, a slight smile on his lips. "One of the deadliest substances known to man."

Bear turned the container over in his hands cautiously. "Radioactive?"

John nodded. "Highly. But in the right doses, nearly undetectable. No taste, no smell. A microscopic amount, absorbed through ingestion, and it starts destroying the body from the inside out. It won't kill him right away, but once the symptoms appear, it'll be too late."

Bear grinned. "You poisoned the old ass? How?"

John leaned forward, lowering his voice. "It was added to his meal. Just a trace, mixed into his food at the pub. Something hearty, heavy flavors to mask anything unusual. He cleaned his plate, none the wiser." He smirked. "By the time symptoms start appearing, it'll look like a sudden, unexplained illness. No one will connect it to what he ate weeks ago."

Bear looked impressed but skeptical, raising an eyebrow. "And you're sure it'll work?"

John gestured to the reinforced container. "I've tested it before. Sometimes having old friends in odd places leads to interesting opportunities. This isn't something you can buy off the shelf. Several people risked their lives to get this to me. The effects are devastating. It's why polonium's been used in assassinations before, undetectable until it's too late. And best of all? By the time anyone realizes, if they ever do, he'll be too weak to do anything about it."

Bear's grin widened. "Brilliant."

John exhaled and set the canister back in its secure storage, sealing it tight. "Just don't touch it. A single mistake with this stuff, and we'd be the ones in the grave."

As they sat, the comm rang. John picked up and spoke with the barmaid.

"There's a reporter here," he said to Bear. "You stay here, and for God's sake, don't go anywhere near that container."

John went through the secret door into the main cellar and through another small anteroom locking each door behind him as he went. He climbed the ladder to the main floor and came out and washed his hands in the small sink in the kitchen.

As he looked through the order window, he saw an attractive redhead sitting at the bar sipping a drink. She looked familiar—a regular, he wondered to himself.

"Hi, I'm John," he said, cheerfully, but hurried.

"Alex Baker, I'm a reporter for the *Courier and Post*."

"What can I do for you?" John asked.

The bartender was beaming. "She's here to talk about the King's visit," she said giddily.

John visibly tensed, and Alex noticed.

"I also like to eat here a lot with my boyfriend, I thought we could do a food review and maybe help boost business. Is there somewhere private we can talk?" she asked.

"Listen, Ms. Baker, I'm very busy today..."

"Oh, this will only take a minute." Alex started walking toward the back of the pub. John instinctively followed, calling after her. She feigned interest in some of the art on the back wall and as John walked next to her, she whispered, "I'm here about the dissidents' meeting... not the food."

Chapter Five

Queens, New York —Late Winter 2053

VINNY CARCIONE WAS RAISED IN Queens by his grandmother Ruth and her sister Anne. The two women were tough, hardened by years of navigating the world that the men in their family had built, a world of blood, loyalty, and power. Ruth never spoke much about the past. Anne, on the other hand, relished the stories. She'd sip her coffee at the kitchen table, the crack of her knuckles filling the silence, and talk about how the Carcione name once echoed through the back alleys of Brooklyn.

But the loudest stories belonged to Vinny's great-uncle, Joe "The Claw" Carcione. His name was whispered with a mixture of fear and reverence. *The Claw* had earned his nickname for his tendency to solve disputes with a claw hammer, a brutal enforcer who made loyalty a matter of life and death. When Vinny was fourteen, Uncle Joe picked him up from school in a black sedan, the smell of leather and stale cigar smoke clinging to the air. That day marked the end of Vinny's boyhood.

"Got a favor to ask," Uncle Joe had said, his voice rough like gravel. "Time you learn how this family really works."

The favor took them to a warehouse in Brooklyn, a darkened space that reeked of oil and damp concrete. Inside, a man named Tim was tied to a chair, blood staining his white shirt. Three men circled him like wolves. Uncle Joe didn't waste time with pretense. The fists came first—sharp, bone-snapping blows that echoed through the hollow space. Tim's cries were low and broken, the kind that only came from a man who already knew he wouldn't leave alive.

Vinny stood still, his stomach twisting with something cold and unfamiliar. But he never looked away. Not once.

When Tim finally gasped out the name they wanted, Uncle Joe gave a satisfied grunt. Then he reached into his coat, pulled out a .45 revolver, and shoved it into Vinny's trembling hands.

"Time to finish it," Joe said. "We'll bury the body. No one will find him."

Vinny's hands were steady. He didn't hesitate. The shot cracked through the empty warehouse. He remembered the ringing in his ears, the way Tim's head slumped forward. He remembered Uncle Joe's rough clap on his shoulder, the grin of approval.

"That's blood," Joe said. "Carcione blood. Don't ever forget what that means."

Vinny never did.

That was *twenty years and seventeen bodies* ago.

Vinny Carcione loved three things: travel, history books, and hurting people. The first two gave him pleasure. The third gave him meaning. He carried it with him like an instinct, a weight that settled deep in his bones.

Medium height, with a lean, muscular frame, he could pass for a boxer. His brown eyes held that gleam, the look of someone who had seen too much and enjoyed most of it. Dark hair slicked back, a jagged scar tracing the edge of his jaw, a souvenir from a fight he'd won, though the other guy didn't survive to hear about it. The scent of cheap, flavored cigars clung to his clothes. You often smelled Vinny before you saw him.

Tonight, the air in the Queens club was thick with smoke and laughter. The backroom was louder than usual, the scrape of chairs and the clink of glasses mixing with the low hum of conversation. Every eye in the room had turned to Vinny.

"*Salute!*"

Uncle Joe raised his glass, and the others followed. The old man's presence still commanded respect, even as his voice cracked with the strain of years. Vinny nodded, his grin sharp. This wasn't just a toast. This was recognition.

Vinny Carcione was now a made man.

It had been a long time coming. For years, he and his crew had handled the family's dirtiest business: extortion, weapons smuggling, settling old debts with fists or bullets. Now, no one could touch him. Not without consequence. The oath had bound him, and in return, the family had given him the power he craved.

"Vinny," Joe said, lowering his glass, "this is just the beginning."

Vinny already knew that.

Two in the morning. The fog was thick, curling in damp tendrils along the edges of the docks. The harbor's skeletal cranes stood motionless against the dark sky. Somewhere in the distance, the hum of a cargo ship's engine echoed through the mist.

Vinny leaned against the side of the delivery truck, the glowing ember of his cheap cigar cutting through the shadows. Five of his men flanked him, their eyes scanning the empty expanse. Every deal had a rhythm. The waiting, the tension—it all built like a symphony before the final note.

"It's about damn time," Marco muttered, his hand resting casually on the grip of his sidearm.

Vinny didn't respond. He had already given the orders. Two men had taken positions within the building, hidden behind crates and steel beams. They had clear sightlines to the loading dock. If the deal went bad, Vinny would know before the first shot was fired.

He'd been around long enough to know that gun deals rarely went clean. Greed had a way of twisting even the simplest exchanges. But that was fine. Vinny wasn't afraid of blood.

Bear cursed under his breath, slamming his hand against the dashboard, creating a spiderweb crack in the plastic. The navigation system flickered uselessly, its glowing map doing little to guide him through the soupy fog. The hulking delivery truck rumbled beneath him, its tires crunching over uneven pavement. He could see the faint glow of the warehouse lights ahead, but the loading dock remained stubbornly hidden.

He slowed to an idle, scanning the mist for movement. Then, a figure emerged.

A short, round man waddled forward, a flashlight bouncing in his hand. The man's breath came in short gasps, sweat already slicking his forehead despite the cold. Bear rolled down the window, but his fingers lingered on the grip of his sidearm.

"You Bear?" the man wheezed.

"Yeah," Bear grunted. "Can't find the damn dock."

The man let out a shrill whistle, and two floodlights flickered on. The loading bay loomed ahead, its steel doors gaping like the mouth of a beast.

"It's right there, buddy," the man said, his grin too eager. "With this fog, I don't blame you."

Bear's gaze lingered on the man for a moment longer. Then, satisfied, he slid his gun back into the holster.

Vinny saw the truck roll in, its engine growling as it pulled up to the dock. From the corner of his eye, he caught the faint shift of a figure crouched behind a stack of pallets—one of his men. The deal was in motion.

Bear stepped down from the cab, his movements deliberate. He was big, the kind of big that didn't come from a gym. His shoulders were broad, his frame dense with the kind of muscle earned through labor and war. A rifle was slung over his shoulder, its black barrel gleaming faintly.

Vinny liked that. Men who brought rifles to business deals weren't cowards. They were realists.

"Bear," Vinny said, his voice cutting through the still air.

"Vinny," Bear replied, just as evenly.

The two men locked eyes. No words were wasted. They both knew why they were here. The only question that remained was whether they'd both leave the docks alive.

Chapter Six

The Appalachian Mountains —Late Winter 2053

HUNDREDS OF MILES SOUTH, A maple block was taking shape. Hammer and chisel were shaving thin layers of wood, revealing a carving of an American Indian hunter with a bear head in his hand. Each tap of the chisel was precise and perfectly timed. Yuri never slowed. He worked methodically, thinking and carving at the same time. To him, the American Indian was already carved. All he had to do is use the chisel to reveal it.

This was what Yuri did to pass the time. He found woodworking to be useful. It required both intellect and precision of action, two things very important in Yuri's line of work. Each evening, he would work on various projects he had started. Many nights he would stay awake until dawn, slowly carving intricate and beautiful objects. They were very high quality and would have fetched a handsome price at auction if the public were ever allowed to see his work. But the public would never see these carvings, because Yuri did not exist.

Here he was now, a man of thirty-five years, living in solitude in the foothills of Appalachia. He lived deep in the woods, under the shadow of a steep hill, miles from the nearest human soul, and the terrain was so treacherous even the wayward backpacker would steer clear. His friends had bought the land for him. They had formed a corporation, which had in turn bought 100 percent ownership in two other corporations, which held as part of their assets the land on which Yuri now lived. These corporations paid their taxes on time, kept the area enclosed by a modest barbed-wire fence, and did nothing to attract attention.

After the land was bought for Yuri, he was flown in on a helicopter and dropped at the site of a manufactured cabin. In fact, everything had been flown in, including the hammer and chisel he was using now. There were no roads to the cabin, not even an ATV trail. The roof was camouflaged, and the cabin was powered by a series of discrete solar panels on the hillside.

A quick-moving stream was nearby. A well was dug and supplied the cabin with purified water. Despite its isolation, it was very comfortable. Nearby, in a clearing near the stream, Yuri had dug a small vegetable garden. He didn't have to grow his own food, shipments came every two weeks, but he liked the security of it and found the work rewarding.

Sometimes, like tonight, the helicopter came for Yuri. Yuri looked up from his carving as the helicopter's noise drew near. Even at this time of night, there was no one nearby enough to be disturbed. A rope ladder descended from the open door. Yuri, a black duffel bag over his shoulder, climbed steadily. Inside, he was given an envelope with a number written on it. Yuri did not speak to the men. He needed to rest and found the rhythm of the motor comforting. He leaned back, his head against the frame, and slept. He slept the fitful sleep one does when sitting up. But it would be enough to keep him fresh and sharp for the long day ahead.

Rural Virginia, Later That Day

His pupils dilated as they adjusted to his sudden wakefulness. The sun was rising quickly and was shining through the once-again open bay door. The helicopter was hovering, and a rope had been dropped. Yuri looked out and saw that he was being dropped in an area not too dissimilar from the one he had just come from. He was over a forest of huge, old oaks and pines as far as the eye could see. One of the men gave Yuri a hand signal which meant 'time to go; good luck.' Again, without a word, Yuri descended the rope to the ground below.

With the sound of the helicopter fading away, Yuri opened his bag and took out a compass and a map. He looked in the envelope and found instructions on when and where he was supposed to be. As was his custom, he took a moment to light a very expensive cigar and enjoyed it as he made his way into the woods.

Before long, Yuri found a game trail and followed it south until he came to a pond. He followed the trail around the edge of the pond and saw that an ATV trail was on the other side. Following this new trail for an hour eventually led him to a gravel road. In the distance, he could see a scattering of farmhouses, barns, and a few silos. He walked as if preparing to carve another great masterpiece. Each stroke of the chisel must be exact, the hammer must hit just right—not too hard and not too soft. Every hit must have a purpose. No movement should be made unnecessarily. As he planned in his mind, he came to the first farmhouse.

It was an old house with light blue paint, chipping badly in many places. There was a smell of barn animals in the air as Yuri walked up the driveway. His bag was gone, and though it was a warm day, he was wearing a long black jacket. As Yuri came near the house, he heard a man speaking in Italian on a pad. He realized the man was behind the house and started to circle around, but thought better of it and approached the front porch instead. Trying the door, Yuri found it unlocked and helped himself inside.

He walked toward the sound of the man. The man was very loud and seemed to be having an argument of some kind. His voice would rise in shrill opposition to whatever the other person was saying. Yuri watched him through the kitchen door. The man was pacing back and forth, talking very animatedly with his hands even though no one was around to see him. "No! I will not tolerate this outrage," shouted the man in English.

Yuri thought about waiting until the man was finished, but decided now was as good a time as any. On the other end of the line, the man heard his Italian friend make a deep gurgling noise and then what sounded like a gasp. Then the call went silent.

The man did not die quickly. There was a lot of blood. And despite his frail appearance, the man had fought back a little when Yuri had sliced his thick neck. He tried in vain to use the pad as a makeshift weapon. Yuri just took it from him and ended the call. The man had fallen to the ground, and the puddle around him was growing steadily. Yuri looked in the man's eyes and watched the life draining out of them. The Italian mouthed "*Why?*"

"Because I must," said Yuri.

That was all the explanation that Yuri ever gave when asked questions like this. He believed it, too. There had been many days like this.

When Yuri was sixteen, his younger twin brothers had hung themselves in his closet as part of a suicide pact. In the note they left, which they had signed together, they said they "*wanted to see what death felt like.*" If they had waited just a little longer, they might have at least seen what it looked like; Yuri's father died of a fast growing cancer just seven months later. Suddenly, Yuri and his mother were alone. Their big family had disappeared. When Yuri turned eighteen, his mother became sick with the same kind of cancer his father had died from. It was painful and unbearable. In mercy, Yuri helped his mother die.

When he was much older, he learned that the Chinese had poisoned the water supply near his home and had caused much of the cancer in that region. He had fled further into Russia and then to Canada, where he had worked for logging companies until he was twenty-one. Even when he was working in the logging camps, Yuri had chosen to live alone. He rarely spoke to anyone; he was a hard worker and held up his end of the job. No one seemed to mind him, or even notice him, except one man. Arvil hated the Russians, and Yuri drew his scorn as a result.

One day, Arvil was showing the other men a gold watch that his girlfriend back home had mailed to him. He made sure everyone saw it. That night, after supper, he broke into Yuri's locker and planted the watch there. In the morning, as he had planned, he accused Yuri of stealing it. When the foreman opened Yuri's locker, he of course found the watch and fired Yuri on the spot.

Yuri had liked his logging job and he had tried very hard not to cause any problems. *Arvil*, thought Yuri, *is a worthless man*. They eventually found pieces of Arvil scattered throughout the forest.

They never found Yuri.

The Italian had nice things. And, though no one would have said anything if he had taken something, Yuri never stole. He was not a thief, and no one would ever accuse him of that. *Ever*. Yuri looked around the house and studied the life of the man he had just killed. He searched it thoroughly. As he was making his way down into the cellar, he heard the sound of a gun being quietly cocked. Very quietly. It was coming from the darkness down at the bottom of the stairs. He could leave no witnesses.

Yuri's assailant had the benefit of being used to the darkness. After all, Yuri had just come from outside. But Yuri quickly took advantage of this by throwing a flash grenade down the stairs. Gunfire erupted in a blind panic. Deafened and blinded, their shots were far from their mark. Yuri simply walked toward the noise. Soon, he had disarmed the man and was dragging him by his hair up the cellar steps.

"Who are you?" asked the man, breathless and terrified.

"I am nobody," said Yuri.

"Please... don't." The man was begging for his life.

"I am simply a businessman," said Yuri. "I must do my job, and I cannot allow anyone to get in the way."

"Where is Carlos?"

"In hell, I'd guess. Don't worry. You will soon join him."

The man began to weep. That, in itself, didn't unsettle Yuri—he had seen men cry before dying. But this was different. There was a strange rhythm to it, a cadence beneath the sobs that pulled at something buried in his memory.

Yuri narrowed his eyes.

Something about the man's face. The way he knelt. The way he whispered—not words, but sounds—just under his breath. Familiar.

Yuri hesitated, blade hovering at the man's neck.

A name surfaced in his mind, unbidden. A face from another time. A boy, once frightened, once broken, now grown.

That flicker of recognition was all the time the man needed.

With sudden, explosive precision, Antonio lunged—not wild or desperate, but practiced. His first strike caught Yuri in the throat, just enough to stagger his breath. The second forced him back a step. Yuri recovered instantly, slashing in tight, efficient arcs, but the rhythm of the encounter had shifted. Antonio wasn't the man Yuri had faced in the cellar seconds ago. Something else had emerged—trained, focused, and driven by more than survival.

Antonio dashed toward the kitchen. Yuri followed, blade drawn, calculating angles.

The refrigerator flew open. A flash of silver caught Yuri's eye.

A deafening blast rang out as the shotgun discharged. Buckshot shredded a cabinet near Yuri's shoulder—close, but not close enough. He ducked left, already drawing his pistol, and came up with deadly focus.

They stood nearly chest to chest. The sawn-off shotgun was pressed to Yuri's heart. His pistol pressed into Antonio's gut.

"Pull the trigger," Antonio said, his voice eerily calm. "I'll live. You won't."

Yuri's mind raced. At this range, neither would walk away clean. But Antonio's eyes... they didn't blink. Didn't twitch.

And that's when Yuri saw it—he wasn't dealing with a man anymore. He was dealing with belief.

Yuri dropped the pistol.

Antonio struck fast and hard, the shotgun's butt catching Yuri behind the ear. The world spun. His legs buckled.

Darkness followed.

When Yuri woke, his arms and legs were bound behind him, duct tape across his eyes and mouth, lashed to a post like a dog. He heard footsteps, the shifting of supplies. Antonio had already gone to find Carlos.

But Carlos was dead. And Antonio, by the only rule that mattered in their world, was now the boss.

He had spent many hours in the field here at the farm in Virginia, one of Carlos' American retreats. He had been Carlos' right-hand man for seven years and was well respected in their business. He was not a rash man, and, like Yuri, was a man of precision and method. He wondered how Yuri had found them and who had hired him. He would get his answers. The first thing Antonio did was to call his uncle, Vincent, in New York.

CHAPTER SEVEN

Queens, New York —Late Winter 2053

THE AIR ALONG THE WATERFRONT was thick with salt and oil. Fog curled in lazy wisps along the empty piers. The distant hum of the city never quite reached this part of the docks, too far from the gleaming towers, too forgotten to care. Bear climbed down from the truck, his boots hitting the cracked asphalt with a dull thud. The looming warehouse ahead of him was skeletal and grim, its rusted frame disappearing into the mist. Only the faint glow of industrial floodlights gave away the presence of the men waiting for him.

Comms buzzed somewhere among the group. The men were hard-faced, clad in worn jackets and heavy boots, their hands resting uneasily near the bulges beneath their coats. Most didn't bother hiding it. The air stank of sweat and stale tobacco, mingling with the rot of the harbor. Bear did a quick scan. No movement in the shadows. No silhouettes shifting behind the pallets. It seemed clean, but he'd seen "clean" go bad before.

The shortest of the group, compact and broad, with the look of a man who had spent more time throwing punches than dodging them, reached into his coat pocket. He yanked out an old phone, an anachronism, cracked at the edges.

"What's up, Tony?" he barked, his thick accent unmistakably Brooklyn. "Shit. When?" His face twisted as he listened, a prominent vein bulging across his forehead. Bear didn't need to hear the words to know the call had turned sour. He'd seen it before. News that made men nervous traveled fast.

"Okay. Hang tight," the man growled. "I'll call you back in a minute."

He pocketed the phone, muttering under his breath before turning back to Bear.

"You know anything going down with the Russians?" he asked, his voice low.

"No," Bear replied without hesitation. "I don't work with them. Never have."

The man gave him a long, measuring look. "Vinny," he said, jabbing a thumb at his own chest, as if the name alone was supposed to mean something. And maybe it did. In this part of New York, *Vinny* wasn't just a name. He was a reputation, the kind that carried weight in back rooms and bloodied alleys.

"Bear," the larger man answered simply, offering no elaboration. Vinny had already heard the name.

"Listen, I'm in a bit of a hurry, so..." Vinny began.

Bear nodded toward the truck. "Money's in there."

One of Vinny's men, a wiry guy with a crooked nose, stalked over to the passenger side. He yanked the door open, retrieving a heavy black duffel bag. Without ceremony, he hauled it back to a folding table set up along the side of the warehouse. Several money counters were already positioned there, the hum of machinery filling the space.

Vinny watched closely as the bag was unzipped and bundles of crisp bills spilled out onto the table. The dull fluorescent light reflected off the tightly wrapped stacks, the weight of it enough to quiet the restless air.

"My men will start loading while he counts," Vinny said, jerking his head toward the truck. "You and I will drink."

He pulled a worn pistol from his waistband and placed it on the table with a metallic clink. "If you don't mind. I mean, if we wanted to double-cross you, there's not much you could do at this point anyway."

Bear scanned the group. He could feel the tension, but not the kind that came before a fight. This was posturing. Theater. Vinny wanted to see how Bear handled it. Without a word, Bear shrugged, slung his rifle off his shoulder, and set it down beside the pistol. A gesture of compliance, but also one that made it clear he wasn't afraid.

The whiskey appeared next. A dusty bottle, likely older than the youngest man in the room. The label had been peeled away, but the amber liquid within gleamed in the dim light.

Vinny poured generously, then motioned to a row of crates. "Sit," he said, his grin toothy and warm. "We'll toast to prosperity."

The glass was rough against Bear's palm. The whiskey burned on the way down, sharp and smoky. Not the cheap kind. Vinny might have been a thug, but he had good taste in liquor.

"Only reason for that much hardware is if you got an army," Vinny said casually, nodding toward the loading truck as his men began heaving crates inside.

Bear's expression remained unchanged. He sipped again, letting the heat spread through his chest. "Maybe."

Vinny laughed, though the sound was more like a low growl. "You know, I was in Texas, too."

Without warning, he rolled up his left sleeve, revealing the faded lines of a tattoo etched into his forearm: a snarling coyote surrounded by barbed wire, the mark of the 45th, notorious for its role in the border conflicts.

Bear's eyes narrowed. He leaned forward, extending his hand. "What unit?"

"Border security. Mostly holding ground around Laredo," Vinny answered, clasping Bear's hand in a firm grip. "You?"

"EA-114," Bear replied.

A moment passed, then Vinny's grin faded. His whistle was low, almost reverent. "Jesus. You guys were the shock troops."

"Yeah," Bear said, the word hollow. "*Wrong side of it*, I figured out later."

Vinny's gaze lingered, but whatever he was searching for, he didn't find. Instead, he nodded slowly, a flicker of respect crossing his face. "Listen, I don't know who you're with, but I trust our guy. Anybody who's been through what you have is okay with me."

With a snap of his fingers, one of Vinny's men handed Bear a small card. It was blank aside from a single number, scrawled in plain ink.

"You can call that number. Leave a message," Vinny said. "I'll be in touch."

The money counters slowed, their mechanical hum giving way to silence. Vinny's man gestured—the total had cleared.

"Three for the cause," Vinny said, pulling out three fat stacks of cash and tucking them into a plain envelope. He handed it to Bear. "Consider it a donation."

Bear took it, though the weight of the money barely registered. His focus was already shifting back to the truck, the crates stacked neatly in the bed. Every box had been marked, every inventory accounted for. The weapons were there, ready to disappear into the resistance.

He hoisted his rifle and climbed into the cab. The engine roared to life, the sound bouncing off the empty dockyards. Vinny raised his glass in a mock salute, his grin never wavering.

"Safe travels, Bear," he called.

Bear didn't answer. He shifted into gear and pulled away from the warehouse, the truck's taillights vanishing into the mist. Behind him, the dock returned to stillness.

CHAPTER EIGHT

THE ITALIANS WERE FURIOUS ABOUT the assassination. After being captured, Yuri awoke to find himself hooded and wearing headphones blasting a Puccini opera at full volume. The choice of an Italian composer was not lost on him. He was functionally blind and deaf. His head throbbed with pain, the relentless surge of music making it worse.

His hands were bound with what felt like shoelaces, cutting into his wrists. His waist and ankles were lashed to a wooden chair, and the restraints were tight enough to keep him trapped but not so tight as to cut off circulation. He could wiggle slightly, but the moment he tried moving his wrists, a sharp pain shot through his shoulder as someone struck him with what felt like either a stun gun or a cattle prod. His muscles seized, and a fresh wave of agony coursed through his body.

He was being held in a meat-packing warehouse in New Jersey, but he knew he wouldn't be there for long. Either the Italians would kill him once they decided they couldn't beat any information out of him, or the Russians would get to him—either to rescue him or, more likely, to silence him before he could implicate them.

It turned out that the latter was already in motion. As a Russian squad closed in on the building, one of the Italians on guard, through sheer stupidity and bad luck, flicked his cigarette too close to a leaking drum of paint thinner. The liquid ignited instantly, flames jumping to the surrounding barrels. Within moments, the fire roared to life, sending thick black smoke curling toward the rafters.

At first, the chaos seemed to work in the Russians' favor, giving them the perfect diversion to move in. But Vinny, unaware that his own man had started the blaze, made a snap decision: he ordered his men to throw Yuri into the back of an armored dump truck.

The men cut the cords binding Yuri to the chair and jabbed him with a shock, forcing him to stumble blindly toward the truck. Rough hands grabbed him, flipping him unceremoniously over the side. The impact knocked the hood loose and sent the headphones clattering away. For the first time, Yuri could take stock of the situation.

Gunfire ripped through the air. The warehouse burned, thick smoke rolling in waves around the chaos. Vinny climbed into the driver's seat and floored it. The heavy truck roared forward, smashing through three of the five Russian operatives, killing two instantly and leaving the last lying broken on the pavement.

Yuri, sensing his chance, wrenched free of his wristbindings and slipped away in the confusion. Behind him, the surviving Russians recovered and gave chase.

While Yuri never revealed his source, the Russian soldiers did—without saying a word. Their gear, accents, and precision made their allegiance obvious. Vinny had suspected the Russian mob was involved, but seeing these men confirmed it.

It would be months before Vinny learned the true reason behind the assassination. The motive was petty in the grand scheme: the Russian president owned a stake in a caviar conglomerate, and Carlos had begun competing with it, mainly by hijacking shipments into Europe and stealing the cargo.

Though the feud had nothing to do with the greater war to come, Carlos's death became a pivotal moment. His murder meant a changing of the guard in the family.

On that day, though, to these men, the *why* mattered far less than the *who*. Vinny was now the acting New York boss until a new leader was appointed. And in that role, he had already made his decision: there would be retaliation.

Texas —Early Spring 2053

Six days after Yuri's escape, mourners gathered to lay Carlos Carcione to rest. His funeral should have been in Italy; that was his home. It was where his mother and father were buried, where his two sons lay in the ground. But at the last minute, it became clear that traveling there would be nearly impossible. With tensions rising across the world, the Empire had tightened restrictions on international travel.

So, it was decided that the Don's funeral would be held in Texas, his adopted home. Many of his Italian relatives were frustrated at being unable to pay their respects in person, but the reality was simple: Carlos' body was in America, and that was where it would stay.

Hundreds of mafiosi attended, joined by a half dozen undercover agents of both the Empire and the rebellion. Even for the well-connected, traveling had become difficult. Checkpoints were everywhere, and security had tightened dramatically.

Outside Volgograd, Russian Federation —Early Spring 2053

While the priest read from the Book of Ephesians in Texas and mourners dried their eyes, halfway around the world, Antonio and three of his best men lay in wait outside a dacha in the Russian countryside. Hidden among the trees, they watched the house, waiting for the right moment.

Then, they moved. In a line, they advanced toward the house. A fuel tank behind the building erupted, sending a fireball into the sky and carving a crater into the earth.

Moments later, an elderly woman staggered through the front door, her husband gripping her arm for support. Behind them, a servant scrambled to escape the inferno.

Antonio and his men gunned them down. Boris Aslanov's mother and father were dead.

Chapter Nine

Moscow, Russian Federation —Early Spring 2053

VIHAAN WAS STUCK IN RUSSIA. Though he had tried multiple times to figure out the logistics of crossing the border, it was clear that any attempt would end in arrest. Nearly three months had passed.

During his time in Moscow, Vihaan had learned much—more than he ever expected. He now understood the true reach of the British Empire's military machine. Even as an officer with high-level clearance, he had never grasped its full scope. The sheer number of paramilitary soldiers and contractors was staggering. But what unsettled him most was the Empire's surveillance network. *Spies were everywhere.*

On his third day in Moscow, Vihaan received a security briefing from an intelligence officer on how to avoid surveillance and abduction. It was a grim lesson. Aslanov, believing Vihaan could play a vital role in the coming battles, assigned a guard to shadow him at all times.

It had been a whirlwind of high-level strategy meetings. But Vihaan's strengths weren't in military tactics. His value lay in his ability to lead and communicate.

To stay connected with his forces, he used encrypted Russian satellite comms. Even so, he was cautious. Discussing operational details—whether with his own men or the Russians—felt like an unnecessary risk. Keeping his secrets was his best defense.

It was Sunday. Moscow had been blanketed by heavy snow overnight. From his balcony, Vihaan gazed at the silent, frozen city. He had rarely seen snow before. *It was beautiful, he thought.*

The shrill whistle of the kettle pulled him back inside. As he poured a cup of tea, the doorbell rang.

In the front room, the bulky guard raised a hand, signaling for Vihaan to stay back. Slowly, he approached the door, gun drawn, and peered through the peephole.

Before he could react, an explosive round ripped through the door.

The apartment filled with the sharp stench of gunpowder and burning flesh as the guard collapsed, blood spilling across the floor in a widening pool.

Two more heavy thuds. The door crashed off its hinges.

Four masked men in thick black overcoats stormed into the apartment. Vihaan, watching from the kitchen, calculated his options. Resist? Impossible. Tactical defeat was his only move.

As he raised his hands in surrender, the nearest man punched him hard in the face. Pain exploded through his skull. He barely had time to react before something heavy slammed into the back of his head.

Darkness took him. The last thing he registered, just before it did, was the strange, clipped accents of his attackers.

Vihaan spent the next several days traveling with a cloth bag over his head. He was bound but otherwise unharmed.

Only one man spoke to him: Blair. Unlike the others, Blair didn't bother with a mask. He was bearded, gruff, and oddly polite.

"No more harm will come to you," Blair had said. "Just cooperate." He even apologized for knocking Vihaan out. By the third day, the kidnappers became less guarded around him. He was no longer a prisoner in their minds—just another object moving from one place to another.

So, Vihaan listened. And learned.

On the fifth day, the truck jolted to a stop.

"We're here," Blair said, pulling the bag off Vihaan's head.

Vihaan blinked against the sudden light. The cold air bit at his face. He was standing in a dense forest. It was raining lightly, the moisture clinging to his skin.

Ahead, a small wooden cabin sat in a clearing, smoke curling from its chimney.

Blair led him up the path. Around them, dozens of armed men stood in a defensive formation.

Inside the cabin, Vihaan froze.

Sitting in front of the fireplace was Edward, the Duke of Vancouver, Governor General of Canada and Pacific Northwest. Edward rose and walked toward him.

"My uncle is searching high and low for you," he said, studying Vihaan. "What he would give to know I have you here now..."

Before Vihaan could reply, the door burst open. A man in snow camouflage strode across the room and handed Edward a tablet. The Duke scowled as he scrolled.

"Damn him!" he barked. "Prepare the transport."

Turning to Vihaan, he said, "Mr. Chadra, you will accompany me."

An hour later, they were in the air. Vihaan sat across from Edward in the private jet, exhaustion weighing on him after a week of near-constant travel. He had lost all sense of time and place, shuffled from vehicle to vehicle, blindfolded more often than not. Now, at least, he could see his captor clearly.

Edward studied him with a cool detachment. "I had planned for us to stay at the cabin longer," he admitted, reclining slightly in his seat. "There was strategy in its location. But that doesn't matter now." He leaned forward, elbows resting on his knees. "I don't intend to kill you, nor do I plan on turning you over to my uncle. For now, I just want to talk." His eyes narrowed. "Why are you in this rebellion?"

Vihaan took a breath, his mind still sluggish from exhaustion. "The Crown has been too restrictive for too long. We should have the right to determine our own fates, without the yoke of the monarchy." He surprised himself with the conviction in his own voice.

Edward scoffed. "Fate is fate. A republic wouldn't change that. What it *would* do is create a power vacuum, one that would be filled with something much worse. You rebels don't seem to understand that governing isn't just about ideals; it's about control. Order. The moment you tear down a system like ours, chaos takes its place."

Vihaan frowned, his back pressing against the leather seat. "What about France? They've been successful enough to menace you for the last hundred years."

The Duke let out a sharp laugh. "*Ha!* The French? They're no democracy. They just swapped a monarch for nepotism. An honest leader hasn't been elected there in a generation. You people don't even know what it is you're fighting for." He was quoting Imperial propaganda.

Vihaan didn't look away. "And yet, despite their supposed corruption, they've managed to rival the Empire, both militarily and economically. Their system, flawed as it is, has still given them enough flexibility to adapt, innovate, and challenge you. Meanwhile, your Empire clings to the illusion of stability while rotting from within."

Edward's smirk faltered, just slightly. Vihaan pressed on. "You talk about order and control, but control isn't the same as strength. You think the Empire is untouchable because of its rigid structure, but rigidity is a weakness. Every empire in history that refused to evolve collapsed under its own weight. The Romans, the Ottomans, the Qing, how long before the British Empire meets the same fate?"

The Duke exhaled through his nose, folding his arms. "And you believe rebellion is the answer? That if you tear down the monarchy, something better will rise from the ashes? You're a soldier, Chadra. You've seen war firsthand. You know that when systems collapse, the people suffer. The chaos you unleash won't be brief—it will be generational."

Vihaan shook his head. "I don't believe in blind destruction. But I also don't believe in a world where people are forced to live and die under the rule of kings who never earned their power in the first place. A monarchy only ensures stability for those at the top. For everyone else, it's just another prison."

The debate stretched for hours, neither man yielding. Vihaan found himself frustrated, Edward was arrogant, but he was also sharp. He had clearly considered every argument before, and had counterpoints at the ready. Yet Vihaan refused to concede. There was something deeper at stake than the Duke's well-rehearsed logic.

Finally, the jet began its descent. Outside, the landscape was featureless in the dark, offering no clues to their location.

As they disembarked, one of the guards reached for a hood, but Edward lifted a hand to stop him. "It's fine," he said. "What difference does it make now?"

They drove into a small town, the convoy slipping through empty streets before entering an underground garage beneath a nondescript apartment building. The ride was silent. Edward was focused on a tablet, frowning often as he read.

When the elevator doors slid open, Vihaan followed him down a dimly lit hallway. There were more guards here, though something about them was different. They weren't dressed like Edward's usual security. Their posture, their weapons, it was all wrong.

Edward stopped at the last door. He turned to Vihaan with something almost like amusement. "I know you're afraid, Colonel Chadra. But I think the last few weeks are about to make sense." He gave a slight smile and reached for the door handle. Then he hesitated, looking Vihaan in the eye. "You do need to get over that fear, though. You're a warrior, and this is a war."

The door swung open.

Inside, standing near a table, was a man Vihaan never expected to see: Andrew Greg. He wore a full rebel uniform, the general's stars gleaming on his collar.

CHAPTER TEN

New York —Early Spring 2053

ALEX HAD NOT GOTTEN EXACTLY what she wanted from the bartender, but she hadn't been turned away outright either. After they talked awhile, he realized that he knew her by reputation and told her he'd be willing to speak with her, *off the record*, later. He had originally said he wanted to see her that weekend, but it had been three weeks, and with the fighting between the mobs, security had been tight.

It was dark now and the city was blanketed with a thick fog that made the air seem to stick to everything. The tops of the high-rises disappeared in the Manhattan skyline giving the appearance that they went on forever. Alex was driving along the East River making her way out of the city. At the bridge she stopped for the checkpoint. The guard looked sleepy and bored. She rolled down her window. Drones buzzed overhead, peering through the night.

"Evening, miss," the soldier said. "Curfew is at 1:00 a.m. tonight on a'count o' this fog."

"I understand," said Alex. "I'm just crossing to get some pie at a diner I like."

"*Wha?* All this for a piece o' pie?" asked the soldier. "That mus' be some special pie," he chuckled.

Alex grinned back and was reaching for her identification when the soldier waved her on.

"Don' you worry 'bout it, miss. Enjoy your pie." The soldier tipped his hat at her and motioned at the sentry to let her pass.

Alex drove carefully over the bridge and down onto the ramp leading into Jersey. After another twenty minutes, she was well into the suburbs. She doubled back twice and pulled into a gas station once, just to see if anyone was obviously following her. Of course, they could have eyes on her from above, and she'd never know. But odds were about equal that they didn't.

She was in the countryside now. The well-lit streets had given way to a two-lane country road. She spotted the landmark she was looking for, an old Texaco sign with an "X" across the star. She turned into the abandoned parking lot and, as she was told would happen, the old garage doors opened. She drove her car into the service bay, where a blinding light immediately filled the room. A hum came from the air and she could feel the static crispness around her as the hair on her arms stood on end. The car lowered into the bay. She was blinded by the intense light.

"Step out of your car, Alex." said a familiar voice over a speaker.

Going by feeling alone, she opened her door and stepped tentatively out onto solid ground.

"You'll need to leave that pad behind," the voice said. The bright lights dimmed, and Alex pulled her pad from her jacket pocket and tossed it into the car.

She waited for her eyes to adjust. The room was slowly coming into focus and she noticed the very strong smell of gunpowder. Then, with a few blinks, she was able to see again. The security scan was over. The room was crowded. At least fifty people, most carrying firearms, were in the room engaged in various tasks. Her car slid back on a glider into a space with a dozen other vehicles.

From behind a glass wall, she saw John motioning toward her. As they walked down a corridor, going consistently deeper underground, Alex began to get the sense that this was the real heart of the dissident movement. Every fifteen meters or so, other halls branched off the main line. The complex was huge.

"How did you build all this?" she asked, but John just kept walking without so much as a grunt. Finally, he turned into a common room with three doors, one on each wall. He pointed to the one on the right and handed Alex a key fob.

"That's your room there. I'll be back in two hours. There's a audio-only phone in there, too, if you need to call your boyfriend, but you should know that the call is monitored." Alex looked down at the key and made her way over to the door. It was heavy steel.

Inside, she found a small bed and bath combo with a desk. On the desk was a pad that said "Please place thumb for identification." Once she placed her thumb on the security icon, the pad lit up and greeted her by name.

She spent the next hour and a half reading fascinating accounts of the battles of the Texas Wars, which she knew too well. She was pleased to see that unlike the Empire's version, here was truth. There were files on the junior officers who had gone into hiding. There were files on the foreign generals who were trusted. This would have been a treasure trove for a historian, but nothing really shed light on any of the new leaders in the rebellion.

A light knock came at her door. She suddenly realized what time it was. She opened the door and saw a man waiting on her. He looked vaguely familiar, and then she realized it was the strange man from her gym. He grinned, "Yeah, we've been following you a while now."

This reminded her that she had forgotten to call Ben. She hesitated a moment, and then, deciding that he'd understand, she followed the man out into the hallway. They moved back down into the corridor, through a mess hall, and past a long row of offices. Clearly, this was an underground labyrinth that had been there a long time. Her head swirled with all the sights and sounds of the place.

At last, they came to a bank of elevators and went down many levels—so many Alex couldn't figure out how far. Out again into another corridor, where they met John, who seemed impatient. This hall was guarded by combat sentinels with machine guns and large cameras on each side. Sentinels like these were very expensive and state of the art—even for the Empire. As they passed, one of them rolled near her while two more took up a defensive posture. Alex froze, scared of the lifeless androids with the automatic weapons. John seemed unperturbed and turned to face the closest droid, apparently to be scanned. "She's with me," he said, and the three sentinels changed posture and continued to patrol the hall.

They came to a conference room with a massive table in the center and chairs all around the walls. It was richly decorated with thick carpet and wood panels. The far end was a bank of video displays and, to Alex's surprise, a uniformed military officer sporting the colors of the old rebellion. John pointed to a seat along the wall for Alex and continued on to the table. People were still arriving. Men and women were huddled in small groups, looking over pads or talking. Other uniformed officers came and went. The room was getting crowded, and nearly every seat was taken. Suddenly, there was a flurry of activity as several people came in at once. The officer at the far end shouted, *"Ten-hut!"* and everyone stood up, all the uniformed personnel at attention. The room fell silent.

In walked a very old man who, despite his age, seemed light on his feet. "Please take your seats," he said, looking around the room. He briefly made eye contact with Alex as he scanned around. She felt like she had seen him before... *the files*. He was the famed Martin Frell. The picture of him in the archive was of a younger man, a man who was supposed to have died in Texas. Though he was a high-ranking general, he was not in uniform. Instead, he was in a simple dark suit with a blue tie.

General Frell looked around the room. "I need eyes up and the tactical status of each of the cells."

The room was abuzz, and Alex suddenly felt very out of place. John came over to her. "You're going to witness history tonight," he said. "You're going to have to decide though, Colonel, whether you're going to just watch or help." She was startled by his use of her former rank. She had hidden that part of her past from everyone. Not even Ben knew what exactly she had done so long ago.

"We need to get our message out, and we believe you are the right person for the job," John said.

Alex got back home just as the sun was rising. She was buzzing with energy and had written an incredible multipart story for the paper in her mind on the way home. She was excited to be a part of something this important and needed to get her thoughts down before she forgot them. She didn't want to be a propagandist for the rebellion, but she was willing to write sympathetically about them, if she could just convince Carl to run the stories. It would be a hard sell, for sure.

She burst into her apartment and started to dig in the coat closet for an old pad she hadn't used in years. It had been rebuilt by a friend of hers to stay off the radar of the government, and she used it to keep things safe and secure. She began to type furiously, recalling everything from the night before, keeping detailed notes. She knew she was putting more down than she ought to, but none of the facts that would endanger the rebellion would make it into her final columns. She just wanted to keep the facts straight.

Ben stirred awake to the sound of rapid, rhythmic typing. It took him a moment to place it—Alex, working. The glow from the living room seeped under the bedroom door, and he could hear her muttering softly to herself. He ran a hand through his hair and pushed himself up, stretching. It was still early, but she had been gone all night. He had expected her to slip into bed quietly, exhausted from whatever lead she'd been chasing. Instead, she was wide awake, possessed by whatever she had uncovered. He walked out to find her hunched over an old, beat-up pad, her fingers moving across the screen with frantic energy. Loose strands of her hair had fallen into her face, but she didn't seem to notice. Her lips moved as she read and typed, a rhythm of thought so deep it was almost a trance. Ben smiled, coming up behind her and pressing a soft kiss to the back of her neck. She gasped, jolting slightly before turning to see him.

"You scared me," she whispered, a grin flickering across her lips.

"You've been at this for hours," he murmured, rubbing her shoulders gently. He could feel the tension in her muscles, the kind that came from being too wrapped up in her own thoughts to even acknowledge her body's exhaustion.

She glanced at the clock and let out a breath. "I just needed to get everything down."

He recognized the manic glint in her eyes, the way her mind worked in overdrive when she had uncovered something big. She was vibrating with energy, her body still thrumming with adrenaline. Without another word, she grabbed his sleeve and pulled him toward the bedroom.

Later, as Alex finally drifted into sleep beside him, Ben lay awake, staring at the ceiling. Her body was curled into his, her breath warm against his chest, but his mind was racing. He carefully slid out of bed, making sure not to wake her, and padded to the kitchen. He put water on for tea, the simple, familiar act grounding him, choosing not to use the amphora. But his eyes kept drifting back to the old pad she had left on the counter.

He frowned. Why had she pulled that relic out of storage?

Ben knew Alex. She was always chasing something, always digging where she shouldn't. But she was also careful, meticulous in guarding her work. The fact that she had left this sitting out, unlocked, was out of character. She had been too caught up in the moment to think about securing it.

He hesitated, then reached for it.

The screen came to life, the words bright against the dim kitchen light. The first lines made his stomach drop.

Ben skimmed through the opening paragraphs, but by the time he hit the middle, he wasn't skimming anymore, he was reading every word, absorbing every chilling detail.

The rebellion wasn't just an idea anymore. It wasn't just whispers or speculation. It was real, organized, structured. And Alex had been inside it.

The more he read, the worse the sinking feeling in his gut became. She wasn't just covering them. She was inside their world now, too close to it, too enmeshed. She had seen their leaders. She had walked through their stronghold. She knew how their cells operated, where their weapons came from.

And now, so did he.

His hands trembled as he reached the final notes. A meeting. A gathering of all the rebel cell leaders. A moment so crucial, so dangerous, that they couldn't even risk communicating about it remotely.

Ben put the pad down as if it had burned him. He stared at it, his breath shallow, his pulse hammering in his ears. He had read every word, every damning detail, every thread connecting Alex to the rebellion. His heart raced as he scrolled back up, his mind screaming at him to do something.

His first instinct was to wake her up. Shake her, demand that she stop. Demand that she see reason. *Demand* that she walk away while she still could. He pictured it—her drowsy, annoyed expression shifting into anger as he tried to explain what she had done. She wouldn't listen. He knew that. Alex never backed down from a fight. She never stopped digging. And if he woke her now, it wouldn't be to convince her, it would be to push her away for good.

His jaw tightened as another thought crossed his mind.

Destroy it.

His gaze flicked to the old pad sitting on the counter. He could do it. One simple action. He could wipe it. Smash it. Drop it in the kettle and watch the circuits fry. He could erase the notes, the files, everything. She'd be furious, but she'd be safe. She'd have nothing left to give the rebellion.

His fingers twitched.

But she'd just start again.

Ben closed his eyes, his gut twisting. If he destroyed her work, it wouldn't stop her. It would only make her more reckless, desperate to rebuild it. She'd see him as an enemy. As an obstacle. And worse, she'd know.

She'd know that he was afraid.

A shudder ran through him. He knew what the smart choice was. If he had any sense of self-preservation, he'd do what the good citizen was supposed to do: take the pad, slip out into the city, and turn it in. Drop it in the hands of the Empire and pray they let her go with just a warning.

But he knew better.

The Empire didn't warn people.

Ben's breath came in ragged bursts now, his mind reeling, clawing for a way out. He looked at the bedroom door, at the dim glow of morning creeping in. Alex was asleep, warm, safe.

For now.

He exhaled.

And then... he did nothing.

With slow, deliberate movements, he turned the pad off and set it down exactly as he'd found it. His hands were still shaking as he reached for his tea, bringing it to his lips. It had gone cold.

Ben sat there for a long time, staring at the screen. At the choices he hadn't made. At the weight of what was coming.

CHAPTER ELEVEN

Chinatown, New York —Early Spring 2053

ANDREW GREG STARED BLANKLY INTO space, a ring of smoke circling his head, a pipe in his hand. He sighed loudly. He was a large man with bushy eyebrows over dark blue eyes. He looked older than his forty-seven years and weary. His beard was mostly gray, but his hair was still chocolate colored with only the occasional white strand.

Andrew wondered where this new rebellion would lead. He had seen all this before and despite being the face of this new rebellion, he was a little jaded. He worried about his young officers. He felt they were too optimistic. They hadn't been beaten enough and battle-tested enough to be sufficiently suspicious.

It had been a long night, and he was tired, but he didn't have time to sleep. Things were moving quickly now, and the betrayal of the Russians had the potential to ruin everything. He cursed softly to himself and thought about the damn Russians and their stupid skirmishes with the Italians. He had no time for the problems they were creating. Couldn't they both see that their fight was only helping the Empire?

Andrew walked over to his desk, the smoke following him. He looked at the map. The Russians had dropped paratroopers into Rome, without any obstruction from the broader international community. Meanwhile, the Italians were occupying most of the Russian sections of New York and Philadelphia. The Empire had largely ignored the street fighting, so long as it stayed in those neighborhoods. But he knew it was just a matter of time until the fighting spilled over and the Empire used it as an excuse to crack down again. A lot of innocent people would die over this nonsense.

Andrew thought about what had happened to Vihaan. He felt bad for having set the meeting with Aslanov. He was lucky to be alive. The Russians had offered to trade Vihaan to the British in exchange for looking the other way as they prosecuted their war against the Italians. That was before Greg had help him disappear.

As he looked at the map, his pad began to ring. He selected a screen nearby to take the call. On the other end was General Frell. An icon appeared showing the line was being encrypted. Then Frell spoke, "We've recruited the Colonel as an information officer," he said.

"She's so much more capable than that," answered Greg.

"Well, this is where she'll start anyway. If she lives long enough without being detected, she'll do more for the cause with her writing skills than her fighting skills. Though, I agree with you, before this is over, we're going to need all the fighters we can find." The General paused and took a deep breath. "Listen, General, I've got a job that needs doing and I think you're the only one that can pull it off."

"I'm all ears," said Greg.

"I want you to go to New York and meet with a man there named Vinny. He's the acting boss of the New York families. You'll meet up with one of our guys, a big fella named Celsus Berning. He goes by Bear."

"Yeah, I've met the guy. He's not reliable. He was a merc and the meanest son of a bitch I've ever met."

"Well, be that as it may, he's the guy that is going to help us meet with Vinny. He's been buying guns from them for a while now and says that the Italians trust him."

Andrew had known General Frell for a long time. He trusted his wisdom. "Okay. Just tell me when to go," he said finally.

"Your driver will be there in an hour." And with that, the generals nodded and the two men disconnected.

That night, Andrew sat across the table from Bear at a small, hot, Chinese bar. The tiny room was lit by a single fluorescent light that flickered annoyingly. The owner, a man of eighty, left the front door open because of the humidity from the cooking. The one large window in the front was hazy with condensation dripping slowly into a puddle on the ancient sill. Bear's face dripped too, but he didn't seem to mind the heat. He told a joke in Mandarin to the old man, who didn't laugh, even though Bear found his own joke so funny he snorted.

"What'd you say to him?" asked Andrew.

"Oh," Bear started laughing again, almost unable to spit out the words, "I said, 'What do you call a fortune cookie that's missing its paper slip?'" Bear paused for dramatic effect, "Unfortunate."

Andrew smiled weakly, "Nice one."

"Say, let's get some grub while we wait. This place might look like a shithole, but it has the best mushroom stir-fry in the city."

"Sure," said Andrew, "and a beer."

Bear ordered in Chinese, and the old man nodded, turning to face the giant wok on an open flame behind him. As he cooked, Andrew gazed into the fire, lost in thought.

"Hey, they're here," said Bear, stroking his thick red beard and covering his mouth at the same time.

Vinny was not a big man. But he walked the way a man who knows what he is capable of walks. He had alert eyes and dark, slick hair and wore a vest that was made to look fashionable, but was clearly bullet resistant. Next to him was one of the biggest men Andrew had ever seen. He was as wide as a tree and took up the entire doorframe, which he had to stoop to enter. The man was so big, he made Bear look small.

"Holy shit," muttered Andrew.

"Yeah," said Bear, "You should see him fight. I once saw him jokingly punch a guy in the arm and accidentally dislocate the guy's shoulder."

Vinny joined the men at the table. The muscle, Ace, as he was known, stayed near the door.

"You guys clear this place?" Vinny asked.

"Yeah," said Bear, "and Bo is a friend."

Vinny looked at the old Chinese man, still stirring the food in the wok, ignoring the newcomers.

"OK, let's get to it then. We are planning a major assault on both the Russians and the Imps in Greenwich Village. We have intel that the Empire is looking to wipe us out and give the gun trade to the Russians. We want to preempt that and eliminate the Russians and their local Imp supporters."

"When?" asked Andrew.

"Tomorrow night."

Andrew scoffed, "I can't get any logistics into place that quickly, much less for something so sensitive that it will inevitably lead to a broader conflict."

Bear and Vinny looked at each other.

"What?" asked Andrew.

Bear slid a pad across the table and Andrew saw a logistics report from the New York cell leader, the Boston cell leader, the Philadelphia cell leader, the Hartford cell leader, and on, and on. This was all highly classified, and Andrew had seen the same report that morning during his briefing.

"How the hell did you get this?" he asked.

"General Frell gave it to us yesterday. He wanted you to know how serious we are," answered Vinny. "We're going to attempt to assassinate the King tomorrow night at the palace."

Bo stopped cooking in the wok and brought four beers and four plates to share the giant bowl of food he'd just made.

"Oh, he won't be eating," said Vinny gesturing to Ace at the door.

Bo flashed a grin to Bear before sitting down to join the men, shoveling some of what was clearly his dinner onto a plate and starting to eat. Bear laughed heartily, as did Bo.

Bear said something in Mandarin, and the old man nodded. He pulled a pad splattered with grease from an apron pocket and handed it to Andrew. On it, he saw a schematic of the King's palace. Skimming, he then saw a profile of the kitchen and a young man who resembled Bo.

"His grandson," said Bear.

Andrew nodded, understanding. "Okay, what do you need me to do?"

"We need a massive diversion," said Vinny. "The New York cell is going to work with us to attack the Russians. We're hoping that all the other cells jumping in at once will force the King to call up his reserve guards and call a lockdown."

"Won't that make things worse?" asked Andrew. "I've seen this battle plan before many times and we suffered too many casualties to make it worth it."

"That's only if our plan is to make territorial gains," said Vinny. "This time, we just want two things: decapitate the Empire and stop the Russians. In the chaos that follows, we'll have our best chance in a generation."

Bear skimmed to the next page on his pad. "This is the plan," he said.

Andrew reviewed the notes and map and nodded slowly. "I understand," he said simply.

"Boss, we need to go," said Ace.

Just as he spoke, there was a small explosion not far from the bar. Then another, closer.

Bear stood up, pulling a large handgun from a hidden holster. Bo slurped his noodles loudly, seemingly uninterested in the sudden commotion. Andrew and Vinny also each had guns at the ready. Ace came further inside.

"Is there a back door to this place?" he asked the old man.

Bo sighed loudly, clearly annoyed at having his dinner interrupted. The man stood, noodle bowl in hand, and walked toward the front door. The familiar pings and pops of rounds ricocheting off concrete and steel were now audible and the crack of small arms going off in the middle distance could be heard throughout the neighborhood. Bo casually leaned into the doorframe, finishing his noodles and surveying the scene. The hiss pop of a bullet skimmed off the frame as Bo stared angrily into the street. He then walked out to the fire hydrant on the curb and kicked it hard, causing it to suddenly tilt askew, revealing a panel underneath. Bo put his palm on the panel, and from behind the sign on his bar, a drone appeared, jetting quickly through the front door and taking up position above the old man. The lighting in the bar dimmed and the counter of the bar flipped up like the lid of a briefcase, revealing an impressive arsenal underneath. Two buildings down, across the street, men suddenly poured out like ants—hundreds of them running toward the sound of the nearby fighting.

Vinny's phone rang, as did Andrew's pad. Both men had received the same communiqué from General Frell: "Fighting has begun. Meet cell leader and engage."

The four men walked to the bar to examine the weaponry, each selecting one to their taste. All of them were veterans of violence and knew how they did their best work. Bear took a shotgun and an M4 rifle, checking them and grabbing extra ammunition. Ace took a massive machine gun that even he needed two hands to carry. Both Vinny and Andrew took rifles with V7 smartscopes. They took up a tactical formation and headed into the street, staying close to the building. Bo took a walking stick that was leaning in the corner, and a handgun, and followed the men out. As the battle-hardened men walked steadily toward the sounds of heavy fighting in tight formation, heads moving and surveying, constantly alert, Bo simply shambled down the middle of the street, the look of an ancient man lost amid the chaos, his tactical drone hovering a few meters above.

On the next block, they saw their first fighting. Imperials in battle gear were bunched behind a sandbag barricade in the middle of the intersection. They had an armored personnel carrier in the middle of their makeshift fort. On top, a man with a .50-caliber gun was preparing to fire into a nearby building. Bear could see muzzle flashes coming from the building and saw the Brits taking cover behind the APC. Bear looked at Andrew and the others, who had seen what he had, and they nodded at him. He was going to charge the Imperials' position. The enemy hadn't seen any of them yet and the element of surprise would work to their advantage.

Just as he started running, a young British soldier protecting his unit's rear saw Bear and started to shout. But the words never left his throat. Bo's drone had fired a missile into the center of the sandbag fortification. All the men around the APC disintegrated. Only the man on the .50-caliber rifle remained. He tried to swivel his gun around to face the new threat. But whoever was firing from the building finally got a good shot in, and the man crumpled.

Andrew and Vinny looked at Bo, still hobbling toward them. The man looked at them and shook his head disapprovingly. Soon, from alleys and other nearby streets and buildings, an army of Chinese men came and began to walk behind Bo tactically surveying the area. Andrew noticed that they were wearing the rebellion's insignia, but it had another mark on it in Chinese.

The group made their way to the sandbags. One of the men flashed a signal to another in the nearby window, who returned the signal. Suddenly, the streets were filled with people. All of them had armbands with the rebellion's symbol, all handmade. Men and women, from all walks of life, were streaming into the streets now carrying various weapons, though with few guns.

Vinny pulled out his phone and a man's face appeared. "Where are you?" asked Vinny.

"I'm at our other place," said the man on the line.

"OK, I want you to get everybody over to the first place. We're about to have company. Tonight's the night."

The man nodded and hung up. Vinny turned to Andrew, "We need to get to Brooklyn, and we need to take most of these people with us."

"We'll be sitting ducks for the drones if we cross the bridge," said Andrew.

"Well, they're all going to be dead unless I gear them up," said Vinny, gesturing to the newly formed army of amateurs.

Andrew surveyed them. They were ragtag for sure. But they were angry and determined. "What do we know about these guys?" he asked Bear, gesturing to the heavily armed Chinese men.

"They're Bo's family," said Bear. "Whether by blood or friendship, they all owe their loyalty to him. When he became part of the rebellion, so did they."

"They will help you however you need, General Greg," said Bo, "You will find that they are very capable soldiers, and most have been training for years for this very night."

Andrew stared at the old man, shocked by his English. Bear laughed heartily at his obvious confusion.

"I've lived here for sixty years, General, do you not think I've picked up a few words in that time? I've found that choosing not to speak so much has allowed me to hear more than I would have otherwise." Bo grinned and then said something in Mandarin. A young man came up and listened as Bo gave him instructions. The man made a gesture to the rest of the men, who then took up positions around the intersection.

Andrew looked out over the assembled fighters, the smoke curling above the ruined barricade. He turned back to Bo and Vinny, his voice steady.

"I've got a plan."

Chapter Twelve

B EN WAS ON HIS WAY home from work when the sirens started wailing. Seemingly all over the city, the sounds of trouble erupted. He watched as a fire truck, then another, and then an army transport screamed by. Sentry droids were in the air everywhere. Ben was more than a dozen blocks from home, but he started to run as fast as he could, his dress shoes clapping loudly on the concrete. His shins were screaming.

Suddenly, rain started pattering around him, first in big fat drops, then just curtains of water. He was soaked through. His sweater vest was clinging to him, weighing him down. He slowed, planning to pull it off, but as he had it over his head, he felt two hands grab his shoulders and push him to the ground. Then he felt a sharp pain in the back of his head, his right arm went numb, and then everything went dark.

He awoke in a cavernous warehouse, lying on a hospital bed. His wet clothes were gone and in their place, he was wearing a hospital gown. He was cold, but sweating. He looked down and saw that he was handcuffed to the bed. Ben's heart pounded as he yanked at the cuffs, the cold steel biting into his wrists. His breathing was sharp and ragged. What the hell was going on? The last thing he remembered, rain, a shove, pain. Then... nothing. There was no one around, and he shouted *"Hello,"* but there was no answer to his call. Water was dripping somewhere, and he could hear the occasional rumble of thunder. Or, so he thought. It occurred to him moments later that it wasn't thunder, but explosions. Deep and loud, but far away.

Ben's shoulder was throbbing. It felt like something hot was poking him just below his collarbone. He must have broken something when he fell.

Somewhere behind him, he heard a cough. He strained his neck, trying to turn to see behind. But it was no use. The way he was tied to the bed made it impossible, and besides, there was really no other light in the warehouse beyond the one spotlight above him.

"Hello?" he tried again. Still, no answer. He could feel the presence of someone else in the room, but clearly, they had no interest in conversation. Ben closed his eyes and laid back. He was pragmatic enough to understand that conserving his energy was the best idea right now.

But somewhere off to his left, a door creaked loudly on its hinges. It sounded old and heavy, and when it closed the sound echoed loudly in the room. He then heard a metal chair scraping the concrete floor as the person behind him stood. He braced himself and began to feel his heart beating in his temples. His adrenaline was pumping. He was scared. Truly scared.

From his right, the person who had been behind him came into view. It was a woman, tall and beautiful, with her hair pulled back into a tight bun. She had an eye patch over her left eye, but her right eye was a sparkling blue. She cleared her throat and spoke, but not to him.

"He's awake. It seems to have all worn off and there doesn't seem to be anything wrong with him."

"My... my shoulder hurts badly," said Ben.

From the shadows, a tall, heavy, light-skinned man with a walking stick approached with a menacing grin.

"Which side?" he sneered.

Ben hesitated, then looked at the woman and back to the man, "Uh, this one," he said, lifting the arm chained to the bed.

"Well, let's get that fixed up, then. Nurse?" said the man, turning toward the woman. She reached out and pressed on Ben's collarbone and then his shoulder blade. Ben winced. "It's not dislocated," she said. "Either just a strain, or possibly a minor fracture, but we'd need an X-ray to confirm."

The man leaned toward Ben, putting his weight on the railing of the bed. He whispered in Ben's ear, "I'm going to ask you a question and it is important that you tell me the truth."

Ben was confused, and he turned his head to face the man when he saw that he was holding a small blade—a scalpel. Lars ran the scalpel along Ben's arm, not enough to cut, just enough for him to feel the cold blade. "See, Mr. Patel, I prefer to start slow. Give a man time to think. To weigh his options."

Ben squirmed. "What do you want from me?"

Without speaking again, the man plunged the blade into Ben's bad shoulder. Ben screamed and felt a stream of warm blood flow down his arm. The man pulled the blade out, causing even more pain. Then he immediately plunged it in again, only this time in Ben's good shoulder. Ben cried out, "Please, you have the wrong person! Why are you doing this?!" But the man still didn't speak. He simply pulled the blade out and then sliced a long line across Ben's face. Ben felt the slice as an intense white-heat—almost like he'd been burned. He racked his brain, trying to figure out why this was happening to him.

Then it dawned on him: Alex. This was about the meeting she'd gone to. The man held the bloody blade in his hand and paused for a moment. Someone else had come into the warehouse. Ben recognized him immediately—it was Lieutenant Marby, the soldier he and Alex had often seen in their neighborhood. He came around to the other side of Ben's bed.

"Hello, old chap," said Marby with a grin. "It looks like you've found yourself in a bit of a spot here. I could help you out here, you know. You'd just need to tell Lawrence here what we need to know."

"But I don't know what you want to know," screamed Ben. "He's not asked me anything."

"Tsk. Tsk. Come now Lars, we can't start cutting until he refuses," said Marby.

"You do your job your way; I do my job my way," said Lawrence, still holding the scalpel.

"Fair enough, good man. Fair enough. But let's at least give the old boy a chance." Marby looked down at Ben and removed his hat. "Now, Mr. Patel, I'm going to ask you only once: tell me—what is your girlfriend's involvement with the rebellion? And mind you, we've got her in the next building over. If what you say contradicts what she says, we'll just kill her."

Ben thought for a moment before speaking, but the hesitation cost him. Lars stabbed him again in his bad shoulder. Ben writhed in agony and gritted his teeth. "I... I don't think she has anything to do with the rebellion. I think. I think..." he started, but didn't get to finish before Lars put his finger deep into one of Ben's wounds.

"Do not lie to me, son," Lars said, leaning in as he spoke. Ben screamed.

"Just tell us," said Marby, "Alex is going to give it up if you don't. If you tell us the truth, I'll let you both live. Lie, and I'll kill her first and make you watch before torturing you slowly to death."

Ben felt like he was in a long tunnel. He could hear Marby, and he wanted to speak, but it was like he was underwater. Suddenly, everything went black as he passed out again.

The girl with the eyepatch felt for a pulse. "He's alive, but his pulse is thready. He's probably not built for much more of this," she said. She pulled a small bag from beneath the bed and prepared a syringe from a vial of opaque-looking liquid. She stuck it into Ben's arm and he gasped awake, startled and sputtering.

"She's just researching an article!" he blurted. "It's nothing, it's just research!"

Marby looked at Lars and Lars shook his head. He knew. From years of experience in interrogations for the Empire, he knew when someone was lying. He was an expert at his job, which was to pull information out of enemies of the state, *no matter* what it took.

Marby nodded back. Lars then pulled a new tool from his jacket. It was a small thing—dull and dark. Ben fixed his eyes on Lars and his hands, already bloody, holding a long, skinny hook. Ben wasn't sure what it was but he was immediately repulsed.

The nurse looked uncomfortable. "Please, Mr. Patel, just tell them what they want to know."

Ben summoned his courage and lied again, "She's never even met them."

Lars shook his head and pulled a file folder out from a briefcase on the floor and tossed it onto Ben's lap, open. On top was an aerial photo of Alex and John, the bartender, standing outside talking. It was night. But it was clear that she had been surveilled and that they thought the old bartender was a member of the resistance.

"Try again, Ben," said Lars as he took the metal hook in one hand and held down Ben's head with the other. Ben felt the cold metal on his cheek. The hook sliding up and resting near the corner of his right eye. "Last chance," said Lars.

"Ben, you have to tell them!" said the nurse. Ben looked more closely at her eye patch and put it all together. He began to shudder. The drugs were wearing off, and he was at risk of passing out again.

"Give him another dose," said Lars.

Ben watched as the nurse injected him with more of the opaque solution. He could feel his pulse quicken and his cheeks getting hot. He realized he was shaking involuntarily. Lars pressed the hook into the corner of Ben's eye, sliding it behind the orb and deep into his socket. Ben could hear the hook moving behind his eye, scraping. It was a pain unlike anything he'd ever experienced. His right eye went dark, and he heard a tearing sound on that side. The nurse looked away. Despite the drugs, Ben passed out again.

CHAPTER THIRTEEN

ALEX WONDERED WHERE BEN WAS. She hadn't been able to reach him all night. With the comms still dead and the weather worsening, her nerves were stretched taut. Something wasn't right. He must have stayed at the office to keep out of the way. The best thing is to stay put. She was just sitting down with a cup of tea and her old pad to review what she'd written when a knock came at the door. Looking through the visor, she saw that it was Mrs. Sadakis. Alex opened the door and greeted her warmly. "Come in, come in!"

Mrs. Sadakis grabbed Alex's arm. "You have to come with me right now. If you have anything about the rebellion, get it now and come with me. Hurry."

Alex's fingers hesitated over the panel. This was insane. How did Mrs. Sadakis even know about this? But the tone in the woman's voice sent a shiver down her spine. No time for questions. Move. She grabbed her old pad and ran to her bedroom, where, under a hidden panel in her closet, she slid out a long footlocker. She dragged it across the floor, leaving scratches in the hardwood.

Back in the living room, Mrs. Sadakis was still standing in the doorway, glancing furtively down the hallway. She came and took the old pad from Alex, freeing her up to wrangle the footlocker with both hands. She followed Mrs. Sadakis down the hall to her apartment.

The two women had just closed the door behind them only moments before they heard the sound of Imperial chatter over comm-links, coming off the elevator and coming down the hall. Looking at the visor, they saw a team of at least a dozen soldiers walking quickly to Alex's apartment.

The soldiers didn't knock before breaking her door off its hinges. They threw a flash-bang into Alex's living room. She and Mrs. Sadakis could smell the smoke wafting down the hall. Alex turned, preparing to tell Mrs. Sadakis to get to a safe place in her apartment, but saw her standing, bracing herself, holding a sawed-off shotgun ready to draw down on the door. Mrs. Sadakis didn't speak but gestured toward the coffee table where a rifle sat. Alex picked up the weapon and stood next to her neighbor, focused on the front door. There they stood for the next twenty minutes, waiting for the worst to come, but it never did.

Alex's grip tightened on the rifle. "They have to know I'm close." Mrs. Sadakis kept her eyes on the door. "They expect you to run." "Should we?" Alex's pulse pounded in her throat. "What if they...?"

A faint metallic clink sounded from outside: footsteps, the sound of boots moving away. After a time, the women relaxed and Mrs. Sadakis lowered her shotgun. "What the hell was that?!" asked Alex.

"They know where you were. They were coming to kill you. We've got to get you out of the city because they are all looking for you now," said Mrs. Sadakis. Alex blinked in confusion. "Who is looking for me?"

Mrs. Sadakis was moving now, pulling down a piece of luggage from a hall closet. She grunted as she struggled with its obvious weight. "The king's soldiers. They know what you did."

Alex helped her pull the suitcase down. It was heavy and hit the floor with an audible thud. Mrs. Sadakis looked toward her door to see if it had drawn any attention. Hearing nothing, she flipped the top open, revealing a surprising number of handguns with boxes of ammunition. She picked up one that looked almost brand new. Alex could smell the gun oil. She was speechless.

"Hurry, dear," said Mrs. Sadakis, "we have very little time." She handed another weapon to Alex and a box of bullets. Alex glanced at the footlocker she'd dragged from her own apartment. Opening it, she revealed an old rebel's uniform with a colonel insignia, a rifle, and several boxes of her own ammunition, all very much illegal. Mrs. Sadakis nodded approvingly.

"Before my husband died, during his last time with me, he introduced me to a commander in the resistance."

"Samuel had met the man at an airport during a layover flight back from Paris. At first he thought the man was sent as a test to see if he'd gone too deep in his undercover mission in France. But, over time, the man gained my husband's confidence and respect. So, one spring morning, the year he died, Samuel introduced me to Andrew Greg." Mrs. Sadakis stopped for a moment to look Alex in the eyes. "Over the years, I came to trust Andrew with my life and I have been devoted to the resistance, the ideas of freedom that Samuel loved, since."

As she loaded her guns, Alex thought about Ben and instinctively reached for her pad. But all she had was the old one with her notes, and it wasn't connected. "I've got to reach Ben. They could be coming for him too," she said.

Mrs. Sadakis hesitated. "Dear, it's likely they already have. I got the alert just minutes before they got here. If they came here, they are at your office too. Do you know where he is?"

Alex didn't. Worry crept in, and she wasn't sure what to do.

"We have to get you out of the city. They're really only after you, but they will use him to get you if they can. A man will be meeting you soon to help you escape. I don't know who, but I was told to look for a blue cap and a green coat."

Alex had nothing but the clothes she was wearing, and she certainly couldn't put on the uniform. Alex activated the visor, the screen unfolding silently like origami in reverse, taking over the far wall and door, making the other side transparent. Looking through the visor, she could see that by now most of the soldiers sent to get her had left once they realized she wasn't there. But a man had remained in the hallway to see if she happened to stroll home. "There's one out there," she said. "How do we get out?"

Mrs. Sadakis answered, "You'll have to go without me, dear. Blue hat. Green jacket. Take the pad, take my sweater, and keep your gun close. Wait for my signal." Mrs. Sadakis handed her a hooded sweatshirt. "Put this on and keep the hood up." She glanced outside. "Oh good, it's still raining; use my umbrella too. That will help." She stood back and looked at Alex. "OK. That will have to do. Get your things."

Alex complied. Mrs. Sadakis put an old shawl over her head and hunched her back, making herself look smaller and more frail than she was. She opened the front door.

"Ma'am, you need to go back inside," said the soldier standing in the hallway. "We're conducting a terrorism investigation."

"Oh, sweetheart," said the woman, "today is my shopping day. I have to get to the market before they run out of oranges." She walked toward the man, appearing unsteady on her feet. "What is all this about?"

The man looked unsure. "Ma'am, I need you to stay inside. I'll come get you once we have the all-clear."

Mrs. Sadakis took another step down the hallway. She was close enough now that she could see the man's dark-gray eyes peeking over the edge of his ski mask. "I'm sorry. I'm a bit hard of hearing. What did you say?"

The man took a step back and raised his rifle slightly. "Ma'am, back up."

Mrs. Sadakis tripped and fell on the floor, face down, groaning loudly in the process. The man didn't move. Still face-down, she said, "Can't you help an old lady up?"

Sighing loudly, the man shouted, "Get up yourself, you old bag." Mrs. Sadakis lay still, barely breathing. Swearing under his breath, the man slung his rifle and bent down, rolling her over harshly. He never saw the glint of steel beneath her shawl. He was dead before he knew what happened.

The only other guard, still in Alex's apartment, came running out, rifle raised. Mrs. Sadakis lay still. The first guard was on top of her, and she was covered in his blood. "What the hell?" said the new guard. "Rob, are you OK?" He came closer. Mrs. Sadakis stayed still as Alex looked, shocked, through the visor. Alex readied her own gun. The second guard pulled Rob off Mrs. Sadakis. "Holy shit!" he blurted. Blood was everywhere, and Rob's face was gone. The man steadied his rifle on Mrs. Sadakis, using his foot to turn her over. She waited until the last moment; then fired again. The bullet grazed the man's head as he screamed and pulled away. Mrs. Sadakis tried to fire again, but the soldier was quicker, firing from the hip. The man slowly walked toward her, rifle still aimed. He walked by the apartment door, and Alex could see the back of his head through the visor. She disabled the visor to remove the interference and pressed her back against the door. Her fingers felt slick with sweat as she raised the gun. She counted her breaths. One. Two. Three. Then she pulled the trigger. The soldier fell, landing on top of Rob.

Alex threw open the door and ran to Mrs. Sadakis. There was little life left in her eyes. A pool of crimson was spreading from beneath her. "Go. Quickly. I lived well and I died well," she said. Alex pressed her hands against the wound. "Hold on, just hold on."

Mrs. Sadakis's breathing was shallow, but she smiled weakly. "Not bad for an old lady, hmm?"

"I'm getting you out of here."

"No, dear. You go. Live free."

Mrs. Sadakis was gone.

CHAPTER FOURTEEN

ALEX STUMBLED TO HER FEET and ran back into Mrs. Sadakis's apartment. She grabbed the suitcase of guns and ammunition, threw in her pad, and wheeled it across the hall to her own place. The left wheel squeaked annoyingly as she rolled past the dead in the now blood-soaked hallway. Her door was still open, and she gingerly glanced inside. The front room was wrecked: furniture overturned, cushions sliced open, pictures shattered on the floor. No one seemed to be inside. She looked back at the three bodies in the hall, then sprinted in to grab her good boots and a sensible sweater. As she cinched the last lace, the squawk of the soldiers' comtags crackled behind her.

"Unit Three, report. Status?" Silence. Then: "Unit Three, check in immediately."

Alex's pulse pounded. If no one responded, reinforcements would come. She yanked the suitcase upright and bolted for the stairs. The wheel squeaked loudly. *Damn it*. The stairwell echoed with every step and squeak. No time to be careful.

With the suitcase in tow, she hurried down the hall and into the stairwell. The case clanged as she dragged it down the flights. She controlled her breathing—muscle memory and training kicking in—blinking back those damn tears she couldn't help.

Outside, the sun had risen over an ash-covered city. Smoke clung to the buildings like a second skin. Sirens wailed somewhere beyond the horizon, and the occasional pop of small-arms fire echoed. The streets looked scoured, like something had swept through and left behind only silence and soot.

She paused at the doorway, planning her route. She needed to find Ben—whatever was left of the *Courier and Post* would be her best hope. She pulled on the cap and jacket Mrs. Sadakis had pressed into her hands the night before. They smelled faintly of cedar and dust.

The streets were nearly empty—no guards, no civilians, no cars. Just long stretches of concrete and shadow. An old dog limped across the intersection ahead of her, ribs showing beneath its matted fur, its head low as it sniffed for anything worth finding. A post-apocalyptic tableau.

Alex moved cautiously, suitcase in one hand, the other brushing against the 9 mm tucked under her belt. She stuck to the edges of the sidewalk, ducking past blown-out storefronts, keeping her head low.

Then she saw them.

The gallows had gone up overnight.

Three sets of heavy wooden beams stood in the plaza near the subway entrance, hastily reinforced with steel rebar and chain. Beneath them, the bodies swayed in the morning light. Imperial justice, raw and absolute.

She slowed, stomach tight. The first body was that of a young man, barefoot, his arms bound cruelly behind him. The second was a woman in civilian clothes, her face obscured by the angle of the sun.

But the third—

She froze.

There, at the end of the row, hung Carl.

Her editor.

His tie was still around his neck, now tangled with the noose. His eyes were half-lidded, his mouth slack, his head lolled forward like a marionette with its strings cut. The breeze caught the hem of his coat and made him sway slightly. A small sign had been stapled to his chest:

"Seditionist Collaborator."

Alex's breath caught. The weight of it slammed into her chest harder than she expected. She'd had mixed feelings about Carl. But he'd fought to protect her, in his own flawed way. He'd tried to keep her safe when everything was burning.

She staggered a step forward, then forced herself still. No time for grief. Not here. Not now. Then she moved, quick and low, keeping the gallows to her back and the shadows in front of her.

Ben would be at the office, or he wouldn't. Either way, she was going.

And she would not forget what she'd seen. Not today. Not ever.

Carl deserved at least that much.

As she walked, a low rumble grew behind her: a personnel carrier. She slouched, pulling up her hood. Left hand on the suitcase, right on the 9 mm at her belt. The carrier slowed and dropped from hover to street level; she glanced over her shoulder.

A man stood on the running board—John, the rebel bartender—smiling and calling her name. The turret gunner kept the weapon trained to the rear.

"Come now. Quickly!" John shouted.

Alex sprinted, dragging the suitcase. A high-pitched trill: a drone. Gunfire erupted—first the drone, then the flak guns on the APC. Projectiles hissed, snapped, and whirred around her. John pulled her and the heavy case through a side hatch. Inside, the turret's steady rhythm drowned out all else. The carrier lurched forward. John handed her a headset; once on, the gunfire muted and she heard him.

"The city erupted last night," he said. "All our cells are active. We came for you as soon as we could. We need your help at headquarters—coordination, analysis, external comms."

She nodded and adjusted her mic. "My boyfriend. I need to find him—he didn't come home."

John's expression softened. "We'll put out a notice, but it's going to be hard in this chaos."

Suddenly the machine gun stopped, and a new voice came over the headset. It was the driver. "Mills is dead! I need someone on the turret!" Alex jumped up instinctively. She was closest. As she opened the inner hatch, the lifeless body of Mills dropped into the APC. He had no obvious wounds but was bleeding from the mouth. She had no time to sort that out. John reached for her, trying to move past her in the cramped space, but she pushed him away and climbed behind the auxiliary machine gun. Silhouetted against a gray sky were a half-dozen drones of various makes. She realized immediately that she was outgunned and felt naked without armor. She checked the gun and ammunition, then swiveled the aim-assist computer in front of her. Mills hadn't been using it for some reason.

The computer interfaced with the gun so the user could control the rate of fire to more accurately hit a moving target. It was designed to overcome the evade-and-resist countermeasures standard on Imperial drones. Invented by the French and smuggled to the rebels, it was priceless. Alex's fingers flew over the controls. Why hadn't Mills used the assist? The default French setting? No; he would have at least tried. A faint error flashed in the corner of the display: "System rebooted during combat." He hadn't had time to recalibrate. That was his mistake. Messages still appeared in French, both on-screen and in her headset. Fortunately, that wasn't a problem for her. She turned the turret and locked in the aim assist. A single calibration round drew heavy fire from the drones; the second round, guided by the assist, pulled slightly left and brought down the nearest drone in a fiery explosion. A pleasant, calm artificial French voice called shots and strategy as she worked. She fired again and again; not every bullet hit, but enough of them did.

The APC roared through the city on wheels. Propulsion had been damaged in the attack, and it couldn't achieve lift. Drones weren't the only obstacle. The Empire had erected barriers and roadblocks on alternating streets, making ground movement difficult. Occasionally they took fire from rooftops near fortified buildings. The carrier was a bullet magnet. Smoke thickened as they neared the city's edge, and more drones filled the air. Alex kept firing efficiently and effectively, her combat experience guiding every burst.

They turned into a side street to avoid a roadblock, and at the far end more rebels were locked in battle. Infantry crouched behind sandbags, lobbing grenades and firing into an Imperial nest on the opposite corner. The driver came over the headset: "Brace yourself!" He drove out of the alley and straight at the Imperials. Panic spread as the carrier banked over their fortifications. Men on the periphery fired, but the machine gun tore through them. Within seconds every Imperial was down. The driver swung back toward the rebels and slowed near their barricade.

"Man, you guys came along just in time!" A young, stocky rebel looked up at Alex, sweat running down his face despite the cool air.

The driver opened his door. "What unit are you with, son?" "We're part of General Greg's detachment." "Where can I find him?" "He's down at the bridge front. We're supposed to hold this intersection to keep imps from advancing. If you see him, tell him we need reinforcements. That nest went up under heavy drone cover—we couldn't stop them. We need ground-to-air." "I'll let him know," the driver said, then shut the door.

As the carrier pulled away, more drones zipped into the alley, forced into a single-file line by the canyon-like buildings. Alex switched to the cannon on the rear mount, selected the flak option, and took aim.

She selected grapeshot from the interface, locked onto the first drone, and fired. The shot tore through its wing, sending it spiraling, but not before it let off a burst of fire. Metal rang like a gong as rounds ricocheted off the APC's hull. "Damn it," she hissed. She barely had time to adjust before another drone broke formation, diving straight at her. She yanked the trigger, letting off a desperate burst. Smoke, fire, then impact. There was a short delay, and suddenly the entire sky above the alley filled with explosive ordnance. Nearly a dozen drones fell in smoking heaps.

Alex slunk back down into the carrier, closing the hatch behind her. John was crouched over Mills. "He's alive, but barely," he shouted over the noise. Blood was everywhere, making the floor slick. The air reeked of iron and smoke—thick and clinging, with a sour edge that comes from a man bleeding out. Alex opened a hatch on the right side near the fire-control systems panel. Inside, she could see, in the dim light, smoke rising from a fried-out propulsion-control unit. The redundant system glowed red as well. Alex reached for a tool fastened to the back of the hatch door but jammed her hand as the whole carrier careened wildly. She tried to regain her balance but was flung the opposite way and fell into the blood on the floor.

Sitting upright, she reached for the headset to find out what was happening. "...maybe nine or ten more minutes depending on the resistance," the driver was saying.

As she listened, she grabbed the tool and disconnected the harness for the main unit and the redundant one, switching them to auxiliary systems normally used for inertial control. After she reconnected the harness, the whole panel lit green. "Driver, you are green on flight. Be careful; I had to sacrifice some control," she said.

Before she finished speaking, the carrier began lifting. "Roger that," said the driver. "Glad to have you aboard."

The APC was airborne again, hovering near the tops of the buildings. Thick smoke helped shield them from snipers. They headed southeast toward the river, and as they began their descent, Mills died from his wounds.

On the ground, Alex followed John to meet General Greg. The rebels had set up a large encampment that resembled a professional military installation. Thousands of fighters rushed about, filling sandbags, fueling vehicles, and loading ammunition from enormous canvas bags. Overhead, hundreds of drones, dirigibles, and conventional craft swarmed the skies. Across the bridge, the rebels held the opposite bank, where a temporary dock was under construction beside a littoral combat ship.

"General," John greeted Andrew Greg.

Greg nodded. Calm despite being one of the most hunted men in the world, he leaned against a bollard and bit into a green apple, smiling. He looked at Alex, stood, and dug in his pocket, pulling out a tattered piece of paper. "You wrote this, didn't you?" he said. She took the printout and saw it was the article she had proposed to Carl.

"Yeah, that was me. Where did you get this?"

"Hell of a thing, pads," Greg said. "Turns out they're not all that secure. Always preferred paper myself. Walk with me a moment."

He led her to a covered pavilion where stacks of equipment were being sorted. Staff came to attention as he entered, then returned to work.

"Alex, we need you at headquarters. You're one of the best communicators I've read, and we need you to get our message out. We figure twenty percent are loyalists, forty percent are with us, and forty percent can be persuaded either way."

Alex paused. The war had begun, and she needed to believe this time would be different. "I could use a drink," she said.

"Me too," he replied, motioning toward a building across the parkway.

"Is it still open?"

"One way to find out," Andrew said.

They walked into the pub, surprised to find it not only open but packed with excited patrons. When the general entered, the room erupted in cheers.

"Well, I guess we know their politics," he said, smiling and waving at the crowd.

Alex made her way to the bar to get them both a pint while Andrew mingled with those gathered, shaking hands and answering questions. He motioned for her to come over. "I'd like to introduce you to Colonel Alexandra Baker, one of the most important people in our movement."

Startled by the sudden assignment of a rank—especially since she hadn't actually agreed to anything—Alex nevertheless decided it was worth it. She handed Andrew their pints and turned to the crowd.

"We've lived under the weight of this tyranny for generations. I fought in Texas and briefly saw what freedom can look like." The crowd cheered. "All of us will need to do our part to make this work."

CHAPTER FIFTEEN

BEN OPENED HIS ONE GOOD eye. His head was throbbing, and he was shuddering uncontrollably. Sobbing, covered in his own blood and urine, he looked at Marby. "Please... please make it stop."

"I need to know about Alex," Marby whispered.

Ben thought back to what he'd read on Alex's pad when she got home from her meeting. He loved her so much, but he also believed she was already dead. No matter what he told them, they were going to kill her—but maybe he could live. He wasn't a rebel; he was a copywriter.

"It's the only way you're going to live through this," said the nurse, seeming to read his thoughts.

Ben squeezed his one good eye shut. He could still see Alex laughing in the kitchen, the smell of warm tea in the air. She would never forgive him. But she was already gone, wasn't she?

He opened his mouth. "The headquarters is in New Jersey. I don't know where," he began. "She's just writing a story about the rebellion; she's not part of it." He coughed, and fresh flecks of blood sprayed out. "She met with them there. It's at an old abandoned gas station. It goes underground somehow. That's where they meet and plan."

Over the next hour, Ben told them everything he knew. Marby gave him some water, and the nurse injected him with pain medication. As Ben began to feel less pain, he was suddenly overwhelmed by grief at his betrayal. But his fear and desire for self-preservation overrode everything else. He held nothing back.

By midmorning, he was dead. They left him in the warehouse, chained to the bed.

Chapter Sixteen

New Jersey, Rebel Underground Headquarters —Early Spring 2053

WITH NEW YORK GROWING IN chaos, the generals met. The war room in the underground headquarters was alive with tension. Screens glowed, maps were spread across tables, and the air smelled of sweat and gun oil. The hiss of the tea kettle was an ever-present and familiar sound. The base stretched deep beneath an abandoned fuel depot, a relic of an age before the Empire's tightening grip choked the last vestiges of free enterprise. The facility had once stored crude oil, but now it held weapons, intelligence reports, and the desperate hopes of a fractured world.

General Andrew Greg stood at the center, his hands planted on a steel table, his sharp blue eyes scanning the reports before him. To his left an intelligence officer was feeding in the latest updates from the global cells. They had intelligence that the Empire was reeling in India after a successful series of coordinated bombings against supply convoys. In Texas, sporadic fighting had broken out in Houston and El Paso, but the rebels were struggling to hold ground. Canada had seen a resurgence of guerrilla efforts, striking at rail lines critical for the Empire's logistics. Even in the Caribbean, a bold attack on a naval supply depot had thrown the Crown's forces into disarray. For the first time in decades, the rebellion was fighting on multiple fronts.

John Norcamp, the bartender turned *veneficus*, paced at the far end of the room, rubbing his hands together. He had always been a calm man, a man of measured action, but the new report he was holding made him anxious. "The King is dying," he said, his voice low but firm. "The poison is working faster than expected."

A murmur rippled through the room. Everyone knew of Norcamp's handiwork, but few had dared to hope that their plan would work so soon. "What's the source?" Greg asked. "Multiple," John replied. "Independent news leaks suggest he's not left his chambers in days. The official reports claim he's recovering from a 'routine illness,' but my contacts say otherwise. The Royal Guard is in lockdown, and there are whispers that a power struggle is already beginning."

Greg absorbed the information, nodding slowly. "If Frederick dies, his brother Charles takes over. We don't know if he'll be any better."

"He won't be," one of the generals muttered, folding his arms. "Charles may be less cruel, but he's just as determined to keep the Empire together."

A middle-aged woman with cropped black hair and a deep scar across her cheek stepped forward. "We can't afford to wait. If the King is incapacitated, now is the time to strike. We should take this fight directly to the heart of the Empire."

Before Greg could respond, a deep, reverberating boom rattled the room. Dust rained down from the ceiling. A second explosion followed, then a third. The lights flickered. The war room sprang into action. "Bunker penetration!" someone shouted.

The blast doors groaned under the force of the impacts, and a red alarm blared through the corridors. Greg grabbed a nearby comm. "All units, defensive positions! Get to the escape hatches now!"

But the bombing was relentless.

The Empire had found them.

A fourth explosion tore through the main tunnel, sending men and women sprawling. The reinforced ceiling held, but strained.

Smoke filled the chamber. Alex Baker, crouched near one of the auxiliary exits, pulled her sidearm and turned to Greg. "We need to move. Now."

The ground shook again, and part of the far wall collapsed, crushing a group of analysts beneath a cascade of concrete and steel. The room was filled with coughing, shouting, and the sharp cries of the wounded. An aide struggled to his feet, gripping his pad. "Command post is compromised! We're losing structural integrity!"

John helped a bloodied officer up, but his face was grim. "They're not just bombing us, they're coming in. We've got Imperial infantry inbound." Greg swore under his breath. "We're trapped."

The ceiling groaned, and another blast ripped through the upper levels. The distant sound of gunfire echoed through the corridors. Alex turned to Greg, her face set with determination. "We fight our way out, or we die here."

The general gave a short nod. He turned to the room, meeting the eyes of every rebel still standing. "We hold this position as long as we can. If you find an exit, take it. If you find an Imperial, kill them."

Another explosion sent a fireball licking through the entrance tunnel. The Imperial assault had begun in earnest.

Alex turned to give an order, just as a large piece of concrete collapsed directly onto her.

Chapter Seventeen

The Republic of Texas —Ten Years Earlier

THERE WAS DUST IN THE air, thick and dry, coating her throat, clogging her lungs. The heat pressed down like a weight, the kind of searing, inescapable heat that turned men into ghosts before the battle even began. The land stretched before her, a cracked and battered valley pocked with scars from battles long lost. Scraggly mesquite trees twisted in the wind like grasping fingers, and the wreckage of old skirmishes lay rusting in the dirt.

This was Texas. The Republic, as it had once been—ten years ago. It was so familiar to her.

The sun was burning against her back, but she barely felt it. The only thing that mattered was the valley.

A long breath. The press of her binoculars against her face. The slow, steady overlay of data filtering across her vision. The rebel drones overhead painted the terrain in spectral white, marking the outlines of detected landmines. Black dots marked the places where men had already died. But the gray, the gray was where death was waiting. The gray was what they couldn't see.

She lowered the binoculars, rubbing at the bridge of her nose, feeling the headache already settling behind her eyes. "Well, shit."

Beside her, Command Sergeant Major Mark Dunning crossed his arms. "That bad?"

"We're boxed in." Alex turned toward him, still staring at the valley, as if it might shift under her gaze and reveal some hidden path forward. "Imperials are closing in from the east. If we don't move, they'll cut us off from the capital."

Dunning chewed the inside of his cheek. "So, what? We go through?"

A muscle in Alex's jaw twitched. She hated this part. The part where she knew what had to be done, but had to say it anyway. She looked at the valley again, at the ghostly marks of mines and wreckage, at the places where good men had already disappeared into nothing.

"Yeah," she said finally. "We go through."

The hovercrafts roared forward, kicking up waves of dust and sand.

The heat shimmered off the metal, distorting the air like a fever dream. Alex braced herself against the command railing as the first explosion ripped through the valley behind them. The blast sent a transport flipping end over end before it slammed into the ground, bursting into flame.

Then another.

Then another.

She barely had time to register the horror before she saw it—one of the crafts listing dangerously to one side, sparks sputtering from the lifters, its pilot struggling to correct. The failure was inevitable. The craft lurched, slammed into the dirt, and skidded across the valley floor before detonating in a burst of fire and metal.

Alex's heart slammed against her ribs. She had seen this before. Had watched it happen too many times. She knew, in some distant part of her mind, that she should be used to it by now. That this was war. That people died. She never got used to it.

Dunning was already moving.

"I'm going," he said, voice tight, reaching for his helmet.

Alex turned sharply. "That's a death sentence."

Dunning gave her a look—the kind that said they both knew she was right, but that it didn't matter. "So is staying still."

Then he was gone.

She watched, helpless, as he leapt onto a flatback speeder and tore across the battlefield, weaving through craters and wreckage like death wasn't waiting just a breath away. He moved like he always did, like he believed he would make it. Alex wanted to believe it too.

She saw the soldiers stumbling from the wreckage, their faces streaked with soot and blood, eyes wild with panic. Dunning reached them, hauled them aboard, barked orders over the roar of the speeder's engines.

He was almost back when the drone hit.

Not him.

Her.

A shriek of incoming fire. A split-second instinct, too little, too late.

The hovercraft lurched beneath her. The sky tilted.

Then—nothing.

Darkness.

For a long time, there was nothing else. Then, something distant.

Faint.

A voice.

"...Alex..."

No. Not yet.

The battlefield pulled her back.

She woke to the bitter stench of burning fuel, the sharp crackle of fire. Her head pounded, her ears ringing. The hovercraft was a ruin around her, torn open like a carcass, smoke curling from the jagged wreckage.

Somewhere beyond the haze, the battle raged on. She could hear it, the pulse rifles, the screams, the roar of engines. The war had not stopped for her.

She pushed herself up, every movement agony, her breath ragged. Blood dripped down her forehead, warm and thick. She pressed a hand to it, feeling the gash just above her temple, but there was no time to assess the damage. She wasn't dead. Yet.

Her pulse rifle lay half-buried in debris. She grabbed it, forced herself upright, stumbled toward the noise.

A shadow moved through the smoke. She lifted the rifle, finger tightening on the trigger. Then,

"Easy, Colonel. It's me."

Dunning's voice cut through the haze.

She exhaled hard, lowering the weapon. He looked like hell, helmet gone, uniform scorched, his left arm streaked with blood, but he was alive.

"How bad is it?" she asked, voice raw. Dunning wiped at his forehead, smearing the blood further. "Bad."

She nodded once, adjusted her grip on the rifle. "Then let's make it worse for them."

She saw the shift in his face, the flicker of exhaustion replaced by something steadier. Something determined. The battle wasn't over. Not yet.

Time blurred.

As the battle raged on, Command Sergeant Major Dunning cut through the chaos, his speeder kicking up a storm of dust and debris as he veered toward the second rebel hovercraft. The crew inside was barely holding their ground, the gunners firing wildly at the swarm of Imperial drones slicing through the sky. Without hesitation, Dunning leapt onto the command deck, gripping the edge as the hovercraft lurched beneath him.

"Take the left flank!" he barked into the comms, his voice hoarse from smoke and battle. "We pin them in, force them to pick a target. They can't take us both at once!"

The hovercrafts roared in unison, engines straining as they weaved through the battered valley, laying down suppressing fire. The air was alive with the shriek of pulse rounds, the deafening roar of explosions as drones spun out of the sky in trails of fire. Still, the rebels were outnumbered, the Imperials pressing hard, determined to crush them before they could escape.

But they wouldn't break.

Through the smoke and blood, Alex could see it—momentum shifting. The Imperials were faltering, their drones falling faster than they could be replaced. The rebels were still standing, still fighting.

Then, the sun crested the ridge.

A golden sliver of light split the battlefield, spilling over the distant mountains. And in that light, Alex saw them.

The Imperials.

A battalion, silhouetted against the dawn, pouring over the ridge like a tide of black and silver. Their numbers were staggering, but they were without air support now—their drones had been decimated. Still, they descended into the unmined edge valley, rifles poised, moving with military precision. They weren't here to win a battle. They were here to destroy this army and capture its leaders.

She saw the hesitation in her soldiers, the flicker of fear as the Imperials advanced. But fear was a weapon, and she refused to let it be used against them. Mines exploded around the soldiers as they advanced into the valley. She could see them wavering and knew that these line soldiers were fully aware they'd been ordered into a minefield to capture a single 'high-value' person. They knew it was as insane as it sounded.

Alex grabbed her comms. "Hold the line! No one runs. No one falls back." Her voice cut through the chaos, cold and sharp. "They think they can take us? Let's show them what a mistake looks like!"

A roar erupted from the rebel forces, a battle cry that rolled across the valley. The Imperials pressed forward, cautious but determined. And then, they stepped fully into the valley of death.

Another landmine detonated with a bone-shaking blast, throwing dirt and bodies skyward. Then another. And another. The ground was a killing field—riddled with traps, concealed explosives, pressure-activated charges, buried shrapnel that shredded carriers like paper and did far worse to these lightly armored infantry.

The Imperial formation collapsed into chaos. Soldiers screamed, stumbling over the dead, firing blindly as explosions ripped through their ranks. Some turned back, but there was nowhere to go—only death at their backs and death ahead.

Alex watched from the command deck, her rifle steady as she picked off any who managed to make it through the minefield.

Dunning's voice crackled through her earpiece. "They're breaking." She nodded, exhaling sharply. "Then let's finish this."

The rebels surged forward, sweeping through what remained of the Imperial forces like a blade through flesh. The battlefield became a slaughterhouse.

And then, silence.

The last Imperial fell, his rifle clattering uselessly onto the blood-soaked dirt. For a moment, no one moved. No one breathed.

Then, the realization hit them all at once.

They had won.

A cry of victory erupted from the rebels, a sound that shook the valley to its core. Soldiers embraced, weapons raised in triumph. Some laughed, some wept. Others simply stood, staring at the battlefield, at what they had survived.

Alex closed her eyes for a long moment, letting it sink in.

Another battle won. Another victory carved into history.

She turned, scanning the faces of her soldiers, the ones who had fought and bled beside her. They looked at her with something deeper than respect. Something heavier than loyalty.

They trusted her. They believed in her.

And that was a weight she would carry forever.

But history had already written its verdict. The Republic of Texas was doomed. And Alexandra Baker was running out of time.

The battlefield flickered, its edges dissolving. The gunfire softened. The smoke thinned.

Something else was pressing in. Something real. Warmth against her hand. A voice, insistent, pulling her upward. "...Alex..."

The past collapsed in on itself, shattering into dust.

She was falling...

And then,

She woke.

CHAPTER EIGHTEEN

The Imperial Palace, New York —Early Spring 2053

THE KING WAS DYING. That much was undeniable, though his physicians remained confounded by the rapid, inexplicable decline. Every test they conducted yielded nothing they could fight, no infection to purge, no antidote to administer. His body was failing, cell by cell, and there was nothing to be done.

At first, he raged.

From his sprawling palace in New York, he barked orders through gritted teeth, lashing out at his doctors, his ministers, anyone who dared enter his chamber. He accused them of incompetence, of sabotage, of treason. When the court physician hesitated before administering yet another round of useless treatments, Frederick seized a crystal paperweight from his nightstand and hurled it across the room. The shattering glass sent attendants scrambling, but the court doctor did not flinch. He had seen this before—the rage of a man who has ruled for too long to accept his own mortality.

Within a week, the King's body had withered into something unrecognizable. His skin, once ruddy and full, clung to his sharp cheekbones, his lips cracked from fever. He passed blood with terrifying regularity. The stench of sickness filled his quarters, despite the perfumes his servants burned to mask it. And still, even from his deathbed, he ruled.

His ministers had pleaded with Charles to come to his side. "Your Royal Highness," the chief physician had said, his voice carefully measured, "the King has asked for you. He has little time left. It would be best if—" "No," Charles had interrupted. His hands clenched at his desk in Bombay. "If it is disease, I will not risk infection. If he is dying, then he is dying. I will not sit at his bedside like some grieving widow."

The physician hesitated. "Your Highness, he is your brother."

Charles exhaled through his nose, his expression cold. "That is precisely why I know he would do the same in my place."

And so he remained in India, governing from afar, knowing that if his brother could fall, then he too was already a marked man.

Frederick did not stop commanding. Even in his final hours, he clung to power with the last of his breath.

"Burn New York to the ground if you must," he snarled at his generals.

"These rebels think they can win a war in my streets? Turn them into ash."

"Your Majesty," one of the officers said cautiously, "the civilian population—"

Frederick's fingers twitched as if they could still curl into a fist. "If they wanted to live, they would have stayed loyal."

His breath came in sharp, uneven gasps. His voice cracked. "Mass arrests. Public executions. Hang them from the bridges. Let them see what it means to defy the Crown."

There was a long silence in the war room. The generals, standing just outside his chamber, exchanged glances, knowing that even if the King perished, his orders would stain the city in blood.

But it was not enough. His mind drifted further, reaching for something more final.

"You know," he murmured, his voice taking on a feverish lilt, "we should have used the nuclear arsenal on Texas when we had the chance."

The room went still.

The men before him, the same men who had once followed his every command without hesitation, exchanged wary glances.

"Nuclear weapons are a last resort, Your Majesty," one of them said carefully.

Frederick's lips curled. "A last resort?" He coughed violently, gripping the armrest of his chair. When he looked up, his sunken eyes burned with something darker than fever. "We are at the end. What do you think this is, if not the last?"

No one answered.

The King gave a breathless chuckle. "Pathetic," he spat, blood spattering the sheets. "You stand before me, the greatest military force in history, and you tremble before peasants."

Another fit of coughing racked his body, and for the first time, his ministers saw it—that moment of inevitability—that he was not long for the world.

By the second week, the morphine dulled his agony, but not his fury.

He lay against the silk sheets, his breath slow, rattling. His vision blurred, shifting between reality and fevered delusion. At times, he called for men long dead—his father, his son, the generals who had won him his Empire. At times, he simply muttered to himself.

"Four hundred years," he whispered, the words barely audible. His fingers twitched at the covers, grasping at nothing. "Four hundred years we have ruled..."

Markson, his private butler, stood at the bedside, watching the life drain from the most powerful man on earth.

The King's lips moved again, but no sound came.

Markson leaned closer, just enough to catch the last breath of words as they slipped from his master's lips.

"Not... enough."

And then, silence.

Frederick, King of the British Empire, Lord Protector of the Americas, Conqueror of India, and Master of the Western World, was dead.

Markson straightened. He smoothed the sheets over the King's skeletal frame, adjusting the royal crest at his breast. He clasped his hands behind his back, bowed his head, and exhaled.

He should have mourned. He should have wept.

But instead, buried beneath the layers of duty and fear, was something else: relief.

Markson turned to the chamberlain, his voice steady. "It is done."

Half a world away, in India, the news arrived like a thunderclap.

Charles sat in his private office, staring at the sealed communiqué for a long moment before breaking the wax. He read the words once, then twice. Frederick was gone. He set the paper down, pressing his fingers together, thinking.

Then, before the weight of it could settle, the doors opened. Advisors entered. Ministers. Aides. The ceremonial robes were thrust upon him. The coronation had already been arranged.

There was no mourning. Only continuity.

As he stood before the gathered dignitaries, the reality of his position pressed upon him with a force he had never felt before.

The King was dead. Long live the King.

And already, the rebellion surged on all fronts, threatening to tear the Empire apart.

As the final words of the coronation ceremony were spoken, his chief advisor leaned in, voice low but urgent. "Your Majesty," he said, "the Russian Foreign Minister is here. In person."

Charles inhaled sharply.

His reign had just begun, and already, the world was at his doorstep.

He turned, adjusting the weight of the crown upon his head.

"Send him in."

CHAPTER NINETEEN

Toronto, Canada —Early Spring 2053

THE SKY REMAINED INK-BLACK as Edward, Duke of Vancouver and Governor-General of Canada and the Pacific Northwest, stepped up to the podium. A sea of cameras flashed before him, their bulbs flickering like distant artillery fire. Only minutes ago, he had spoken by video to his father, the newly crowned King Charles. The call had gone as he expected, poorly.

Edward had delivered the decision that had weighed on him for many months. Twenty minutes ago, he had been the heir apparent to the throne. Now, he was defecting. He could no longer serve the Empire. The turmoil following the King's death had given him a rare chance for a clean break. But he knew it would not be clean. No defection ever was.

Charles had been stunned. Not by the loss of his son's loyalty, but by the sheer audacity of it. Edward, his own blood, was turning his back on dynasty and destiny. He was turning his back on *him*.

Edward had kept his voice even, though his heart pounded. The rebels' cause is just, he had told his father. The Empire is too brutal, too corrupt, too broken to mend. And you—he had hesitated then— you lack either the ability or the will to make things better.

The connection had cut out in silence.

Now, he stood alone at the podium, facing the world, his moment of no return upon him. The marble halls around him amplified his voice, making it sound stronger than he felt.

"As you all know, my uncle, King Frederick passed away last night," Edward began, his tone measured. "My father, Charles, has been crowned."

He paused, letting the words settle. A deep breath. A heartbeat. Then, "But the Empire is not invincible. Nor is it eternal."

A murmur rippled through the gathered officials and press. Some stiffened. Some exchanged glances. He pressed on.

"My father, our King—*the* King—believes that Canada belongs to him by sheer right of precedence. That its people are mere subjects under his rule. He is wrong." Edward's grip tightened on the podium. "This land belongs to the people who built it. Who fought for it. Who bled for it. This continent has a right to self-rule."

The murmurs grew louder now, a rising tide of unease. But he did not falter.

"Today, I renounce my allegiance to the Empire," Edward declared, his voice ringing through the chamber. "And I declare Canada for the rebellion."

The hall erupted—gasps, cries, the frantic clicking of camera shutters.

Bombay, India

King Charles rarely ventured beyond the towering walls of his sprawling compound, an opulent fortress of marble and steel that stood as both a sanctuary and physical projection of his dominion over the subcontinent. The compound—a symbol of the Empire's excess, expanded to meet the paranoia of the modern age—was guarded by a regiment of elite soldiers, their crimson-clad figures a stark contrast against the dusty streets beyond the gates.

From his high-walled terrace, Charles could see the city stretching endlessly, a chaotic expanse of industry. The weight on his shoulders had just become so much heavier.

CHAPTER TWENTY

Toronto, Independent Canada — Early Spring 2053

A FAMILIAR VOICE, STEADY BUT weary. "You're awake."

Andrew Greg stood at the foot of the bed, arms crossed over his broad chest, his face etched with exhaustion.

Alex blinked, the light overhead searing her vision. Her throat was raw, her body stiff. She tried to sit up, but the dull ache in her ribs flared into sharp pain. She looked around, confused.

John was leaning against the far wall, rubbing the back of his neck. "You don't remember?"

She swallowed hard. "The bunker." The words scraped against her throat like sandpaper. "Flames... smoke... an explosion..."

"Yeah," John muttered. "That about sums it up."

Andrew sat at the edge of the bed, his expression dark. "The bunker was hit. They wanted to wipe us out completely. You got caught in the blast and were unconscious when we carried you out."

John smirked slightly, but there was no humor in it. "Dragged you out, more like. You weren't exactly light with all that dead weight."

Alex ignored him, her mind catching up to the situation. "How did we get out of the city?"

Andrew leaned back slightly. "A lucky break. The Duke sent men to extract us. He's broken with the Empire."

That caught her attention. "The Duke... defected?"

John nodded. "Turns out the King's latest crackdowns didn't sit well with him, either. He's thrown in with us, declared Canada a free state. It's not just whispers of rebellion anymore. This is war."

Alex exhaled sharply, trying to process it all. She could still hear the explosion in her mind, still feel the heat licking at her skin. But she had survived.

The handle turned, and in stepped Colonel Vihaan Chadra. His uniform was immaculate, his posture steady, but his eyes—his eyes told a different story. Beneath the discipline, there was exhaustion, a quiet grief that hadn't yet found words.

"Good to see you back, Alex," he said, his voice calm, yet weighted.

She barely had time to register the tension in his stance before he took a measured breath and spoke again.

"We have news of Ben."

The room tilted.

Vihaan hesitated just for a moment, as if searching for the gentlest way to deliver a blow that could never be softened.

"He was the source of the rebellion's location." His jaw tightened. "They tortured it out of him. He's gone."

The air in the room became suffocating. Alex's fingers clenched against the sheets, her breath frozen in her throat.

Ben.

Her mind recoiled, trying to reject the words.

She saw him standing at the kitchen counter, smiling. She heard his laugh, his soft reassurances when she came home late from chasing a lead. She felt his warmth beside her, his heartbeat steady as they lay in the quiet of the night. And now he was gone.

Her chest tightened, her vision blurring.

John cleared his throat, uneasy. "It... it happened before the bunker was hit. While you were still inside."

Alex inhaled sharply, a jagged breath that barely reached her lungs. "How?" Her voice was barely more than a whisper.

Vihaan's jaw twitched. "They took him the night before. The timing wasn't a coincidence. Someone was feeding them intel. Whether it was just Ben... or someone else, we don't know. But once they had him, they had confirmation. Your name, your past, your involvement."

"And then," John added grimly, "they came for all of us."

Alex's hands curled into fists, nails biting into her palms.

Tortured. They had tortured him for information.

She had known this war would take lives. But this... this was Ben.

For a long moment, she said nothing. Her body trembled, her pulse hammering in her ears. Then, finally, she forced herself to breathe. He was gone. And she would not let his death be in vain.

Her voice was steady but laced with quiet fury. "What's our next move?"

Vihaan sighed, running a hand through his hair. "We lost a lot of people."

John sat down, his usual bravado absent. "Josh Wells was killed."

Alex exhaled sharply. Josh had been one of the rebellion's primary strategists, a former intelligence officer turned defector.

"And Zane Douglas," John continued. "He was running comms when the blast hit. Didn't make it out."

Alex closed her eyes. Zane had been young, only twenty-six, but one of the best logistical minds they had.

Vihaan's voice was grim. "And Commander Seaton."

Alex's breath caught.

Commander Isaac Seaton had been the rebellion's field commander of the joint forces, managing global strategy alongside General Frell. A former admiral of the Imperial Fleet, he had defected five years earlier, bringing with him military experience and tactical genius that had kept the rebellion alive.

She looked at Andrew. "Then... who..."

John exhaled. "Andrew was chosen. The council of surviving officers held an emergency vote. Seaton had no designated successor, but there was no time for debate. The rebellion needed leadership, and fast. It was unanimous."

Vihaan nodded. "With the support of the remaining officers, he's been leading since we got out of the city. The rebellion needed stability. There are still many—too many—still unaccounted for."

Alex studied Andrew carefully. He looked exhausted, but there was something else beneath the weariness, a quiet, unshakable resolve. This was the weight of leadership.

"I want you to be my chief of staff," Andrew said.

Alex let out a short breath. "What?"

Andrew leaned forward. "Because I trust you," he said, smiling. "And, frankly we're short on people with leadership experience. You have a strategist's mind, a soldier's instincts, and a journalist's ability to see the truth through the lies. You'll be useful in this fight."

Alex exhaled slowly. The war had already claimed so much—her past, her home, the man she loved.

Now, it was asking for something else.

A role she hadn't sought, but one she could no longer turn away from.

She met Andrew's eyes, her jaw tightening. "I accept."

"Then, congratulations, General," Andrew said.

John exhaled. "And there's one last thing you need to know."

Alex turned to him.

John leaned forward slightly, a slow, satisfied smirk tugging at the corner of his lips.

"My poison worked."

Alex didn't blink. She just nodded.

"How long ago?" she asked.

John shrugged. "Around the same time the bunker was hit. He went fast toward the end. Charles has already been crowned."

Alex exhaled, shaking her head. "So the Empire falls to a weaker man."

Andrew nodded. "And that means we have an opening."

Alex sat back, her mind already calculating the next steps. Ben was gone. Their leaders had fallen. The King was dead. The war was entering a new phase.

CHAPTER TWENTY-ONE

These are the times that try men's souls. The summer soldier and the sunshine patriot will, in this crisis, shrink from the service of their country.
Thomas Paine, The American Crisis —December, 1776

Toronto, Independent Canada —Early Spring 2053

MIST SPRAYED ACROSS THE FACE of Colonel Vihaan Chadra. He stood on the roof of the gold-plated Royal Bank Plaza in Toronto, fog rolling in from Lake Ontario, veiling the city below in a ghostly shroud. Normally, he would be offered a panoramic view of the streets, the skyline, and the distant shore, but today, all he could see was a murky expanse, the world outside blurred and indistinct. It suited his mood. He had been in Canada for weeks, and while the initial meetings had been cordial, the underlying tension grew thicker each day. The distant rumble of cannon fire drifted through the air, not a singular boom, but a relentless, rhythmic pounding, steady, methodical, seemingly creeping ever closer.

"Tea?" asked the Duke, breaking the silence. His voice was calm, almost too calm given the circumstances—a forced calm. He moved with an air of understated grace, his tailored suit sharp against the misty backdrop. But Vihaan didn't miss the way his fingers curled slightly too tightly around the delicate porcelain cup, or the way his jaw clenched at each distant explosion.

"Oh, thanks kindly," Vihaan said, accepting the cup with the ease of a man who had spent years drinking tea in war zones—sometimes in moments stolen between battles, sometimes from metal canteens in burning fields. The warmth seeped into his hands, a pleasant contrast to the damp chill. He took a sip, savoring the delicate bergamot flavors of Earl Grey.

The Duke, however, barely touched his tea. Instead, he cast a wary glance toward the mist-cloaked cityscape, his foot tapping lightly against the stone floor. His shoulders were stiff, his breath controlled but shallow. Vihaan recognized it for what it was: a man unused to war, standing in its shadow for the first time.

"You seem unsettled," Vihaan observed.

The Duke exhaled through his nose. "I am unsettled."

Vihaan simply nodded. He had expected as much. The Duke of Vancouver had spent his life behind walls of polished marble, moving through halls of diplomacy and wealth, untouched by the raw, unfiltered brutality of war. He had made a bold choice in defecting from the Empire, but war was not policy. War was not a well-rehearsed debate or a neatly drafted speech. War was chaos. And for all the Duke's careful composure, the chaos was beginning to wear on him.

Every so often, the faint echo of artillery fire punctuated the stillness more loudly, a distant but constant reminder of the struggle for control. A sudden blast, closer than the others, made the Duke's hand twitch slightly, though he masked it well.

Vihaan found himself wondering if the mist would ever lift, or if it would forever shroud their efforts—and moods—in uncertainty.

"Ours," he murmured, more to himself than to the Duke. His eyes narrowed, trying to make out the invisible line between the lake and the sky. Somewhere out there, his men were fighting, securing the waters, ensuring that supplies and reinforcements could flow freely into Ontario.

The Duke followed his gaze, swallowing hard. "You sound confident," he said.

"I have to be," Vihaan replied simply. "Confidence wins wars. And hesitation loses them."

The Duke exhaled, shaking his head. "You make it sound so simple."

Vihaan took another sip of tea before setting the cup down on the railing. "It is. You hold the line, or you don't."

The Duke turned away from the view, rubbing the bridge of his nose. "You know, before I defected, I thought I understood what war meant. I thought I was prepared for what this fight would cost."

Vihaan studied him carefully. "And now?"

The Duke let out a humorless chuckle. "Now, I hear gunfire outside my window. I see the streets empty, shops shuttered, entire districts gone silent except for the movement of soldiers. Do you know how many civilians are sheltering in place? Hundreds of thousands. Families holed up in basements and subway tunnels, praying they won't wake up to an Imperial drone strike. And when they do step outside, it's not to live their lives, it's to join the rebellion."

Vihaan's expression darkened. "The volunteers?" The Duke nodded. "Since I declared Canada free, we've had thousands enlist from Toronto alone. More every day. Most of them have never held a rifle before." He looked Vihaan in the eye. "I tell myself that's a good thing. That it means the people believe in this cause. But part of me wonders... how many of them will survive?"

Vihaan didn't offer false comfort. "Not all of them," he admitted. "But enough will. Enough to make a difference."

The Duke clenched his jaw. "I hope you're right." He turned back toward the skyline, but neither man spoke for a long moment.

Then, in the distance, the cannon fire grew louder once more. "We should be getting reports by now," said the Duke, his voice smooth but with an edge of impatience. He was not a man used to waiting, and the prolonged silence from the field intelligence was clearly unsettling him. Vihaan knew that this operation, though a small piece of the larger puzzle, was critical. If they could maintain control over Lake Ontario, they could cut off one of the Empire's key supply routes and weaken their hold on the region.

Alex walked gingerly out to the balcony as both men turned to greet her. Vihaan was glad to see her up and moving again. The previous night had been her last in the hospital, and clearly she was ready to get to work. "Colonel Chadra, how have you found your time in Toronto while I was... unavailable?" she asked.

"The Duke has been a most respectable host and an incredible tactician in the field," Vihaan replied, glancing at the Duke, who offered a modest nod in acknowledgment. It was true; the Duke had been instrumental in fortifying their positions around the lake, using his intimate knowledge of the area to anticipate enemy moves. But Vihaan could sense the underlying strain, the pressure that came with every decision, every command. It was a delicate balance, one that could tip at any moment.

Alex's smile widened, though it didn't quite reach her eyes. "Good. Good. We need all the help we can get. I hear that you've had some success in securing the lake?"

"Yes, General," said Vihaan, his tone steady. "We've managed to blockade the key entry points, and our patrols have intercepted several supply ships attempting to slip through. There was a skirmish near the Scarborough Bluffs yesterday, but our forces managed to drive them off without sustaining heavy losses. We're holding, but I don't know how much longer we can rely on these victories. The Empire won't stay passive for long."

"Indeed," said Alex, her expression growing serious. "I've been getting reports that suggest they're planning a counteroffensive. We need to be ready. The situation is changing quickly, and we can't afford to lose momentum. Not now, not when we've finally managed to make some headway."

Vihaan's eyes drifted back to the fog. Somewhere, just beyond that veil, the Empire was regrouping, preparing to engage. He had seen it before, the way they would draw back, let you think you had the upper hand, only to lash out with a force that would crush everything in its path.

"We're reinforcing our positions," Vihaan said, his voice low. "I've deployed additional patrols around the eastern edges of the lake. If they try to push through, they'll meet resistance, but... I think they know that. If they come, it won't be with a small force."

"Let's hope we can delay them long enough," said the Duke, setting his cup down. "The Canadians are stretched thin, and we're relying on our allies from New York to hold the line."

From the balcony, Alex Baker imagined she could hear it all. The sharp percussion of gunfire rattled through the streets of New York and Vancouver, punctuated by the deeper, more ominous roar of distant naval bombardments, and the constant buzz of drones. The Empire was committing its forces, pressing north with brutal determination. Intelligence reports confirmed it. Charles had moved tens of thousands of troops into position, reinforced by the British Navy, whose warships now loomed along the Atlantic coastline. Canada would not slip from his grasp easily.

She pulled her coat tighter against the cold. The rebellion had won victories before, but this felt different. The full weight of the Empire was descending on them now. If they lost here, they lost everything.

Vihaan stood beside her, his posture rigid, his expression unreadable. But she knew him well enough to see the tension in his stance. He was already strategizing, anticipating, preparing for what came next.

"Charles is throwing everything at us," Alex said, her voice steady. "If we hold here, we prove the Empire is not invincible. If we fail, there won't be another chance."

Vihaan nodded, his eyes fixed on the horizon. "We can hold," he said. "But not indefinitely. We need reinforcements. More supplies. More alliances."

Alex exhaled, turning to face him. She studied him for a long moment before making her decision.

"You're not staying in Canada," she said. "You're going to Bombay."

Vihaan's brow furrowed slightly. "Bombay?"

"You've earned your promotion, General Chadra," Alex continued, letting the weight of the words settle. She didn't rush. She wanted him to feel the full weight of what she was giving him, and what she was asking in return. "This isn't just another deployment, Vihaan. You will lead the fight for India. We are making you the commander of rebel forces there. The war is shifting. We hold here, but we win there."

Vihaan's jaw tightened slightly. He had fought battles before, commanded men, made decisions that sent soldiers to their deaths. But this was different. This was no longer just fighting for survival. This was shaping the course of a war that would either break the Empire or leave them crushed beneath it.

"If we're going to win this war," Alex continued, "we need to control the subcontinent. India is the epicenter now. And I need someone I believe in to oversee it. The cells there are fragmented and need leadership."

Vihaan's expression remained unreadable, but she saw the flicker of something in his eyes, acceptance, and perhaps even the burden of knowing what this meant.

A promotion like this was not an honor. It was a responsibility. A heavy one.

Alex took a step closer. "You're the only one who can do this," she said, quieter now, almost personal. "Not just because you're the best commander we have, but because you understand what's at stake. You know what it means to fight for a country that deserves better. You know what it means to make the impossible happen."

Vihaan inhaled slowly, glancing out over the mist-covered city. He had been preparing for this war his whole life. And now, Alex was handing him the future of his homeland.

"When do I leave?" he asked. "Immediately."

She pulled a sealed dossier from inside her coat and handed it to him. He flipped it open, his eyes scanning the documents inside. No pads this time. His shoulders tensed slightly.

"The Russian Foreign Minister is willing to meet with us," Alex said. "He'll be in Bombay in three days. You'll be the one negotiating their assistance."

Vihaan's fingers lingered over the page.

"Russia," he murmured, his voice neutral, but Alex caught the subtle edge of hesitation.

"They were going to trade me to the Empire," he said.

"The Russians have been playing both sides," she admitted. "But if they're offering a meeting, we have to take the opportunity. They can see that the rebellion is spreading and with Frederick dead, they've made a new calculation. If they're serious about assisting us, it could shift the balance of the war."

Vihaan closed the dossier, rolling his shoulders as if settling a weight across them. "And if they're not?"

Alex looked back toward the distant battlefield, where the rumble of war grew louder by the hour.

"Then you'll have to find out before they strike," she said.

There was a long silence between them, broken only by the distant howl of sirens.

Finally, Vihaan nodded. His voice was firm. "I'll be ready."

Alex placed a firm hand on his shoulder. "I know you will."

He turned and walked toward the stairwell, his footsteps fading into the mist.

She remained on the balcony, watching as flashes of gunfire lit up the distant skyline.

CHAPTER TWENTY-TWO

THE AIR WAS THICK WITH humidity, the scent of rain mingling with the ever-present smoke from the city's factories and the faint tang of the sea. Inside the previously designated governor's palace, now the seat of the King in India, King Charles sat behind a massive teakwood desk, fingers steepled, studying the man across from him.

Anton Breshkev, Russia's Foreign Minister, exuded the patience of a man who already knew the outcome of the conversation. He sat with one leg crossed over the other, his sharp, wolfish eyes gleaming in the dim lamplight. His salt-and-pepper hair was neatly combed, and his finely tailored suit, despite the Bombay heat, was immaculate. He had played this game before.

Charles had never been a patient man.

His late brother, King Frederick, had thrived in the meticulous dance of diplomacy. He had relished the quiet victories found in closed-door negotiations, the art of bending nations to his will with the threat of brute force. That was his form of diplomacy. He could be surprisingly patient, allowing foreign leaders to exhaust themselves making their points. He would wait because he could wait. He would outlast and outmaneuver any of the world's lesser leaders. Frederick had believed in control—of people, of narratives, of history itself. But Frederick was dead, and now the world was unraveling at a pace that no courtly intrigue could contain.

Charles had inherited a war, not a throne, and wars were not won through talk alone. He no longer ruled from the position of strength that his brother had.

The weight of the Empire pressed against his shoulders as he sat in the overstuffed chair. The room was vast, lined with gilded columns and heavy silk drapes that barely stirred in the suffocating heat, despite the air conditioning running at full speed. Outside these walls, the streets pulsed with unease. British troops patrolled in greater numbers, convoys rolled through the avenues, and whispers of rebellion curled through the alleyways like smoke from a fire yet to fully catch.

Across from him, Breshkev sat in perfect composure. The man radiated a quiet amusement, as if he were indulging in a private joke at Charles's expense. He adjusted his cuffs with deliberate care, his movements slow, methodical—an unspoken assertion of power, of patience. Russia was not desperate. Russia could afford to wait.

Charles, however, was in no mood for spectacle.

"Let's get to it," he said flatly, his voice cutting through the heavy air like a blade.

Breshkev's lips curled, the ghost of a smirk playing across his face. He exhaled through his nose, as if he had expected nothing less from the impatient new monarch. He reached for his tea, lifting it with the precision of a man who had spent a lifetime in negotiation halls, where power was measured in pauses and glances rather than bullets and battalions.

"Vihaan Chadra is coming to India," Breshkev said at last, savoring the words as though tasting a rare delicacy. "With Russian assistance. Or so he believes."

Charles remained utterly still. He did not scowl, did not react, but something coiled tight inside him. Vihaan. The traitor. The upstart commander who had defied the Crown time and time again. The man who now dared to think himself a diplomat, a statesman, capable of negotiating with Moscow? The arrogance of it was almost laughable.

"Go on," Charles said evenly, though his fingers curled against the carved armrest of his chair.

Breshkev swirled his tea before taking a slow sip, watching Charles over the rim of his porcelain cup. He let the silence linger, stretching the moment just enough to force Charles to feel its weight. Then, as if finally deciding that enough time had passed, he placed the cup down on the polished mahogany desk between them.

"He was in Moscow not long ago," Breshkev continued. "Andrew Greg, your favorite fugitive, joined by video. And, of course, they were received. President Boris Aslanov himself met with them. It was quite the affair."

Charles's jaw tensed. The president of Russia, entertaining rebels? Allowing Vihaan Chadra to walk through the halls of the Kremlin like a recognized leader? It was an insult, a provocation.

"I assume you welcomed them with open arms," Charles said, his voice a razor's edge.

Breshkev did not flinch. Instead, he smiled, an expression that contained neither warmth nor sincerity.

"We welcomed them, yes," he said smoothly. He spread his hands in a gesture of mock innocence, his gold cufflinks catching the dim light. "We listened. We learned. And now, we are in a position to act."

Charles leaned back in his chair, his eyes locked onto the Russian's. He could hear the echoes of Frederick's voice in his head: never let them think you are desperate. Never let them see the cracks beneath the surface.

"And you claim they are vulnerable," Charles said, his tone neutral. "Prove it."

Breshkev's lips curled into a smile. "They overestimate their position. Their victories have come too quickly. They believe momentum is on their side, but in reality, they are exposed. Their forces are scattered, their supply lines fragile. They rely on new alliances that are not yet tested. The Canadians—idealists, poorly armed. Their leader—your son—ill-equipped to lead a wartime government, if you'll forgive me saying so. The Indians—desperate, splintered, clinging to the hope that Chadra can deliver them. The Americans—led by Greg, a man who plays at war but has not truly been tested in decades."

He let the words settle before continuing. "They need us more than we need them. That was clear in Moscow."

Charles studied him. "And yet, you entertained them. You let them believe Russia might help their rebellion."

Breshkev shrugged. "It costs us nothing to let fools hope. The longer they believe they have Russian backing, the more reckless they become. That is how we will break them."

Charles nodded slowly. He had underestimated Russia. While he had been focused on securing India, the Russians had been playing both sides, waiting for the best offer.

"And what is it you want in return?" Charles asked.

Breshkev's expression didn't change, but there was something hungry in his eyes now.

"When your war is won, when the rebels are crushed, Russia will claim Italy and the entire Mediterranean. The Empire has no real need for them."

Charles exhaled slowly, absorbing the demand. It was bold. Frederick had always dismissed Russian ambitions, but Charles was not his brother. If sacrificing Italy meant securing his throne, then so be it.

Still, he let the silence stretch. He wanted Breshkev to feel the weight of the decision.

"And if I refuse?"

Breshkev's smile did not falter. "Then we will wait. We will let Chadra fight you. We will let Greg bring the Americans deeper into this war. And when you and your rebels have bled each other dry, Russia will step in." He leaned back, his voice almost casual. "But why let it come to that? You are a pragmatist, Your Majesty. The question is not whether you will win. The question is how much you are willing to sacrifice to ensure victory."

Charles drummed his fingers on the desk. The Empire could survive without Italy. It could not survive losing India.

Slowly, he smiled.

"Done," he said.

Breshkev inclined his head, as if they had simply concluded an ordinary business transaction. "Excellent. Then let us begin."

CHAPTER TWENTY-THREE

THE DUKE INDEED FOUND HIMSELF ill-equipped to run a wartime government. His first order of business was to determine what percentage of his father's military was with him, and how many were going to fight still for the King.

The numbers weren't just a matter of statistics, they were a matter of survival. The Imperial Army had been built to conquer, not to divide. For years, it had been an unbreakable machine, moving from continent to continent, enforcing the Crown's rule with brutal efficiency. Now, that same machine was splitting at the seams, and the Duke needed to know how deep the cracks ran before the whole thing collapsed.

He sat in the dimly lit war room of his newly repurposed headquarters, a former government building in downtown Toronto. The walls were still lined with the old flags of the Empire, the symbols of a dying world order. Maps were spread across the table, marked with strategic assets, troop movements, and supply lines, but none of it told him what he needed to know: who was actually willing to fight for him?

Across from him, General Martin Frell leaned back in his chair, arms crossed, watching the Duke with the patience of a man who had already survived more battles than he cared to count. Frell had been presumed dead after the bunker bombing, but his sudden reappearance had been met with both shock and relief.

The Duke hadn't pressed him for details at first. There hadn't been time. But now, as they sat in the war room, he finally asked, "How did you make it out?"

Frell exhaled, rubbing his temple. "Damn miracle, really. I was in one of the secondary command rooms when the first strike hit. The whole place started caving in. By the time I realized what was happening, half the exits were blocked."

He shook his head, as if still processing it. "Lost a lot of good people. Commander Seaton, Zach Mulcahy, General Brian Ziegler, were with me—they didn't make it."

The Duke frowned. Seaton had been the de facto leader of the rebellion. With him gone, there had been no clear chain of succession. That explained why Frell wasn't in command now—he had disappeared when the movement needed leadership the most.

"I was pinned in the lower levels with a few others," Frell continued. "By the time we dug our way out, the whole damn place was a crater. We spent the next few weeks sneaking through Imperial-controlled territory, trying not to get shot. Eventually linked up with some partisans who exfiltrated us into Ontario." He gestured around the room. "And here I am."

The Duke nodded. It was a testament to Frell's resilience that he had survived at all, but he wasn't the leader the rebellion had needed in its darkest hour. That role had gone to Andrew Greg, who had held the movement together in the days and weeks following the bombing, rallying the remaining forces and taking command.

"Do you regret not being there?" the Duke asked, watching Frell closely.

Frell didn't answer right away. He stared at the map instead, his fingers tracing along the marked Imperial strongholds. "Doesn't matter," he said finally. "Greg's the one who stepped up. I may be a damn good general, but I'm not the one who's going to win this war."

There was no bitterness in his voice, only pragmatism. Frell was a fighter, not a politician and his years were catching up with him. He had no desire to sit in war rooms making speeches. He was here to win battles, not to lead nations.

The Duke respected that.

"Then let's make sure we win," the Duke said, shifting the conversation back to the task at hand. "I need numbers. Who do we actually have?"

Frell exhaled and leaned over the table, tapping a thick, calloused finger against the map.

"If you're asking how many men are on paper, we still command nearly two hundred thousand Imperial soldiers in Canada. If you're asking how many of those men will actually fight for you... the real number is lower. A lot lower."

The Duke crossed his arms. "How low?"

Frell didn't answer immediately. He picked up a marker and drew a hard, deliberate line through Toronto, Ottawa, and Quebec City, carving up the map as if it were already a battlefield.

"The Canadian-born soldiers, they're with us. At least sixty thousand, maybe more. Most of them signed up to protect their homeland, not to die for an Empire that's already lost half the world. They're the backbone of what we have."

The Duke nodded, but Frell wasn't finished.

"The British officers?" He shook his head. "That's a different story. Most of them came up through the old academies in New York. Their careers, their lives, their families—they're all tied to the Crown. They'll fight for King Charles, even if it means tearing Canada apart. Worse still, they control logistics, supply chains, and high command. We might outnumber them on the ground, but if they cut off our fuel, our munitions, our reinforcements? It won't matter."

The Duke's stomach was unsettled, but he kept his expression even.

"And the rest?"

Frell sighed and scratched at his beard. "That's where things get messy. The Indian and African regiments, the Caribbean divisions, the stray battalions from Australia—some will fight for the King, some won't. They weren't sent here to die in a civil war. Hell, some of them are already wondering if they should go home and fight for their own revolutions instead of dying in someone else's."

"And the conscripts?"

Frell gave a humorless chuckle. "They're running. Twenty, maybe thirty thousand men will just disappear. You know how this goes—when an empire crumbles, the first thing soldiers do is decide whether it's worth fighting for. Half the conscripts didn't want to be here in the first place. Now that it's a civil war? They'll slip away in the night and take their rifles with them."

The Duke took a deep breath and let his gaze drift back to the map. The reality was starting to sink in. This wasn't a simple fight for independence, this was a war against a system that had spent generations conditioning its soldiers to serve without question.

Charles still had the Imperial Navy, the air force, the most elite special forces units, and enough loyal officers embedded in their ranks to cripple the rebellion before it could truly get started. The Duke had the will of the people, but will alone wouldn't be enough if his own officers sabotaged him from within.

"This won't be won on numbers alone," the Duke said finally. "We need to act before Charles does."

Frell nodded but didn't immediately respond. He tapped the map in front of them, his fingers tracing along garrisons that were still technically under their control: Ottawa, Montreal, Quebec City, Halifax, Calgary—but control meant nothing if those within were waiting for orders from the King.

The Duke caught the hesitation in Frell's expression. "What?"

Frell exhaled. "We've still got too many men loyal to Charles embedded in our command structure. And I don't just mean a few stray officers. I mean entire chains of command, men trained since birth to serve the Empire, not question it."

The Duke leaned back in his chair, letting the weight of the statement settle. He had known this was coming, but knowing it and deciding what to do about it were two different things.

"We can't just let them stay," Frell continued. "They'll stall orders, leak intelligence, undermine morale. Hell, some of them will flat-out defect the second Charles sends a counterstrike."

The Duke nodded grimly. "If we purge them all at once, it'll cripple us just as much as them. We still need officers. Someone has to run logistics, oversee supply lines, keep discipline."

"If we pull out every Imperial-trained commander, we'll be left with chaos." Frell gave a humorless chuckle. "The King's officers built this army for the Empire, not for us. And if we're not careful, they'll make sure it dies for the Empire, too."

The Duke pressed his fingers against his temple. "We need a test. Some way to figure out who's with us and who's just waiting to turn us over."

Frell thought for a moment, then leaned over the table. "Loyalty oaths. Public and binding. Swear to Independent Canada, renounce Charles. No hedging, no half-measures."

The Duke raised an eyebrow. "And if they refuse?"

Frell didn't hesitate. "Then they're prisoners. Or worse, depending on the risk they pose."

Silence hung in the room for a moment.

The Duke folded his arms. "Imprisoning hundreds, maybe thousands of officers and senior commanders would gut our leadership overnight. Even if we replace them with loyal men, they won't have the experience to lead at that scale."

Frell sighed. "Then we prioritize. The most dangerous ones, the ones with ties to the monarchy, to Charles's inner circle, we lock up immediately. The rest? We reassign, isolate, and monitor until we're certain."

The Duke thought it over. "So we offer them the oath first. Publicly. If they refuse, they're prisoners of war. If they take it and still betray us, we deal with them as traitors."

Frell grunted. "That's the cleanest way. No room for doubt."

But the Duke wasn't convinced it was enough. Fear alone could inspire loyalty, but it could also make a man reckless. Some would take the oath just to buy time, waiting for the first opportunity to sabotage them from within. He needed something stronger, leverage.

"We'll need insurance," the Duke said finally. He looked up at Frell. "We need to know everything about these officers. Their weaknesses, their families, their secrets. The ones we don't imprison, we control."

Frell exhaled sharply. "Then we'll need a security force, not just military police, but something designed to root out threats before they happen."

"The old Imperial Secret Police?" the Duke asked, already thinking ahead.

Frell smirked. "Not exactly. They served the King. We need our own."

The Duke nodded slowly. "Then we build one."

The Canadian Security Bureau, or whatever they chose to call it, wouldn't be a simple military police force. It would be a weapon of control, one that operated outside the chain of command, answering only to the highest levels of leadership. They would monitor officers, infiltrate military units, and keep watch over garrisons.

And then there were the spies, the men and women already embedded within Charles's army, already feeding information to the rebellion. They had compiled files on hundreds of officers—who had mistresses, who owed money to crime families, who had taken bribes, who had smuggled goods under Imperial authority. The Carcione family, in particular, had been collecting dirt on military officials for years across the entire continent. That information would now serve a new purpose.

"If they won't pledge loyalty to the Republic," the Duke said, "then they'll pledge loyalty to their own survival."

Frell's expression darkened. "Blackmail."

The Duke didn't flinch. "We use whatever tools we have. I want a full dossier on every officer above the rank of captain, their history, their debts, their vulnerabilities. The ones we can control, we keep in line. The ones we can't?" He glanced down at the map. "We remove."

Frell crossed his arms, nodding. "It's ruthless."

"It's necessary," the Duke corrected.

They wouldn't purge every officer; they couldn't afford to. But they could make an example of the first few, ensuring that fear and leverage did the rest of the work. A man didn't have to love the Republic to serve it; he just had to fear the consequences of doing otherwise.

"Then we start now," the Duke said. "Draft the loyalty declaration. All officers above the rank of captain will be required to swear their allegiance by the end of the week."

Frell stood. "And the ones who refuse?"

The Duke's expression was cold. "We make an example of them. The rest will understand what's at stake."

The meeting ended with a new set of orders, communications officers dispatched to every major garrison, spies activated to collect intelligence on questionable officers, and the first steps taken toward establishing a network of security enforcers to keep the northern rebellion from collapsing before it even had a chance to win.

Chapter Twenty-Four

EVEN IN EARLY SUMMER, THE cold air of a freak storm system bit against Vihaan's skin as he stepped onto the airfield. Through layers of bandages that concealed most of his face, he could feel the sting of the wind cutting through. The tarmac was slick, the runway lights barely cutting through the darkness. The sky above Toronto was empty, but it wouldn't stay that way for long.

The Duke had made it clear, this was a race against time. If Vihaan wasn't airborne within the hour, the British would come down on them like a hammer.

"Keep your head down, you're supposed to be hurt," the rebel medic muttered as he adjusted the sling around Vihaan's arm, making a show of handling an "injured officer." The charade was thorough—bandages over his forehead, a fake IV line tucked under his coat, and a military-issue stretcher waiting just in case they had to sell the act harder.

Vihaan pulled his coat tighter and kept his movements slow, deliberate. A man who had just barely escaped death wouldn't be walking with confidence. He forced himself to shuffle slightly, favoring one side, moving like a soldier who had taken shrapnel to the ribs.

Frell stood beside him, arms crossed, his breath misting in the cold night air. "Medical transport is fueled and ready," he muttered. "Pilot's one of ours. But we've got a problem."

Of course, they had a problem.

Vihaan didn't respond immediately, letting the weight of the words settle before glancing at Frell. "How bad?"

Frell exhaled sharply. "We picked up radio chatter. The British know someone high-ranking is trying to get out of Toronto. We don't think they know it's you yet, but they've locked down every official airstrip, every major road leading north. They're setting up checks on outgoing flights."

Vihaan's stomach tightened. If the British figured out he was here, this airfield would be a crater before sunrise.

The Duke's intelligence network had been working around the clock to throw Imperial spies off their scent, leaking false reports of a rebel offensive toward Buffalo, staging decoy convoys heading south, and even having a fake Vihaan appear at a hospital in Montreal, posing as a wounded officer in critical condition. But intelligence games could only buy them so much time.

"We'll have to assume we've got a tail," Vihaan muttered. "Can't afford a direct flight."

Frell nodded. "Already planned for that. You're not flying to India."

That made Vihaan pause. "Excuse me?"

Frell smirked. "You're flying to Greenland."

Vihaan frowned. He hadn't been expecting that. "The hell is in Greenland?"

"A runway where no one's looking for you," Frell said flatly. "The Danes aren't exactly taking sides in this war, and their airspace is clear of British patrols. From there, you transfer to a Scandinavian merchant vessel heading for the Middle East. Neutral-flagged, no direct Imperial oversight. The ship will dock in Oman, where our contacts will get you the rest of the way to India."

It was a longer route, riskier in some ways, but the logic was sound. Any plane flying toward India would be tracked, intercepted, or shot down before it hit Pakistani airspace. But an emergency medical flight to Greenland? Nobody would look twice.

Vihaan nodded slowly. "And the backup plan?"

Frell's smirk faded. "We don't have one. If you don't make it to Greenland, you're dead."

Vihaan appreciated the honesty.

The fake medic nudged him forward. "Time to go. Plane's fueled. British radio is getting more active. We either move now, or we're running for the tree line instead."

Vihaan climbed the steps into the medical transport craft, settling into one of the rear seats. The interior smelled faintly of sterilizing agents and warm engine ozone, the synthetic scent clashing with the tension in the air.

The pilot, a grizzled man with long sideburns, glanced back through the open cockpit. "Hope you're not the superstitious type, General."

Vihaan raised an eyebrow. "Why?"

"We just filed your flight under a defunct biometric ghost ID. Technically, you're flying as a corpse." The pilot offered a tight smile. "Try not to die again before we land."

Before Vihaan could respond, the engines whined to life. The low thrum of the mag-rotors vibrated through the floor as the medevac craft began taxiing down the darkened tarmac. Outside, Frell stood at the edge of the hangar, watching silently as the aircraft disappeared into the haze.

The first ten minutes of flight passed without incident. Too smooth.

Vihaan kept his breathing steady, staring through the rain-streaked window at the cloud-tangled moonlight. Every minute they stayed aloft without challenge felt stolen.

Then came the first transmission.

"Unidentified medevac craft, this is Imperial SkyGrid Command. You are entering a high-sensitivity corridor. Transmit encrypted ident-code and flight telemetry immediately."

The pilot swore under his breath. "That's a hard ping from NOR-SKYCOM. They're running spectral gate analysis. It means they flagged our emission signature—probably running crosswave intercepts."

"They're triangulating every outbound vector from near rebel airfields," Vihaan said grimly.

"Yeah," the pilot nodded. "And they're not buying the ghost ID much longer."

"We have to respond," he added. "If we ignore them, they scramble jets. If we answer wrong, they scramble jets."

Vihaan glanced toward the radio, thinking fast. "Put me through."

The pilot hesitated, then flipped the switch. Vihaan deepened his voice, shifting his accent just enough to mimic the clipped, proper tones of an Imperial officer.

"Imperial Command, this is MedEvac 446. We're on an emergency evac route per Directive Black Lantern, surgical triage transport from Sector Nine. Confirm clearance authorization code Delta-Zero-Twelve. Our eCM is active due to patient instability. Stand by for burst-ident pulse if required."

Silence.

Then:

"MedEvac 446, maintain current heading. Confirming Black Lantern clearance. Maintain radio contact."

Vihaan exhaled. The falsified clearance—an injected signal loop through an obsolete Imperial medical codebase—had worked. For now.

The pilot eyed him. "That bought us time, but SkyGrid is still tracking our EM footprint. They'll know we're a non-standard signature the moment they run deeper scans."

"They're not verifying," Vihaan said. "They're stalling."

"Someone tipped them off," the pilot muttered. "They're not just screening flights—they're hunting you."

The radio stayed silent. The tension in the cockpit was a live wire.

"They'll keep soft-scanning us," the pilot muttered. "But if they get positive ID, they deploy those damn Raptor-class intercepts."

Vihaan watched the horizon darken. A storm was building over the Labrador Sea.

"How long to Greenland?" he asked.

"Three hours—unless we shift vectors."

"We need to disappear before they lock our path," Vihaan said. "Options?"

The pilot tapped a blinking section of the nav-display. "There's a convective cell moving fast over the Labrador shelf. A thunderstorm cluster big enough to blind SkyGrid's multi-azimuth radar. But we'll be bouncing like popcorn in a steel pot."

Vihaan nodded. "We'll take it."

Before the pilot could bank the craft, the radio flared again.

"MedEvac 446, Imperial Command. Confirm attending med-officer and transmit biostat of casualty. Over."

"They're probing," the pilot said. "They're readying a hard challenge."

Vihaan grabbed the comm again, and forced his voice into something steady, something near annoyed, the voice of a man used to barking orders without challenge.

"Command, our casualty's vitals are unstable. Bio-data locked behind medical override. Confirm Delta-Zero-Twelve. We are under magnetic storm interference. Routing delayed."

He let the words sit, letting the imperious tone do the work. Imperial officers weren't used to being questioned, especially not in emergency situations. If they stalled, they risked looking incompetent.

A long pause. Vihaan could almost hear them arguing on the other end, trying to figure out if pushing harder was worth the risk.

Then:

"MedEvac 446, stand by."

He turned toward the cockpit window, staring out at the expanse of darkness stretching beneath them. The sky was still clear, but in the distance, he could see the looming outline of storm clouds moving in from the Atlantic. A jagged web of lightning flickered across the horizon.

"Cut the transponder," Vihaan said.

"You sure?"

"They'll use our emissions to triangulate a lock. Let them think we're losing systems in the storm."

The pilot killed the signal burst transmitter. The aircraft's ID beacon vanished from Imperial SkyGrid's mesh net.

Seconds later, the turbulence hit—violent and relentless. The medevac dropped into the storm's edge, its fuselage shaking as wind shear buffeted the hull.

"They'll think we're a crippled evac bird caught in a cell," the pilot said.

A new ping echoed on the radar.

"Two fast movers," the pilot growled. "Thermal profiles say SkyRaptor interceptors."

"They know," Vihaan said quietly.

"They're not here to escort. They're armed."

"They were waiting for a positive ID."

Vihaan scanned the storm readouts. "Can you drop out of SkyGrid view?"

"Barely. We ghost out at two hundred meters above sea level, but it's risky."

"Do it."

The plane dropped suddenly, pitching into a near free fall as the pilot sent them plunging deeper into the storm. The radar display stuttered, obscured by ionization. They rocked violently as they entered the thick of the storm. Rain hammered against the fuselage, the wind howling through the metal frame. The cabin lights flickered.

The interceptors hesitated—either confused or waiting for confirmation.

Then, the fighters veered off.

"They bought it," the pilot whispered. "They think we crashed."

"Keep us low," Vihaan said. "Keep us invisible."

The pilot nodded, adjusting their vector toward Greenland's hidden coast.

They had survived the first gauntlet.

But Vihaan knew this was only the beginning.

They weren't safe yet. But for the first time since he stepped onto the tarmac in Toronto, he wasn't about to die.

The pilot straightened their course, adjusting the throttle. "We'll make Greenland soon. Hope you don't mind the cold."

Vihaan closed his eyes for a moment. The British had nearly killed him. Someone inside the rebellion had betrayed him. And India was still a long way off.

The plane rocked as they cleared the worst of the storm, emerging into the calmer air beyond. Rain still streaked across the cockpit windows, but the worst of the turbulence had passed.

The pilot let out a slow breath, adjusting the throttle to stabilize their path. "We're ghosts for now," he muttered. "But that won't last forever."

Vihaan rubbed his temple, feeling the tension that had been tightening like a vise since he'd stepped onto the plane. "How long before they figure it out?"

The pilot's jaw tightened. "A few hours if we're lucky. Less if they're really looking."

Vihaan glanced at the instrument panel. Greenland was still an hour away. The safest thing to do was lie low, keep radio silence, and hope their pursuers took long enough to put the pieces together that by the time they did, Vihaan would already be out of their reach.

But Vihaan had been fighting this war too long to believe in luck.

He knew that somewhere, an Imperial intelligence officer was already running flight logs, comparing takeoff manifests, cross-referencing emergency dispatch records. They had the resources, the manpower, and the patience to sift through every lie, every false trail.

And when they did, when they realized Vihaan Chadra hadn't died in the storm, they'd come looking again.

The pilot adjusted their heading. "We'll be making our approach soon. Weather at Narsarsuaq is clear."

Vihaan didn't respond immediately. His mind was already racing ahead, thinking about the next step. This was just the first hurdle, if he couldn't get out of Greenland without being seen, the rest of the plan wouldn't matter.

"How clean is this landing?" he asked finally.

The pilot's lips pressed into a thin line. "Cleaner than anything else we could've pulled off. It's a small airstrip, remote. Hardly anyone will be there at this time of night."

"Hardly anyone," Vihaan repeated, unconvinced. "And what about the ones who are?"

The pilot hesitated. "It's not a British-controlled zone, if that's what you're asking. But that doesn't mean there aren't eyes."

Vihaan already knew what that meant. The Empire had long fingers. Even in places where they had no official control, there were always sympathizers, informants, paid collaborators. If even one person at that airstrip recognized him, word would get out before he ever boarded the next leg of his journey.

"Then we assume we're being watched," Vihaan said. "We get in and out as fast as possible."

The pilot didn't argue. He adjusted the controls again, checking the altimeter. "We'll be on the ground in forty minutes. I suggest you get ready."

Vihaan didn't need to be told twice.

The air was colder than anything Vihaan had felt in years. The moment he stepped off the plane, the bitter Arctic wind cut through his coat like a blade, carrying the sharp scent of salt and ice. His boots crunched against the snow-covered tarmac as he followed the pilot toward the small terminal building ahead.

The airstrip was almost abandoned. A few hangars, a control tower that looked like it hadn't seen real activity in years, and a handful of lights illuminating the frozen ground.

Too quiet.

Vihaan adjusted his collar, keeping his head down as they moved. "Who's meeting us?"

The pilot kept his voice low. "A Scandinavian merchant captain. Goes by Rasmus. He's been running cargo between here and the Middle East for years, no Imperial ties. His crew is mostly Danish and Chinese, neutral enough that nobody asks questions. He'll get you on board and into Oman."

Vihaan nodded. "And how much does he know?"

The pilot smirked. "Enough to get paid, not enough to ask questions."

That would have to be good enough.

They made their way toward the hangar where the next transport was supposed to be waiting. Vihaan scanned the perimeter as they moved. No obvious threats. No soldiers. No uniformed personnel at all, in fact.

But his gut told him something was wrong.

There was a sedan hovering near the edge of the runway, close enough to see the landing but far enough to look inconspicuous. The engine was still running. The windshield was tinted, making it impossible to see inside.

"What about that?" Vihaan asked, keeping his voice low.

The pilot didn't answer right away. That was all the confirmation Vihaan needed.

"We move now," Vihaan said.

They crossed the tarmac quickly, stepping inside the hangar. The merchant captain, Rasmus, was already there, waiting.

"Trouble?" Rasmus asked, his Danish accent thick.

"Unknown," Vihaan said. "We need to be moving soon."

Rasmus didn't argue. He gestured toward an old truck. "This will take us to the docks. Cargo hold's prepped. Your papers are inside.

You'll be a crewman for the next leg. My men don't know who you are, only that you're part of the shipment."

Vihaan nodded. It was a solid cover, better than anything else they could've managed on short notice. He was already stepping toward the truck when he heard the door open behind him.

He turned, hand instinctively reaching for his weapon.

A man had entered the hangar. He was dressed in civilian clothes, his coat lined with fur, his posture too straight, too rigid for a simple worker. He looked at Vihaan, his lips curling into a thin, knowing smile.

"General Chadra," the man said, voice smooth. "I was hoping I'd catch you."

The moment stretched thin.

Vihaan didn't answer, didn't move. He was already calculating the distance, already watching the man's hands, already assessing how much time he had before this turned into something messy.

The man took a slow step forward, still smiling. "I don't work for the British," he said. "If I did, you'd already be dead."

That didn't make Vihaan feel any better.

"Who do you work for?" he asked.

The man shrugged. "People with interests." He glanced toward the plane, then back to Vihaan. "And right now, those interests align with keeping you alive. But that depends on whether you listen."

Vihaan exhaled slowly, keeping his expression neutral. "I don't have time for games."

The man's smile widened. "No, you don't. Which is why I'm here to warn you."

Vihaan tensed.

"About what?"

The man's voice dropped slightly, his tone shifting.

"The British weren't the only ones tracking your flight," he said. "There's a bounty on your head. And if you get on that ship, you're sailing straight into a trap."

Vihaan's pulse quickened. He looked at Rasmus, then back at the man. "Who put out the bounty?"

The man's smile faded. "Your friends in Moscow."

The words landed like a punch to the gut.

The Russians. Breshkev. He knew not to trust the bastards.

Vihaan clenched his fists, forcing himself to breathe evenly. The betrayal wasn't a surprise. The timing was. He was about to board a ship that wouldn't reach Oman, that would never make it to India.

And now, he had to decide.

Take his chances with Rasmus and risk walking into a death trap, or find another way out before it was too late.

Vihaan met the stranger's gaze. "And what do you suggest?"

The man smiled again. "A different boat."

Vihaan studied the man in front of him, his expression betraying nothing. The stranger had the relaxed confidence of someone who wasn't worried about getting shot, which meant either he had backup nearby or he believed Vihaan wouldn't risk killing him. Either way, it meant he was dangerous.

Behind him, Rasmus frowned, shifting his stance slightly. The merchant captain wasn't a soldier, but he wasn't an idiot either. He could feel the tension thickening in the air.

"I'm going to need a little more than 'a different boat,'" Vihaan said evenly.

The man smirked. "Of course. But first, let's be clear. If you get in that truck, and Rasmus here takes you to your next stop, the moment you step off that ship in Oman, there will be a bullet waiting for you."

Vihaan glanced at Rasmus. The captain scowled but didn't protest. He knew the world he operated in.

"And how exactly do you know that?" Vihaan asked.

"Because someone was paid to make sure you never set foot in India," the man said, slipping his hands into his pockets as if they were having a casual conversation. "You've pissed off the wrong people, General. Breshkev was never going to let you get that far. The moment he realized you weren't as useful to Russia as he thought, he did what men like him always do."

"Sold me out," Vihaan muttered.

"Sold you out," the man confirmed. "The British still want you dead, but they'd prefer to get their hands on you first. The Russians? They don't care how you die, as long as you don't make it to India. And the bounty they put on your head?" He chuckled. "That's just to make sure every gun-for-hire in the world has a reason to keep an eye out for you."

Vihaan didn't allow himself the luxury of frustration. He had suspected something was wrong when the British intercepted his flight so quickly, but this changed the game completely. If Breshkev had ordered a bounty on him, it meant Russia wasn't just hedging their bets anymore. They had already chosen a side.

"I assume you have a way out of this," Vihaan said, voice calm.

The man smiled. "Now you're catching on."

Vihaan crossed his arms. "You're not Russian. You're not British. So who exactly are you working for?"

"For now?" The man shrugged. "People who think you're more valuable alive than dead."

"That's not an answer."

"It's the only one you're getting."

Vihaan could hear Rasmus shifting uncomfortably behind him. He wasn't the only one who didn't like being left in the dark. But this wasn't the time for trust.

"How do I know I'm not just walking into another trap?" Vihaan asked.

The man smiled again, but this time there was something colder behind it. "You don't. But I'd take my chances if I were you." He gestured toward the parked car outside.

"The moment you turn your back, someone is making a call. The Russians aren't stupid. They knew you'd come through here. If I hadn't intercepted you, someone else would have."

Vihaan's gut churned. The car outside. The engine still running. Not watching for them. Waiting for confirmation.

"We need to move," the man said.

Vihaan looked at Rasmus. The captain let out a long breath. "I don't like this," he muttered.

"Neither do I," Vihaan admitted.

Rasmus hesitated for a moment before finally nodding. "Go. Get out of here." The pilot also nodded.

Vihaan turned to the stranger. "Where are we going?"

The man grinned. "To the last place the Russians will expect."

Vihaan barely had time to grab a spare coat from the hangar before he was following the man across the icy airstrip, cutting a sharp path away from the terminal and toward the tree line beyond.

The wind howled as they moved, whipping at Vihaan's coat. The ground beneath them was hard-packed snow and ice, the terrain treacherous underfoot.

"Where's the car?" Vihaan asked.

The man shook his head. "No car. Too easy to track. We're taking a boat."

Vihaan glanced toward the coastline in the distance. The dark silhouette of the fjord stretched out beyond the airfield, the waters eerily still beneath the overcast sky. A single fishing vessel sat near the shore, near the docks, its lights dimmed, the crew barely visible in the shadows.

"This was your plan all along," Vihaan muttered.

The man shrugged. "Call it insurance. I don't take contracts I can't control."

Vihaan didn't bother asking who this man was really working for. He was a professional, and in their world, professionals didn't talk unless they wanted to get killed.

As they neared the docks, and the boat drew closer, Vihaan caught sight of three men waiting on the boat. They were dressed in thick winter gear, their faces obscured by scarves and hoods. But

Vihaan knew body language. These weren't fishermen. They stood too rigid, too aware of their surroundings.

"Your crew?" Vihaan asked.

"My insurance policy," the man said. "You think I'd try pulling this off alone?"

They stepped onto the docks, boots thudding against the wooden planks. One of the men stepped forward, nodding to the stranger before glancing at Vihaan. "Is he in?"

The man smirked. "He's in."

The crew wasted no time. Vihaan followed them onto the boat, stepping below deck as they prepped for departure. The interior was cramped but efficient, the space clearly designed for smuggling rather than fishing.

Vihaan turned to the man who had just saved his life. "Where are we going?"

The man leaned against the bulkhead, arms crossed. "I wasn't lying when I said the Russians don't expect this. They think you're heading to Oman. They think you're boarding Rasmus's ship."

Vihaan's stomach clenched. "So where am I actually going?"

The man grinned. "Morocco."

Vihaan frowned. That wasn't part of the plan.

"That's halfway across the world from India," Vihaan said slowly.

The man nodded. "And that's exactly why it'll work. The Russians are smart, but they're also predictable. They'll have eyes on the Middle East, Pakistan, even China. But North Africa? That's not on their list."

The fishing boat carried them only as far as the edge of a radar blind zone, where the real transport awaited—a decommissioned Arctic survey ship, retrofitted in secret by the Italian Navy. The *Maria Grazia* had a dull civilian hull and fake maritime registry, but beneath her rust-streaked exterior she was fitted with long-range stealth drives, signal scramblers, and hydrogen-fed power cores. Originally built for climate research, she had been quietly converted into a deep-sea courier vessel during the early years of the global fracturing. Now, she cruised dark and silent beneath the satellite nets, invisible to drones, ghosting down the Atlantic seam with two passengers who no longer existed on paper.

Vihaan exhaled. The logic made sense, but it didn't mean he had to like it.

"Once we hit Casablanca, you'll have options," the man continued. "I have contacts who can get you into Egypt. From there, you can slip into the Red Sea, link up with resistance forces in Yemen. You take the long way around, but you stay alive."

Vihaan didn't like it. But he didn't have a choice.

He ran a hand through his hair, exhaling sharply. India had never felt further away.

CHAPTER TWENTY-FIVE

St. Petersburg, Russian Federation —Summer 2053

CHARLES DIDN'T SLEEP ANYMORE. Even before his brother's death, his nights had been restless, filled with dreams of collapsing thrones and cities burning beneath strange flags. But since Frederick's death, only five days past, Charles found himself caught in a different kind of insomnia. Not dread. Not grief. Clarity.

The Empire was bleeding. New York was no longer stable. Canada was gone.

He stood in the center of his temporary office in the old imperial palace at Tsarskoye Selo. It was suspiciously quiet here. The Russian servants moved like ghosts. Even the air outside seemed to muffle the sharpness of his thoughts.

Behind him, an aide cleared his throat. Then a junior officer stepped forward, tablet in hand. "There's one more matter, Your Majesty. A detachment intercepted six defectors near Albany. British nationals, former soldiers, wounded in the last push south. They'd been convalescing in a rebel field hospital. Our team brought them to the military complex in Syracuse for treatment. There's debate among the officers about how to proceed."

Charles turned slowly, half-listening, "Which detainees?"

"A group of British soldiers, wounded. Captured during the retreat from the canal district. They're being held in the prison hospital just outside the city. They've... defected. Refused to follow orders. Some are believed to have aided rebel movements."

Charles crossed to the table and picked up the report. A brief scan told him everything he needed. Injured men. Formerly loyal. Possibly poisoned by rebel lies, or perhaps just broken by war.

"We've had them under watch for a week," the aide continued. "The governor is requesting instruction. Trial? Transfer?"

Charles stared at the page. Once, months ago, he would have sent them into exile. Or buried them in a remote prison. But now, something had shifted. The whispers of his brother echoed in his mind—not Frederick as a monarch, but Frederick in his final, fevered days. The man who had ordered mass executions without trial. The man who ruled through terror and was never truly challenged.

For the first time in his life, Charles saw it clearly: cruelty was a kind of currency. And the Empire was running out of softer options.

"No trial," he said flatly.

The aide hesitated. "Sir?"

"They swore an oath," Charles said, his voice suddenly distant, like it was reaching through layers of memory. "They raised their hands and pledged loyalty, to me. And now they wear the colors of traitors?"

The room stiffened.

"They're injured, sire. Likely coerced, or misled..."

"No," Charles interrupted. "They are not misled. They are a message."

He stepped to the table and tapped twice on the glass surface, pulling up a live feed of the Syracuse compound—sterile white halls, medical cots, combat medics moving about.

For a moment, the screen dimmed and his own reflection glinted back at him—drawn, sharp-eyed, regal and cold.

But it wasn't his own eyes that stared back. It was his brother's. He could see them: stern, sunken, *regal.* Eyes that had ordered purges, watched executions. The eyes of a man Charles had once vowed not to become. And yet here he was.

"They think I've softened," Charles murmured. "That grief has dulled me."

They were wrong.

"Broadcast their names," he said, voice steadier now. "Make sure their former units see. Let it be known they'll be executed at sunrise. No blindfolds. No courtesies. Stripped naked and shot."

A sharp intake of breath somewhere in the room.

"Have the executions filmed," he added. "Let every soldier in the Empire see what betrayal earns. And what loyalty preserves."

The silence that followed was not fearful. It was stunned.

Admiral North took a cautious step forward. "Sire, if I may—"

"You may not," Charles snapped. "If you want to win this war, don't flinch."

As he exited, the room remained frozen, anchored by what had just been decided.

In the corridor, flanked by aides and the rustle of his robes against polished tile, Charles allowed himself the briefest flicker of satisfaction. There had been doubt in that room. But now? Now there was obedience. Frederick would have approved.

The sound of heels against marble echoed through the palace, where Charles had been granted temporary use of the old imperial palace for the summit. Outside, St. Petersburg's heat shimmered through the palace windows, and inside the gilded halls, the rooms were too warm. Charles tugged at his collar and nodded curtly as the Spanish foreign envoy entered with exaggerated grace, followed by his German counterpart—a man who barely looked old enough to drink, let alone speak for a nation fractured by its own recent unrest.

Anton Breshkev was already seated, his posture as effortlessly smug as ever. Charles hated the man—his smirks, his silences, the way he never seemed to sweat—but today, he needed him.

Charles remained standing. "Gentlemen," he began. "We are here to finalize what history will call the coalition that restored order to the world. Or, if we fail, the last indulgence of monarchs and ministers before the crashing of an age."

The Germans chuckled politely. The Spanish minister bowed his head slightly. Only Breshkev responded directly.

"I prefer not to think in such apocalyptic terms," he said, sipping from his ever-present tea. "But I do agree with the premise. There are stakes. Your Empire is bleeding, Charles. So is the Crown's credibility. What you propose must offer more than survival—it must offer legacy."

Charles forced a smile. "Legacy is exactly what I intend. Let's speak plainly. Spain wants Gibraltar returned. Germany wants trade rights and security guarantees in the Americas. And you, Anton, want the Mediterranean."

"And recognition," Breshkev added smoothly. "Of our right to oversee regional stabilization in the former Italian territories. Including naval superiority in the Adriatic."

Charles inclined his head. He sighed, "if you help crush this rebellion, if you deliver the support I've asked for, then yes. Italy is yours."

Behind the glint of polished crystal glasses and silent servants, the room thickened with unspoken agreement. Charles saw it in their eyes. They didn't trust him. But they trusted the chaos less.

"We'll see," said Breshkev. "But don't mistake proximity for strength."

Montreal, Independent Canada —Summer 2053

Meanwhile, across the Atlantic, the newly designated Independent Canada was hosting its own summit in a much less ornate but far more energetic chamber in Montreal.

The Duke leaned against the edge of a rough-hewn table as the French delegation arrived. Unlike his father's grand halls and dramatic monologues, the Duke offered handshakes, nods, and coffee in enamel mugs.

"You'll have to excuse the décor," he said. "We're spending more on ammunition than drapery these days."

General Laurent of France laughed, clapping him on the shoulder. "You have a charm, Duke. Your father would have staged this in a palace."

The Duke smiled wryly. "That's the difference between us. He's trying to rebuild a throne. I'm trying to win a war."

In the background, maps of Quebec, Ontario, and the Great Lakes were spread out, full of new French troop positions and naval movement charts.

"We're prepared to open a second front," Laurent said. "With your permission, we'll begin landings near Halifax by week's end."

"You have it," the Duke replied. "And you'll find that our people are not just ready to fight—they're ready to win. They've seen what freedom could look like."

The Frenchman raised a brow. "And what will that freedom look like when the war ends?"

The Duke didn't hesitate. "No empires. Only nations free to choose their leaders. That's what we're fighting for."

General Laurent studied the Duke for a long moment, then gave a slow nod. "France remembers what that kind of talk can cost. Revolution is never clean."

The Duke poured him another cup of coffee. "No. But neither is submission."

Behind them, aides murmured over intelligence reports, tapping coordinates on digital maps. A series of red dots blinked to life along the southern St. Lawrence, French naval movements aligning with Canadian rebel positions.

Laurent sipped his coffee and leaned in. "There's one thing we need clarity on before we move our full fleet into position."

The Duke's posture didn't shift, but something in the room did—a stillness, like a held breath.

"Which is?" he asked, though he already knew.

"Your father." Laurent's voice was low but deliberate, just loud enough for everyone in the room to feel the weight of the question. "If this rebellion succeeds, and the world begins to shift, France cannot afford ambiguity. If the King survives, we risk finding ourselves on the wrong side of the next chapter."

The words settled like ash.

Edward—because that was who he was in this moment, not the Duke, not a commander—looked down into his mug as if the answer might be hiding in the swirl of steam.

"I've thought about this," he said slowly. "More than I'd like to admit."

Laurent didn't interrupt.

"I don't want to see my father dead." Edward's voice was quiet, edged with something brittle. "I still remember the man he was, before the crackdowns, before the purges. Before my uncle poisoned his mind. He wasn't always a tyrant. There was a time... a time I thought he might even change."

He let the silence stretch for a beat before continuing.

"I've considered options. Exile. Permanent house arrest. A negotiated surrender with guarantees. I would take that deal in a heartbeat, if I believed he'd accept it."

Laurent watched him closely. "But you don't."

Edward shook his head. "No. Not unless the Empire is shattered beneath him. He's too proud. Too certain that history will bend to his will. And if he refuses to surrender..."

He trailed off, then looked up, eyes clear, voice firmer now.

"If he refuses, then yes. I will do what's necessary. I won't let his legacy rise from the ashes to haunt us again. The world deserves a clean break from the age of tyrant kings."

Laurent exhaled slowly, considering. "Then we're aligned."

Edward nodded once, but there was no triumph in his expression. Only weariness, and the quiet grief of a son who had made peace with the cost of his cause.

Before the conversation could deepen further, a young Canadian officer entered and whispered something into the Duke's ear. His brow furrowed for a moment.

Laurent gave a low sigh. "You're building a real alliance."

The Duke turned to the map. "We're building a future."

A brief silence followed, then the sound of boots on the floor as a second group of French officers entered the room, led by a sharp-eyed admiral with a steel cane. She saluted the Duke crisply.

"Admiral Lemoine. Naval command."

The Duke returned the gesture. "I trust you've reviewed the Strait plans?"

"We have. With your air support and our carriers, we'll have superiority in five days. But there's a catch."

"Always is."

"Fog, jamming, and complete silence over Newfoundland. We think the Empire is moving something in under cover—subs, maybe. Or worse."

Laurent turned to the Duke. "You've got the will. Now comes the test of your reach."

The Duke walked to the table, laid a finger over the northeastern quadrant of the map, and looked up.

"Let them come," he said. "We're not playing defense anymore."

Laurent smiled. "Spoken like someone who was never meant to be a prince."

The Duke looked out the tall windows, toward the clouds over the river. "No," he said. "But maybe I was meant to end the monarchy."

Buffalo, American Northeast

Inside a fortified command post just outside Buffalo, Alexandra Baker rubbed her temple as she skimmed the latest draft of a coalition statement. The tension in the room was wire tight. Maps blinked with troop positions. The war had changed shape.

The door opened without fanfare, but the man who entered moved like someone used to being heard. He was tall, angular, dressed in a dark wool coat with an old Republic of Venice pin on his lapel.

"I am Minister Luca di Sorrento," he said in flawless English. "I bring formal recognition from the Italian Republic. Italy stands with the rebellion."

Andrew Greg looked up from the comms table and didn't bother hiding his skepticism. "Wholeheartedly?"

Luca nodded once. "The vote in Rome was impassioned and decisive. It was not only about what Charles has done, but what he intended to do. We have... sources. It has come to our attention that the King offered to hand Italy over to Russia in exchange for their support. Our homeland, traded like a colony. Like spoil."

Alex sat forward. "How sure are you?"

Luca's eyes met hers. "Sure enough to burn our last bridge with the Crown."

Greg leaned back, his voice low and sharp. "He really offered you up."

Luca nodded grimly. "He treats Italy as if it were his to give. But we are not a prize to be bartered. The Italian people, at home and abroad, have seen what the Empire offers. Suppression. Silence. And now, the threat of Russian rule? It has enraged them."

Alex glanced at Andrew, a thread of urgency in her voice. "The diaspora—"

"They are already moving," Luca said. "From New York. From Philadelphia. From Chicago. The Empire underestimated their reach. They think of Italians as immigrants, not as patriots. That was their mistake."

He unlatched a slim briefcase and slid a folder across the table. Inside were satellite photos of troop mobilizations, naval activity off Sicily, and encrypted correspondence indicating coordination between Rome and key Italian rebel contacts in the Americas, including Vincent Carcione.

"We can deliver logistical support within a week," Luca continued. "Arms, advisors, naval corridors. And more importantly, coordinated messaging through our global networks. But Italy will not fight to liberate another empire. We want guarantees. We want a seat at the table. When this war ends, we intend to shape what comes next."

Greg didn't hesitate. "You'll have it. We don't need pawns. We need partners."

Luca narrowed his eyes. "And the Empire? It must end."

Alex answered this time. "Not just ended. Replaced. With something built by the people who bled for it."

Luca nodded slowly.

Greg tapped the edge of the folder. "We'll coordinate with Montreal and Quebec. This changes the diplomatic map overnight. We need to go public. Today."

Alex's voice was firm. "We need a joint statement. Your flag. Our movement. Global unity. Not in theory. In optics. In message. No more hiding in the margins."

Luca allowed himself the faintest smile. "We Italians are used to being underestimated. But we do know how to make noise."

Greg leaned forward. "Let's make it thunder."

CHAPTER TWENTY-SIX

The North Atlantic Sea —Summer 2053

ABOARD THE *MARIA GRAZIA*, THE sea was quiet now.

The storm that had threatened to rip the sky apart near Greenland had faded behind them, leaving only the steady groan of the ship's engines and the creak of old wood shifting beneath steel reinforcements. Vihaan stood on the deck, wrapped in a wool coat too thin for the wind, watching the endless horizon. Somewhere out there, across continents, India waited. But it felt like a memory more than a destination.

Footsteps approached behind him.

"You're lucky," the man said. "Few get to die once and live to watch the funeral."

Vihaan turned to face the stranger who had pulled him out of a death trap with nothing but quiet authority and a dangerously good plan. The man lit a cigarette with a match cupped from the wind and held out a hand.

"Luciano Bellandi," he said. "Italian intelligence. Technically no longer on payroll, but I still answer Rome's calls when things get strange."

Vihaan shook it. "You're the one who intercepted the bounty."

Luciano nodded. "Russia issued it through private syndicates. Not the usual state channels. Very old-world, very deniable. But messy. That's when I got interested."

Vihaan folded his arms. "You weren't working for the rebellion then?"

"No. I was working against the Russians." Luciano exhaled smoke into the wind. "The moment I saw your name on their target list, I started digging. Found out you were alive. Found out you were heading east. Then I found out my own government was quietly pivoting toward your side."

Vihaan raised an eyebrow. "You intercepted all that solo?"

Luciano grinned. "I'm very good at my job. I had to call in a lot of favors to pull this off."

He leaned against the rail, growing serious. "Rome has officially aligned with the rebellion. A formal envoy is already in upstate New York meeting with your people—Greg, Baker. It's not just political. Italy's committing resources, military advisors, logistics. We're done pretending neutrality."

Vihaan absorbed the news in silence.

Luciano continued. "But we're not out of danger. Russia's not giving up. They've moved agents into North Africa. Casablanca's no longer clean. We'll land there, but we don't stay."

Vihaan nodded slowly. "What's the route?"

Luciano dropped his cigarette overboard and pulled a folded map from inside his coat, spreading it on a cargo crate. "We offload in Casablanca. From there, we meet a trusted contact near Fes. He'll get us into Egypt through an overland route—military caravans, bribes, and a few uncomfortable nights in abandoned safehouses."

"After Cairo?" Vihaan asked.

"We join a resistance courier group in Suez. They'll take us to Yemen under a Saudi defector's papers. From there, a rebel flight is waiting. Flies once a week to Bombay with humanitarian supplies." He paused. "That's your last ride."

Vihaan stared at the lines on the map. "And the Russians?"

"They'll be looking in the Middle East, Pakistan, and along the old intelligence corridors. They won't expect you to come up from the south straight into the hornet's nest."

Vihaan let out a breath. "It's insane."

Luciano shrugged. "That's why it'll work."

After nearly six weeks at sea, the *Maria Grazia* docked just before dawn. Fog rolled in off the Atlantic, coating the port in a wet film that softened shadows and made movements feel dreamlike.

Vihaan and Luciano slipped onto the docks with forged merchant IDs and a crate of fake manifests. Within minutes, they were moving—on foot first, then by jeep, then under the tarp of a water truck heading inland.

In Fes, they changed clothes in a centuries-old madrasa repurposed by smugglers. In the alleyways of Luxor, they traded papers with a retired Egyptian general who demanded nothing but a single, whispered prayer in exchange. Near Suez, they posed as relief workers delivering medical supplies to a rebel hospital outside Mocha.

Every stop was another gamble. Every name dropped, every passphrase given, every contact trusted by someone who might already be dead.

Luciano never lost his calm. Vihaan never lost his edge.

They were hunted men moving through a world that no longer believed in clear lines.

But when the humanitarian plane lifted off from the Yemeni coast, neither of them looked back.

Bombay, India —Summer 2053

The moment Vihaan stepped off the aircraft in Bombay, the humid night air hit him like a wall. It smelled of brine, smoke, and overripe mangoes. He had never been so glad to breathe it.

He moved quickly through the hangar, where rebel fighters and medics worked side by side, unloading cargo under strict radio silence.

Luciano peeled off, disappearing into a group of operatives with a simple nod. His job was done, for now.

Vihaan was escorted into the main building, through reinforced corridors lined with comms equipment, past a sealed map room, into a small communications chamber.

A screen flickered to life.

Then Alexandra appeared.

Her face was sharper than he remembered, leaner, exhausted, but alert. The moment she saw him, her posture changed. She leaned forward, eyes narrowing. Not quite smiling. But something close.

"You look like hell," she said.

"You should see the other guy."

A long silence passed. Just the two of them, separated by oceans and war, staring at each other through low-bandwidth pixels and too many miles.

"You made it," she said softly.

"Barely."

"I heard about the Russians," she added.

"I'm not surprised."

Her voice grew quieter. "There's more coming."

Vihaan nodded. "I know. But now I'm here."

She nodded back.

"You ready to fight?" she asked.

He looked directly at the screen, jaw tight.

"I never stopped."

CHAPTER TWENTY-SEVEN

Bombay —Summer 2053

KING CHARLES SAT INSIDE A secure war room beneath the old Parliament building, flanked by hollow-eyed generals and intelligence officers who hadn't slept properly in weeks. The overhead lights buzzed against the humming fans that did nothing to break the heat.

He barely heard them anymore.

"...multiple Russian destroyers have been stationed off the coast of Vancouver and Puget Sound. Civilian ports have been mined. Two carriers are operating under Arctic cover, possibly staging south toward San Francisco and Los Angeles. Canada has requested expanded anti-ship capabilities, but their Western Command is stretched thin."

Charles's fingers drummed slowly against the arm of his chair.

"And Italy?" he asked.

Admiral North shifted in his seat. "Blockaded on three sides. Russian subs near the Strait of Gibraltar. Air raids on Naples, Cagliari, Genoa. Civilian casualties rising. Their coastal defense network is holding—for now—but they're begging for reinforcements that won't be coming."

Charles nodded without looking up.

"And the Germans?" he asked, already knowing.

General Rostand stepped forward. "Full-scale arms production underway. Troop transports spotted near Baden-Württemberg. We estimate a full invasion force will cross into Alsace-Lorraine by the end of the month. The French are fortified, but if the Germans push through, northern Italy will fall within a fortnight."

"And the French?"

"Confident," Rostand said. "Too confident, perhaps. But they're dug in, and their supply lines are solid. They're even drawing volunteers from Quebec now."

Charles sat back in silence.

He had known this day would come. A world war. Not in name, but in fact. His father had told him once: "The world won't explode all at once. It will fracture. Quietly first. Then all at once."

It had begun as whispers in America. Then a spark in Canada. Now, flames were breaking out across the map.

"What are we looking at?" Charles asked flatly.

"Sir—" said Admiral North, not bothering to sit. "It's everywhere."

General Rostand stood beside him and activated the feed uplinks. One by one, real-time battlefield footage queued up across the central monitors, taken from security feeds, satellite footage, and comms of Imperials.

"We're receiving fragmented reports," she said, "but these aren't small insurgencies. These are offensives against some of our weakest outposts. Some look spontaneous—some... don't."

She didn't elaborate. The first feed loaded.

Darwin, Australia

Rain fell sideways off the gulf, thick and sharp with sea brine, as the crowd surged up the wharf road. They moved like a tide: dockworkers, schoolteachers, teenagers in reflective vests and patched jackets, all howling slogans, in that distinctive Australian way, that bounced off the dented corrugated siding of the old port authority building. Faces were masked with goggles and soaked scarves, many carrying signal-scramblers stolen or pieced together from blackmarket technology and salvaged batteries, low-grade jammers to confuse drone targeting.

Above them, an Imperial recon drone banked in from the east. It stuttered mid-air as its proximity sensor failed to lock onto individual threats.

"The swarm AI flagged the crowd as 'unidentified commercial maritime traffic' and held its fire," said the Admiral.

A convoy of Imperial transport trucks sat across the road, barricading the pier. Behind them, two armored trucks loomed, turrets idle but tracking, their auto-targeting systems waiting for a breach of the pre-programmed no-go perimeter. Sirens blared overhead. A synthetic voice issued a garbled final warning in three languages. The crowd didn't slow.

A molotov arced forward and smashed against the side of the first truck. Flames burst across the reinforced windows. The second firebomb followed, thudding into the engine block of the adjacent carrier. Smoke billowed. Soldiers spilled from the vehicles in confusion, their visors fogging from the coastal heat and static interference.

From atop a rusted tugboat chained to the jetty, a woman in a neon vest raised a pressure-cooker bomb wrapped in copper wire and weatherproof tape. She hurled it overhand. The explosive struck the armored turret of the lead carrier and detonated in a burst of white-hot shrapnel. It didn't explode so much as implode—metal screeching like a dying beast, the hull crumpling inward with a sharp metallic scream.

A new burst of static buzzed through the air. One of the resistance engineers had hacked the drone's frequency, splicing an open-loop command to flood its system with false positives. The drone, confused, listed sideways and hovered above the flaming wreckage, useless.

Then the crowd surged. Hunting rifles cracked. Bricks flew. Tear gas canisters were thrown back before they could deploy. Old flare guns fired point-blank at sensor arrays. The checkpoint crumbled in minutes, and the remaining officers fell back toward the waterline, calling for aerial evac as comms began to fail.

By nightfall, two armored vehicles had been repainted with crude white spray-paint, their sides emblazoned with a new flag: a crown, engulfed in fire. The words beneath:

NO MORE MASTERS. NO MORE GODS.

A new feed appeared on the screen.

Honiara, Solomon Islands

The market was a sea of activity. The remnants of an old Coastwatcher mast leaned overhead, its rigging tangled in netting and tattered Imperial signal flags. Beneath it, the garrison formed up for the morning report, thirty soldiers in dust-flecked armor, their boots slick with rain and spilled oil.

Constable Masi stood among them, motionless. His uniform was pressed, boots shined, his badge catching the early sunlight like a signal mirror. To the officer beside him, he looked like every other loyalist in the ranks. Calm. Predictable. Until the moment he moved.

He didn't speak. He didn't hesitate.

One smooth motion: his sidearm cleared its holster, barked twice. The command sergeant crumpled to the ground, blood soaking the coral-pink pavement. The second shot struck the uplink tech beside him. Silence reigned for less than two seconds before the square exploded into motion.

Rebels hidden among the vendors surged forward. Fishermen, mechanics, sailors with coilguns built from repurposed drone parts and stolen transmitter guides. Someone hurled a sack of ball bearings into the patrol line just as a shortwave scrambler ignited near the mast, killing Imperial comms.

Masi sprinted for the shack beneath the tower, the transmitter station the Empire used to relay encrypted updates to the Pacific fleet. A corporal lunged for him with a shock baton, but Masi dropped him with two shots and kicked open the door. He sealed it behind him with a mechanical lock, then wired the failsafe: a narrow black transmitter, palm-sized, rigged to mimic a burst weather alert. It had been smuggled into the station three nights ago, hidden inside a crate of old books, meant to be used as kindling.

On the table sat the old broadcast console, outdated but functional. Masi slammed the signal override key and flipped the toggles by muscle memory. The system hissed to life, blinking green.

Outside, Imperial drones buzzed low overhead, searching for targets. But their recognition software, once pristine, had been corrupted. Hours earlier, rebels had uploaded false-positive databases through a hijacked uplink. The drones now identified anything moving as "non-combatant"—even the rebel fighters were now torching the last APC on the far end of the market.

A woman's recorded voice cut across the comms grid, washing through every Imperial earpiece in a hundred-kilometer radius. It wasn't a speech. It was a hymn. Old and rhythmic, laced with code. Coordinates disguised as verses. Evacuation orders disguised as prayer. Pirate poetry threaded with truth.

And beneath it, looping once every minute, a message stitched in both English and pidgin:

"The tide is ours now. We choose the island. We choose the sky."

Within twenty minutes, the tower was lost. The garrison either fled, surrendered, or bled out in the square. Imperial warships offshore tried to jam the broadcast but failed, Masi had hardwired the signal through the old undersea cable lines, once Imperial, now theirs.

By nightfall, rebel banners flew from every government building in Honiara, stitched from fishnet, parachute fabric, and scorched uniform sleeves.

The Empire never reclaimed the island. It never even tried.

Tripoli, North Africa

The desert wind came first. Hot and gritty, it whispered through the cracked streets and rusted scaffolding of the Imperial armory's eastern wall. Loose tarps snapped against chain-link fences. Warning sirens stayed silent. No one inside noticed the change in the air.

Then came the roar.

They arrived in waves. Women on motorbikes, cloaked in desert robes and scarves, rifles slung across their backs. The first group broke from the dunes with engines screaming and tires spinning sand into the sky. The guards at the checkpoint reached for their weapons too late. One rider hurled a homemade explosive—a repurposed oil can packed with ceramic shards and powder. It landed beneath a sentry tower and ignited in a vicious crack of smoke and flame. The outer wall shook. Men inside the bunker began shouting.

While the perimeter scrambled, the second wave came from the south. More riders, moving fast, arced around the rear compound and lit the fuel depot with a cluster of Molotovs. Flames rolled across the sand and burst against the concrete. From nearby rooftops, women with carbines opened fire, targeting cameras, floodlights, and mounted drones. A signal jammer the size of a toaster, sent from an old shipping crate, had already scrambled the base's proximity alarms. When the fire suppression units lifted off their rails, they hovered in place—confused, stuck on false telemetry loops injected by rebel hackers three days prior.

From the alleyways of the old city, a third wave surged forward. Fighters on foot, some barely more than teenagers, some bent with age. They wore scavenged armor plates and carried bolt-action rifles passed down through three generations. Several carried weather drones modified to drop nails, screws, and glass across the courtyard. Every approach had been planned. Every step calculated.

By late afternoon, the armory gates lay open. Ammunition crates had been seized, burn marks etched into the yard where the last defensive line had fallen. Officers tried to barricade themselves in the inner depot, but the rebels used welding torches to peel back the steel doors and left the interior to burn. Fuel tanks erupted in the night with dull concussive thumps that echoed for miles.

From the balcony above the loading bay, a woman in a crimson scarf raised a flare gun and fired into the darkening sky. The smoke that spiraled upward bloomed in colors long outlawed under the Empire: saffron, black, and rust-red. The tribal flags once banned had returned to the sky, unchallenged.

Across the outer gates, someone painted the new name of the stronghold. They used a strip of torn cloth as a brush and ash from the destroyed communications bunker as ink. DAUGHTERS OF THE DESERTED

That night, a rebel broadcast station hijacked the city's signal and played a loop of the assault. No commentary. No propaganda. Just the sound of engines and women shouting across the sand.

Guiana, South America

The first shots came before dawn.

In the lowland sprawl of Paramaribo's southern quarter, among the concrete tenements and rusting comm towers, the streets erupted in violence. Rebel units—mostly dockworkers, former soldiers, and sugar field deserters—moved in coordinated silence beneath the cover of the morning mist. Their target: Fort Zeelandia, an old Imperial logistics node surrounded by blast fencing and surveillance drones.

The drones fell first. Using homemade jammers mounted on motorcycles and guided by signal mappers running point with stolen military tablets, the rebels pushed the scout network into blackout. One by one, the flying sentries lost their bearings and spiraled into alleyways and rooftops, crashing like mechanical birds.

Then came the push.

A column of rebel fighters advanced through the east canal district, flanking the outer perimeter of the fort. Explosives planted in storm drains collapsed the gate's defense corridor. From the rooftops, snipers opened fire. Their bullets found the gaps in armor—throats, shoulders, the soft undersides of helmets. Imperial troops returned fire, laying down suppressive bursts with auto-rifles and rooftop-mounted railguns. But the fort was too exposed, the lines too thin.

Inside the command center, comms fell silent. Dozens of support staff and officers attempted to hold the inner complex. Some fought back. Most died in place.

An old fishing trawler, retrofitted with armored plates and a crude rocket pod, barreled through the south checkpoint and ignited its payload inside the motor pool. Flames engulfed the lower yard. Munitions cooked off in staccato bursts. Smoke rose high above the mangroves, black against the blood-orange light of dawn.

By the time the sun cleared the tree line, the Imperial flag had been pulled down. In its place, a red cloth with a black handprint.

Spray-painted on the walls of the burning command center:

THIS IS NOT BRITAIN. THIS IS SOUTH AMERICA.

The footage ended. Not in ten-second clips, but in a barrage of flame, defiance, and blood.

From the Pacific to the Caribbean, the Empire was bleeding. These weren't isolated sparks—they were coordinated uprisings. Tactical. Deliberate. Global.

Charles stared at the final frozen frame on the war room screen. Black smoke. Burning banners. A soldier's body draped over the hood of an armored truck. It was no longer a rebellion. It was a reckoning.

"And here?" he asked quietly, without looking away. "What of India?"

Rostand hesitated. "Holding, sir. But we lost three command vehicles outside Delhi last night. Rebel bomb. Killed General Patel, Minister Cohen, and Admiral Levy."

Charles's jaw tightened. His old friends. Men who had stood beside him for decades. Loyal to a fault. Loyal enough to die in his name.

He closed his eyes. Just for a moment. Reaching back, maybe, to some simpler image of them before the blood, before the fire.

"Prepare a state funeral," he said. His voice was flat, but the grief cut through. "Tomorrow. They deserve more than a passing footnote."

The next day, Luciano Bellandi adjusted his cufflink, slow and deliberate, and scanned the rooftops one last time.

The crowd was quiet. Too quiet.

Funerals were supposed to be loud in India—wailing, chanting, smoke—but this one was imperial, hollowed of tradition, drowned in flags. A performance of loyalty. A eulogy for men who had orchestrated airstrikes and blacksite disappearances.

He was forty-seven meters from the platform.

Dressed as a visiting military attaché from Rome, his credentials were perfect. A minor assistant to the Italian envoy. No weapon. No wires. Just a polished pin on his chest and a very old debt in his heart.

The bomb was built into the base of a ceremonial offering urn near the main stage. It had taken two weeks, three false credentials, and a midnight swim through the sewage canals beneath Bombay to get it there. It had been worth it.

Cohen. Levy. Patel. The architects of the Bombay Crackdown. The ones who signed the order that turned the Dharavi ward into a free-fire zone during the riots. Ten thousand dead. Half of them children. The rebels knew the King favored them and had counted on this funeral.

Luciano had walked those ashes. He had watched the Empire pave over the bodies and call it progress.

"Your King is a careful man," he had said to the envoy afterward. "But careful men make slow mistakes."

Now, as the carriages drew near and Charles took his place beside the podium, Luciano slid a hand into his coat pocket.

The transmitter was small. Thumb-sized. Encased in leather. His finger rested against the activation switch, but he didn't press. Not yet.

He scanned the square again. Dignitaries everywhere. Soldiers with autoloading rifles. Drones hovering. Everything in its place.

Then he saw her—the decoy.

She wore a sari, face veiled, pushing a wheelchair draped in Empire colors. Inside: a body. Real or fake, he didn't know. She was insurance. If something went wrong. If the blast missed.

She looked at him once. Just a flicker.

Luciano gave the signal: a small tilt of his chin.

And then he looked up.

Charles stood on the dais, dressed in funeral black, gold trim across his chest, arms behind his back. He looked old today. Not tired. Not weak. Just... thinner somehow. As if the war had begun to hollow him from the inside.

Luciano didn't care.

This wasn't about Charles. Not directly. This was about a message. A precise, bloody reminder that the rebellion had teeth. That even allies of the Empire would not be safe.

He pressed the switch.

Nothing happened for a full second.

Then, a loud, sharp pop—like fireworks. The urn shattered in a white-hot burst of light and sound. The platform cracked, wood and stone erupting into the air. Glass sprayed like shrapnel. Bodies slammed into pavement. Screaming. Gunfire. More screams.

Luciano didn't move. Not yet.

Smoke billowed across the square as soldiers scurried. The crowd stampeded. Somewhere nearby, someone else shouted for a medic.

A second blast, smaller, went off near the back of the square. The decoy. A distraction.

Luciano used the chaos.

He ducked behind a guardrail, stripped off his coat, and tossed the pin into a trash receptacle. Underneath the uniform was a street vendor's shirt—sweaty, stained, anonymous. He grabbed a bag prepacked with spoiling vegetables and limped into the dispersing crowd like just another man trying to survive the day.

As he passed the edge of the square, he saw the stretcher.

Charles was alive. Bleeding from his head, dazed—but alive. He was surrounded by security and military personnel being rushed to an ambulance nearby.

Luciano didn't flinch.

He wasn't here to kill the King. Not yet.

He was here to kill faith. To kill the illusion that the Empire could grieve its own with dignity. To kill the idea that the center still held.

He vanished into the back alleys of Old Bombay before the emergency perimeter closed, just another face in the blur of terror and revolution.

Behind him, sirens wailed.

Chapter Twenty-Eight

THE SOIL TREMBLED UNDERFOOT WITH the distant thud of kinetic shells, and even through the reinforced visor of his command helmet, Vihaan could see the shimmer of heat rising off the fractured ground. There was ash in the air, and something sharper beneath it—hot ozone, the tang of scorched circuitry.

This was India. His India. The nearest base to Bombay, now a war zone. The place he had fought to return to. The place he had come to take back.

General Vihaan Chadra crouched on a ridge of shattered stone, watching through a HUD overlay as drones traced glinting arcs through the sky above the Imperial base below. The facility was half-buried in the earth, ringed by anti-air towers and kinetic rail cannons, pulsing with blue heat as they charged.

They called it Base 14-Kilo. A hardened Imperial command hub with subterranean tech vaults, research wings, and a functioning fusion core. If the rebels took it, they'd gain access to enough cutting-edge weaponry to change the balance of the war.

And if they failed, they'd lose more than momentum. They'd lose Bombay.

Vihaan's voice came through the comms—crisp and controlled. "Scouting units, report."

A flash of static, then a voice, female, sharp, close. "This is Recon-One. Mines ahead, smarttrip class. Heat-triggered. Our crawler marked three lines running east to west across the approach valley."

Vihaan narrowed his eyes. "Estimated depth?"

"Surface, sir. Shallow-set. Designed to slow hovercrafts."

Vihaan swore under his breath. The Imperials were using terrain denial protocols, slowing their movement, channeling them into kill zones. Textbook Frederick-era tactics.

But this wasn't the Empire of ten years ago. And these weren't the rebels of ten years ago either.

"Deploy counter-drones," Vihaan ordered. "Sweep ahead and scramble their mines and probe the field. We've got the EMP script loaded?"

"Confirmed," came another voice. "Stormcaller AI online and syncing now."

The Stormcaller drone suite, one of the rebellion's most volatile battlefield tools, launched overhead with a high-pitched scream, scattering like a flock of burning birds. Each drone carried a micro-EMP burst, designed not to destroy tech, but to disorient sensors and blind defenses for thirty critical seconds.

"Armor teams, advance on my mark," Vihaan said. "Grids Nine through Thirteen. Keep it tight. No wide formation. We move like a needle, not a hammer."

Beneath the ridge, rebel hovercrafts stirred, their engines humming like hornets. Vihaan could see the dust plume rising behind them already—massive armored skiffs, retrofitted with scavenged railguns and armor plates painted with the sigil of the resistance: a broken crown, aflame.

"On your call, sir," said a voice beside him.

Vihaan didn't answer. Not yet.

He stared at the Imperial base, watched the pulse of its perimeter defenses, timed the arc of the patrol drones as they swept the western approach. Now.

"GO."

The rebel line surged forward.

The first wave moved fast, low-flying assault carriers kicking up gouts of dust as they skimmed the earth. Mortar fire erupted from the Imperial line almost immediately—plasma rounds and smart-guided shells that tracked movement heat signatures and curved mid-flight like sharks in water.

But the Stormcaller drones were already in play.

Bursts of static flickered across the enemy turrets as their sensors overloaded. Targeting systems blinked out. Two railguns went dark.

"Now! Cut west! Push through Zone Twelve!" Vihaan shouted into the comm.

Rebel skiffs flared hard to the left, slipping past the worst of the kill zone. Behind them, infantry squads ran low and fast. Vihaan dropped from the ridge and joined the lead unit, his boots slamming into the packed dirt.

They hit the perimeter fence like a tidal wave. Plasma cutters whined. Rifles snapped. One Imperial drone zipped overhead—and was immediately taken out by a shoulder-mounted rail spear that turned it into slag mid-air.

Vihaan led the charge through the breach.

Inside the compound, the fighting was close, brutal.

Hallways flashed red with emergency lights as alarms shrieked overhead. Rebel slicers had jammed the Imperial surveillance feed and overclocked the fire doors, but that hadn't stopped the defenders from mounting a disciplined stand. The Imperial guards weren't green recruits—they were hardened regulars, dug in and waiting.

Vihaan ducked behind a column as gunfire tore through a nearby squad, bullets sparking off concrete, the staccato crack of rifles echoing down the corridor. This wasn't drone warfare from a distance. This was rifles at thirty feet. Sidearms at ten. Blades when it got worse.

A rebel went down hard across from him, clutching a bleeding shoulder, pinned behind an overturned gurney. The man's rifle had jammed. Vihaan didn't think—he moved.

He broke cover low and fast, rounds snapping past his ear, and reached the man in seconds.

"Stay down," Vihaan barked, dragging him by the vest collar back behind a bulkhead. A second later, a grenade detonated where they'd just been. Pressure and smoke punched through the corridor, deafening.

The wounded rebel gasped, dazed. "Thought you were command—"

"I am," Vihaan said, slapping a fresh magazine into the man's rifle. "Now get back in the fight."

Under the old Imperial model, a general wouldn't be within a hundred klicks of a frontline engagement, let alone on the floor, bleeding beside a corporal. But Vihan's rebellion had no room for titles that hid behind walls. It was personal. Everyone pulled weight. Everyone earned their place.

And when the troops saw Vihaan out front, rifle in hand, taking fire, dragging comrades out of the blast radius, they fought harder.

He pushed forward with his squad, clearing room by room.

The Imperials had set up choke points—sandbags, steel plates, overlapping fields of fire. Vihaan's team had to breach with old-school flashbangs and close-quarter drills. A rebel beside him took a shot to the thigh and went down screaming. Another was dragged out of the fight with burns along one arm after catching a blast from a portable launcher.

At one point, Vihaan's knife was in his hand before he could raise his rifle, and the fight was blade against sidearm in a cramped maintenance corridor lit only by flickering emergency strobes. The Imperial officer he dropped was fast, trained—but not prepared for someone who fought like he had nothing left to lose.

They finally pushed through to the command core.

Vihaan kicked in the door to the central vault and shot the first officer before the man could raise an alert. The second reached for the wall comm—Vihaan shot the console before he could activate it.

"Secure the room!" he barked. "Download everything. Then wipe it."

His breath was ragged. His face streaked with ash, sweat, and blood—some his, mostly others'.

"Status on the armory?" he called out.

"Secured," a voice answered. "They've got serious gear. High-grade repeaters, rail-cored rifles, a few things we've never seen before."

Vihaan's eyes swept the room. Half the displays were still functional—maps, troop movements, encrypted communications. Their value would be in the seconds, not hours.

"Tag the gear. Take what we can. If it's bolted down, you know what to do."

Outside, the sound of gunfire was finally fading. The enemy fallback lines had collapsed. A fresh wave of rebel fighters poured into the main corridors, calling clear.

Vihaan keyed his comm. "This is General Chadra. The base is ours. Repeat: Bombay's tech hub is under rebel control."

There was silence. Then Alexandra's voice, calm and clear: "Nice work, Vihaan."

He looked out at the carnage—dead Imperials, wounded rebels, smoke curling from bullet-scarred walls.

He wiped blood from his brow and smiled grimly. "Just getting started."

The command room still smelled like blood and ozone.

Vihaan stood at the main console, staring at the flickering overhead map. It was grainy, patched together from salvaged Imperial systems and rebel uplinks, but it showed the truth well enough.

A reaction force was en route.

"They'll be moving fast," said Lieutenant Khan beside him, pointing at the route through Pune. "Three hours, maybe less. Armor, drones, heavy infantry. The usual show of force."

Vihaan's jaw tightened.

He turned to the comms officer at the far console. "Have we finished the scans?"

"Mostly. We've mapped all critical tech sectors. We've pulled the blackbox data from their R&D servers and tagged what we couldn't carry."

Vihaan exhaled through his nose. They could level this place and vanish before the reaction force arrived. That had been the fallback plan: blow the vaults, torch the weapons, leave nothing behind.

But this base mattered.

It wasn't just a depot. It was an Imperial testing site, one of the few in the region with advanced weapons prototypes still intact. If they could hold it, even for a few days, they could extract, replicate, and redeploy Imperial tools at scale.

And more than that—taking it had sent a message. Holding it would make history.

He looked at the map one more time.

"We hold," he said.

Khan blinked. "Sir—"

"We hold," Vihaan repeated. "Get word to Colonel Argyle's unit near Surat. I want them moving south now. They'll intercept the reaction force in the field, slow them, bleed them, break momentum."

"Yes, General."

Vihaan moved through the main corridor, his boots tracking blood and ash across the tile as he passed triage teams working in every available space—hallways, storage closets, disused labs. Rebel medics shouted orders, scrambling to stabilize the wounded while field surgeons operated under lantern light and generator hum.

He turned to the lead medic stationed at the mobile triage console just outside the converted lab.

"Final count?" he asked.

The medic, an older woman with a silver streak of dried blood across her cheek, didn't hesitate.

"Two hundred sixty-eight dead on our side. Seven hundred thirty-one wounded. About a quarter will need evac or long-term care. We've started airlifting the critical ones to safe zones in Pune and Surat."

Vihaan's jaw tightened. He had known it would be bad—any base this fortified wasn't going to fall without blood—but hearing the numbers made the cost feel real.

"And the Imperials?"

"Seven hundred twenty-one confirmed dead. Just over a thousand wounded—about four hundred serious, the rest light or stable. Five hundred forty-four were captured in the final breach, mostly from the lower vaults and drone hangars. We've identified twenty-seven officers among them. A few hundred still unaccounted for—presumed buried or burned."

Vihaan nodded slowly, absorbing it all. "No retaliation. No brutality. Give them medical aid. Keep them under guard. Anyone with officer clearance gets tagged and pulled for debrief."

"And if they resist?"

"Remind them this isn't Frederick's army."

The order was clear. The rebellion didn't stoop to Imperial methods. Not if they wanted to build something better after the dust settled.

The scale of the fight had been massive—just over five thousand troops across three divisions. The rebels had come in with a narrow numerical advantage, twenty-seven hundred to the Empire's twenty-five hundred. But the defenders had fortified walls and top-line weapons. It had evened the field.

For every meter gained, someone had paid in flesh.

He looked past the medic to the field boards, where names were still being added—red for dead, yellow for wounded, blue for critical. The boards were full. Another board was being taped to the wall.

"Tell the teams in Sector Six to start rotations," he said. "Anyone who can walk and hold a rifle goes on security detail. Everyone else gets water and rest. I want this place locked down before sundown."

"Yes, General."

Vihaan turned to Khan, who had been watching silently from the doorway.

"Put together a list of the fallen. Name, unit, hometown. I want it transmitted to every rebel camp and posted in every city that stands with us."

"You want casualty lists public?"

"I want their sacrifice seen. We didn't come here to vanish our dead. We came to win something that matters. And that means honoring the price."

Khan nodded.

Vihaan looked back at the sea of stretchers and triage mats. In the Empire, generals observed from towers or floated above the battlefield in silent drones. They never smelled burned cloth or listened to the whimpering of a kid who had just lost both legs.

He moved further into the base, stepping over shattered glass and shell casings. His boots crunched against a pile of tangled data cables that someone had yanked from the comms mainframe.

"Any luck unlocking their weapons?" he asked as he entered the holding chamber where a rebel tech team worked at a row of crates.

One of the slicers, barely twenty, sweat-slicked and jittery, looked up. "We got lucky, sir. Pulled partial override codes from one of the officers you captured. We combined it with a dump from an old Intelligence blacksite file—stuff we got last year out of Bhopal. Fragmented code keys, but enough to spoof the authorization layer."

Vihaan stepped closer, eyes narrowing at the open crate in front of them. Inside: a compact carbine with a built-in power cell that glowed faint blue.

"So we can fire them?"

"We can now. Not everything, but most of it. And we're writing a patch to bypass the biometric locks on the rest."

"Timeframe?"

"Two hours. Four if we lose power."

"You won't," Vihaan said.

He tapped his comm. "All units: reinforce perimeter. Dig in. No fallback. No burn orders. We hold this base. If the Empire wants it back, they're going to have to take it."

CHAPTER TWENTY-NINE

THE RAILCAR HUMMED LOW BENEATH their feet, cutting south across old freight lines that hadn't seen regular traffic since the Empire shuttered civilian logistics. Ten years later and Texas was still being punished. Outside, the plains stretched wide and golden under the weight of late afternoon light. Patches of prairie grass swayed in the wind, undisturbed by the war crawling toward them.

Inside the armored cabin, Alexandra Baker sat opposite Andrew Greg at a folding steel table covered with reports, radio logs, and an untouched thermos of bitter coffee. They had barely needed to speak on the ride, so much already understood.

But silence had never felt quite like this before.

"We'll link up with the Texas Expeditionary Force at dawn," Greg said, tapping a point on the worn highway grid near Austin. "From there, we roll west to connect with the Gulf Coast resistance cells and consolidate into a formal command. Dallas and Houston are already preparing for urban engagements. Port Sabine's still in play."

After the last war, the Empire had rebuilt Dallas as an industrial compound. The city had been effectively leveled and but the strategic location and geography suited the Empire's needs.

Alex nodded, tracing her fingers over the map. "We take Dallas, we break the Empire's mid-continent supply line. We take Houston, we open the Gulf. It's not just about ports anymore. It's about splitting their theater in two."

Greg leaned back. "It's ambitious."

"It has to be."

Her voice was calm, but her eyes lingered on the place where the red ink met the coastline. Texas was more than just strategy. It was memory. It was where she'd learned to fight, and where she'd lost the illusion that winning would come easy.

"Your old unit's already calling it the Texas Front," Greg said. "They're dug in and waiting."

Alex smiled faintly. "They always did like the sound of their own legend."

He watched her for a moment, then looked away. "They're ready for you."

She didn't answer immediately.

"I'm not the same soldier I was a decade ago," she said finally.

"Good," Greg replied. "That soldier nearly burned herself out trying to carry the war on her back. This time, we do it together."

She looked up at him then—really looked—past the field uniform and the tired posture, past the command responsibilities. He'd changed, too. He was still careful with his words, still the strategist who weighed every move before committing. But he had learned to lead from the field, not just the command tent. And somewhere along the way, she had started trusting him more than anyone.

Maybe that was dangerous.

She pushed the thought aside.

"And the command structure?" she asked. "Us taking control—it's going to raise questions."

Greg nodded. "We'll keep the optics clear. You take tactical command of the southern front. I'll remain as division authority, strategic oversight. Not direct battlefield orders."

"A way around the aide-to-superior issue," she said dryly.

His expression softened. "We're at war. But we're not blind."

For a moment, the air between them changed. The railcar still hummed. The sun dipped lower in the sky, casting long shadows through the armored glass.

"We make this work," he said quietly. "All of it. The campaign. The politics. The future."

Alex looked out the window. The fields were giving way to dry scrubland, the start of old ranch country. The kind of place where people disappeared into land and silence. The kind of place that never forgot who it belonged to.

The convoy rolled into Austin under the cover of nightfall, the skyline dimmed, most of the city still dark except for the flickering power nodes the resistance had rigged back to life. The streets were quiet—too quiet for a capital of a revolution—but the silence didn't feel like fear.

It felt like waiting.

Alex stepped down from the lead vehicle and inhaled deeply. Dust. Cedar. Warm concrete. The smell of Texas hadn't changed.

Greg followed her, glancing around the perimeter as rebel sentries moved to secure the street. A few of the Texas Expeditionary Force—her old unit—stood at the ready outside the old courthouse turned command center. Their uniforms didn't match, but their posture did. Loyal. Hardened. Ready.

She didn't greet them yet.

Instead, she turned to Greg. "Before we do the formalities... there's somewhere I need to go." Greg gave a small nod. "I'm with you."

They walked across a forgotten corner of the city, skirting silent blocks and overgrown lots until they reached the edge of a small, chain-linked cemetery tucked between two collapsed buildings. No streetlights. No markings. Just weather-worn headstones and the brittle rustle of grass in the wind.

Alex led him through the gate, stopping in front of a simple stone slab, low to the ground.

GABRIEL BAKER 2034–2042

A HERO KILLED IN ACTION

She knelt. "My brother. He was eight," she said. Her voice didn't shake, not yet. "Too young to fight. Too young to understand what was happening. But he followed me. Even when I told him not to."

Greg stood silently beside her, watching her shoulders tense.

"We were ambushed outside San Angelo. It was supposed to be a supply run. Nothing dangerous. I let him carry a radio, gave him something to do. He thought that made him part of it."

She reached forward, brushing her fingers across the rough edge of the stone.

"A drone strike took out the transport behind ours. Debris hit him. Shrapnel to the neck. There wasn't enough time."

Now her voice cracked.

"I buried him myself. We were on the move. There was no time for anything else. I carved the stone from an old slab and came back after the siege to place it."

She hadn't planned to cry. She had promised herself she wouldn't again. But here, on this dirt, with Greg standing beside her and the war closing in again, there was no room for promises. She thought to herself again... *you can't hate your tears enough to stop them.*

They came quietly. No sobbing. No dramatic collapse—just tears.

Greg crouched beside her without a word and placed a hand gently on her back. He didn't speak. He didn't try to fix it. He was simply there.

After a long moment, she leaned into him—not all the way, just enough that their shoulders touched.

"He would've hated that it took this long to come back," she said.

Greg's voice was quiet. "He'd be proud of what you're building."

She didn't answer, but the way she let her head rest briefly against his shoulder said enough.

For a minute, the war fell away. The titles. The ranks. The politics. It was just two people, in the dark, at the grave of a boy who never had a chance to grow old.

Two hours after dawn, the morning heat hadn't yet peaked, but the sun was already burning through the haze as Alexandra and Greg stepped into the repurposed city council chamber. The ceiling tiles were gone, replaced by hanging solar lights. Folded maps covered the walls, along with live drone feeds projected onto patched-together smartglass panels.

The Texas Expeditionary Force was already assembled—dozens of officers and cell leaders in mismatched uniforms, old ranchers in dusty boots beside young tacticians in patched body armor. All of them turned when Alex entered. A few saluted. Most didn't, but they watched her closely.

She could feel it. The weight of their memory. Their loss. And something more dangerous than doubt: expectation.

She stepped up to the front of the room.

"I know many of you," she said. "And most of you know me. I bled on this ground with you ten years ago. I left to fight a different kind of war, but I never stopped thinking about this one."

A murmur rippled through the room—approval, perhaps, or quiet acknowledgment.

"Now we're back," she continued, glancing briefly at Greg beside her. "And this time, we're not holding the line. We're breaking it."

Greg took a step forward, his voice measured but clear.

"We're organizing every southern resistance group into a unified command structure. The Empire has stretched itself thin trying to contain the rebellion in the east, but they've neglected the southern corridor. That's our opportunity."

He tapped the map behind them, where Texas was split into color-coded zones.

"Our targets are Dallas and Houston. Dallas because it's their western administrative hub—command, supply, and psychological control. Houston because it gives us the ports. You cut their access to the Gulf, you force a maritime shift they can't afford."

An older woman in the second row—grizzled, sharp-eyed, her vest stitched with the faded insignia of the original T.E.F.—raised a hand.

"They're dug in tight," she said. "Especially in the rail spines between Austin and Houston. You're talking about a hundred miles of Imperial armor and drones, and you want us to walk into it?"

Alex nodded. "No. I want to bait them out."

She turned and highlighted a wide corridor west of College Station.

"We don't hit Houston directly. Not at first. We push east through secondary roads, flare up in small towns, disrupt their logistics. We let them think we're too fragmented to hold ground. Then, when they shift units west to resecure the corridor..."

Greg picked up the thread. "We hit Dallas. Hard. From the north and east. Once they scramble to defend it, we double back and cut down the I-10 axis toward Houston. This is about misdirection and timing, not brute force."

A younger officer leaned forward. "What's the projected force strength?"

"About 9,000 active rebels across all southern cells," Greg answered. "Another 3,000 in support and logistics roles. We expect to face around 5,500 Imperial troops in Dallas—double that between Houston and Galveston. But we control the roads. We control the narrative."

"And we control the will," Alex added. "Every rebel here is a volunteer. Most of their troops in this region are press-ganged and as likely as not to join our side. The rest are outsiders and mercenaries. We know what we're fighting for. They just know they're not allowed to lose."

A long silence followed. Then the old officer stood.

"You've got my unit," she said.

And just like that, the room shifted.

One by one, the leaders gave their nods. Not with salutes or ceremony, but with that subtle, unmistakable mark of trust among soldiers—willingness to follow.

Greg turned to Alex once the room began to disperse. "You had them the second you walked in." Alex gave a tired smile. "Maybe. But now we've got to win Texas."

The offensive began at dawn.

From the pine thickets north of Conroe to the flat, wind-blasted ranchlands outside Victoria, rebel columns advanced in staggered formations. It wasn't a blitz. It was a slow grind—a series of controlled maneuvers designed not to take ground but to bleed the Empire, to draw them west into the trap Alexandra had built piece by piece.

The Empire took the bait.

By day three, Dallas had begun to shift. Fast-response units redeployed northward. Rail columns surged along I-45. Air patrols diverted west, chasing ghost units and decoy convoys. And as the pressure there mounted, the real move began.

Alexandra stood inside the mobile command carrier just outside Beaumont, watching real-time drone feeds and thermal overlays. The air inside the vehicle smelled of sweat, oil, and the static of overclocked processors.

"Enemy reinforcements en route from Fort Polk," her comms officer called out. "Two armored brigades. ETA ninety minutes."

Alex leaned over the tactical table. "They'll try to pin us between the Sabine and the old I-10 corridor. Shift the southern line, have Leal's battalion fake a fallback, then collapse the flank the second they commit armor. Leave the minefield intact."

The officer hesitated. "That'll leave Leal exposed."

"She knows the risk. If they can't commit, we never break the chain."

She tapped the port screen. "Where's Greg?"

"In Austin, coordinating the northern push. He's holding four divisions in reserve, waiting for confirmation we've engaged the Houston command structure."

She keyed a direct line to him.

"Andrew. We've drawn them out. Houston's vulnerable. You're go."

His voice came back instantly. "Copy that. North cell just hit their comm array in Tyler. They're deaf and limping. Tell me when you breach the city perimeter and I'll move the last wave south to support."

Then the line clicked off—no wasted words.

This was the part they hadn't been sure would work.

The battle for Houston lasted four days.

Fighting ranged from neighborhood to neighborhood, the line shifting by the hour. Imperial armor was vicious in the open but useless in the tangle of highways and shipyard bottlenecks. Drones strafed rebel artillery units while rooftop snipers dueled at dusk with outdated infrared scopes and outdated munitions versus new sonic resonance LR weapons.

Then there was the block by block. It was dirty, close, personal.

Alex's mobile command unit took shrapnel on day two. She refused evacuation, patching into comms manually and guiding battalions street by street through the digital wreckage of old city schematics.

She spotted traps the field units missed.

Her orders came fast, clipped: "Don't follow the gridline. Cut down Canal. Use the flood tunnels. They won't expect a subterranean push."

She wasn't watching from above. She was in it.

Greg held it all together from Austin, juggling supply lines, feeding real-time troop intel, approving emergency drops and medical airlifts. On the third night, he overrode a senior field commander who wanted to pull back from Galveston.

"If we lose the ports, the Gulf is gone. We hold."

"But sir—"

"We. Hold."

And then, when the fighting reached its bloodiest point—when the rebels had secured the dockyards but were being bombarded by Imperial gunships offshore—

The ocean changed.

The rebels had taken the beach, but they were being slaughtered by the vessels blockading the coast. Munitions fell like rain. The air was black with smoke.

Then a lookout on the east watchtower shouted something impossible. "Ships!"

At first, no one believed it.

Then they saw them—dozens of ships rising over the eastern horizon, fast and silent. Some were military craft, painted in the old colors of fractured Caribbean nations. Others were converted merchant haulers, flying patched-together sails above modified missile platforms.

The largest bore the flag of the old Dominican navy, the aft covered in rebel red.

Greg's voice cut across the emergency channel. "We just got word. Caribbean alliance forces broke away. This is their fleet."

The rebel fighters on the ground didn't cheer. They wept.

The first Caribbean missiles hit the British warships minutes later. Two exploded before they could respond. A third tried to retreat and was torn open by coordinated fire.

The blockade shattered by a ragtag group of vessels that the Empire had deemed too small to pay notice.

By nightfall, the Gulf was open.

Total rebel losses: 1,902 killed, 4,800 wounded. Imperial losses: approximately 2,300 killed, 5,000 captured—including three field generals.

But Houston was free.

The ports were operational.

And for the first time in fifteen years, a rebel-controlled shipping corridor linked the continental rebellion to the wider world.

CHAPTER THIRTY

New York —Late Summer 2053

NEW YORK WAS STILL THE Empire's capital. Not in title—King Charles ruled from India now—but in function. Parliament convened in the Core Tower, a brutalist slab of steel and black stone that jutted over the East River like a blade. It was the centerpiece of Imperial authority, built nearly a century earlier and expanded after the London bombing, towering above the rest of the city as a permanent symbol of unshakable control. From its throne-room annex, royal envoys presided over affairs of state in the king's absence, ensuring the illusion of continuity even as the world fractured around them.

Surrounding the tower, the machinery of Empire operated in tireless coordination. The Ministry of Internal Order, housed in the financial district, ran the global surveillance and policing systems that kept the outer territories docile and under constant observation. The Imperial Revenue Authority, based in Midtown, monitored and enforced economic compliance across four continents, channeling everything from luxury tariffs to food ration quotas through its encrypted systems. Near Central Park stood the Office of Cultural Integrity, its pale façade concealing the Empire's most powerful propaganda and censorship division, controlling what could be printed, streamed, or even remembered.

Uptown, near the university, the Board of Scientific Stewardship was now sealed and garrisoned. There, all research and innovation passed through ideological filters, with scientists permitted to study only what the ministries deemed useful to Imperial longevity. On Governors Island, behind naval-grade shielding, the Naval Directorate—Atlantic Command coordinated the Empire's sea power from New York to the Arctic, directing missile platforms and fleet rotations that kept the coasts of the rebellion under constant threat.

Above the city, blimps hovered in silence, sensor-laden sentries with full kill authority. Beyond them, satellite weapons hung in low orbit. And below, the subways had been converted into sealed, pressurized transport corridors, capable of moving entire companies of soldiers from Brooklyn to Harlem without ever surfacing. The skyline bristled with rail turrets, drone nests, and signal jammers. The bridges were rigged with failsafe detonators. The harbor was ringed with sonar buoys, magnetic mines, and submersible torpedo drones.

It was the most fortified city on Earth. But in the shadows of skyscrapers and tenements, a guerrilla war raged.

Their aim was simpler: disruption. Chaos. To pin down the Empire's elite, burn their fuel, drain their patience, and make New York bleed resources while the broader war was won elsewhere.

Vinny Carcione ran operations out of a half-collapsed warehouse in Brooklyn's Red Hook district. He commanded the resistance like an old syndicate don, trading favors for weapons and coordinating ambushes from abandoned subway maintenance tunnels. His men ran counter-surveillance rings and hit-and-run units with clockwork precision.

Bo, the quiet elder of Chinatown, had turned his people into a ghost army, disappearing into alleys and basements, striking with clinical efficiency, then vanishing again. His network of informants, smugglers, and rooftop sharpshooters gave the rebellion its eyes and ears in Manhattan.

And Bear—Celsus Berning—trained new recruits from the wreckage of Queens, running brutal exercises through derelict parking towers and underused aqueducts. He knew how to break Imperials in hand-to-hand combat and how to teach others to do the same.

Together, they made the city ungovernable.

The safehouse was beneath an old shipping terminal, long since buried under newer construction and forgotten zoning codes. A single fluorescent bulb flickered above the steel table, surrounded by crates of stolen supplies, maps taped to the walls, and a battered radio playing low jazz from a rebel frequency that barely cut through the static.

Vinny Carcione sat at the head of the table, a cheap, flavored cigar burning between his fingers, vest unzipped over a black dress shirt, sleeves rolled up to the elbow. Bo was to his left, sipping tea in silence, eyes half-lidded but watching everything. Bear stood in the back, arms crossed, a grin threatening at the corner of his mouth like he was waiting for someone to say something stupid so he could laugh about it later.

Their lieutenants sat around the table—street soldiers, cell runners, smugglers turned tacticians. All of them tired. None of them broken.

"All right," Vinny said, flicking ash into a jar. "Bo's people hit the west station grid this morning. Knocked out comms from Midtown to Harlem for two hours. That's a first."

One of the lieutenants, a wiry guy from the Bronx named Tango, let out a low whistle. "You cut power to the surveillance loop?"

"Correct," Bo said softly. "They will restore it fully tomorrow. We will do it again the day after."

Vinny nodded. "That blackout let Bear's crew pull two full crates of ammo off a supply truck on FDR Drive. No shots fired. No alarms. They didn't even know they'd been hit until lunchtime."

Bear cracked his knuckles. "Told you the key was hiding the spike strip in plain sight. Bastards thought they hit construction debris."

Laughter rippled through the room.

Vinny smirked. "So, congratulations. We've harassed the Empire into high blood pressure. Now comes the part where they try to remind us who's in charge."

"Let 'em," said Big L, one of Bear's lieutenants. "We've got half of upstate under the rebel flag. Albany's locked. New Haven's reinforcing Boston. And last I heard, the Canadians are sending a brigade south."

"They are," Bo said. "Elite urban recon. Highly trained. They're waiting on insertion orders."

"And supplies," added Vinny. "Which we still don't have."

Tango raised a hand. "Why not pull from the Philadelphia lines? We've got some loyalists smuggling meds and rations out of Camden."

"No," Vinny said firmly. "Philly's being watched. Naval Command is off the coast with enough firepower to glass it if we give them an excuse."

Bear scratched his beard. "So what you're saying is… we need to cause a mess big enough to distract them without causing a mess big enough to kill us all?"

"Exactly," Vinny replied.

"Good," Bear said. "That's my specialty."

Laughter again, lighter this time. It was late, and they'd all lost people. But something in the room had shifted. The city hadn't been winnable a year ago. Now it wasn't about winning—it was about dragging the Empire down, block by block, until it cracked.

Vinny spoke, "We control the outer boroughs. We control the underground. What we need now is a symbol. Something they can't ignore. Something the people still loyal to the Crown will see and begin to question."

He looked at the map. A red X marked the Core Tower. "Soon," he said. Bear snorted. "Sooner than they're ready for."

Bo set his teacup down. "There's one more issue before we talk about the tower."

Vinny leaned back. "Go on."

"The Second Sons of Liberty are active again. Four raids this week. One was messy—too many civilian injuries. But the others were surgical. Clean. Effective."

A quiet beat passed.

"They're still freelancing?" Bear asked.

Bo nodded. "Operating without coordination, pulling their own ops, intercepting supply routes we already mapped. They nearly blew our extraction tunnel from Midtown."

Vinny's eyes narrowed. "They already hit John's pub once to send a message. They're not subtle."

"No," Bo said, "but they're gaining support. Especially with the younger fighters. Their propaganda's slick. They're calling for a 'Second Declaration'—total removal of loyalist sympathizers, Crown civilians, anyone who won't take a loyalty oath to the new republic."

Bear crossed his arms. "They want a purge."

"They want a spectacle," Vinny said. He took a slow drag from his cigar. "But they're not wrong about needing a symbol."

"So we pull them in?" asked Tango.

"We don't pull," Vinny said. "We steer."

Bo gave a slow nod. "I've already made contact through a proxy. They're willing to meet—if we offer them a headline."

Bear scoffed. "So we throw 'em a bone?"

Vinny pointed to the map. "We throw them the tower's east facade. Flashiest sector. Heaviest surveillance. They go loud—smoke, fire, every camera rolling."

Bo added, "It draws fire from Bear's push and hides the ghost route for my team."

"And it gives them what they want," Vinny said. "But under our coordination. Our timing. Our trigger."

"If they break ranks?" Bear asked.

"They won't make it out alive," Vinny said flatly. "But if they play it right—they'll get their spectacle. And we get Parliament."

No one argued.

The meeting had broken up an hour ago. The lieutenants had dispersed back to their sectors, maps folded under arms, voices low and determined.

Now Vinny and Bo walked side by side through the hushed streets of Red Hook, a pair of shadows moving under the cracked lamplight. The air was thick with the scent of industry. Smoke curled up from a distant fire—one of theirs, maybe. Maybe not.

Vinny lit a fresh cigar and offered one to Bo, who declined with a quiet shake of the head. He puffed once, then again, letting the silence settle before speaking.

"They want to make me a colonel."

Bo raised an eyebrow but said nothing.

"The Italians," Vinny continued. "Command up in Montreal. They want to make me an official liaison to the American front. Give me a rank. A pin. Probably a fancy hat."

Bo gave a small, unreadable smile. "You'd look good in a hat."

"Yeah," Vinny said, smirking. "And real uncomfortable."

They kept walking, the drone of a faraway Imperial patrol buzzing faintly overhead. Bo's own drone stayed high and quiet in the fog above them, listening, watching.

Vinny's tone dropped slightly. "I told 'em I'd think about it. Truth is... I don't know."

Bo nodded, still silent.

"I've spent my life running a different kind of organization," Vinny said. "One built on blood, trust, favors. My father ran it before me. His father before him. We didn't take orders from anyone. We gave them. But now..."

He gestured broadly toward the ruins of the waterfront, toward the flickering lights of the makeshift barracks and the quiet streets crawling with revolution.

"Now I'm fighting someone else's war."

Bo finally spoke, his voice soft but firm. "It stopped being someone else's war the moment they put checkpoints in Little Italy.

The moment they started dragging your people into cells and pretending they were statistics."

Vinny didn't answer at first.

They turned down a side street where vines had overtaken a chain-link fence. Somewhere nearby, a child was laughing, too young to know better.

"I know," Vinny said finally. "It's just... I was good at the family job. We had rules. Quiet rules. Nobody touched civilians. We kept our corners clean. I knew what I was."

"And now?" Bo asked.

Vinny sighed. "Now I don't know if I'm a soldier or a ghost of the past."

Bo stopped, put a hand on Vinny's shoulder, and looked him in the eye.

"You're both. And we need both."

Vinny smiled faintly. "You always know the right thing to say, huh?"

"No," Bo replied. "But I know when to say nothing at all."

They stood for a moment, two men who'd survived more than most, who knew the weight of power and the cost of choosing to wield it.

Then Bo turned and started walking again.

Vinny stayed a moment longer, looking up at the sky through the smoke.

"I'll think about it," he muttered to no one in particular.

Then he followed.

Several days later, the air in the safehouse was sharp with sweat, coffee, and anticipation. The table at the center of the room had been cleared of weapons and replaced with three-dimensional schematics of the Core Tower district. Small digital markers blinked at intersections, rooftops, ventilation shafts, and subsurface utility lines.

Six new figures stood around the table—lean, alert, dressed in slate-gray tactical gear without insignia. Canadian commandos. The best of the Quebec-Cascadian Reconnaissance Group. They moved like ghosts and barely spoke unless they had something worth saying.

"They'll breach with us from underneath," Vinny explained, pointing to a sewer access tunnel in the Lower East Side. "Their team comes up through the water main, cuts power at the East Substation, and scrambles surveillance before our first team crosses the bridge."

"We'll take fire," said Bear, seated on a crate with a combat vest half-zipped and a shotgun across his lap. "No way we get past the perimeter without waking the nest."

"We're not trying to be subtle anymore," Bo said. "That time is past."

The Canadian squad leader, a man known only as Leclerc, nodded. "Our job is to make them see one breach and miss the three others."

"And the kill team?" one of Bo's lieutenants asked.

Vinny's voice lowered. "That's us."

A shadow moved near the back of the room.

Several fighters stood slightly apart from the rest—lean, young, sharp-eyed. They wore black tactical gear patched with a faded flag with thirteen stars reworked into a new crest: a snake coiled around broken shackles. The Second Sons of Liberty.

Vinny turned toward them. "Your fireteam hits the east facade."

One of them, a tall man with a scar through his eyebrow and a too-calm voice, stepped forward. "We're not running cover."

"You're running the distraction," Vinny said, "in the most watched corridor in North America. We need noise, fire, confusion— and discipline."

"And if we go off-script?" the man asked.

Bo's voice was like gravel. "You won't get a second scene."

The man studied them, then nodded once. "Understood."

Bear muttered under his breath, "Hope they like theatrics more than martyrs."

Vinny didn't smile. "They'll get their revolution. And we'll get the building."

He pointed at the innermost ring of the Core Tower—the annex beneath the chamber of Parliament where Imperial ministers met when the king wasn't present. He tapped a red dot.

"This is where we put the knife in."

It began at midnight.

Three simultaneous explosions rocked the East River perimeter—two from the sewers, one from a disguised trash compactor packed with ammonium nitrate and bike chain. The blast ripped through a convoy of Imperial transports on FDR Drive and lit the skyline in orange.

Rebel drones screamed overhead, drawing Imperial gunfire toward the decoys. Meanwhile, the real infiltration teams moved under the surface—through storm drains, electric service tunnels, even old bootlegger routes long forgotten by modern cartographers.

Bo's team emerged from an elevator shaft in an abandoned hotel across from the Core Tower. They were already inside the security perimeter before the first gunfire had even started on the surface.

Bear led the forward team with a battering ram and a short fuse. His crew took the north barricade by force—flamethrowers clearing pillboxes, shotguns at close quarters, a wall of fury punching through the front line.

Vinny moved with the central strike group. He didn't speak. He didn't need to.

They breached the outer hall of the Core Tower at 12:42 a.m. Two minutes after that, they took the sub-basement. Five minutes after that, the Canadians had dropped comms for the entire tower and blacked out the lights.

The rebellion was in the heart of the capital.

Imperial soldiers fought like wolves—well-trained, armored, and fearless. But they hadn't expected an attack this deep, this fast, and certainly not from three angles at once. Confusion spread through the upper ranks as command protocols failed. Junior officers were issuing orders by hand.

On the east front, the Second Sons of Liberty ignited a spectacular diversion, storming the outer barricades with firebombs and sonic charges, broadcasting their assault live across hijacked Crown networks—turning chaos into propaganda.

A counter-assault team tried to retake the central stairwell, only to find it mined with remote charges. When the floor came down, it took half their unit with it.

Vinny reached the annex doors at 1:04 a.m.

He fired three shots into the lock. Kicked the rest open.

Inside, three ministers were still at the table—stunned, frozen.

Vinny raised his weapon.

"You're coming with us." He didn't flinch, but this wasn't about revenge. Not yet. The rebellion needed leverage more than it needed martyrs.

Bo stood on the rooftop, staring out at the smoke curling over Manhattan. Below, firefights still burned across Midtown, but the battle was nearly over. Rebel flags—some hand-stitched, some printed—were waving from balconies and rooftops.

Vinny emerged beside him, bruised, limping slightly, but alive. Bear followed, his gun pointed at the back of the ministers and several Imperial officers.

Bo didn't speak at first.

When he did, it was quiet. Almost reverent. "You did it."

Vinny shook his head. "We did."

He looked out over the smoldering skyline, chest heaving.

Far in the distance, sirens wailed. Gunfire cracked. But it didn't matter.

Parliament was gone. And the city, at least for one dawn, was theirs.

CHAPTER THIRTY-ONE

Bombay India —Early Fall 2053

THE KING'S ROOM SMELLED LIKE antiseptic. Twelve days had passed since the funeral. The explosion that shattered half the procession, killed two of Charles's closest allies, and left him bleeding on the marble. He had survived—barely. A piece of shrapnel had sliced through the side of his skull, and while the surgeons said the operation was successful, the man who woke up nine days later was not the same.

He was angrier. Sharper in some moments, duller in others. And when his temper flared, it came like a lightning strike—instant, blinding, gone.

Now he lay propped up in a reinforced hospital bed in the center of his private medical wing. Machines beeped quietly. Monitors blinked. A physician stood in the corner of the room with two guards, giving the King just enough space to pretend he still had privacy.

Charles's eyes snapped to the ceiling lights. "Turn them off," he barked.

"They're on the lowest setting, Your Majesty."

"I said, off."

The lights dimmed. The guards stiffened.

He ran a hand through what was left of his hair. His left side moved more slowly now. The tremor hadn't gone away. He hated the way the words sometimes caught in his throat. Hated the pity in the doctors' eyes even more.

He was the most powerful man alive. Let them fear him—never pity him.

A general entered the darkened room—a young officer from the palace garrison, pressed uniform, clean boots, eyes twitching just slightly at the corners. The oppressive scene made the man shiver. Charles turned to him, snapping the silence like glass.

"Report."

The general stood rigid. "It has been two weeks since the fall of New York, sire. Parliament is gone. Core Tower was destroyed. Minister Langen and four others were confirmed captured. Three are presumed dead."

Charles stared at him. His voice came out brittle. "And the fleet?"

"Still holding off the coast, but we've lost command and control. Naval HQ in the Atlantic Directorate was compromised three days ago. Philadelphia remains functional, but containment is slipping."

The King's face darkened. "And the Indian base?"

"Still under rebel control, Your Majesty. We believe General Chadra is still leading the defense. Skirmishes in Delhi, Rawalpindi, and Hyderabad have kept our forces tied up. There's been no opportunity to mount a coordinated retake effort."

Charles was silent for a long time.

Then: "Summon every garrison between here and the Ganges. I want the entire corridor fortified. Lock the roads. Sweep the airspace. No one moves without clearance from this office."

"Yes, sire."

"And send the order to New York... what's left of it. Ministers. Parliament officials. I want them evacuated and brought here. If they're not on a flight within twenty-four hours, they're on their own."

The general hesitated. "Sire, there is no secure air corridor to New York—"

Charles slammed his fist into the bed rail. "Then make one."

The general flinched. "Yes, sire."

He turned to leave.

"Wait," Charles called out. "How many are dead?"

"On which front?"

Charles narrowed his eyes. "Ours."

The general's mouth was dry. "Too many to count accurately."

Charles sank back into the pillows. His head ached. The room seemed smaller than it had a moment ago.

He wasn't losing the war. He wasn't. But he could feel something he hadn't felt since Frederick's final year.

The center was no longer holding. And the walls were drawing closer.

The King refused to be wheeled into the meeting.

Two aides had tried to assist him. One now had a broken wrist. The other a black eye and a promise that if he so much as touched the King's shoulder again, he'd be sent to the frontlines in Rawalpindi without boots.

So he walked.

Slowly. Stiffly. But he walked.

The meeting room had been cleared of local security. Only his most trusted guards stood by the doors. Two Russian envoys waited inside, flanked by four black-suited operatives with pale eyes and colder expressions. The flag of the Eurasian Alliance hung behind them like a veil of threat disguised as diplomacy.

Charles entered the room without ceremony. He remained standing.

"You're late," he said.

Anton Breshkev stood slowly. Of course it was him. The same man who had smiled during the Moscow summit. The same man who had offered support in exchange for territory, Italy then, and now more.

"We've come as promised," Breshkev said smoothly, hands folded behind his back. "Forty thousand troops. Armored divisions. Anti-air. Orbital-linked artillery. All under General Sokolov's command. They'll arrive in full within seventy-two hours."

Charles stared at him.

"And you expect what in return?"

Breshkev shrugged. "The usual. Corridor access. Docking rights. Temporary oversight of regional stabilization protocols."

Charles laughed once, a sharp, humorless bark that echoed in the marble chamber.

"Let's not pretend. You want occupation."

"We want order," Breshkev replied, stepping forward. "The rebellion is out of control. You've lost New York. You've lost Delhi. Your enemies now control both ends of your former Empire. You need a spine. We're offering one."

Charles's hand trembled. He clenched it into a fist.

"You come into my house and offer me support like I'm some broken client state?"

"You invited us," Breshkev said calmly. "After the funeral bombing. You asked for help. I'm here to give it. Or would you prefer I leave and let the Canadians come through Karachi instead?"

Silence.

Charles looked at the map glowing on the far wall. Rebel positions lit up like embers across northern India. He couldn't hold Bombay without help. And he knew it.

"You'll answer to me," Charles said, voice low. "Sokolov doesn't give a single order unless it comes through this palace."

"Of course, your Majesty," Breshkev said, smiling.

It was a lie, and they both knew it.

"But let's not pretend this is weakness," Charles added. "This is strategy. When I retake India, when the rebellion collapses and your men return home, history will show this was a moment of consolidation. Not surrender."

Breshkev inclined his head. "Then let's begin consolidating."

Imperial press were ushered into the room.

The men shook hands, neither smiling. Cameras flashed. The official record would show unity.

But even in the stillness of the room, Charles could feel it.

Something had changed.

CHAPTER THIRTY-TWO

FIVE DAYS AFTER THE SUMMIT in Bombay, the ground began to tremble.

They came before dawn. The sound arrived first, low and distant, like a rolling storm that never stopped moving. At first, some thought it was shelling. Others mistook it for thunder. But Vihaan knew better. That deep, rhythmic quake in the ground—the way the dust shifted on the floor—it was the sound of armor. Russian tanks. British dropships. Drones by the hundreds. A modern siege force moving with industrial precision.

The rebel base outside Nashik had stood longer than anyone expected, fortified by stolen tech, camouflaged bunkers, and weeks of preparation.

It hadn't mattered.

The allied Russian-Imperial force hit with synchronized force, overwhelming defenses before the rebels could fully respond. The first strikes targeted communications and radar, hypersonic missiles tearing through the outer ridge like it was paper. One shot shredded the comms tower. Another hit the forward command post. Within minutes, they were blind and partially decapitated.

Vihaan sprinted across the open tarmac, shouting into a handheld radio that crackled with static and distorted feedback. "Fall back to the bunkers! Now! Repeat, fall back!" The signal was barely punching through the jamming field, which had grown worse by the minute since the first wave of artillery. Around him, the ground vibrated with the concussive rhythm of incoming fire. He ducked behind a scorched transport just as a rail round screamed overhead and ripped a fuel station apart in a geyser of fire.

A few meters ahead, a trio of medics dragged wounded fighters toward the triage tent—one man missing a leg, another limp and bloody across the chest. A drone dipped low over their heads, blinking with red targeting sensors, but it exploded midair in a burst of sparks and shrapnel, hit by a lucky shot from a rebel sharpshooter on the north wall. Vihaan didn't stop. He vaulted over a shattered blast shield, smoke stinging his eyes, and reached the central runway just as a fresh barrage hit.

The sky lit up in a sickly orange glow. A salvo of guided missiles tore through a line of armored personnel carriers near the eastern barracks, flipping two vehicles and setting a third ablaze. The blast wave rolled across the tarmac with brutal force, flattening tents, scattering bodies, and knocking Vihaan hard to one knee. His ears rang. Dirt filled his mouth. The ground itself seemed to shift beneath him. Someone screamed nearby, high and ragged—and then fell silent.

There was no time to regroup. No second line of defense. The enemy was already inside the wire.

Russian shock troops advanced in tight, ruthless formations, their armor matte black and faceless, weapons synced to helmet feeds. Behind them, Imperial drones zipped between buildings, painting targets and relaying coordinates in real time to artillery units positioned miles away. The southern gate had been reduced to twisted metal, its defense team buried under the rubble of their own machine gun nests. From the north, a flanking force breached the perimeter through a collapsed maintenance tunnel—one Vihaan hadn't even known was exposed. The base was being eaten from the inside out.

The eastern wing fell first. What was once a command dormitory turned into a furnace after a plasma burst detonated the backup generators. A dozen rebels died trying to pull their friends from the inferno. The air was thick with burning plastic, scorched wiring, and the iron stink of blood. Vihaan saw one of his junior officers firing blindly from a collapsed doorway, then watched him vanish in a white-hot blast from a shoulder-fired missile.

The western ridge didn't fare any better. Booby traps, trip mines, and fallback trenches slowed the attackers for minutes, not hours. The enemy came prepared—autonomous breach bots crawling ahead of the infantry, sniffing out mines, mapping obstacles, neutralizing defenses before human boots hit the ground. Every movement was rehearsed. Every target, precise.

This wasn't a siege. It was a purge.

The Russians had come to erase the base and everyone inside it—and they were doing it with mechanical efficiency.

Suddenly, the unmistakable resonance of a Russian SKP-class orbital breach platform tore through the atmosphere—a shrill, oscillating whine that heralded the deployment of one of the most advanced siege systems ever fielded. Only one was known to exist, a city-sized construct held in low-Earth orbit and precision-guided through quantum tether triangulation. Its destructive capacity was second only to nuclear warheads, but without the fallout. In a fortunate turn for the rebels, Britain's own SKP-class platform had been quietly decommissioned shortly before the war began, plagued by intermittent harmonic destabilization and logistical failures. Plans to replace it with a smaller, modular platform fleet—optimized for atmospheric maneuvering and low-latency targeting—had stalled due to budgetary delays and shifting strategic priorities.

What followed was not a conventional bombardment, but a directed energy lattice cascade—a scalar field weapon designed to bypass shielding and molecularly disassemble high-density alloys along a precision vector path.

Titanium plating, boron-carbide composites, and even the polythermal ceramic shells of hardened bunkers vaporized in nanosecond bursts, leaving behind narrow, glowing furrows like surgical incisions. There was no shockwave. No residual heat signature. Just a corridor of immaculate devastation. The SKP didn't destroy indiscriminately—it cut. It carved clean lanes through the base infrastructure, eliminating resistance with ruthless, algorithmic precision.

Russian infantry advanced in its wake, clad in adaptive exo-stealth rigs that shifted their EM profiles with every step, invisible to most targeting systems. There was no risk of friendly fire. The corridor had been cut for them—unforgiving, surgical, and absolute.

At the first sound, Vihaan ducked behind a shattered supply container, heart pounding, breath ragged, rifle clenched in white-knuckled hands. His command was collapsing around him. The defenses he had built, the fighters he had trained—everything was burning.

And they were still coming.

By the time Vihaan reached the inner command bunker, the walls were vibrating with the shock of sustained assault. He was covered in dust, bleeding from a cut on his cheek, his rifle nearly empty. Around him, the last dozen members of his command team tried to coordinate evacuations and fallback routes, but every plan died within minutes of being spoken. The waterway extraction had collapsed. The secondary tunnels were compromised. No one could reach the rebel cells in Hyderabad or Delhi—skirmishes across the region were keeping Imperial forces too active to break away, but not active enough to help.

Vihaan realized then: they weren't just losing the battle. They were being erased.

Paris, French Republic — Military Operations Hub

The moment the report came in from India, a silent alert passed through a restricted system buried beneath École Militaire.

"Cascade," the algorithm flagged. "SKP activation confirmed."

General Étienne Moreau stood over the war table, eyes narrowing at the pulsing trajectory streaking across the Indian theater. "So, they've unleashed it."

"They've gone active with the orbital breach platform," his aide confirmed grimly. "They are clearing the base in India."

Moreau tapped a secure key on the console. "Prepare Marabout."

Across the room, a cyber-ops officer stiffened. "Sir—are we certain we want to burn the channel?"

"It's time," Moreau said flatly. "They've shown their hand. We show ours."

Years ago, during the SKP's multi-year phased construction, French operatives had infiltrated a subcontractor in Vladivostok that produced subquantum telemetry nodes—tiny relay modules responsible for linking platform movement and scalar targeting across the orbital mesh. Using a modified additive printer, the French had embedded a microscopic photonic kill-switch, hidden not in code, but in the resonance profile of the hardware itself. The alteration couldn't be detected via firmware audits. It was physical—a ghost in the circuits.

The hack had lain dormant for years, transmitting only the faintest telemetry pings—heartbeat pulses confirming its hidden presence. When the British SKP prototype kept failing during a live tests three years prior, investigators blamed internal design flaws and unstable energy routing. The complexity of the design made this the most plausible answer. The French said nothing.

In truth, the same exploit had triggered the collapse. One attack. One burn. And then silence.

The Russian platform had remained untouched—observed but never triggered. Not yet. Activating it would have exposed the sabotage, and the French couldn't afford that—not with British eyes still combing over their own disaster.

But now, India was burning.

And the time had come.

That same kill-switch—cold, quiet, and surgically precise—was ready to fire again.

Moreau gave the order. "Engage Marabout."

The cyber officer inserted a quantum-locked cipher disk. The encrypted pulse was fired into low Earth orbit via stealth commsat relay, targeting the SKP's hardened relay architecture.

At that moment, hundreds of kilometers above the Earth, the Russian platform's telemetry began to drift. Targeting locks failed. Scalar phase aligners twitched and desynchronized. Internal feedback loops overloaded, triggering a cascade abort protocol. Within twenty seconds, the platform had dumped its capacitor stores into the void and shut down propulsion.

To Imperial command, it looked like an overload failure. Another mystery to investigate. Another moment too late.

Back in Paris, the screen dimmed as the signal terminated.

Nashik, India

Luciano Bellandi appeared in the chaos, grabbing Vihaan by the arm and pulling him down a side corridor. "We're done here. Come on."

"There's no way out," Vihaan said. "They've taken the outer gate."

"There's always a way," Luciano snapped. "I blew the reservoir gate. The old sewer line's flooded. We're going through it."

The air was thick with smoke and heat as they moved through the lower tunnels. Vihaan helped carry a wounded comms officer who had taken shrapnel to the thigh. The water rose quickly—ankle deep, then knee. Bodies floated past them. One belonged to a young woman who had joined the rebels just two weeks earlier. Vihaan forced himself to look at her face—to remember it.

By the time they emerged into the hills north of the base, only a few hundred remained. Out of the 3,200 fighters who had held the compound, only a few hundred made it out. Many were wounded. All were silent. The survivors gathered in trenches and ditches beneath a smog-stained sky, the dirt dry and cracked, the wind too warm. Vihaan stood on a small rise, wrapped in a torn cloak, his boots soaked, his rifle slung but useless. His face was streaked with ash and blood. He said nothing for a long time.

Then, without orders or ceremony, they began to march. No one spoke until the last Imperial drone vanished from view.

They walked for long, treacherous nights, losing more along the way, until they crossed into view of a rebel Pakistani patrol—unlikely, but welcome, volunteers—that had been making its way south to reinforce Nashik.

As Vihaan spoke with the patrol's commander, Luciano joined him, arms crossed. "We lost the momentum," he said.

Vihaan didn't argue. "But we're still breathing."

He looked over the survivors—young men and women who had believed they were fighting for a turning point. Instead, they were watching the war turn on them. The loss of Nashik wasn't just a defeat. It was a message.

"We regroup here," he said finally. "Pakistan becomes the front. Get me every surviving medic, engineer, and radio tech. I want the wounded stabilized. I want new shelter before nightfall."

Luciano nodded, but there was hesitation in his eyes. "And after that?"

Vihaan turned back south, where the rising sun glinted off distant smoke columns. His hands clenched.

"Then we remind them we're not dead."

They reached the last ridge into the Pakistani border just before dusk on the fifth day.

The survivors straggled in groups—wounded, shell-shocked, on the Pakistani haulers. They had nothing but what they could carry, and most had left even their packs behind during the retreat. Their eyes were sunken, their faces streaked with ash and sweat, and none of them had slept more than a few hour in the past several days.

From the high ground, they could see the plains below, hazy in the fading light. Far to the west, across a shallow bend in the terrain, the lights of Pakistani border towns twinkled faintly through the dust.

Vihaan stood with Luciano and three remaining officers, one of them a medic with a tourniquet still wrapped around his own thigh.

"We won't last another night out here," the medic said bluntly. "We're out of plasma, out of antibiotics. We've got more wounded than not who won't survive unless we get them to shelter. Real shelter."

Vihaan didn't disagree. He could see it on the faces of the fighters gathered across the ridge, many slumped in silence, rifles laid across their laps, helmets off, eyes fixed on the horizon like it might answer them.

Luciano produced a worn pad, placing it on a flat stone. "There's an old supply route here," he said, pointing to a thin trail weaving down the ridge. "Used to be a smuggler road. Mostly agricultural traffic now—tractors, supply wagons, occasional military patrols."

"Is it watched?" Vihaan asked.

"Sometimes. Depends on the hour," said the Pakistani commander. "But if we move in small formations, with cover from above..."

The man looked up at the thin overcast sky. "I might be able to get us some air cover. Not military—civilian drones. Recon units we've kept off the grid. Silent, slow, but they'll help us avoid roadblocks."

"And once we cross?" the medic asked.

"There's a safehouse in Rahim Yar Khan," Luciano said. "Old contacts. They would know to expect us if we make the signal."

Vihaan folded his arms, staring down the ridge. His body ached. His ribs were bruised. His hand still shook from the effects of the concussion wave. But his mind was clear.

"We move at midnight," he said. "No lights. No unnecessary comms. Split into four units. Staggered timing, fifteen-minute intervals. We send the injured first, with the medics. I'll take the last group."

The officers nodded.

"What about food?" one of them asked.

Vihaan turned to the camp. "We're not stopping to eat."

He crouched beside a young rebel, barely twenty years old, bandaged along the temple, cradling a broken rifle.

"What's your name?" Vihaan asked.

The boy looked up, startled. "K-Kartik, sir."

"You ever been to Pakistan, Kartik?"

The boy shook his head.

"Well," Vihaan said, rising. "Tonight's your first lesson in diplomacy."

By midnight, the first group was already moving down the ridge.

Vihaan watched them go in silence, the stars barely visible above. They would make it, or they wouldn't. There was no middle ground anymore.

When his turn came, he pulled the scarf tight around his neck, adjusted the weight of his rifle, and looked over at Luciano.

"Still with me, spy?"

Luciano smiled grimly. "We didn't come this far to die so easily."

They started down the trail, disappearing into the dark.

Behind them, India burned. Ahead, Pakistan waited.

And between the two, a ghost army crossed the earth in silence.

CHAPTER THIRTY-THREE

Rahim Yar Khan, Pakistan —Early Fall 2053

THE MEETING ROOM WAS AN old storage hall in the basement of a shuttered textile factory outside Rahim Yar Khan. It still smelled faintly of fuel and rust, though the rebel medics had tried to air it out. Folding chairs ringed a long, weather-warped table. Portable floodlamps buzzed overhead, and a single cracked monitor flickered in the corner, streaming intercepted Imperial radio chatter in a loop.

Vihaan stood at the head of the table, a scarf draped around his shoulders and dried blood at the cuff of his sleeve. His face was drawn, but his posture still held the echo of command. Around him sat four of the senior Pakistani rebel leaders—two in mismatched combat uniforms, one in civilian clothes stained from recent travel, and the last, Colonel Faheem, in crisp desert fatigues and a trimmed mustache that hadn't moved once since the meeting began.

The mood was cautious. Respectful, but heavy.

"We lost more than just a base," Vihaan began. His voice was calm, even. "Nashik was a symbol. It was the proof that the Empire could bleed. That they couldn't control every inch of the subcontinent."

No one interrupted, but no one nodded either.

"We need to reestablish a foothold. Everything hinges on this. The rebels across this entire region need to know we're still in the fight."

Faheem leaned forward, his hands clasped on the table. "You've brought barely more than a hundred men, many wounded. You've got maybe a dozen functional weapons platforms and no air cover. You lost a garrison that most of us assumed was unshakable. Forgive me, General, but you're not in a position to reestablish anything."

Vihaan didn't react to the tone. He let the weight of Faheem's skepticism hang in the air before responding.

"I understand how it looks. But I'm not asking you to follow us. I'm asking you to work with us. Pakistan and India were divided long before the Empire returned. But they didn't care about that border. They built garrisons on both sides. They installed checkpoints without asking whose land they were on. They punished Urdu and Hindi speakers alike."

One of the younger officers, Major Kamran, shifted in his chair. "Maybe. But when they're gone, that border won't vanish. And neither will the memories."

Vihaan nodded. "You're right. History doesn't disappear. But it doesn't have to be a prison either. We've all lost something in this war. Families. Homes. Cities. What we do next, together, determines whether that loss means anything."

The civilian—a man named Niaz, who ran the intelligence network in Multan—spoke for the first time. "Our people are watching closely. Many are ready to fight. But they want to know they're not just replacing one foreign occupation with another. They want to know this war isn't just about restoring Delhi's control."

Vihaan stepped away from the table, moving slowly around the room. "It isn't. I'm not here to reclaim India. I'm here to destroy the Empire that's buried all of us. If that means I stand beside Pakistani fighters in Karachi, or Afghan units in Kandahar, or Bengali rebels in Dhaka, I will. This isn't a nationalist war. It's a liberation."

There was a long pause.

Colonel Faheem looked at him with something new in his eyes. Not warmth. Not trust. But curiosity. A willingness to listen.

"And if our troops die defending territory your government once claimed as its own?" Faheem asked.

Vihaan stopped walking. "Then they won't die defending a flag. They'll die fighting tyranny. That's the only banner that matters now."

For the first time, the silence in the room didn't feel hostile. It felt like breathing space.

Faheem sat back in his chair. Kamran glanced at Niaz, who gave the faintest nod. Something was shifting. Slowly. But it was real.

Vihaan returned to the head of the table. "With your permission, we're setting up temporary command two clicks west of here. If your people can help us secure the corridor, we can begin operations in Punjab by the end of the week."

Faheem exhaled. "We'll see what can be done."

Vihaan didn't press further. He knew this would take time. Trust came in inches, not leaps.

But tonight, they had taken a major step.

After the meeting with the Pakistani rebel command, Vihaan remained behind in the quiet of the old textile basement. The others had scattered—to coordinate supplies, organize sleeping quarters, or simply vanish into silence—but he stayed at the long wooden table, its surface scratched with age and worn maps. His fingers traced the edge of the Indian border, now meaningless on paper but still alive in every conversation with his hosts. The air hung still and heavy, like something just waiting to shatter.

He stepped into the dimly lit comms room adjacent to the meeting space and powered up the encrypted link himself. The screen flickered twice before resolving into the grainy image of Alexandra Baker, seated in what looked like a field command post. The feed was faintly washed in blue, her features sharpened by the harsh overhead light.

She looked exhausted. Her hair was tied back, streaked with sweat and dust, and there was something harder in her eyes than there had been a month ago. Behind her, blurred figures moved between crates and tactical maps. Even in the stillness of the frame, the air around her felt kinetic.

Vihaan didn't speak immediately, but she beat him to it anyway. "You're alive."

"Barely."

The pause that followed wasn't awkward—it was weighted, shaped by grief and survival, the kind of silence only shared by those who've bled for the same cause in different time zones.

"We heard," she said. "About Nashik."

He nodded once. "It wasn't a battle. It was an execution. They knew everything—our fallback paths, our comms, even our blind spots. They didn't just crush us. They hunted us."

"I've seen the intel. Russian armor took the lead. British drones tracked the stragglers. Every move was coordinated. And then the SKP..." she trailed off. "They're not just allied anymore. They're fused."

He exhaled, rubbing his temple. "Not enough made it out. We've reestablished comms, found shelter here with the Pakistanis. But it's a fragile arrangement. History doesn't vanish overnight."

"And the front?"

"Shattered. I'm trying to rebuild. Quietly. But I need time—time we don't have."

Alex leaned forward, elbows on the table, her eyes narrowing as her voice dropped. "Then we buy you some."

He studied her face. "What are you thinking?"

"I think we're still fighting this war like it's two-dimensional—the Empire and the rebellion. But that's not the shape anymore. It's a triangle now. Russia's not lurking in the shadows anymore. They're trying to become the war's architects. If they lock down northern India, they won't stop. Not with the Empire bleeding and the Gulf wide open. Next comes Myanmar, Bangladesh, Nepal. Maybe more. This ends with Russian boots at every border if we let it."

"And the Chinese?"

"They're watching. Nervous. But they're still quiet. They haven't chosen sides, but they're watching Russia the way a tiger watches another predator edging toward its cubs."

Vihaan didn't look away. "You think you can turn that anxiety into action?"

"I think I have to."

She leaned back slightly, the tent light catching the old scar across her collarbone. She never mentioned it, and he never asked.

"China's neutrality has always been conditional. They've hedged their bets, traded with both sides, played the long game. But now they're watching Russia set the region on fire, and they know exactly what that means for their interests. If Russia gets too strong, the balance across all of Asia goes with it—the Belt routes, the mountain corridors, every soft alliance they've built from Laos to the Red Sea. It all starts to unravel."

His voice dropped. "You think they'll send ground troops?"

"I think I can make the case. Not just that it's necessary, but that it's their last real shot at shaping what comes next. If they stay neutral and Russia wins, they'll be boxed in for a generation. But if they move now—decisively, visibly—they get a voice in redrawing the world. As partners."

He was quiet, weighing the risk.

"You'd go yourself?"

"I have to. No envoy can deliver this. They won't trust a diplomat from New Europe, and they won't take a video call from Andrew, not without layers of posturing and protocol. But me? I'm not asking them to believe in philosophy. I'm asking them to believe in math."

He managed a faint, humorless smile. "And what does the math say?"

"That we lose this war without them."

The line buzzed faintly, static and the faint echo of something metallic striking stone outside Vihaan's bunker. He didn't turn his head.

"You'll go off-grid," he said. "Deep cover. Alone?"

"I'll bring two. Maybe three. People I trust. No insignia. No titles. Just clean intel and a good pitch."

"If they say no—"

"They won't," she interrupted. "Not when they see what Russia's really after."

Vihaan watched her for a moment, something unreadable moving behind his eyes. Then he nodded.

"If anyone can do it, it's you."

Alex's voice softened just slightly. "I'll speak to the Italians first. I'll need a corridor through Kashmir—quiet, unofficial. No escorts. Just clearance."

"And if the Chinese agree?"

"Then I ask for an armored division in Ladakh."

He arched a brow. "That'll light a fuse."

"That's the point."

Another long pause followed, quieter now—the kind that holds after two people say what they didn't think they'd have to say.

"Stay alive," she said.

"You too."

The screen flickered, then cut to black. The room dimmed with it.

Vihaan sat still for a while, watching the dead glass, the last impression of her face lingering like heat. Behind him, Luciano stepped into the room, his voice low.

"How'd it go?"

"She's going to China," Vihaan said without turning.

Luciano blinked, processing. "That's bold."

"No," Vihaan replied. "It's our last hope."

CHAPTER THIRTY-FOUR

Berlin, British Imperial Germany —Fall 2053

THE EMPIRE HAD TAKEN INDIA. With the fall of Nashik, the British and Russian alliance moved swiftly to consolidate power across the subcontinent. In Bombay, the banners of imperial occupation still snapped over domed rooftops, and Russian armor patrolled the arterial roads once held by rebels. What had begun as a precarious partnership between the two Empires now hardened into open camaraderie—joint checkpoints, bilingual signage, shared command posts. The occupation wasn't temporary. It was strategic. Permanent.

And it emboldened them.

From his command post in Berlin, General Klaus von Rennstadt of the Imperial German Army stood at the head of a sprawling situation table. Maps of France, satellite feeds of the Maginot Line, and a dozen predictive models blinked and scrolled on the wall behind him. For over a decade, France and the Empire had been locked in a chess match—each side entrenched, probing, skirmishing, but never fully committing. That changed now.

The fall of New York had sent shockwaves through the Imperial ranks. Though the King ruled from India, New York had remained the nerve center. The rebellion hadn't fully taken the city, but they had shattered its grip. The ministers had been forced to flee. The aura of invincibility had been ruptured.

Von Rennstadt knew that if they were ever going to strike, this was the moment. France was vast, militarized, and battle-hardened. But it was also alone. The British had once counted on Germany to stay defensive, to contain French forces from expanding eastward. Now, with the British distracted by uprisings in India, rebel control in New England, and increasing insurgencies in Africa and the Caribbean, that leash had slipped.

Moscow, Russia —Fall 2053

Inside the Kremlin, meanwhile, another map was being studied.

In a sealed conference room beneath Moscow, President Aslanov met with his closest military and intelligence advisors. The Russian government had stood by the Empire during the Indian campaign, citing "regional stability" and "shared post-colonial responsibilities." But that cooperation had always been transactional—and temporary.

Now, with India under joint occupation and Britain weakened, the Russians saw opportunity. Not alliance. Opportunity.

"They are stretched thin," said Minister Breshkev, tapping a red-marked corridor along the Alps. "Their supply chains into southern Germany are vulnerable. If we were to secure Bavaria and move south into Lombardy—"

"We would take Vienna and Milan in a month," Aslanov finished, eyes narrowing. "And hold them indefinitely."

It was not yet a war plan. Not officially.

But it would be.

Italy, now fully aligned with the rebellion, had become a symbol of resistance—openly supplying arms, safe harboring rebel agents, and even launching raids into the Balkans. The British and Russians had largely ignored these provocations while India hung in the balance. But now, Italy would be next. The Russians had no intention of ever letting the Empire control Italy again.

They also had little trust in Germany, whose generals had grown louder, more reckless. France might be an enemy of the Empire, but it was a threat to Moscow too. If war engulfed Europe, Russia intended to be the last one standing.

The global rebellion was the spark. But the fuel had always been imperial ambition.

And in dark rooms in Berlin and Moscow, those ambitions were about to ignite.

Paris, Republic of France —Fall 2053

In Paris, the grand war room beneath the École Militaire hadn't been used in decades. Not officially. Its steel doors were disguised behind a wall of archives, and its elevator hadn't run on city power since the blockade of '39. But when Admiral Lemaire stepped through its threshold, trailing a half-dozen aides and intelligence officers, it lit up as if it had never been dark.

Across the central table, General Victor Léandre was already pacing, a glass of espresso in one hand and a stylus in the other. The main screen behind him flickered with live satellite feeds of the North Sea—dozens of vessels in formation. German destroyers, Russian subs, and at least one heavy Imperial carrier group idled just north of Heligoland.

Lemaire studied the feed for a moment, her expression unreadable. "They think caution means fear."

Léandre tapped the edge of the table without glancing up. "Good. Let them stare into the dark while we slip the knife in somewhere else."

For nearly a decade, France had been the sole continental power not under Imperial sway. After the fall of New York and the Russian conquest of India, the world had expected France to go quiet. To pull back. Instead, they'd activated six naval strike groups and put three more on ready reserve status. Paris hadn't flinched.

Now, the French Navy—the largest in the world—was about to move.

"We have confirmed satellite images that the Germans have pulled significant air and drone assets toward Strasbourg," said Major Sévigné, pointing to a looping feed of traffic along the border. "They're preparing for a frontal assault across the Rhine."

"And we're going to let them," Léandre said, finally stopping his pacing. "We let them keep building. Let them position their reserves, string their fuel lines, reinforce the forest trails. Meanwhile, we make it look like we're about to cross into Lower Saxony through the north."

"You want a feint?" Lemaire asked.

"A feint they can't ignore," Léandre said. "We leak troop movements, drone flight paths, chatter in Dutch and Flemish resistance groups—just enough noise to force them to reposition north."

"And while they're shifting north," Lemaire began.

"We strike their fleet in the sea."

He turned, tapping the projection. The North Sea lit up in red and blue formations.

"Operation Trident. Carrier Group *Delacroix* will move through the Shetlands under civilian marine cover. We launch preemptive strikes against the Russian support flotilla just east of Skagerrak. If we can cripple their logistics before they know it's real, we push the Germans into panic and fracture the Russian naval link entirely."

Lemaire's eyes narrowed, but she nodded. "You'll risk escalation. If you hit the Russian fleet—"

"They won't escalate," Léandre cut in. "Not until they stabilize India. And if we hit first, they won't stabilize anything."

Around the room, aides exchanged glances. No one questioned the boldness. France had been on the defensive for too long. This wasn't just about survival anymore. It was about shaping the war before someone else decided where it would be fought.

Léandre stepped back from the screen and looked to Lemaire. "Your navy's the sharpest blade we have. Is it ready?"

Lemaire didn't smile, but her voice carried the weight of steel. "It was ready before the world remembered we existed."

CHAPTER THIRTY-FIVE

The North Sea, 200 km off the German Coast —Fall 2053

THE NORTH SEA WAS COLD enough to crack steel, and the fog rolled over the waves like ash from a distant fire.

Carrier Group *Delacroix*, thirty-one ships in all, moved under strict blackout orders just west of Jutland. At the front, the *Maréchal de Villars* sliced through the heavy sea with steady purpose, her hull sheathed in a layered ECM field that turned her signature into little more than a drift of static on enemy radar.

Inside the command deck, Admiral Lemaire stood at the chart table, one hand braced on the edge as the other adjusted the digital overlay projecting real-time feed from their vanguard drones.

"They've left the fuel column exposed," she murmured.

Commander Durand nodded beside her, jaw clenched. "Just like we hoped. Russian fleet is holding fast south of the Skagerrak. German patrols are guarding the perimeter, but their main guns are facing west. Not north."

"They're watching the Dutch coast," Lemaire said. "Let them. Deploy forward wings. Initiate the Prometheus net. And tell Captain Giraud he may fire at will."

On the deck of the *FS Liberté*, Lieutenant Camille Baudin double-checked the arming panel for the forward torpedo batteries. She barely noticed the freezing wind curling down the collar of her coat.

"Drone feeds confirm contact. Six Russian support vessels and four German tenders in quadrant seven," the gunnery officer called out.

Camille nodded. "Prometheus protocol is green?"

"Green and standing by."

She tapped her headset. "Bridge, this is Baudin. Commencing fire."

The *Liberté* shuddered with release as a spread of torpedoes surged from their tubes beneath the waterline, disappearing into the black. Seconds later, the horizon lit with flame.

The Russian refueling barge *Volzhsky* erupted first, an expanding ball of heat and smoke that rose like a second sun. Flames tore sideways across the sea, licking at the hulls of two more transports even before the shockwave reached the French line.

The enemy's response was immediate. The air crackled with electronic screams as German and Russian carriers launched their countermeasure: swarm drones, thousands of them, airborne and aquatic, clustering like metallic starlings. They surged across the sky in shifting clouds, diving in synchronized bursts, while beneath the surface, their submersible counterparts created a lattice of autonomous threats meant to overwhelm any defense grid by sheer numbers and unpredictability.

Camille Baudin watched the tactical screen bloom red. "Here they come."

She didn't flinch.

No one on the French bridge did. Because they had something no one else did.

The Prometheus counter-swarm system activated.

Mounted on reinforced towers across the lead destroyers and command ships, Prometheus had been developed in total secrecy over five years by the French Naval Research Directorate. While the rest of the world invested in bigger swarms and smarter kill chains, France had pursued a different solution—one that didn't just fight drones, but neutralized the entire concept.

The system deployed a dual-layer defense net. The first: a spread of low-frequency sonic pulses tuned to destabilize the swarm's mesh networking. Like a virus scrambling synapses, it broke their ability to think as a collective. Many simply spiraled away, twitching mid-flight or sinking beneath the waves. The second: concentrated UV-laser arrays that painted targets in wide arcs, slicing through communications bands and burning out sensor clusters in precise, invisible flashes.

No other navy had it. No one else had seen it tested in open water. The Germans didn't even know it existed.

And now, their greatest weapon was collapsing in real time.

Camille looked to her gunnery tech. "Status?"

"Seventy-five percent of the aerial swarm is down. The rest are scattering."

"Submersibles?"

"Directionless. Drifting. We've blinded their hive protocols."

Camille exhaled slowly. This was no fluke. It was doctrine.

In under a minute, the sky above the *Liberté* began to rain.

Hundreds of German and Russian drones, stripped of coordination and scrambled mid-flight by the Prometheus net, dropped from the air like slagged hailstones. Some detonated midair as their failsafes tripped; others simply fell, spinning wildly, slamming into the sea with plumes of spray. Several struck their own ships in a cruel irony of reverse targeting; one embedded itself in the communications tower of the Russian destroyer *Almaz*, disrupting its bridge feed for nearly forty seconds. That was all the time the French needed.

On the *Villars*, Lemaire stood unmoved as dozens of red enemy markers blinked out in real time. Her hands remained clasped behind her back, her voice cool and low.

"Advance strike group. Push hard. Get me the *Granitovyy* and *Königsfeld* before they dive."

The bridge acknowledged her with a flurry of action. Orders were relayed through tight-beam comms. Artillery crews loaded fresh cluster rounds. Sub-commanders confirmed torpedo tubes green.

Three nautical miles ahead, the French missile cruiser *Touraine* opened fire.

She had been lurking just beneath the low cloud cover, camouflaged by heat baffles and jamming fields. Her broadside came all at once—twelve cluster shells howling through the air, trailing smoke and shrapnel bursts. They landed amid the German screening line with such violence that the *Heiligenstadt*, a mid-range escort ship, was torn nearly in half. Water flooded her engine room before the flames finished it.

To starboard, the *Valois* took a direct hit from a Russian rail shell, her stern engulfed in fire and black smoke. Still, she held course. Her captain, Captain Maestri, an old Corsican with lungs full of salt and a voice like broken gravel, bellowed orders through his throat mic.

"Bring the forward guns online. We don't run, not in this war."

Her bow guns roared seconds later, sending a blistering burst of high-velocity rounds into the flank of the *Brandenburg*. The German cruiser reeled but didn't fall.

From the southern edge of the battle, the French submarine *Fleur de Nuit* breached momentarily, rising like a predator from the depths just long enough to release two shipkillers at close range. The torpedoes, powered by hydrodynamic rail-cavitation, struck the *Königsfeld* amidships. The destroyer buckled with an awful groan and cracked like dry wood. Within minutes, she had vanished beneath the surface.

On the *Villars*, a low chime lit up Lemaire's console.

"Admiral," Durand said, "we've got a secure civilian transmission. Origin point: Dallas."

She raised a brow. "General Greg?"

The screen blinked to life, grainy, disrupted by battlefield interference. Andrew Greg's face appeared, dusty and lined, lit red by emergency strips inside a rebel mobile command center. The rumble of artillery echoed in the background. Behind him, people moved with the exhaustion of those who hadn't slept in days.

"You're making headlines, Admiral."

"We're not done yet."

Greg smirked faintly. "Keep the pressure on. They've already pulled two destroyers off the Canadian coast to cover losses. And New England's reporting a gap in the blockade. You're bleeding them dry."

Lemaire gave him the barest smile. "Do you need anything from us?"

Greg shook his head. "You've done more than enough. Just make it hurt."

The line cut.

The battle entered its fourth hour.

Flotilla Grande—three French cruisers and two stealth corvettes—swung wide around the burning wreckage of the Russian supply column and closed on the German command ships still holding position near the eastern shelf. Torpedoes launched in staggered waves from different depths, confusing sonar profiles. Railguns chattered. Sea-skimming missiles wove serpentine trails between smoke columns and mastheads.

Onboard the Russian battlecruiser *Volkhov*, Admiral Viktor Stoyanovich gripped the brass edge of his command rail with white-knuckled fury.

"They shouldn't have been able to blind us. That's not possible."

His chief of signals, a pale man in a sweat-streaked uniform, said nothing. The drone systems had been their edge, their spear, their shield. Without them, the *Volkhov* was a steel target—massive, slow, and blind.

"Redirect all firepower to quadrant C," Stoyanovich barked. "We push through the flank. Overwhelm their smaller vessels before they can circle."

But he knew the window had closed. The French weren't reacting. They were controlling.

And they were about to finish it.

From the *Touraine* and *Fleur de Nuit*, the French launched their second wave: offensive swarm drones of their own design, smaller than a man's forearm, silent, and packed with kinetic payloads and micro-plasma torches. They darted low over the surface and skimmed beneath the waves, weaving through radar blind zones and target dead angles with terrifying precision.

The Germans and Russians had no effective countermeasures. Their own defensive software, fried by Prometheus, left them open to infiltration. Within minutes, French swarms were crawling the hulls of their ships, melting sensor clusters, drilling through exposed weld seams, and detonating interior compartments. Some swarms clustered at the waterline, directing concentrated EMP pulses that knocked out targeting gyros. Others simply dove into exhaust vents and exploded.

Elsewhere, on the bridge of the *Ostmark*, a German officer was screaming into a headset.

"I need comms with Berlin now! We've lost the *Königsfeld*, the *Heiligenstadt*, and half our supply drones! We are being carved to pieces, where is reinf—"

The line cut midword as a cluster round struck the ship's communications mast and turned the upper bridge into a fireball.

Overhead, French air drones swooped low and detonated flak pods midair. The bursts scattered kinetic chaff and overloaded optical targeting systems on enemy decks, further blinding their gunners. In the chaos, a squadron of French marines, launched hours earlier via stealth gliders, descended silently onto the deck of the Russian intelligence trawler *Petrovsk*. They breached the bridge, neutralized the crew, and dropped magnesium charges into the data core before vanishing back into the smoke.

By now, the sea shimmered with heat distortion and wreckage. Flames licked along oil-slicked water. Ships lay gutted and silent or still burning, their metal frames hissing in the cold air. Lifeboats drifted. Cries of orders and panic echoed across open water.

Three hours ago, it had been a corridor of commerce. Now, it was a machine graveyard.

By the time the *Villars* pulled back beneath the shelter of returning fog, sixteen Imperial vessels had been confirmed destroyed. Another nine were burning or adrift, some gutted midships, others dead in the water with black smoke rising like funeral banners. The French fleet had taken damage—a cruiser lost, two others battered—but its core was intact, and more importantly, it had completed its mission.

The enemy's logistics corridor in the North Sea was gone.

But that wasn't the only objective.

At 0732 hours, Admiral Lemaire gave the final order: "Withdraw. Mask our trail but make it look like the landing force is inbound."

Her bridge crew exchanged glances. No explanation was needed. They knew their next moves would feed a carefully constructed illusion.

Already, the French were seeding false signals: encrypted bursts mimicking amphibious transport traffic, garbled radio chatter suggesting staging areas near the Dutch coast, and intentionally leaked sensor echoes pointing toward naval infantry units forming up in the fog. The enemy would see what they were meant to see—a full invasion force preparing to come ashore.

In Berlin, confusion would turn to fear. They'd scramble to reinforce the northern coast, pulling divisions from the Rhine, diverting fuel, repositioning air wings. Exactly as planned.

Camille Baudin remained at her station, gaze fixed on the viewport as wreckage drifted past—charred hulls half-submerged in black water, torn plating twisted like ribbon, lifeboats spinning empty in the swells. Ships lay split like cracked shellfish, their insides open to the cold. The sea itself was streaked with fire and oil, a moving graveyard under a blood-colored sky.

She felt no surge of triumph. Only purpose.

This wasn't victory. It was deception, sharpened into strategy.

The Empire's grip on the North Sea had been shattered. In its place, France had planted a ghost—a phantom invasion force that would haunt enemy radar and cloud their judgment. A full-scale amphibious landing that would never come. But it would look real. It would sound real. And it would force Berlin to act on illusion.

By the time they realized the truth, it would be too late.

In Moscow, encrypted channels lit up like firecrackers. In Berlin, officers shouted across fractured comms for answers that weren't coming. And across the rebellion, from Quebec to Paris to Delhi, the word moved faster than the smoke could settle:

The French Navy hadn't just survived. It had seized initiative. And changed the shape of the war.

CHAPTER THIRTY-SIX

We must all hang together, or most assuredly
we shall all hang separately.
Benjamin Franklin —Summer 1776

Beijing, China —Late Fall 2053

ALEXANDRA BAKER DESCENDED INTO BEIJING under an assumed name, her credentials a patchwork of rebel forgeries and Italian covert clearances, designed to slip through the kind of layered scrutiny only the Chinese bureaucracy could muster. With her was Celsus "Bear" Berning. Their path had not been simple. From Texas to Cairo, Cairo to Tashkent, then overland into Xinjiang, through the old Soviet tunnels once trafficked by arms dealers, later by political defectors, and now, once again, repurposed for diplomacy.

The city revealed itself slowly, unfolding not with light, but with order. From the clouds, Beijing was a map of precision and restraint, a city untouched by war not out of mercy but because no one had dared. For a century, no bombs had fallen here, no occupation had taken root.

Not because China was untouchable, but because any would-be invader knew the cost. Where others projected force, China had learned to absorb it, to consolidate, to retreat inward, to endure.

It had never joined the Empire.

And it had never forgiven the one place that had been taken from it: Hong Kong.

British rule had begun, as all their claims had, with a treaty written under duress. The Treaty of Nanking in 1842, the spoils of opium and Empire, had ceded Hong Kong Island to Britain "in perpetuity." What followed was a century of colonial expansion disguised as administration. First the island, then the Kowloon Peninsula, then the so-called "leased" New Territories. A patchwork of acquisitions, legal fictions, and military facts on the ground.

During one of the world's many moments of distraction, Britain had recently reasserted its grip. Under the pretense of stabilizing economic markets and cracking down on corruption, Imperial forces had swept through the city. First the financial district, then the courts, then the streets. The dissidents disappeared first. Then the journalists. Then the artists. The blackout lasted five years. There had been no war. Just silence.

New York had called it a restoration.

Beijing had called it something else. It had not retaliated. Not then. It had buried the wound beneath policy and time and focused instead on internal strength, building walls not of ideology, but of economy and steel. It had endured humiliation without reply. But it had never forgotten.

Now, as Russia moved south and the Empire bled itself dry across three continents, China watched. And in the watching, it calculated.

Alex entered the capital unnoticed, accompanied only by Bear and a quietly embedded Italian attaché with deep contacts inside the Ministry of State Security. There was no motorcade, no flag, no protocol, just a state-marked sedan that passed silently through four layers of automated security and vanished into a compound disguised as a telecommunications research center somewhere beyond the fifth ring road.

The building was airless and immaculate. Soft white corridors stretched in angular silence. Unmanned drones moved overhead on ceiling tracks like predatory birds following prewritten loops. Biometric locks were hidden in walls designed to look like nothing at all. No portraits. No slogans. Only fluorescent light and the deep, mechanical hum of buried servers.

They were led to a narrow, windowless room three levels underground. The walls were seamless concrete, the lighting deliberately subtle. It could have been a bunker or a data center. Possibly both. Bear scanned it without comment, counting exits, blind spots, the distance to the nearest vent.

Vice Marshal Liang Yulan sat across the table, perfectly still, her hands folded, her expression unreadable. She hadn't spoken. Not yet. She simply studied Alex with the clinical patience of someone who could afford to wait.

Alex kept her hands visible on the table. "I came here because your analysts already know what's happening. You've seen the troop movements. The fuel logistics. The silence from the Empire. You know what Nashik means."

Bear translated, crisp and clear, never embellishing, never hesitating. His voice was low, neutral, but not passive. He was watching Liang as much as he was speaking, tracking the micro-reactions, the stillness of her breath. He knew when words landed and when they missed. The Vice Marshal had her own translator, of course. That was part of the performance. But Bear wasn't translating for her. He was translating for the room.

Liang didn't blink. "You're not the first foreigner to tell us what we already know."

She spoke in impeccable English. Her voice was even, shaped by discipline more than accent.

Bear paused, then offered Alex a dry glance and leaned back in his chair. The corners of his mouth turned up, just barely.

"Well," he muttered, mostly to himself, "that saves us a step."

Then he went quiet again, watching, listening, reading the room like it was just another battlefield.

"No," Alex replied. "But I might be the last who says it before the map changes."

She reached into her satchel, not fast, not slow, and placed the tablet on the table. With a swipe, images began to cycle. Russian formations crossing the upper Ganges, British forward observers operating under Russian logistics command, thermographic footage of Indian civilians being herded into temporary containment zones.

"They're not helping the Empire," she said. "They're building something of their own. The British are a mask. Russia is the face."

Liang's gaze didn't move.

"China has spent decades building a perimeter of silence," Alex continued. "A kind of disciplined distance. And it's worked. You've remained unentangled. But now someone else is drawing new borders, on land, over sea, through fiber, and they're not asking for permission. They're asking whether anyone will stop them."

Liang lifted a hand and paused the tablet.

"You think we fear encirclement."

"I think you already are encircled," Alex said. "I think they want to test whether you'll accept it."

"And your rebellion?" Liang asked. "Is that the force that will stop them? A handful of rogue provinces and defecting generals?"

"No," Alex said. "We don't have the strength. Not alone. But we're the only ones willing to bleed for the idea that empires don't get to last forever. And we're holding the line. For now."

She leaned forward slightly.

"I didn't come here for ideology. I came here because your ports depend on southern trade routes. Because your energy grid depends on contested crossings in Myanmar. Because your satellites run through blind spots over India. And because if the Russians close those doors, the only leverage you'll have left is history."

Liang's lips pressed into a thin line. "You mistake our restraint for inaction."

"No," Alex said softly. "I'm counting on it being preparation."

That caught something behind the Vice Marshal's expression. Not a smile, but a recognition.

"What do you want?" Liang asked.

"An armored division in Ladakh. I want tanks the Russians can't ignore, drones that can fly without flag, and a visible footprint large enough to freeze their next move."

"And if we decline?"

Alex didn't hesitate. "Then in six months, you'll be negotiating your border policy with Moscow."

Silence filled the space like pressure in a sealed chamber.

"You will have our answer in two days," Liang said finally, her voice smooth.

Alex stood. "You'll have it by tonight."

Liang arched a brow.

"I'm not here to build a case through channels," Alex said. "I came here because you already know the math. I'm not asking you to believe in my cause. I'm asking you to decide whether you want to write the future, or read about it after it's too late."

This time, Liang didn't respond at all. She simply turned and exited the room.

Alex remained standing for a beat, letting her own pulse settle.

Outside, Beijing carried on in the hush of its own rhythm. But far to the west, in armored vaults beneath the provincial command of Gansu, encrypted systems began to light. East of Chengdu, a mechanized battalion that had been designated "inactive" since 2031 received new orders. Along the western frontier, five logistic hubs were shifted from civilian to defense control without a single public broadcast.

Her journey south was nothing like her arrival.

They left Beijing before sunrise, dressed in plain couriers' uniforms, hair and beard dyed several shades darker, names reduced to a blank passphrase embedded in a military hardlink. The convoy was unmarked, just a set of rugged transports moving along freight routes that did not exist on any civilian map. Her escort was tight-lipped and unmistakably elite: three officers in gray fatigues who neither introduced themselves nor spoke unnecessarily. They moved through checkpoints that opened without inquiry, across provincial lines that had been redrawn in secret.

The Chinese were mobilizing. Quietly, but without hesitation.

From inside the reinforced windows of her vehicle, her guards pointed out the changes to Alex. Railcars that had once carried steel and grain now moved tanks beneath tarpaulins. Civilian fuel stations displayed handwritten "closed" signs, their contents rerouted by unspoken order. In Chengdu, she glimpsed columns of infantry boarding unmarked transports under floodlights. Outside Xining, long-range missile trucks rolled over the highway under cover of darkness.

The silence was over. China had made its decision.

Pakistan —Late Fall 2053

Their entry into Pakistan was conducted with clinical precision. It had been two weeks since her meeting with the Chinese. There was no welcome party, no red carpet, just a drone hover ferry that took her across a low valley at dawn, escorted by a signal-scrambled flight path that blinked once on rebel radar, then vanished.

Vihaan met them at the edge of the ridge near their new base, a half-buried compound of concrete and steel, patched together from old military stores and newer rebel ingenuity. Inside, the main chamber had been stripped to its bones and rebuilt as a combined field hospital and communications center. He looked leaner than she remembered. Hardened. But when he saw them step down from the transport, something in his posture eased.

"You came back," he said.

"Told you I would," Alex replied.

Bear was already moving, arms outstretched before gripping Vihaan's hand tight and clapping a broad palm against the man's shoulder. "Hell of a way to stay alive, old man," he said. "I'd say you look good, but the cratered eyes give it away."

Vihaan gave a dry smile, the kind that didn't reach his eyes but meant more than words. "Still the biggest bastard in any room, I see."

"I try."

They walked together through narrow corridors lit by battery lanterns, passing medics hunched over triage slates and field engineers stripping drones for spare parts. The air smelled of solder, bleach, and tired breath.

In the planning room, a low stone chamber with half a ceiling and a table bristling with pinned maps, Bear paused at the edge and looked around slowly.

"You've done a lot with not much," he said to Vihaan.

"We ran out of 'much' two weeks ago," Vihaan replied.

Bear glanced at Alex, his tone shifting just slightly. "You sure about this one?"

She nodded. "I was sure before I ever left for Beijing."

Bear exhaled, then reached into his coat and pulled out a small field comms unit. "Encrypted line. Preloaded with ghost frequencies. You'll need it if things go sideways. I left two fallback channels tied to New York." He handed it to Vihaan. "Don't let this place turn into Nashik."

Vihaan took it without a word.

Bear turned back to Alex. "I've got a window, two hours tops. Imperial hardliners are making noise in Queens. Thought they'd scatter, but some of them are digging in. Greg needs me stateside."

She stepped closer. "You'll make it through?"

"I always do. But don't get used to me being the one who leaves quietly."

She almost smiled. "That wasn't quiet."

Bear's grin faded as he looked between the two of them. For a moment, he seemed about to say more. Then he nodded once.

"Don't die," he said, and disappeared down the corridor.

In the planning room, nothing more than a stone chamber with half a ceiling and a full table of maps, they stood side by side as she opened her satchel and placed down a single data pad.

"They're in," she said.

Vihaan exhaled slowly. "How many?"

"Full division, armored. Advance units begin staging in Ladakh within two weeks. Air support will follow. Target range includes the northern corridor from Srinagar to Meerut. If we're in position when the hammer drops, we can cut the Russians off mid-push."

Vihaan blinked, once. Then again. "They're really doing it."

"They're already doing it," she said. "They just haven't been seen yet."

He sat back, eyes scanning the map. His finger moved to trace the old Delhi corridor, the supply artery to the Imperial command still based in the central capital.

"If we hit from the east..."

"We don't hit from the east," Alex interrupted. "We come from the heart."

He looked up.

"China's presence in the north will draw every remaining Imperial reserve. British command will assume the attack is a classic northern push. But we don't give them that."

She tapped the center of the map. "We hit from the inside. You take your re-formed units, the Pakistani battalions, the Indian cells hiding in the center, and we drive into the capital before they know we've regrouped."

Vihaan stood. "We'll need supply lines."

"You'll have them. The Italians are moving equipment through Iran. The French are redirecting satellites. And the Canadians, believe it or not, have offered recon drones for the south."

"And local support?"

Alex allowed herself a faint smile. "The Empire's done more to radicalize the interior than we ever could. Rice farmers near Nagpur. Desert fighters in Jaisalmer. Engineering students in Lucknow building rail bombs in basements. They just need to know the tide has turned."

Vihaan ran a hand through his hair, staring at the board as if trying to see the future in real time. "We're not ready."

"You'll have twelve days."

He turned to her. "We'll make it work."

Outside, the valley winds howled through the broken windows. The sun crept slowly above the horizon, casting long shadows across the battered ground.

Vihaan didn't sleep.

Instead, he moved through the stone corridors of the ridge installation, checking inventories by hand and issuing orders without ceremony. The Chinese had promised two weeks. He intended to be ready in one.

By morning, every surviving engineer was working double shifts. Field medics had converted a storage room into a mobile surgical wing, and new recruits were being drilled in fire teams across the ravines. They had weapons again, some old, some fresh off Chinese transports, and a new supply chain to keep them fed, fueled, and lethal. For the first time in months, Vihaan had a functioning command grid.

Maps were spread across a long table in the command tent, weighted down by stones. Vihaan stood at the center, surrounded by unit leaders, Pakistani and Indian, young and old, all hardened by defeat and ready to make it count. He traced a path down from the north, marking transit points, communication gaps, and potential resistance clusters.

"We hit them from the spine," he said, his voice low but firm. "Not the border. That's where they're looking. We move southeast through the inner valleys, consolidate rebel cells near Indore, then cut toward the central rail corridor. If we time it with the Chinese, the Imperials won't be able to pivot fast enough."

A captain in a sand-dusted turban pointed to a red X over a key depot. "That line's exposed. If we take it, we can shut down their armored supply route east of Bhopal."

"Take it and hold it," Vihaan nodded. "We need more than raids. We need permanence. Every stronghold becomes a command post. Every bridge we seize, we fortify."

An aide passed him a communique, coded but clear. Another rebel force in Rajasthan had begun moving east under cover of night. Small, but growing.

Vihaan looked up at the gathered officers.

"We've been broken, scattered, nearly erased. But the people didn't stop fighting. They're waiting for a flag to rally behind. Let's give them one. Two weeks from today, we move, not just to liberate, but to retake our country."

Murmurs of assent filled the room, then hardened into silence.

Vihaan looked out toward the hills where new tents were rising, new alliances forming. The Empire and Russia had taken Nashik, but they hadn't taken resolve. That lived on. And soon, it would march south.

CHAPTER THIRTY-SEVEN

Bombay, India —Late Fall 2053

CHARLES SAT BENEATH THE CARVED teak lattice of his private study in Bombay, gazing out at the humid expanse of gardens beyond the palace walls. The faint scent of flowering citrus drifted in through the open shutters, but he took no comfort from it. A Russian voice droned in the background, one of Breshkev's men, reading a report from the North Sea, but the King wasn't listening. He already knew what it said. The French had shattered their naval hold. The fleet was gone. The northern corridor was lost.

Nine days had passed since the Chinese had begun to move, but the dread had been building much longer. At first, it was whispers, odd logistics reports, satellite traffic over Tibet, unexplained redeployments in western China. Then came confirmation: entire armored divisions moving west. Supply hubs activated overnight. Rail lines humming at full capacity through Gansu and Sichuan. It wasn't a drill. It was a declaration.

Charles turned away from the window. General Tansley, still in uniform and holding an encrypted tablet, shifted uncomfortably under the weight of the Russian advisor's stare.

"He's always here now," the King muttered, just loud enough for Tansley to hear. "Watching. Waiting to see if I flinch."

"He's not just watching," Tansley said quietly. "He's coordinating. The airbase transfers, the new encryption keys, everything runs through Moscow now."

Charles narrowed his eyes. "Then maybe it's time we remind the world who holds the scepter."

He reached for a fresh report. "The Italians grow bolder. Their ports have opened to rebel fleets. Intelligence says they've begun training foreign fighters. Volunteers from Spain, from Croatia, even from old imperial officers defecting from Africa. That ends now."

Tansley's expression was tight. "What do you propose?"

Charles's gaze darkened. "A combined assault. Carrier-based strikes on Italy's southern coast. Naples. Bari. Knock out their naval yards. Show them what defiance costs."

"And the French?"

"The French will wait," the King said coldly. "The Germans were fooled by their theatrics, but we won't be again. Their navy made its point, but they won't land. Not yet. Once we've secured the Mediterranean, we deal with Paris."

He stood, crossing to a table where a large map of Europe stretched beneath a pane of glass. His finger traced a new route, one bypassing the Alps entirely.

"Tell the Germans to reroute through Austria. No more feints. No more posturing. I want boots in Verona by month's end. From there, they press south."

"And if the Chinese reach the subcontinent before we finish?"

Charles didn't answer immediately.

Instead, he glanced at the Russian in the corner. The man inclined his head faintly, as if waiting for permission to speak. The King ignored him.

"We contain them. We force them into mountain corridors and bleed them in terrain they don't know. If they want to fight in the Himalayas, let them. We'll fight with fire."

Off the coast of Sicily

The Imperial Navy formed a wall of steel and salt. Aircraft carriers and guided missile frigates moved in coordinated formation, their silhouettes like teeth rising from the deep. From Malta to the Ionian Sea, the British fleet, what remained uncommitted in the Atlantic and Pacific, had redeployed southward, abandoning ambitions in the north to focus on the heart of the rebellion: Italy.

The *HMS Resolute*, flagship of the Mediterranean Task Force, led the formation. Her decks buzzed with activity as flight crews armed and launched wave after wave of fighters into the overcast skies. Strikecraft peeled off in formations of four and six, their engines screaming as they broke formation and dipped low toward the coastline.

Over Naples, the sky erupted.

Imperial aircraft swarmed in, flanked by escort drones and signal-jamming countermeasures. The first wave targeted the naval yards, dry docks, ammunition stores, communication towers. Explosions bloomed across the waterfront, sending columns of black smoke spiraling into the sky.

Below, Italian anti-aircraft fire laced the horizon, filling the air with tracer rounds and flak bursts. But the assault had been timed with brutal efficiency. The Imperials had studied these ports for decades, knew their ranges, their response times, their dead zones.

In Bari, the old fortress walls crumbled under precision rail strikes. Hangars exploded. A coastal garrison lit up like a signal flare and was gone in moments. Civilians fled inland. Resistance fighters, caught unprepared, fired blindly into the sky before being silenced by the next strafing run.

From the command deck of the *Resolute*, Admiral Forsythe watched without expression, his gloved hands clasped behind his back.

"Secondary targets?" a young officer asked.

Forsythe's reply was calm. "Rail lines. Communications relays. And fuel. Especially fuel."

The second wave obeyed. Fighters swept inland, unleashing payloads on infrastructure, cutting off supply routes, isolating southern Italy from its own defenders. By the end of the first day, three ports had been struck, two refineries disabled, and one rebel command hub reduced to ash.

It wasn't just a military assault, it was psychological. A reminder. A message to every rebel government watching from afar: the Empire still had reach. Still had teeth.

But behind the admiral's stillness, concern lingered. The strikes had succeeded, yes, but they were not unopposed. The Italians had responded faster than expected. New radar arrays had come online mid-sortie. Coordinated drone swarms, some of them using unfamiliar signal patterns, had harried the tail end of the retreat. And though Naples still burned, a large segment of its anti-air batteries remained intact.

The Admiral stepped away from the main console and approached the encrypted terminal in his quarters. He keyed in a direct line.

"Status update for King Charles," he said. "Initial strikes successful. Resistance moderate but increasing. Recommend accelerated operations if we are to hold the Mediterranean uncontested."

A pause.

Then he added, "And request urgent confirmation: will the Germans press through the Alps alone, or are we to expect Russian reinforcement on that front?"

He did not await an answer. No one did anymore.

Out on the water, the British fleet turned eastward, pushing toward Calabria and the narrow throat of the Tyrrhenian Sea. The plan was to sweep the coast clean, to box in the Italians from sea and sky while the Germans descended from the north.

Victory, the King had said, would begin here.

But far below the surface, a different current stirred. Italian subs, long silent, were beginning to prowl again. And in the port ruins of Bari, a rebel technician crawled from the wreckage of a communications tower, clutching a hard drive that had survived the fire.

The French Navy had achieved its North Sea goals and was now at sea. The room beneath Toulon's central naval command center was cold and sealed with layered encryption protocols. Admiral Lemaire stood at the central display table with her command staff, watching real-time footage fed through long-range reconnaissance and stealth drones positioned above the central Mediterranean. The image was unmistakable: the British Navy was consolidating.

Carrier groups, destroyers, drone barges, and missile cruisers, enough steel and firepower to hammer half a continent, were now staging in the waters between Sicily and Libya. Supply lines streamed in from Malta and Gibraltar. Jet trails laced the skies above Corsica.

"They're preparing for a full campaign against Italy," said Rear Admiral Sorel. "Air strikes are already hitting the Ligurian ports. Naples is under blackout."

Lemaire didn't blink. Her eyes were on the map. She tapped the Strait of Gibraltar.

"If they control the Mediterranean, they own the center of the war. We won't win this from behind a seawall."

Her operations chief hesitated. "We're still recovering from the North Sea engagement. Damage crews are rotating nonstop. Fuel reserves are limited."

"We don't need time," Lemaire said. "We need audacity."

She keyed the holographic overlay, illuminating a projected route south: through the Bay of Biscay, around Spain, and straight into the deep blue chaos that would soon divide history.

"Begin the redeployment."

There were no debates.

Within the hour, the bulk of the French Navy, a bruised but not broken armada of high-speed cruisers, drone carriers, stealth destroyers, and deep-range submarines, slipped away from port and into open waters.

They moved in blackout silence. No beacon pings. No transmissions. No engine signatures over civilian frequencies. Each ship was cloaked in the new VeilleurNet counter-surveillance mesh, a hybrid of quantum interference fields and synchronized laser scatter arrays. Developed in the Vosges R&D corridors and tested during the Iceland drills, VeilleurNet confused standard orbital imaging and bent radar reflections into ghost signals.

To British satellites, the sea appeared empty, save for the faint shadows of phantom fishing vessels drifting harmlessly along old trade routes.

"Their eyes can't follow us," muttered Sorel as the fleet passed into the Bay of Biscay. "Not in real time."

"Then they'll feel us first," Lemaire replied.

The journey would take just under six days from their current position, assuming no delays. They would reach the western mouth of the Mediterranean under cover of weather, silence, and blind spots the Empire didn't yet know it had.

And when they arrived, Lemaire intended to hit hard enough to break history.

The Alps, Northern Italy

The air in the Alps was razor-thin, brittle with cold and altitude. Snow had fallen the night before, masking the old smuggling roads in a sheen of quiet white. By dawn, it was churning under treads.

German armor moved south in tight, disciplined columns, Leopard XIs and Panzerjäger drones creeping down mountain corridors like steel insects. Infantry followed behind on foot, their exosuits hissing softly with every step, adjusting for terrain and temperature. Above them, signal jammers floated in near-silent hover, blotting out communications and bouncing surveillance pings into static.

The invasion had begun before anyone in Italy knew to call it that.

Major Lukas Ehrenthal crouched near a rock outcrop above the Brenner Pass, peering through a digital scope set to heat trace. He watched as Italian scouts retreated through a saddle between ridges, too few, too slow. He tapped the side of his helmet.

"Seventh Division is holding contact at Altino. Light resistance. We'll press to the basin by midday."

A distorted confirmation chirped back, Gottwald's voice, from the command vehicle somewhere east, buried in snow netting.

"They don't have enough guns to hold the ridge," Lukas muttered. "Not yet."

"Then move."

And so they did.

By noon, German forces had secured the pass entirely. Drones swept ahead, mapping the valley and tagging hostile signatures. A hidden mortar nest opened fire from a frozen vineyard, but was silenced within seconds by loitering munitions keyed to sound triangulation. Further down, an abandoned farmhouse rigged with tripwire charges was bypassed completely by scoutbots crawling under its foundation, disabling the explosives before infantry ever arrived.

No frontal charge. No glorious stand. Just methodical, unstoppable pressure.

This wasn't a blitz. It was a siege by motion.

In the rear, mobile artillery was already rolling into position. Self-propelled howitzers began shelling targets beyond Verona, calibrating impact spreads by the second. Their barrels steamed in the alpine cold, resetting after every launch with robotic precision.

A single French-made tank, salvaged by the Italians and retrofitted with smuggled sensors, attempted to make a stand on a ridgeline east of Lake Garda. It got off one shot, burned the side panel of a German APC, and then was reduced to shrapnel by a hypersonic rail burst from an unseen overwatch drone.

Major Ehrenthal arrived twenty minutes later and stepped through the wreckage without speaking. His aide handed him a pad. The map had changed, again. New red zones blinked open like wounds, showing where the Empire had advanced through another checkpoint, another defense line, another town.

"We'll reach Verona by dusk," the aide said.

"No," Ehrenthal replied, narrowing his eyes toward the southern horizon. "We'll surround it. Let them think they have time. Let them concentrate their defense. Then we close the trap."

And behind him, high above the column of troops winding its way down the mountain, the Imperial banner rippled in the cold wind, unfurled from the frame of a command drone drifting watchfully overhead.

CHAPTER THIRTY-EIGHT

Outside Peshawar, Pakistan —Late Fall 2053

THE CALL CONNECTED JUST AFTER dusk; the sky was fading into that half-light blue that came before the stars, and the wind moved restlessly through the open shutters of the command tent. In Dallas, Texas, it was still morning. The difference made the moment feel stranger, like they were speaking across two separate worlds.

Alex's face flickered to life on Andrew Greg's screen, dusty, focused, and framed by the worn canvas backdrop of a mobile base.

"You're in one piece," he said.

"More or less." Her voice was quiet but not weary—just measured. "Vihaan sends his regards. The Chinese are moving faster than expected. We're holding north of Nashik, but the lines won't hold forever."

Andrew nodded, leaning back in his chair. He looked as worn as she felt. His hair was a little more disheveled than usual, pipe unlit for once, his sleeves rolled to his elbows. The Texan heat was pressing down even at this hour, visible in the sheen on his forehead.

"I've heard the reports," he said. "They've already sent mechanized scouts into Arunachal. If they're serious, they'll be in the ridge passes within days."

"They're serious," she said. "I met with the vice marshal myself. I don't think she smiled once."

"That's how you know they mean it."

For a while, neither of them spoke. The silence wasn't awkward, though—just lived-in, like two old soldiers standing in a hallway, not needing to say what they were both thinking.

"How's Dallas?" she asked finally.

"Hot. Crowded. Half the Gulf's trying to move north ahead of the next offensive. Houston held, barely. We lost three bridges outside Galveston, and the water plants are down to half pressure. But morale's good. They know help's coming."

"Because of what you're doing," she said.

Andrew shook his head. "Because of what we're all doing."

He tapped the side of his comm screen, then looked at her again. "You ever think about it?"

"About what?"

"The end. What it looks like. What comes after."

Alex didn't answer right away. She stood, walked a few steps to the open flap of her tent, and looked out. Beyond the field, a mountain ridge caught the last line of light. Chinese supply convoys were visible in the valley below, just silhouettes and engine growls, but real.

"I used to think it would just stop one day," she said. "We'd raise a flag, and that would be that. But now..." She trailed off, then looked back at him. "Now I think it's going to bleed out slowly, like a fever breaking. And we'll have to decide what to do with the quiet. That's the part no one prepares you for," she added. "We train for resistance, not for what comes after, not for the loneliness of survival."

Andrew nodded. "And what would you do with it?"

"Honestly?" Her eyes softened just a little. "I'd sleep for a week, maybe two. Then I'd find a lake somewhere—cold water, trees, silence. You?"

He smiled faintly. "There's a cabin out west I haven't seen in twenty years—middle of nowhere, big porch, bigger sky. If I'm still breathing when this is done, I might just disappear there for a while."

He didn't smile when he said it, not really, but something in the way his eyes lingered on hers, steady, unguarded, made her pulse skip half a beat.

"Might be nice," she said.

Their eyes met again, held just a bit longer this time.

"Could use company," he said, almost offhand but not.

"I'll bring whiskey," she replied, just as quiet.

That was as far as they took it. No declarations, just a possibility set gently on the table between them.

"Be careful out there," he said.

"You too. And try not to piss off too many Texans while you're at it."

Andrew smirked. "No promises. They keep trying to teach me how to two-step."

"Well, if the war doesn't kill you, that might."

They stared at each other once more before the call ended.

Outside her tent, the wind shifted, carrying the sound of distant engines and something else—maybe hope, maybe just movement. But it was enough.

Alex took a deep breath and turned back to the map. There was still war to plan, but now there was something else too, something waiting on the other side.

CHAPTER THIRTY-NINE

Nashik Valley, India —Winter 2053

COLONEL SERGEI ANTONOV PACED, HIS polished boots grinding soot and grit beneath each step. The walls were plastered with maps layered in red ink, lines of advance, fallback positions, artillery ranges. Every inch of rebel movement was meticulously tracked. Yet even with Imperial might at his back, Antonov couldn't shake the gnawing unease that burrowed beneath his ribs.

The air above Nashik was heavy with the sting of scorched earth and diesel. Blown dust coiled lazily from the ruins of the old base, lingering like a bitter ghost. Jagged slabs of concrete and twisted steel beams jutted from the ground, the skeletal remains of shattered barracks. What remained of the central structure was shrouded beneath a heavy canvas, the makeshift Russian command post. Inside, the air was stale and humid, thick with the weight of unspoken doubts.

"The Indians are gathering strength," said his intelligence officer, his voice low and deliberate. "Pakistanis are funneling them weapons and supplies. Volunteers are flooding in from the villages. The tempo is accelerating."

Antonov scowled, but the concern in the man's voice was contagious. "They're fools. They think the Chinese mobilization makes them untouchable." His voice dropped. "They'll learn."

General Bradford Tansley, the highest-ranking British officer on-site, remained still, his arms crossed as he scrutinized the map table. His sharp blue eyes, once icy with conviction, now betrayed a flicker of uncertainty. "They're emboldened," he said. "They hear rumors of a fractured Empire. The Chinese see opportunity. The rebels see victory."

Antonov's lip curled. "The Chinese can drown us in bodies, but they've never fought a modern war. Russia built the machine they think they can topple."

Tansley's jaw tightened. "And if they don't need to fight like us? If brute force is enough?"

The Russian's fists clenched. "Then we remind them why their ancestors feared us."

Outside, the low growl of machinery echoed through the valley. Russian engineers toiled under the sun, assembling bunkers from salvaged steel and rubble. Mobile artillery crews hauled fresh batteries into position. The valley bristled with anti-aircraft guns, their barrels trained skyward. Nashik was no longer just a battlefield; it was becoming a fortress again.

The bunker's canvas flap parted, and a junior officer entered. His face was streaked with sweat and grime, but his salute remained sharp. "Sir. Confirmation from satellite intel. The Chinese divisions are advancing faster than expected. Eight armored columns. Possibly more. And the rebels... "

Antonov's brow furrowed. "How many? Eight!?"

"And every liberated village adds to their numbers. Defectors. Civilians. Trained fighters. The insurgency has become a standing army."

Tansley exhaled sharply. "They aren't just fighting us. They're winning loyalty and the will of the people."

Antonov's fist came down hard on the map table. "Then we break them. Here. Now." His voice was low, seething. "We have air superiority, layered defenses, and enough artillery to reduce these hills to ash. Every step they take will cost them blood."

The officers exchanged uneasy glances, the steel in Antonov's voice doing little to mask the mounting fear. Orders would be followed. Defeat was not an option.

But the truth was evident. Russia had not come to India for a prolonged war. Every fortified trench and anti-air emplacement here was another delay in confronting the rebellion's grip on North America. The war was spreading faster than they could contain it.

"We finish this quickly," Tansley said, his voice lower now. "Then we redeploy."

Antonov nodded, his expression grim. "No mercy."

Beyond the cracked walls of the bunker, the sun scorched the valley floor. Smoke still leaked ominously above the ruins. But on the distant ridge, shadows gathered. Figures moved in the haze, like specters rising from the wreckage.

General Zhang Wei stood with the kind of stillness that made others restless. His uniform was stripped of any unnecessary adornment, no gaudy epaulets, no gleaming medals. Only the modest insignia pinned to his breast pocket hinted at his authority. Unlike his Western counterparts, Zhang had no need for embellishments. Experience was enough.

He had never commanded a battlefield on this scale, but he'd walked through the aftermath of a thousand smaller ones. The scorched fields of West Africa. The shattered streets of Aleppo. The hollowed-out villages of the Caucasus. The Empire had dismissed those conflicts as "regional disturbances," beneath the weight of intervention. But Zhang had studied them. Learned from them. He knew how poor planning rotted armies from within, and how to hasten the decay.

General Vihaan Chadra approached, his uniform still streaked with the dust of their long southward march. Though he carried no polished rank, the worn fabric bore its own marks of command. The two men clasped hands, their mutual respect unspoken. It came not from shared culture, but recognition. Recognition of the weight of the moment, the lives of the men and women in their hands.

To Vihaan's side, Alexandra Baker watched in silence. Her bearing was rigid, but exhaustion clung to her like the dust of the battlefield. She hid it well. Her name had traveled faster than the rebels' own victories. The foreign general who had stood when others fled. Word of her defense at Nashik had spread like wildfire, whispered even in the shadows of cities still under Imperial rule. To the rebellion, she was proof that the Empire could bleed.

Zhang shook her hand with a brief nod. "General Baker. General Chadra." His English was flawless, his voice low and even. "Your people are determined."

"Determination only carries us so far," Vihaan replied. The pride in his voice was muted but present. "We're still facing a force that outguns us."

Zhang's mouth curved into the faintest smile. "Then we remind them that steel alone does not win wars."

A battered table stood beneath a canvas tent, the edges of its maps weighed down by ammunition boxes and half-empty water canisters. The parchment bore the scars of hurried planning, lines drawn, erased, redrawn. But all attention remained on the marked positions of the Chinese armored divisions. Movement. Momentum.

"The Russians think we've come to reinforce," Zhang said, his finger tracing the jagged ridges of the Sahyadri mountains. "They expect a slow, careful advance. Guarded. Hesitant. But we aren't here to hesitate."

"They think you'll play it safe," Alex said.

"They think we'll bleed slowly," Zhang corrected. "But we are not here to bleed."

Vihaan's brow furrowed. "Then what is our intent?"

Zhang tapped a single line cutting through the valley. "We punch."

The word landed like a stone. No theatrics. No bravado. Just certainty.

"They believe we'll test the line. Probe. Calculate. Instead, we will drive straight through. Full mechanized assault within the first forty-eight hours. No half-measures. We break their formation, fracture their command. And when the British think we've overcommitted, we show them how wrong they are."

Vihaan's gaze remained locked on the map. "And if the Russians hold?"

"They won't." Zhang's response was sharp. Absolute. "Their lines are stretched. Their supply chains dangle from the Caspian like a frayed rope. And the British?" He looked to Alex. "They don't know how to fight without total control of the skies."

"We take that from them," she said.

"Temporarily," Zhang allowed. "Our air divisions won't arrive in force until the second day. Until then, we let the British believe they rule the air. They'll grow bold. Commit. And then we close our fist."

Vihaan's jaw tightened. "This won't be clean."

Zhang didn't flinch. "It will be decisive."

A heavy silence fell, the kind that came before irrevocable decisions. Outside, the rumble of engines stirred the dry air. Supply convoys inched into position. In the distance, banners fluttered, some bearing the rising sun of China, others the green and saffron of India. They moved as one. For now.

"Your people," Zhang asked quietly, "are they ready?"

Vihaan didn't hesitate. "They've waited a lifetime for this."

Alex's voice cut through the stillness. "And when we break them?"

"Then we go south," Vihaan answered. "And we take back India."

Zhang gave a single, measured nod. "Then we have our plan."

Yet even as the words settled on her, the weight of those who wouldn't survive pressed heavier against Alex's chest. Victory demanded its own kind of sacrifice.

There were no grand speeches. No calls to glory. Only the sharp scrape of chairs as the generals rose. Orders would be given. Battles would begin. The echoes of empires would clash once more.

As the tent emptied, the valley remained silent. But far beyond the ridgeline, the ruins of Nashik stood in defiance. The Imperial flags still flew, battered but unbroken. Not for long.

The battle began like a storm breaking across the valley. Hours of relentless missile fire pounded the earth, churning the plains into blackened craters. Then, with the shriek of treads grinding over shattered asphalt, the first Chinese armored divisions surged forward. Massive columns of tanks and infantry crawled toward Nashik's jagged ruins. Overhead, the sky burned with the streaking remnants of missile contrails and the brilliant flares of drone bursts, a brutal, contested chaos.

From their fortified command bunkers, Russian and British officers tracked the onslaught. Screens flickered with fragmented data, every sensor and satellite struggling to keep pace with the scale of the engagement. Chinese combat algorithms adjusted in real-time, their strategic calculations twisting the battlefield with relentless precision.

Colonel Sergei Antonov's gaze remained locked on the central display. The Russian's square jaw tightened, deep furrows etched into his face. Even after decades of war, the sight of massed armor advancing with such certainty unsettled him. The rebellion no longer moved like a fractured insurgency. They were a military force, disciplined, deliberate, unrelenting.

"The eastern gate," a Russian officer barked, his voice cracking through the tense hum of the bunker. "Four armored divisions, supported by aerial drone swarms. The British defenses are strained."

Antonov grunted. "They're committing."

"They're forcing us to," General Tansley said. The British officer paced beside the table, his hands clenched behind his back. Dust still clung to his uniform from the previous day's bombardments. "But it's not reckless. Every advance is calculated. Drone suppression. Missile screens. They're not wasting armor."

Antonov's voice dropped. "Then they think they can win."

Tansley's pale blue eyes narrowed. "They're counting on our pride to bleed us dry."

Outside, the valley roared. Russian mobile artillery platforms responded in defiant bursts, hypersonic slugs tearing through the air, hammering into the distant ridges. Mushrooming plumes of fire and debris marked the hits. Yet the rebel formations pressed on. Smoke-blackened silhouettes emerged from the haze, infantry marching alongside the hulking shadows of Chinese tanks. Every casualty was absorbed by the immensity of their force.

Nashik's ruins sprawled behind the Imperial lines, their skeletal remains twisted into makeshift bunkers. Defensive fortifications bristled with rail batteries and automated gun emplacements. Engineers moved with desperate urgency, reinforcing gaps, dragging plates of steel across bombed-out roads. Above them, Russian and British drones tangled with rebel swarms, the air thick with the shriek of pulse cannons and the metallic snap of intercepted munitions.

In the bunker, a junior officer leaned over the console, his face pale. "Confirmed breach in Sector Four. They've severed the western supply route."

"Reinforcements?" Antonov barked.

"Failing to hold, sir. Casualties are mounting."

Antonov's knuckles whitened. "Send drones. Jam their comms. I want them blind."

"They're not blind," Tansley said bitterly, motioning toward the main display. "They're watching. Learning."

The truth was glaring. Every Russian artillery strike, every defensive shift, was met with terrifying efficiency. Rebel predictive algorithms, fueled by vast networks of AI, calculated each Imperial countermeasure in seconds. The Chinese had brought more than steel. They had brought foresight, and it was strangling the defenders.

Antonov slammed his fist on the table. "They're turning our own doctrine against us."

Tansley's voice was grim. "And they're winning."

Another officer called out, urgency spilling from his tone. "Enemy mechanized units are reinforcing the breach. Chadra's divisions are pushing through the gap."

Antonov's jaw tightened. Vihaan Chadra. The rebel general. The defector. Every Russian and Imperial knew his name, a symbol of India's defiance. Chadra's forces moved with ruthless coordination, exploiting every weakness the algorithms exposed. He didn't hesitate. He didn't relent.

"We've lost nearly forty percent of our interceptors," the officer continued. "Chinese electronic warfare systems are overwhelming our comms."

Antonov growled. "They brought their toys."

"So did we," Tansley shot back.

But even as the Russian general issued his orders, the central display shifted. A red flash marked the obliteration of an Imperial armored convoy, rebel-guided artillery shells striking with pinpoint accuracy. Antonov's stomach turned. They weren't merely predicting Imperial moves.

They were anticipating them.

"They're faster than we are," Tansley muttered. "Too fast."

Antonov's mind raced. They could not sustain this. The British had already begun pushing for redeployment to North America, eager to stem the rebellion's spread across the colonies.

A low static crackled through the bunker as a field officer's voice broke through the comms. "General, reports of sabotage in Sector Seven. Rebel infiltration teams. Artillery batteries compromised."

Antonov didn't flinch. "Seal the tunnels. Flush them out."

"They knew," Tansley said quietly, his voice barely above a whisper. "They knew every weakness."

The words hung heavy.

Outside, the storm raged. Missiles streaked through the sky. Fires blossomed along the ridges. And through the smoke, the rebellion surged forward, a tide that could not be stemmed.

The rebel forward command was alive with controlled urgency. Chinese mobile command nodes shifted constantly across the battlefield, small enough to evade Imperial countermeasures but powerful enough to coordinate their vast forces in real-time. Predictive algorithms fed from thousands of data points, every artillery strike, drone intercept, and troop maneuver was calculated in seconds. The result was a war fought with both brute force and frightening precision.

At the heart of the forward command, Alexandra Baker stood beside Vihaan Chadra. General Zhang's projection flickered on the main display, the Chinese commander's face illuminated by shifting tactical data. Behind him, the hum of operations buzzed, technicians adjusting algorithms, analyzing patterns, anticipating the next Imperial response.

"Their reinforcements are stacking too heavily in the west," Zhang said, his voice calm. "They assume we'll keep the pressure there."

"They will assume wrong," Vihaan replied, tracing the projected movements of Indian and Pakistani sabotage teams on the map. The rebels had struck deep, cutting supply lines and crippling fuel convoys. Even now, small teams disrupted Imperial logistics behind enemy lines. "We keep them guessing. Let them spend their reserves."

Alex's eyes flicked across the incoming reports. "Our rotations are outpacing theirs. We're cycling fresh divisions every twelve hours. The Imperials are stretching past their endurance. Their response time is slipping."

"And the drones?" Zhang asked.

Alex swiped the display, highlighting the latest aerial skirmishes. "VeilleurNet's systems are holding. Full-spectrum disruption, laser-based countermeasures, soundwave scramblers. The Russians haven't adapted."

The screen showed the aftermath of a recent drone engagement, Chinese interceptors reducing an entire Russian swarm to tangled, molten fragments. The countermeasures worked. The Imperials had no immediate answer.

Vihaan's expression hardened. "The east gate is the weakest. If we keep the pressure steady, it will collapse."

"They will not yield quietly," Zhang cautioned.

Outside, the rebel war machine churned forward. Supply trucks snaked through the wreckage of Nashik, their tires kicking up plumes of red dust. Mobile field hospitals operated in the shadow of ruined buildings, medics using AI-assisted triage systems to prioritize the wounded. Drones zipped overhead, carrying supplies and relaying real-time surveillance.

The cost was visible. Even as rebel ranks swelled, the toll of the battle left its mark. Exhaustion carved into the faces of soldiers. Blood pooled on makeshift operating tables. Yet with every shift change, more volunteers arrived. Defectors from the Imperial armies. Civilians hardened by years of occupation. The rebel insignia now adorned hastily patched uniforms, a sign not of unity by birth, but of defiance.

Deep beneath the shattered remains of Nashik, the mood was very different.

In the steel-walled corridors of the Russian bunker, the air was stale, tinged with the lingering residue of burned fuel. General Antonov moved with deliberate purpose, his heavy boots echoing with each step. The tremors of distant artillery fire thrummed through the floor, a constant reminder of the battle raging above. Elite units wearing augmented suits lead bands of soldiers wherever reinforcements were needed. But not all soldiers were equipped equally and some, mostly recent conscripts, didn't even have basic body armor.

Behind him, General Tansley caught up, his face lined with weariness. "Morale is breaking. The men are questioning whether we can hold."

"We will hold," Antonov barked. "Because we must."

He stopped before the thick bulkhead leading to the secondary command chamber. Beyond it, Imperial officers monitored the battlefield, their stations lit by the dim glow of sensor data. Antonov drew a slow breath, the weight of expectation pressing down on him.

"We fight for more than Nashik," he said quietly. "If we fall, the world sees weakness. And weakness invites annihilation."

Tansley said nothing. He understood. Every day the Imperials held Nashik was a day the rebellion's advance slowed. If the Empire could bleed the rebels long enough, reclaiming the advantage was still possible. But even Antonov knew the truth gnawing beneath the surface.

The rebels weren't just fighting harder. They were fighting smarter.

The valley was a maelstrom of fire and steel.

The battle unfolded with brutal symmetry, chaotic violence directed with mathematical precision. Over half a million soldiers clashed, the air thick with the roar of engines, the incessant whine of drones, the hiss of missile trails, and the distant, thunderous blasts of artillery.

On the northern flank, Chinese armored divisions led the charge. Towering tanks bristled with railguns and active defense systems, their mechanical forms flanked by swarms of autonomous drones. Above, Chinese fighter squadrons maintained pressure on the defenders, while mobile jamming units scrambled Russian and British communications. It was a relentless advance. For every vehicle lost, another took its place.

General Zhang Wei's voice came calmly over the comms. "Signal Wave Two."

The order triggered a ripple through the battlefield. Hundreds of needle-like drones surged forward in chaotic spirals. Russian flak cannons roared to life, spraying the sky with pulses of energy and explosive shells. Blue light tinged with fire, the signature of anti-aircraft autonomous batteries, streaked in all directions. But the swarm fractured, sending false signals to confuse targeting systems. Decoys tumbled in fiery plumes while the true assault slipped through. Fuel depots erupted. Communications towers collapsed. Even the city's reinforced artillery lines buckled under the onslaught.

To the south, the rebel offensive was no less fierce. Indian and Pakistani divisions moved in synchronized waves, their mechanized forces adapted for the uneven terrain of Nashik's ruins. Guerrilla squads slipped between collapsed buildings and crumbling highways, detonating explosives at chokepoints. Saboteurs, guided by weeks of reconnaissance, disrupted Imperial supply chains and left roads choked with burning wreckage.

At the front, Vihaan Chadra's armored column pressed ahead. From the turret of his vehicle, he watched plumes of fire climb the sky. The radio crackled as his voice barked orders.

"Sector three, push now! We take those anti-air batteries before their drones regroup!"

An explosion thundered in the distance. Smoke curled through the broken cityscape, the bodies of toppled drones littering the streets. But the price was steep. Every block seized came with casualties. Blood mingled with shattered concrete. Medics worked under the shelter of blasted walls, dragging the wounded from the wreckage. And yet, the momentum did not falter.

"Report from the east flank!" A British lieutenant's voice cracked through the bunker's stale air. "Indian mechanized units have breached the secondary trenches."

Tansley's mouth twisted, the grim confirmation tightening the lines across his face. "They're driving for the command hub."

Antonov's jaw clenched, his weathered hands gripping the edge of the steel console. The tactical display pulsed with red markers, enemy divisions converging like circling wolves. But even now, the Russian general's voice was steady.

"Then let them come."

Across the southern flank, Alexandra Baker's command post buzzed with urgency. The dim tent was thick with the glow of drone footage, satellite telemetry, and the endless chatter of exhausted scouts. Operators relayed coordinates and casualty reports, their fingers dancing across worn consoles. The weight of the battle pressed into the space like a storm cloud.

Alex's eyes traced the map, its shifting lines revealing the precarious balance of the front. Zhang's armored push had done its job; the Russians were reinforcing the west, pouring resources into a defense that was already cracking. The southern sector, weakened and exposed, now lay within her reach.

She didn't hesitate.

"Deploy the second wave," Alex ordered, her voice low but clear. "Chadra's forces have clearance to advance. And get our infiltrators in place."

A chorus of affirmations followed. On the map, faint green lights blinked to life, signals from the rebel sabotage teams now embedded deep behind enemy lines. Former Imperial engineers, Indian partisans, and hardened defectors emerged from the shadows of collapsed sewer tunnels and crumbling industrial ruins. They moved with lethal precision, relaying weaknesses in the Russian fortifications.

Minutes passed in tense silence. Then the first detonations shattered the air.

Explosions flared along the southern defenses, plumes of smoke curling into the ashen sky. Concrete walls buckled. Ammunition depots erupted in bright orange bursts. Cries of alarm echoed through the Russian comms, the once-disciplined ranks thrown into chaos.

Alex's comm crackled. Vihaan Chadra's voice, steady and resolute, broke through the static.

"We're moving."

And with that, the tide shifted.

Indian mechanized divisions roared forward, their tank treads grinding over scorched debris. The final remnants of Imperial barricades splintered beneath the assault. Farther to the north, Zhang's Chinese flanks expanded, like an iron vice closing in. For every shell the Russians managed to fire, two rebel artillery strikes answered. For every fortified position the Imperials attempted to hold, a swarm of Chinese drones forced another collapse.

But victory was still elusive. Even with the Russian lines faltering, Nashik loomed ahead, a wounded city clinging to the last remnants of Imperial pride. Smoke curled from shattered towers. Rubble choked the highways. The ruined skyline stood like a monument to defiance, Imperial banners clinging to skeletal towers, daring the storm to finish what it began.

And the defenders, though battered, were far from broken.

"Don't get comfortable," Alex muttered, more to herself than anyone else. "They're not done."

The hum of the command center carried on, the weight of what lay ahead unspoken.

The walls of Nashik trembled beneath the weight of the final assault. Columns of rebel tanks pushed relentlessly through the shattered remains of the southern gate, their turrets swiveling as they fired point-blank into the crumbling Imperial defenses. Smoke billowed in every direction, thick with the acrid stench of burning fuel and scorched metal.

Antonov's voice roared through the comms, but his orders were swallowed by the overwhelming tide of destruction. Russian artillery crews abandoned their guns as advancing rebel infantry breached the outer line. A final wave of explosions sent debris raining down like shrapnel, and the remaining Imperial banners that clung to the ruined city fluttered and burned.

"Sector Eight is lost!" A British officer's voice cracked through the comms, his panic barely restrained. "We can't hold the eastern corridor!"

Antonov's jaw clenched, his weathered face streaked with soot. "Pull them back! Cover the withdrawal!"

But there was no line left to hold. On every monitor, red markers representing the rebels swarmed the map, their momentum unstoppable. Vihaan Chadra's mechanized divisions crushed through the last remnants of the defensive barricades. Chinese drones still hovered high, raining precision strikes on any regrouping Imperial units. From the west, Indian and Pakistani irregulars swept into the exposed flanks, their banners gleaming amid the haze.

"General," Tansley's voice was low, bitter. "They've breached the command sector."

Antonov didn't respond at first. He watched as a section of the base's perimeter collapsed on-screen. The main bunker's steel plating turned inward with a deafening groan, the Russian insignia torn away in an instant.

"Evacuate," Antonov growled. "Fall back to Bombay."

The words felt like ash in his mouth.

Tansley nodded sharply, already issuing orders. The plan was clear. A staggered retreat, units peeling back in tight formations, offering cover as others escaped. Russian and British artillery would provide the last, desperate salvos. But there would be no illusions of victory. Only survival.

Outside the ruined city, the retreat began.

Imperial gunships roared low over the valley, their battered hulls gleaming in the smoke-filtered sunlight. Infantry columns scrambled over collapsed barricades, their uniforms caked in soot and grime. Engineers detonated whatever supplies remained, denying the rebels any spoils. Trucks packed with wounded rumbled eastward, kicking up clouds of ash as they sped away from the encroaching rebel forces.

Along the outer roads, Antonov's elite armored divisions formed a protective wall, their massive rail cannons still firing with mechanical precision. But even the most hardened crews could see the inevitable. Chinese drone swarms darted between the lumbering tanks, unleashing pinpoint strikes that sent fireballs into the sky.

Vihaan Chadra's voice echoed through the rebel command network. "Keep the pressure. Cut their lines. No mercy for the occupiers."

His forces obeyed. Indian and Pakistani regiments surged forward, their banners now planted along the scorched outskirts of Nashik. Cheers rang out through the rebel comms as the last Imperial defensive points collapsed. The city was theirs.

Yet the fighting would not end with Nashik.

Hours later, the Imperial retreat funneled into the outskirts of Bombay. The once-proud highway leading to the city had been hastily fortified, barricades of concrete slabs and overturned transports lined the road. Beyond the defensive lines, the city loomed beneath a sky tinged with the dim glow of distant fires.

The palace rose like a dark monolith in the center of it all. Thick columns of reinforced steel surrounded its polished facade, a final bastion of Imperial authority. Guards in gleaming black armor stood in formation beneath its towering gates. The crimson banners of the Empire still hung, though the dirt and soot streaked across their fabric told the truth of the war.

Antonov's convoy arrived at the command perimeter, its armored transports coated in grime. Tansley stepped out first, his once-immaculate uniform torn and bloodied. Imperial officers gathered near the gates, their expressions steeled but weary. Among them stood the remnants of the officer corps, men and women who had held the line until the bitter end.

The Imperial Guard, their presence unmistakable, formed a disciplined ring around the palace. Unlike the others, their armor gleamed without a trace of soot. The ceremonial gold trim caught the muted light, a symbol of defiance that stood in contrast to the chaos that surrounded them. Though they numbered nearly ten thousand, even they knew the truth.

Antonov stepped forward, his gaze fixed on the distant horizon where the smoke still twisted skyward. He said nothing at first. His officers waited, their eyes searching his face for resolve. But the Russian general knew words would bring no comfort now.

"We regroup," Antonov said finally, his voice cold. "We hold Bombay. Whatever comes next, we meet it here."

He turned toward the palace, the guards opening the massive gates as he passed. Inside, the corridors were lit by harsh fluorescent lights. The remnants of the war council awaited him.

And somewhere beyond the city walls, the rebellion gathered strength.

Chapter Forty

The Kremlin War Room, Moscow —Winter 2053

THE AIR INSIDE THE KREMLIN War Room hung thick with the hum of monitors and the acrid tang of stale coffee. Glowing arcs of troop movements illuminated the polished conference table, while distant missile launches and the chaotic sprawl of battlefield reports flickered across the walls. Russia's most senior generals sat in tense silence, their faces hardened by the weight of decisions already made. Every flash of light on the map was a reminder of the world they were about to break.

President Boris Aslanov stood at the head of the table, his sharp gray eyes scanning the digital battlefield. His once-dark hair had silvered with the strain of years at the helm, though the lines etched across his face seemed to speak less of age and more of resolve. There was no ceremony in the room, no grandeur to mask the grim calculations taking place. The only sound was the rhythmic tapping of fingers against polished wood, as aides input the final orders that would set Russia's betrayal in motion.

"The mobilization is complete," one of the generals reported, his voice low and steady. "Six armored divisions, four airborne, and full logistical support. The western corridor is prepared."

Aslanov's gaze remained fixed on the map, where crimson markers representing the Russian Home Guard stood in wait along the borders of Poland and Germany. German divisions, their forces stretched thin along the Alpine front, were still locked in combat. The offensive into Italy had demanded everything they could spare. Entire armored columns crawled through narrow mountain passes, their focus locked southward. Further west, French fleets lingered in the Mediterranean, their victory in the North Sea coming at the cost of exhaustion. The British, desperate after their collapse in India, had little left to offer. And in the East, Russia's forces remained whole.

"They still believe we stand with them," the general continued. "Our satellite feeds confirm their eastern defenses remain minimal. Regional garrisons. Old fortifications. The Germans think their back is secure."

A thin smile flickered at the edges of Aslanov's mouth, though it held no joy. "Then they are fools," he said.

The Kremlin had always viewed Germany's ambitions with a wary eye. Their rapid expansion, their bold offensive through the Alps, it was the arrogance of an Empire convinced of its own inevitability. Russia had played the part of an ally, its shipments of fuel and arms fueling the German advance, while quietly watching as the Empire weakened itself. Every day Germany bled for the peaks and ridges of northern Italy was another day their eastern flank grew vulnerable. Now, with British forces faltering and colonial rebellions igniting across the Empire's territories, Russia saw its moment. There would be no more patience. No diplomatic maneuvers. Only the certainty of steel and fire.

"And the Germans?" Aslanov asked, though the question was more for his own satisfaction than out of any uncertainty.

"They will know soon enough," the general replied, his voice void of illusion. "But by then, it will be too late."

The map flickered as the final confirmations arrived. From Belgorod to Smolensk, Russian columns rumbled to life. Tank divisions crawled westward through the dense forests, the massive war machines casting shadows beneath the morning sun. Hover trains carrying supplies by the hundreds. Overhead, squadrons of Su-57 fighters slipped into formation, their missile bays heavy with payloads. Military convoys blurred across the snowy plains, every movement following a preordained rhythm. Operation Volga was not simply a battle plan; it was a campaign of conquest.

The hum of servers deepened. A low chime echoed through the room. The order had been transmitted.

Aslanov said nothing at first. He let the silence linger, the weight of the decision settling over the gathered commanders. Russia's ambitions had been held at bay for long enough. Now, with the world's most powerful armies consumed elsewhere, the path was open.

"We won't get another chance," Aslanov said, his voice carrying the finality of a man who understood what victory would demand. "The Americans won't interfere. The British are collapsing. The French will scream, but they are too worried about a land attack. And the Germans..." He let the thought hang before he continued. "They will watch their country burn."

No one objected. The decision had already been sealed. Whatever feigned alliances once stood were now nothing more than forgotten words. Russia would reclaim what had long been denied. The Baltics. The heart of Poland. Germany.

And with that, the room fell into motion. Orders were relayed, encrypted signals pulsed through distant satellites, and across the Russian steppes, the war machine surged forward.

Central Mediterranean Sea, Near Sicily

The Mediterranean shimmered beneath the relentless midday sun, its vast blue expanse scattered with the dark silhouettes of warships. The French Navy, bolstered by its recent victories in the North Sea, had pushed south with ruthless determination. Now, sleek destroyers and missile frigates cut through the waves, their guns trained on the distant British fleet. Smoke lingered on the horizon where the first clashes had already begun, while fighter squadrons screeched overhead in tight formation. The air thrummed with the tension of imminent destruction.

Northern Italy and the Alpine Front

Yet for the German high command, it was not the sea that drew their focus, but the swift advance of their divisions in Italy. The campaign had gone almost as planned. German armor, supported by mechanized infantry and loitering combat drones, carved a steady path southward. Italian defenses crumbled beneath the sheer weight of the offensive. Abandoned towns lined the valleys, their streets scorched and empty. Resistance was sporadic, hastily assembled militia units, undertrained and outgunned, were no match for the disciplined German forces. Victory, it seemed, was merely days away.

Reports from the Alpine front confirmed as much. Major Lukas Ehrenthal's divisions had secured the critical passes, cutting off northern Italy's military supply routes. Every mile gained brought German forces closer to encircling the remaining Italian holdouts. Commanders exchanged clipped, confident updates. The Imperial banners of the British and German armies flew unchallenged along the northern ridges. Even the looming threat of French naval superiority did little to shake the belief that Italy would soon fall. The balance of the war, it seemed, had tipped in the Empire's favor.

But the illusion shattered in a single night.

Eastern Germany, Near Dresden Winter Morning, 2053

Major Lukas Ehrenthal stood ankle-deep in slush, staring down at what was left of the 14th Panzer Battalion.

Smoke rose from the wreckage, thick and oily, as if the earth itself had cracked open to scream. Dozens of armored vehicles lay twisted across the hillside. Some were still burning, others torn apart in perfect, surgical strikes. The field radios crackled with static and panicked voices. One begged for medics that would never come. Another screamed coordinates that no longer existed.

"Well, shit," whispered Captain Leonhardt beside him, his breath fogging in the cold. "They hit us with everything. We didn't even see it coming."

That was the part Ehrenthal couldn't understand.

His men had been dug in near Dresden for five days, preparing for a push to reinforce the Italian front. They'd run the drills. Checked every drone corridor. The Russians were supposed to be allies sent to help them in this final push.

But then the sky had gone dark with drones. Not the erratic, half-blind kind used by the Empire, but swarms. Coordinated, intelligent, surgical. Within minutes, their outer batteries had been silenced, communication lines severed, and half the command vehicles destroyed.

Ehrenthal wiped a smear of ash from his visor and stared across the valley where the Russian columns now moved without resistance. Tanks rolled in tight formation, their rails glowing with residual heat. No banners. No warning. Just steel and silence.

"They knew where to strike," he muttered, voice low. "Every comms node. Every forward fuel station. They knew our entire line."

Captain Leonhardt didn't reply.

From the ridge behind them, Sergeant Kirsch ran forward, helmet crooked, face pale with soot. "Sir," he barked, "Kampfgruppe Dietrich is gone. Air support never made it. Uplink's fried, and the west corridor's jammed with retreat traffic. Command wants us to fall back to Leipzig."

"Leipzig?" Ehrenthal blinked. "That's... two hundred kilometers west."

"Yes, sir. They say it's the only place we can mount a stand."

He almost laughed. But it caught in his throat like a blade.

Half their armor was already lost. Their drone crews were dead. Supply lines cut. Reinforcements? He knew better. The Empire's whole damned bulk was bleeding elsewhere. Charles couldn't spare so much as a rifle, let alone a battalion.

"No stand," Ehrenthal said flatly. "We don't hold. We run."

He turned toward the wrecked convoy behind them. One of the APCs was still mobile, engine coughing, rear hatch twisted. Inside lay the wounded—soldiers barely old enough to shave, their exosuits scorched and their helmets shattered.

He stepped inside, knelt by a boy with shrapnel in his shoulder. The soldier looked up, delirious, blinking blood from his lashes.

"Is it over?" he asked, voice barely audible.

Ehrenthal couldn't answer.

Behind them, another explosion rumbled across the field. A Russian artillery shell, precise and unhurried, tore into the hillside bunker they'd used as a forward listening post. Earth and flame shot skyward. A second shell followed, then a third. Patterns. Always patterns.

"Sir, we have to go," Leonhardt urged. "They're leapfrogging toward Dresden. We'll be cut off if we wait."

Ehrenthal looked once more at the field where his men had stood just hours ago.

Then he gave the order.

"Full retreat. Tell any unit left breathing to punch west. Forget the chain of command. Forget the maps. Just move."

They piled into the remaining transports, engines groaning as they lurched across churned mud and frozen asphalt. Snow flurries swept in from the northeast, veiling the burning wreckage of once-proud Imperial armor.

As the convoy rolled past a civilian junction, Ehrenthal saw a lone Imperial flag fluttering from a bombed-out school.

It looked absurd now. Empty. Like a lie told by a man already halfway through the gallows drop.

Berlin, Imperial German Headquarters

General Anna Wolff stood in the center of the command chamber, eyes locked on the holomap that showed red lines sweeping westward like blood in a glass of water.

"Where are the reserves?" she demanded. "Where are the bombers? Where is the Emperor's response?"

Silence.

An adjutant cleared his throat. "The Empire has nothing left to send. The French are redeploying to defend Marseilles."

"And Charles?"

"Recovering from the Nashik bombing. His war council is split. Half the Indian colonies are in revolt. There's... nothing."

General Wolff stared at the screen, hands clenched behind her back. Her officers stood in dead silence. The data was unrelenting. Dresden gone. Leipzig surrounded. Cologne and Hamburg marked in red. In the hallway outside the command chamber, the lights flickered once, then steadied, like a heart that wasn't sure if it still wanted to beat.

This wasn't a front collapsing.

This was an Empire falling.

CHAPTER FORTY-ONE

KING CHARLES WAS LIVID. "Traitorous wretch! How dare you!" The walls of the palace war room seemed to close in, the ornate gilded trim doing little to soften the oppressive weight of failure. Smoke curled lazily from the barrel of the King's revolver, its sharp scent mixing with the lingering odor of spilled blood. The Russian advisor's lifeless body slumped on the polished marble floor, a dark pool spreading beneath him, staining the immaculate stone. Servants and officers stood frozen along the edges of the chamber, their eyes darting between the corpse and the man who had killed him.

The King's chest heaved, his face flushed red with rage. The trembling in his hand betrayed the adrenaline still coursing through him, but his eyes remained locked on the massive screen that dominated the far wall. President Boris Aslanov's visage flickered against the black backdrop of the Kremlin's command chamber. The Russian leader's expression remained eerily calm, his posture unshaken by the violent outburst he had just witnessed.

"Russia must do what is best for Russia," Aslanov said, his words deliberate, unwavering. "Your palace will not hold forever, even with our support. We are prepared to offer you asylum."

The offer dripped with calculated pity. Aslanov's tone was that of a man who had already measured the King's worth, reduced him to a bargaining chip. The betrayal had been complete, not merely a military maneuver, but a carefully timed humiliation. Russia had held Britain's eastern flank for as long as it suited their interests. Now, with German defenses crumbling and the rebellion in India delivering blow after blow, Aslanov saw no further need to pretend at loyalty.

The King's lips curled, but no words came. His fury was too raw, too absolute. He could feel the eyes of his remaining ministers boring into him, waiting for his response. The chamber's elegant chandeliers swayed gently above, their crystals shimmering in the muted light. The absurd normalcy of it all only deepened the storm within him.

"We are not beaten," Charles finally growled, his voice thick with defiance. "This is a setback. Nothing more."

The hollow echo of the declaration lingered, unanswered. Even the distant hum of the palace's emergency generators seemed subdued, as if the walls themselves doubted his words. Aslanov's expression didn't change, though the faintest trace of amusement flickered at the corners of his mouth.

"A setback?" Aslanov repeated. "Your armies retreat from the Mediterranean. Your fleets burn. Your colonies are in revolt. And now, the Germans will fall without even a proper defense. There is no path forward, Your Majesty. Only the long shadow of what you have lost."

The words struck like a lash, but Charles refused to flinch. He felt the pulse of centuries coursing through his veins, the unyielding legacy of the Empire. His ancestors had stood firm through rebellions, wars, and betrayals. He would not be the one to break.

"You think you can lecture me?" he spat. "You, who play at honor while stabbing your allies in the back? Russia will choke on its own ambition. The Germans may falter, but your borders will bleed for it."

Aslanov's gaze remained steady. "Perhaps. But Russia will endure. And when your palace falls, as it will, we will not wait to pick through the ashes."

Charles stepped forward, his fists clenched so tightly his knuckles gleamed white. "You dare speak of my palace? This palace has stood longer than your republic has drawn breath. The Empire is not some crumbling state to be scavenged. We will rally. We will fight."

The screen dimmed slightly as the Russian president's image flickered, the transmission lagging ever so slightly. Yet even the distortion did not hide Aslanov's disdain.

"Fight, then," he said simply. "But know this, the world no longer trembles at the sight of your banners. The Empire is not eternal. It only seemed so, because no one had dared to prove otherwise. Until now."

And with that, the screen went dark.

General Cartwright, the most senior British officer remaining in the room, cleared his throat. His uniform was still immaculate, but his face was lined with the weight of grim recognition.

"Your Majesty," he said carefully. "We must prepare for what comes next."

Charles's eyes flicked toward him, still ablaze with fury. But beneath the anger, a bitter resolve took hold. The Empire's enemies may have struck with devastating force, but he would not cower. Not while a single ship bore the Union Jack. Not while the crown still rested upon his head.

"They believe this will break us," the King growled. "They believe we will kneel." He struck the table with his palm, the war maps trembling beneath the force. "But I am still King. And there are weapons in our arsenal that no rebellion, no Russian betrayal, can withstand."

The room remained silent. Cartwright's expression did not shift.

"The submarines are still in position," Charles continued, the thought settling into something dark and resolute. "The nuclear fleet. The codes remain intact. The Empire has held them in reserve for a moment such as this." His voice lowered, though it only seemed to gather in strength. "It is time the world remembers what it means to defy the Crown."

He spoke the words slowly, deliberately, letting them coil through the silence. The officers flinched, their hands tightening at their sides. But no one spoke. Only Cartwright dared to meet the King's gaze.

"Your Majesty," the general said, his voice even. "Nuclear deployment is no demonstration. It is annihilation."

"And what has the world given me?" Charles snapped. "Humiliation. Rebellion. Betrayal. If they will not submit to the rightful rule of the Empire, they will learn to fear it."

He turned, his finger jabbing toward the flickering digital map. "New York. Moscow. Rome." The names dripped from his tongue like a curse. "And if Bombay remains in rebel hands, then it burns. Let the ashes serve as their crown."

A murmur rippled through the officers, shock, disbelief. But still, none dared contradict him.

"Your Majesty," Cartwright tried again, his voice taut, "the fallout alone will cripple half the world. Our allies will turn against us. The Americans may strike in return. Moscow has its own arsenal, and the Russians will not hesitate."

"Good," the King spat. "Let them feel what it means to challenge us." His chest heaved, the tremor in his hands barely concealed. "Do you imagine they will hesitate to strike us when the time comes? No. But we will be first. We will show them the Empire's strength. We will end this war before they have the chance."

A silence deeper than before settled over the room. The chandeliers above swayed gently, their golden crystals casting fractured reflections across the bloodstained marble floor.

Then the King's eyes darkened further, his thoughts twisting toward something crueler.

"And the Russians here," he said, his voice low, like the first crack of a storm. "Every Russian soldier stationed near this palace, every one who dared to stand on our soil, thinking us weak, they die."

The officers stiffened. Cartwright said nothing, though a flash of alarm flickered across his otherwise stoic face.

"The Russian battalion remains garrisoned at the outer walls," the King continued. "They were our 'allies' in name, but no longer. They are spies, saboteurs. I will not have Aslanov's dogs watching as my palace stands on the brink." His eyes swept over his officers. "The Imperial Guard will carry out the order. Every Russian within the palace grounds is to be executed without mercy."

The silence grew unbearable. Even the hum of the emergency systems seemed distant, as if the chamber itself recoiled from what had been spoken.

Cartwright's jaw tightened. "Your Majesty, the Russian garrison is nearly our equal in number. Open conflict within the palace walls..."

"...will prove the strength of those loyal to me," the King cut in. "The Guard was forged for this very moment. I will not stand surrounded by traitors. They die tonight."

"But the consequences," Cartwright pressed, his voice low. "Even if we win, Aslanov will know. It will escalate—"

"It already has!" the King roared, his voice cracking. "This is not a time for cowards and diplomats. The Empire will never fall while I still breathe!"

The words echoed through the chamber, the finality of them cutting through any further protest. Charles' trembling hand gripped the edge of the table, but his eyes burned with resolve.

"Carry out the order," he commanded. "The Russians die. And the fleet prepares to launch."

The officers shifted uneasily, their fear now warring with obedience. Cartwright did not move. The King's gaze bore down on him.

"General," Charles said, his voice lowering dangerously, "do I need to repeat myself?"

Cartwright inclined his head, the slightest bow of deference. "No, Your Majesty."

The King's shoulders eased, though the storm within him did not subside. Without another word, he strode from the chamber, his footsteps ringing through the vaulted hall. The doors closed behind him, sealing the room in tense silence.

The body of the Russian advisor remained sprawled on the floor, the dark crimson stain spreading further across the marble. Cartwright's eyes lingered on it.

"Contact the Guard," he said, his voice steady, though the weight of what was to come pressed heavily against him. "They will be told to prepare for combat."

The officers murmured in acknowledgment, but Cartwright's mind was already turning. The King's paranoia had crossed a line. Ordering the deaths of Russian soldiers, soldiers who believed they had stood alongside the Empire, was not only madness, it was suicide. And the nuclear launch? That was the end of everything.

He turned to his aide. "Send word to the commanding officers outside the palace. Report only that internal threats have been identified. Do not mention the Russians. Do not escalate."

The aide's eyes widened. "Sir, the King, "

"The King is unwell," Cartwright said sharply, though he did not dare say more. "We follow orders. But we ensure the Guard moves cautiously. No one fires unless they are fired upon."

"And the fleet, sir?"

"Standard readiness only. Issue technical reports. Mechanical failures, maintenance delays. We'll keep the submarines tethered and the warheads inactive." He lowered his voice. "We are buying time. If the King cannot be reasoned with, we will find another way."

The aide hesitated, then nodded. As the officers dispersed, Cartwright remained, his gaze lingering on the dimmed map. The British red still clung stubbornly to the world's edges, though the Empire was no longer what it claimed to be.

"God help us," he murmured under his breath. "And may He save the Empire from its King."

The air was thick with the weight of anticipation. Around the palace grounds, the uneasy stillness of a city at war seeped into every shadow. Guards shifted in their posts, the gleaming stonework of the

Imperial compound reflecting the cold, metallic hum of surveillance drones overhead. The Union Jack still flew above the palace spires, but beneath it, loyalty had grown uncertain.

Through their comms, the British soldiers received the orders without flourish, vague, deliberate. "Prepare for an imminent threat. Reinforce positions. Stand ready." Not a word about the Russians. Not a hint of the truth. Only the demand for vigilance, wrapped in the cold language of protocol.

But the Russians had heard different orders.

Far from the polished marble and gold filigree, in dim bunker rooms and behind armored doors, President Aslanov's voice had already whispered through encrypted channels. His instructions were clear. "The King has lost his mind. The British will not stand with him. Do not wait. Strike first. Secure the palace."

The Russian officers had not questioned it. They knew the King well, a man who clung to power with trembling hands. They had stood in those same war rooms, felt the air grow thick with his desperation. Now, as the sun dipped behind the western ridge and the shadows of the palace walls darkened, they made their choice.

A sharp breeze stirred the air. Along the perimeter, the Russian garrison moved deliberately, their fingers resting just a little too lightly on the triggers of their rifles. The British Regulars, some uneasy and others oblivious, mirrored the tension. The King's Guard, clad in their distinctive dark armor, kept their watch in silence, a stoic line of figures standing shoulder to shoulder. Their loyalty was absolute.

But then the moment came.

A crack. The first shot echoed from the eastern side of the courtyard. No warning. No preamble. Just the violent report of a rifle.

It struck true, a British captain, mid-step, his body crumpling to the polished stone with a crimson spray. Shouts erupted as the Russian officer responsible turned, his weapon already raised to fire again. But the British were faster. A burst of gunfire tore through the air, and the Russian fell, twisting to the ground.

That was all it took.

The courtyard exploded into chaos. Russians turned on the closest man to them, sometimes an enemy, sometimes an unsuspecting ally. Soldiers grappled, blades flashing in the dark. The muffled crack of suppressed pistols mixed with the ragged sounds of fists colliding against armored bodies. Blood smeared the pristine stone, pooling in the cracks of the marble like ink bleeding into parchment.

Inside the palace, the King's Guard responded with ruthless precision. They had no doubts. No hesitation. They unleashed their weapons with practiced efficiency, driving back the Russian soldiers who had breached the outer halls. The echoes of gunfire roared through the corridors, ricocheting off the towering columns. Ornate tapestries trembled as the palace became a battlefield.

But the Russians had not come unprepared.

Outside the compound, the distant hum of drones filled the air. Like metallic vultures, they ascended in formation, a swarm of sleek, black forms illuminated only by the pulsing blue of their sensors. Russian officers, concealed beneath armored transport covers, barked commands in clipped tones.

"Identify targets. Sweep the grounds. Neutralize Imperial forces."

The drones obeyed. They darted low across the courtyards, their lenses scanning for Imperial heat signatures. British defense systems, still in confusion, hesitated to return fire. Some soldiers took cover, shouting in vain for clarity, while others fired blindly at the ominous silhouettes above. Every burst of tracer fire illuminated the night, casting erratic flashes of orange and gold.

Amid the turmoil, Russian and British alike fought with whatever weapons remained. Some discarded their rifles in the tight confines of the palace halls, knives and fists taking their place. Blood smeared the marble columns as soldiers slammed each other into the stone, the clash of combat reverberating through the grand chamber doors.

The King's Guard, augmented and clad in reinforced armor, moved like specters through the smoke. Enhanced by the most advanced combat systems in the Empire, their speed and strength made them formidable. Russian soldiers fell beneath their blows, but the numbers wore against them. Every corridor, every shattered doorway was a trap waiting to spring.

Outside, the garrison fought viciously. Russian troops, emboldened by Aslanov's orders, poured from fortified positions. For every drone the British managed to shoot down, two more rose to take its place. Fires licked at the edges of the courtyard walls, the ornate iron gates twisted and scorched.

And still, no clear victor emerged.

The King's madness had unleashed a storm of betrayal. Brother turned against brother. Soldiers who had once fought side by side now killed without hesitation.

Within the palace, the echoes of the King's voice still lingered. The orders he had given, "Kill them all."

But now, the blood staining the marble said otherwise. Neither side would emerge whole.

Vihaan sat on the edge of a crumbled wall, the jagged stones still warm from the day's fighting. Smoke curled lazily from the end of a thick cigar, its ember glowing faintly in the dim light. The distant silhouette of the palace loomed beyond the haze, its once-proud spires barely visible through the ashen sky. Fires still smoldered along the shattered perimeter, and the distant echoes of sporadic gunfire whispered from the ruins.

Beside him, Alexandra sat in silence. Her face was streaked with dust and sweat, but her eyes remained sharp, reflecting the faint glow of the embers. There was no need for words just yet. They both understood the weight of what was coming.

"I was thinking of my father," Vihaan said at last, his voice low. The words seemed to drift through the smoke, unhurried.

Alex didn't interrupt. She knew when to let the silence carry its own meaning.

"He was a man who believed in service," Vihaan continued, his gaze fixed on the distant palace. "Not just to the Crown, but to his city. Bombay was his life, every cracked street, every market, every family living in its shadows. He spent years on the Council, believing he could make things better. Believing that if he played by their rules, he could protect the people."

He took a slow draw from the cigar, the smoke curling upward like a lingering memory.

"I never questioned it. Not then. When they drafted me, I thought it was just part of that same duty. I thought I was carrying on what he believed in. But the Crown," Vihaan's jaw tightened. "The Crown doesn't reward loyalty. It uses it. It used him."

He paused, exhaling a thin stream of smoke. "I should've gone to art school. That's what I wanted. I used to dream of painting the streets of Bombay, the sun spilling gold over the market stalls, the fishermen along the harbor. I wanted to capture how the city felt, not how it looked."

Alex's gaze softened, the tension in her shoulders easing as she listened.

"But I traded it for a uniform," Vihaan said, his voice thick with bitterness. "And when my father spoke out, they didn't just punish him. They punished me. They sent me to the Solomon Islands, buried in the shadows of their nuclear stockpiles. Radiation burns on my hands. The stink of chemical waste. Every day, wondering if I'd be next."

His fingers traced the edge of the cigar, as though grounding himself in its rough texture.

"When my father died, they called him a traitor." Vihaan's voice trembled, though his eyes stayed locked on the distant palace. "They scrawled the word on his forehead like it could erase the decades he gave them. But I know the truth. He wasn't a traitor. He was the last honest man in their rotten halls."

A long pause followed. The words hung heavy in the air, settling like the ash that still drifted across the battlefield.

"I wish he could see this," Vihaan said softly. "I wish he could stand beside me now and watch that flag fall. I wish he could know that their lies didn't win. That we're still standing."

Alex reached over, her hand resting gently on his. "He'd be proud of you, Vihaan." Her voice was steady, but the emotion behind it was undeniable. "Not just for fighting. For surviving. For still believing in something when they tried to break you."

Vihaan nodded, though the ache in his chest remained. "We'll finish this," he said. "For him. For Bombay. For all of them."

The words settled between them, their resolve unspoken but understood.

Then, from the shadows, an aide stumbled toward them, his chest heaving as he fought for breath. His uniform was stained with dirt and sweat, the strain of the past hours evident.

"Sir," the aide panted, doubling over as he tried to catch his breath. "It's begun. The palace, the Russians and the King's Guard, they're fighting. Full-scale combat within the walls. Drones confirm it. Chaos."

Alex was already on her feet. "The King's turned on them," she said, more to herself than anyone. "He's lost control."

Vihaan's eyes burned with renewed determination. "The garrison?"

"Disorganized. Half their officers are dead. The rest are fighting or retreating. There's no clear command."

Vihaan didn't hesitate. He flicked the smoldering end of his cigar into the dirt, the embers scattering like dying stars. "We surge," he said, his voice low and certain. "Now."

The aide barely had time to nod before Vihaan turned to Alex. "Get the staggered waves moving. No delays. We hit every breach. Every wall. I'll lead the charge."

"Vihaan—"

"I have to," he cut in. "The King's Guard won't break easily. They'll fight to the last man. But they'll know who I am. They'll see me, and they'll know why we're here."

Alex held his gaze, the fire in her eyes mirroring his own. There was no use arguing. She understood the weight of this moment, and what it meant for Vihaan.

"Then I'll see you inside," she said firmly.

Without another word, Vihaan moved, his voice carrying across the rebel encampment. Orders spread like wildfire. Soldiers sprang into motion, weapons checked, armor strapped. The hum of drones overhead guided the sharpened tide of resistance.

And as Vihaan reached the front lines, the distant echoes of the palace still roared, the sound of a kingdom devouring itself.

Chapter Forty-Two

THE PALACE LOOMED AHEAD, VEILED in smoke and flame. Its alabaster walls, once pristine, were smeared with blackened streaks. The imperial banners still clung to the towers, though the Union Jack had begun to fray, its edges curling from the heat of the fires below. Beyond the gates, the sound of gunfire and the screams of the dying echoed through the night.

Vihaan stood at the head of the column, the grit of the scorched earth beneath his boots. The air was thick with the stench of cordite and burning fuel. Above them, the hum of rebel drones swept in relentless arcs, scanning the ground for hostile movements. But even the machines could not make sense of the chaos that awaited within the palace walls.

He adjusted the strap of his rifle, the weight of it familiar. This was no longer the boy who had dreamed of painting the harbor at sunrise. This was a man forged by the relentless crucible of war. And now, as the King's final redoubt trembled, Vihaan knew there was no turning back.

He raised his voice, cutting through the rumble of the distant artillery.

"We take the palace! No hesitation! No mercy!"

A chorus of affirmations followed, the rebel forces surging forward. Alex's staggered waves moved like a tide crashing against the embattled walls. Soldiers poured into the shattered outer gates, leaping over crumbled barricades and twisted wreckage. The distant palace guns roared in defiance, but already their fire had grown sporadic. The King's defenders were breaking.

Vihaan sprinted forward, his boots kicking up dust and fragments of stone. He could hear the rattling of distant machine gun nests and the whistle of mortars arcing overhead. The rebels returned fire in relentless bursts, hammering the enemy positions as they forced their way into the outer courtyard. Bodies lay strewn across the ruined marble, imperial uniforms soaked in blood. Some writhed, clutching at their wounds, while others lay unnervingly still.

Inside the courtyard, the King's Guard stood firm, the last remnants of Imperial might. Clad in advanced combat suits, their visors gleamed through the smoke. The augmented plating enhanced their strength, their movements impossibly fast. They fought without hesitation, the steel gleam of their rifles cutting through the night.

"Push!" Vihaan roared, his voice hoarse. "Break their line!"

He fired as he advanced, his rifle kicking hard against his shoulder. A King's Guard went down, the blast tearing through the seams of his armor. Another leapt into cover, returning fire with ruthless precision. Molten slugs sparked against the ancient stone columns. Rebel soldiers staggered and fell.

A grenade arced through the air, its trail glowing as it detonated just feet away. The force lifted Vihaan from his feet, slamming him hard into the broken ground. His ears rang, his vision blurred. But the pain was secondary. He staggered up, his hands trembling against the rifle's grip.

"General!" A lieutenant's voice cracked through the comms. "Left flank!"

He spun, just as a King's Guard soldier lunged forward, wielding a combat blade slick with blood. Vihaan ducked low, the blade missing his throat by inches. With a brutal shove, he rammed the butt of his rifle into the guard's helmet, the impact shattering the visor. The soldier crumpled, and Vihaan finished him with a single shot.

But the King's Guard did not break. More emerged from the smoke, their armor scorched but unrelenting. They fought with terrifying efficiency, their training evident in every motion. A rebel beside Vihaan collapsed with a gurgling cry, blood pooling beneath him.

Still, they pushed.

Vihaan's squad forced their way through the shattered archways, the palace doors blown from their hinges. The grand entrance hall lay in ruins. Marble statues toppled, crystal chandeliers shattered across the floor. Blood smeared the walls, mingling with the soot and smoke. The King's Guard retreated deeper into the labyrinth of the palace, drawing the rebels into claustrophobic corridors.

A memory flickered through Vihaan's mind, his father's voice, steady and certain, echoing in the chambers of his thoughts.

"The Crown doesn't reward loyalty. It uses it."

Rajan had stood in the same city, beneath the shadow of this palace, believing change could be reasoned into existence. He fought not with a rifle, but with words, words that were twisted against him, branded treason. The image of his father's lifeless body, marked with the Empire's final condemnation, burned behind Vihaan's eyes.

What would Rajan think of him now? Would he see a man fulfilling the promise of justice, or only another soldier consumed by the endless cycle of war? The blood on Vihaan's hands was no longer just the blood of his enemies, it was the blood of those who had followed him. Each fallen rebel weighed upon him, a silent judgment. And still, he pressed on.

"You deserved to see this," Vihaan whispered beneath his breath. "You deserved to see the Crown fall."

"Keep moving!" Vihaan commanded, his voice hoarse and raw. "We've got them!"

But the truth was grimmer than his words. There was no elegant advance, no clean strategy, only the relentless grind of bodies against bodies, steel against flesh. The rebels surged forward through the shattered palace corridors, their boots slipping on pools of blood that streaked the marble like crude brushstrokes. Every hallway was a gauntlet, every room a grave waiting to be filled.

The King's Guard fought like men who knew they had no future beyond these walls. They struck with vicious precision, their armored limbs snapping bones and crushing skulls with the brutal efficiency of machines.

A rebel to Vihaan's left was thrown against the gilded paneling, his scream cut short as a blade found his throat. Blood sprayed across the intricate gold filigree, staining the delicate patterns in a dark crimson bloom. The guard who killed him didn't hesitate, spinning to engage the next rebel in line.

Vihaan fired before the guard could land another blow. The rifle kicked hard against his shoulder, and the guard staggered, the force of the impact shattering his visor. But even through the jagged shards, the soldier's eyes burned with a terrifying resolve. He lunged.

Vihaan sidestepped, the swing of the guard's combat blade cutting the air where he had stood. Without thinking, Vihaan slammed the butt of his rifle into the exposed wound, the cracking of bone barely audible beneath the din. The guard faltered, and Vihaan drove him to the ground, a final shot silencing him.

The body twitched once, then went still.

There was no time to process. Another explosion rocked the hall, sending debris cascading from the ornate ceiling. Crystal fragments from the shattered chandeliers scattered like jagged stars. Smoke curled through the broken beams, the remnants of the once-grand palace reduced to a battlefield of choking ash and fire.

"Push through!" Vihaan shouted, the command barely audible over the clamor. "Stay on them!"

The rebels obeyed, storming the inner chambers with grim determination. There were no clean kills now. Only the desperate clash of combatants in confined spaces. Rifles emptied and discarded. Combat blades met with the shriek of metal on metal. The air was thick with the scent of gunpowder, sweat, and blood.

In the narrow corridors, the King's Guard fought without mercy. Vihaan caught glimpses of the carnage, rebels pinned against the walls, their bodies writhing beneath the crushing force of armored fists. Others stabbed and hacked with jagged bayonets, driving their blades into the gaps between the guards' plates, crimson seeping through the cracks.

Screams mingled with the constant thud of rifle fire. Blood smeared the polished marble beneath their feet, mingling with the dust and debris. The golden murals that once celebrated imperial conquests now bore the splattered remnants of the Empire's final battle.

Vihaan's own shoulder burned with every recoil of his weapon. His breath came in ragged gasps, the smoke clawing at his lungs. But still, he pressed forward.

"Vihaan, report!" Alex's voice cracked through the comms, urgent but steady. Even in the chaos, she commanded the battlefield with unrelenting focus. "Left wing is holding, but we need reinforcements in the south corridor. The King's Guard is digging in."

"Understood," Vihaan growled, wiping the sweat from his forehead with the back of his sleeve. "We're cutting through. Keep the pressure on."

Another blast shook the palace. The ancient columns groaned beneath the force, chunks of stone crashing down in clouds of dust. A rebel to Vihaan's right collapsed with a ragged cry, the shrapnel tearing through his side. His comrades pulled him to cover, but Vihaan couldn't linger.

Every step forward was earned in blood.

A King's Guard charged from the shadows, his combat suit flickering with the dull hum of energy shielding. Vihaan fired instinctively. The first shot struck the plating, sending a ripple of static across the armor. The second found its mark. The guard staggered, but it was not enough. He roared through his shattered helmet, lunging with terrifying speed.

Vihaan barely managed to sidestep, the guard's blade scraping along his arm, tearing the fabric and grazing skin. Pain flared, but Vihaan retaliated. He drove the butt of his rifle upward, catching the guard beneath the chin. The blow sent him stumbling, and Vihaan didn't hesitate, a single shot to the exposed throat. The guard crumpled.

There was no time to breathe. Another rebel fell. Then another. And still, the King's Guard did not yield.

"Vihaan!" Alex's voice broke through the comms again. "They're retreating to the throne room. You're nearly there, but watch for traps. The Guard will hold to the last man."

"Copy," Vihaan panted. "We end this."

He pushed forward, the weight of the moment pressing down upon him. The King's voice still echoed in his mind, the madness of a man clinging to a crumbling throne. But Vihaan did not falter. He could see the towering gilded doors of the throne room just beyond the smoke.

Then, in the chaos, Vihaan saw him.

A young rebel, barely more than a boy, lay sprawled against a toppled column. Blood seeped from his leg, pooling beneath him. His rifle had fallen from his trembling hands. A gash marred his face, and his eyes were wide with fear.

"Help me!" the boy gasped. "Please!"

Vihaan didn't hesitate.

"Cover me!" he barked, diving toward the wounded soldier. He slid across the marble, his knees striking hard as he reached the boy's side. Blood stained his hands as he pressed them against the wound, trying to stem the flow.

"You're alright," Vihaan murmured, though his own voice shook. "Stay with me."

The sounds of battle raged on. Explosions shook the palace. Gunfire ricocheted through the chambers. Vihaan barely registered it. The boy's ragged breathing filled his ears.

Then came the shot.

It punched into his shoulder, the force jerking him backward. The impact seared through him, white-hot and unrelenting. His vision swam. Pain bloomed like fire beneath his skin. He gritted his teeth, clutching at the wound. Blood slicked his fingers.

Through the haze, he saw the shooter, a King's Guard, rifle still raised. Another shot would follow. Vihaan knew it.

But he didn't move.

He twisted his body over the wounded soldier, shielding him. The boy's terrified eyes locked with his, the realization of what Vihaan had done dawning in that instant.

Vihaan's own rifle shook in his grip. He fired. Once. Twice. The guard staggered, sparks bursting from his armor. The third shot struck true, and the guard crumpled.

But Vihaan didn't stop. He fired again. And again. His teeth clenched, his shoulder burning with unbearable pain. His weapon clicked empty, but his trembling fingers pulled the trigger once more, nothing left.

The guard lay still. The sound of battle continued. But for Vihaan, the world had narrowed to the taste of iron in his mouth and the pulse of agony in his shoulder. He sagged against the marble, his breath ragged.

The wounded boy reached for him, his own bloodied hand trembling. Vihaan forced a weak smile, the corners of his lips barely lifting. "Just hold on," he whispered. "You're not done yet."

But as the shadows crept in, Vihaan's gaze drifted. The world blurred. And then, everything was still.

CHAPTER FORTY-THREE

THE WAR ROOM WAS DARK, its polished oak table illuminated only by the pale glow of flickering screens and red emergency lighting. King Charles stood alone. Cracks spidered across the ornate ceiling, dust falling in lazy streams. Occasionally, small chips of plaster fell, but the King noticed none of it. His trembling hands hovered over the console, the final, irreversible command waiting to be sent.

The words on the screen pulsed insistently:

AUTHORIZATION CONFIRMED. AWAITING SECONDARY CODE.

The submarine, somewhere beneath the Arctic waters, had received the King's order. Only one vessel had remained within range, its silent hull drifting under the ice. Every other submarine in the fleet had ignored the transmission, too far or unwilling. But this one obeyed. The command key had been turned. The missile hatches awaited their call.

The King's reflection stared back at him from the polished screen, a gaunt figure, sweat clinging to his brow. The sound of distant explosions filtered through the thick walls, but he did not turn. Even as the palace fell around him, his resolve remained.

"They will pay," he whispered, his voice ragged. "All of them."

Moscow. The heart of Russia. The seat of Aslanov's treachery. One strike would reduce it to ash, a testament to the Empire's final, terrible reach.

The console beeped.

SECONDARY AUTHORIZATION REQUIRED. INPUT NOW.

His fingers trembled over the keypad. The numbers were seared into his mind, the sequence engraved by years of drills and rehearsals. But even as his hands moved, a sickening awareness gripped him, the end had come. He no longer commanded the skies. His fleets burned. His armies shattered. The Russians and the rebels would flood his palace. And yet, this one act would ensure the world never forgot the power of the Empire.

The King clenched his jaw. His index finger hovered over the first digit.

But then, the comm unit crackled.

"Your Majesty," a trembling voice broke through the static. "We've lost contact with the outer gates. Rebel forces are within the palace walls. They're advancing on the throne room. Sir—"

A burst of gunfire drowned the voice. Then silence.

The King's eyes flickered. The tremor in his hand grew. He glanced to the door, half-expecting it to burst open. Sweat trickled down his temple. Still, the screen blinked.

SECONDARY AUTHORIZATION REQUIRED.

He grit his teeth. One more command. One more step.

But the booming echoes of heavy footsteps pulled him away. The sound of combat swelled, close, too close. The corridors beyond the war room were alive with shouting. Then, a voice through the comms, sharp and commanding:

"This is General Cartwright. The rebels have breached the eastern wing. The King's Guard is in full retreat. Your Majesty—"

Static swallowed the rest.

The King swore, slamming his fist against the console. The screen flashed in protest, but the prompt remained a second longer before COMMAND ABORTED appeared on the screen.

He turned back to it, but the door shuddered. Voices roared from the other side. Heavy gunfire erupted, and then, a violent silence. The King staggered backward, his heart pounding. The sound of metal scraping against stone filled the chamber as the locking mechanism failed.

And then the door burst open.

Alexandra stormed into the war room, the muzzle of her rifle sweeping the shadows. Behind her, rebel soldiers flooded in, their boots crunching over debris and glass. Smoke drifted through the shattered archway. The King stumbled backward, his hands raised slightly, though his eyes burned with furious defiance.

"Hold your fire," Alex ordered, her voice steady. She lowered her rifle, though her finger hovered near the trigger. The King's gaze flicked between her and the line of soldiers, his chest heaving.

"So it comes to this," he spat, his voice low. "You wear the mask of justice, but you are nothing more than a traitor. A pawn."

"You're the only traitor here," Alex replied, stepping forward. "We intercepted the order. Your submarine. Moscow. How many millions would you have killed just to make a point?"

The King's eyes narrowed. "A point? You think this was only about vengeance? The world needed to see the Empire's strength. If we fall, we fall as gods, not as men."

"No," Alex said coldly. "You fall as a coward."

Behind her, one of the soldiers ripped the King's insignia from his uniform. The embroidered lion and crown crumpled in the soldier's fist. The King flinched, but did not lower his gaze.

"The throne room," Alex said, motioning to her soldiers. "We're taking him there."

The King's head remained high, but the illusion of power had crumbled. The Empire that once stood behind him was gone.

The rebels wasted no time. A technician in patched fatigues dragged a portable broadcast unit into the chamber, its blinking sensors humming as it locked onto Alexandra. The drone, weathered from months of combat, hovered unsteadily, but its lens remained fixed on her, transmitting the moment to a world still holding its breath.

"We're live." The technician's voice was low, almost reverent.

Alex stepped forward, the bloodstained marble beneath her boots a grim reminder of the cost of this moment. The Empire's strength had never been absolute. It had been fear, polished and gilded, passed down through the generations. And now, the world would watch as that fear crumbled.

"My name is Alexandra Baker," she began, her voice steady, though the weight of it shook through her chest. "I stand in the heart of what was once the British Empire. Behind me, the throne that commanded nations. The walls that bore witness to conquests and coronations. And now, to its final reckoning."

The King's glare never wavered, though the flicker of shame beneath his facade was unmistakable.

"For centuries, the Empire ruled through force and fear. It burned cities, enslaved nations, and silenced those who dared to defy it. It called its victories peace and its tyranny order. But today, the people have spoken. Today, the Empire falls."

She turned, the camera capturing the shattered grandeur of the throne room. Blood streaked the once-pristine columns, the tattered banners hanging like the ghosts of forgotten pride. The rebels stood shoulder to shoulder, their rifles lowered, but their resolve unbroken.

"To those who fought," Alex continued, her gaze unwavering. "To those who fell. To those who dared to believe in a world without kings, this victory is yours. But it is not the end. The Empire's chains are broken, but now we face the task of rebuilding. Not through fear. Not through domination. But through justice."

The camera lingered on the King once more. No throne awaited him now. Only judgment.

"The era of monarchs is over," Alex declared. "The people will decide what comes next."

She stepped back, the broadcast capturing the full weight of her words. And across the world, in occupied cities and liberated towns, in the depths of prison camps and the ruins of once-great capitals, the people saw what had once seemed impossible.

The throne room, once the jewel of the Empire, was in ruin. Stained glass windows had shattered, casting jagged shards across the marble floor. The towering columns bore the scars of gunfire, the gilded walls smeared with soot and blood. The Union Jack, still hanging above the grand dais, swayed gently in the smoke-choked air.

Alex stood before the throne, the King leaning against it.

She leaned closer to the King, her voice lowering. "You are just a man."

A long silence followed. Then the King's lips curled into a bitter sneer.

"You think you've won."

"I know we have," Alex replied.

The camera held steady. The world was watching.

There was nothing but rage, exhausted, consuming rage, in the King's eyes. It burned through the ruin of the throne room, gleaming with the weight of betrayal and defeat. His face, once proud and composed, twisted into something hollow. The echoes of Alexandra's words still lingered in the air, but it wasn't her voice he heard. "The Empire is not eternal. It never was. You hold it together with fear and force. But even the mightiest walls will crumble when the people no longer believe in them."

Frederick's words, once scorned and dismissed, now rang with cruel clarity. The King had branded his brother a coward, a traitor to the Crown. But it was Frederick who had seen the truth, a truth the King had refused to face. The Empire was never carved from stone. It was built from the trembling hands of those who feared it. It endured not by right, but by submission. And the moment that fear was shattered, the whole fragile edifice collapsed.

The weight of it crushed him. The grandeur of the chamber had faded into smoke and ruin. The golden lion banners, once symbols of unquestioned dominance, now hung in tatters. Blood smeared the intricate carvings of oak and stone. The bodies of his fallen guards lay scattered, their polished armor stained with dirt and soot. And the great throne, his throne, loomed behind him, untouched but meaningless.

"You think you've won," he spat, his voice low, rasping. "But you've done nothing but invite chaos. The wolves will feast. The world will tear itself apart without the Crown."

"Then let it," Alexandra replied coldly. "Better chaos than chains."

The King's lips curled into a sneer, but there was no strength left in it. Only bitterness. Only the remnants of a man who had built his life upon the illusion of power.

And now, the illusion was gone.

The camera drone hovered silently, broadcasting every flicker of his expression to the world. Millions were watching, rebels, loyalists, the uncertain masses. The King's humiliation was complete.

But the rage did not subside.

Slowly, he straightened, his eyes narrowing. There was no tremor in his hands, no faltering in his resolve. His breath steadied. His shoulders squared. Even in defeat, he clung to what dignity remained, the belief that he would dictate his own fate.

Then, in one swift motion, he reached beneath his tattered robe.

The guards tensed, rifles snapping into position. Alexandra's eyes widened, but it was already too late. The glint of polished steel flashed in the dim light, the unmistakable gleam of a revolver.

The King's fingers curled around the worn grip, the weapon trembling only slightly. An heirloom, passed from king to king. The lion crest, still etched upon its barrel, was the last vestige of a blood-soaked legacy.

For the briefest moment, the world seemed to hold its breath.

But the King did not hesitate.

Before a single voice could rise, before the guards could shout their warnings, he pressed the barrel firmly to his temple.

His gaze locked with Alexandra's, and in it, there was no plea. No fear. Only the desperate resolve of a man who refused to let history judge him.

The gunshot shattered the silence.

A single crack. A plume of smoke. The sound echoed through the throne room, mingling with the distant roar of battle.

King Charles III, King of the British Empire, Lord Protector of the Americas, Conqueror of India, and Master of the Western World, was dead.

The body crumpled to the marble floor, the crimson stain spreading slowly beneath him. The crown had long since fallen, but now, so had the man who wore it.

For a moment, no one spoke. The camera drone hovered motionless, capturing the final image of the fallen king. The rebels stood frozen, their weapons lowered. Even the distant hum of comm chatter seemed to fade, as though the world itself was holding its breath.

Alexandra's eyes remained fixed on the body. She felt no triumph. No satisfaction. Only the weight of the moment, the irrevocable truth that the Empire's last sovereign had met his end by his own hand.

The war was over. But the echoes of its consequences had only just begun. With a steadying breath, Alex turned toward the camera. The world was still watching. And now, it would demand to know what came next.

CHAPTER FORTY-FOUR

THE AIR WITHIN THE TEMPORARY command room was stifling. The remnants of the Imperial palace, still smoldering in the aftermath of battle, stood as a fractured monument to a world that no longer existed.

Alexandra Baker leaned over the scarred table, her hands splayed across the maps and documents that detailed the fall of the Empire. The war had been won. The king was dead. But now came the harder part, deciding what would rise from the ashes.

Andrew Greg paced near the balcony, the humid air from the Arabian Sea carrying the distant murmur of the city. The people were celebrating. Flags of rebellion waved from shattered windows, and the songs of liberation echoed through the streets. But victory was not governance. And for all their triumph, the world was still uncertain.

The Duke of Canada sat silently, his posture stiff. His resemblance to Charles was striking, the same sharp nose, the same pale eyes that once gleamed with imperial pride. But there was no pride in him now. Only exhaustion.

"You don't have a choice," Greg said finally, his voice low but firm. "The people need stability. They need to know the fighting is over."

The Duke's jaw tightened. "They need freedom. Not another monarch."

Alex didn't argue. "No one's asking you to rule. They're asking you to hold the pieces together while the world decides what comes next."

The Duke's hands remained clasped, his knuckles whitening as the weight of the decision lingered. The shadows of the war room wrapped around them, the dim glow of the overhead lights casting a harsh contrast against the scorched walls. Through the cracked windows, the smoke from the still-burning outer districts curled lazily into the night.

He shook his head again, though his voice held less certainty than before. "I renounced my claim. Years ago. I walked away from all of it. What legitimacy do I have?"

"More than any other," Greg countered. His voice was calm, but the slight tilt of his head betrayed the quiet insistence beneath it. "You're not your father. You stood against him when it mattered. That means something."

The Duke's gaze flicked between them, searching for any sign of deceit. But there was none. Greg and Alex had no love for the monarchy, that much was clear. Yet their appeal was not about crowns or tradition. It was about necessity.

Alex shifted slightly, the leather of her jacket creaking. Her arms were crossed, but the tension in her shoulders was unmistakable. "The alternative is chaos," she said, her words low, steady. "Every colony, every territory, they'll declare their own governments, but without structure, it'll descend into regional conflict. You don't have to lead forever. You don't even have to lead for long. Just long enough to oversee the transition."

He wanted to argue. She could see it in the flicker of resistance behind his eyes. But the truth had already begun to sink its teeth into him. Whatever resentment or shame the Duke carried, it didn't outweigh the reality that the Empire was gone, and something had to follow.

"Isn't that what your father believed?" Alex added quietly. "That power was the only thing holding it all together?"

The words hit their mark. The Duke's jaw tightened, but his silence spoke louder than any retort.

A breeze stirred through the broken window, tugging at the worn curtains that still clung stubbornly to their rails. The sound of the city below, restless and uncertain, hummed through the air. People celebrated in the streets, but victory alone would not rebuild the world.

"And after that?" The Duke's voice dropped, barely above a whisper. "After the treaties are signed and the Empire is gone?"

"You walk away," Greg said simply. "For good."

The simplicity of the answer seemed to rattle him. The notion of wielding power without seeking to keep it was a concept foreign to men like his father. But Greg's words held no malice, only resolve. There was nothing left to conquer. Only the ruins to tend to.

The Duke's gaze lingered on Greg, but eventually shifted to Alex. Her eyes held the same conviction, though something else stirred beneath the surface. She understood what they were asking of him, and perhaps even understood the burden better than she cared to admit.

"Look," Greg continued, his voice gentler now. "You don't have to do this alone. We're not putting the crown on your head and walking away. Every decision, every treaty, you'll have counsel. From the Commonwealth. From us. You'll have time to put things right."

"And then you're free," Alex added. "Truly free."

The Duke's hands curled into fists once more, but this time it was not with defiance. The fight had left him. He closed his eyes, and for a moment the room was silent. Only the hum of distant generators and the distant crackle of ruined stone shifting beyond the palace walls remained.

Then, slowly, he nodded.

The tension in the air didn't vanish, but something shifted. Greg stepped back, exhaling as though he'd been holding his breath. Alex didn't move, her gaze still fixed on the Duke, searching for any trace of regret. But there was none. Only resignation.

"You won't regret this," Greg said, though the assurance seemed as much for himself as for the Duke.

The Duke scoffed softly, though there was no humor in it. "That remains to be seen."

"Then we'll make sure you don't," Greg replied. He reached for the comms unit resting on the table. "I'll inform the council. They'll begin drafting the terms for the Commonwealth transition. And the declaration, it'll need to be official."

The Duke gave a brief nod, but his gaze didn't leave Alex.

"You were in the throne room," he said quietly. "When my father..." He trailed off, unwilling to finish the thought.

"I was," Alex answered.

The Duke studied her, the shadows beneath his eyes deepening. "You didn't stop him."

"No," she replied, her voice steady. "But I made sure the world saw how it ended."

A flicker of something passed through the Duke's expression, perhaps understanding, perhaps resentment. "And now you're asking me to stand where he fell."

"We're asking you to stand so no one else has to," Greg said firmly.

Another silence passed. The Duke nodded once more, but the strain in his posture remained.

Alex turned toward the door, though the heavy atmosphere lingered behind her. Greg followed, though not before giving the Duke a parting glance.

"You won't be alone in this," Greg said. "And you'll never be your father."

The Duke didn't reply.

Outside, the night air was thick, though the heat had finally begun to subside. The distant sounds of celebration still echoed through the streets. Alex walked ahead, her steps brisk and determined. Greg caught up quickly, his stride falling in line with hers.

"You think he'll go through with it?" Greg asked.

Alex didn't answer right away. She kept her eyes ahead, watching as the fractured skyline of Bombay loomed over the remnants of the palace. "He will," she said finally. "He doesn't want the crown. That's exactly why he'll take it."

Greg nodded, though the tension in his shoulders hadn't eased. "And when it's done?"

Alex's jaw tightened. "Then we see what the world decides for itself."

The question hung between them, unspoken. What role would they play when the last embers of the Empire's rule finally burned out? For now, it didn't matter. The fight wasn't over, not yet.

Greg's shoulder brushed against Alex's as they continued down the narrow street, the proximity lingering longer than necessary. The contact was slight, almost accidental, the kind of fleeting touch that could be dismissed without a second thought. But neither of them acknowledged it. Neither of them pulled away.

It was a strange comfort, the closeness. For months, their bodies had known only tension, bracing for the next explosion, the next ambush, the next loss. Now, with the fighting over and the rebellion's victory secured, the absence of immediate danger left them untethered. The silence was deafening. Even the distant echoes of celebration couldn't fill the space that war had carved inside them. And yet, here in the quiet, the warmth of Greg's shoulder against hers was something solid, something that didn't demand explanation.

Greg's hand brushed the edge of his coat, absently tracing the patch that once bore his rank. There was no longer an army to command, no orders to give. Just rubble and questions. But next to Alex, the weight of uncertainty felt less unbearable.

"Get some rest," Greg said quietly, though the words felt hollow. His eyes held the truth that neither of them would. Not yet. The adrenaline of victory was fading, but sleep would remain elusive. The ghosts of the fallen still lingered, and the weight of what came next pressed down like a storm cloud.

"You too," Alex murmured, though her voice too lacked conviction. She didn't move. Neither did he.

The dim glow of the city framed their silhouettes, fractured glass reflecting the fires that still burned in the distance. Alex's gaze flickered toward the ruined skyline, her jaw tightening as if bracing herself. Greg knew that look. The resolve. The unwillingness to admit how much it hurt. He'd worn it often enough himself.

"You don't have to keep carrying all of it," he said, the words escaping before he could stop them.

Alex's brow furrowed, though she didn't look at him. "Carrying what?"

Greg's voice softened. "Everything."

For a moment, she said nothing. The breeze stirred her hair, and the shadows played across the sharp angles of her face. She was the face of the rebellion now, the hero who had stood in the palace while the King's final act stained the marble floor. But Greg saw beyond the image. He saw the exhaustion she tried to bury. The guilt she masked behind every decisive command. The grief that settled in the lines around her eyes.

"I'm not the only one," she finally replied, her voice barely above a whisper. "We all carry it."

Greg held her gaze. "Yeah. But you don't have to carry it alone."

The words lingered between them, unspoken meaning threading through the silence. There had been moments like this before, fleeting glances across command tents, brief exchanges on bloodied battlefields. But war had given them no space for anything more. Only duty. Only survival.

But now?

Alex's lips parted, as though she might respond, but the words caught. Instead, she nodded once, a small, fractured movement. Greg didn't press. He simply stood beside her, their shoulders brushing once more.

"We should head back," she said eventually, her voice steadier now. "There's too much left to do."

Greg nodded. "Yeah."

But neither of them moved.

The closeness lingered, a quiet understanding passing between them. The war was over, but something else was beginning. Neither of them were ready to name it. Not yet.

But they weren't running from it either. Not anymore.

The Duke of Canada sat alone, the dim lamplight casting long shadows across the cracked walls of the room. It had once been a guest chamber in the palace, reserved for visiting dignitaries and favored ministers. Now, the torn velvet curtains and scorched wallpaper stood as a testament to the rebellion's final siege. There was no comfort here, but comfort was the last thing he wanted.

A small desk, salvaged from the wreckage, bore the weight of scattered documents, declarations of surrender, transition agreements, diplomatic overtures. The ink was still fresh, as if the words might disappear the moment he turned away. At the corner of the desk sat the only object that held his attention. A faded holograph, stained with the smoke of battle.

Vihaan stood at the center of it, his smile unguarded. It had been taken during the early days of their uneasy alliance, back when the fragile lines between enemy and friend had begun to blur. The sun had been setting over the makeshift command post, washing the desert sands in amber light. Vihaan had laughed, some remark about the absurdity of it all, a prince and a rebel, standing side by side.

The Duke traced the corner of the base with his thumb. He missed that laugh. He missed the way Vihaan had challenged him, without malice or condescension. He had been a man of conviction, so unlike the hollow courtiers the Duke had grown up surrounded by.

They had called each other brothers in the end. Not in blood, but in understanding. And now Vihaan was gone.

The thought twisted inside him, bitter and sharp. His father's death had not struck him like this. There had been no grief when Charles had fallen, only the cold certainty that the world was better without him. But Vihaan's loss was different. It was a loss that stripped away the false promises of the crown. Without Vihaan, the victory felt thin, almost meaningless.

The Duke stood abruptly, pacing the narrow room. His boots echoed against the cracked marble floor. The walls felt closer now, the air thick with the weight of decisions not yet made.

The Duke thought of the others. The royal family had been scattered in the final days of the war. Some fled to the furthest reaches of the Commonwealth, clutching at crumbling titles like lifelines. Others were not so fortunate. Reports of imprisonment filtered in from across the globe. Distant cousins, lesser nobility, second sons, all deemed enemies of the people.

And then there were the rumors. Executions carried out in the name of justice. Revolutions demanding blood. Every victory seemed to demand a reckoning, and the sins of the Empire were vast.

It wasn't only guilt that gnawed at him. He had grown up among them, the uncles who traded stories over brandy in rooms gilded with imperial pride, the distant cousins who danced at state balls and smirked through debates in parliament. Some were fools, others were cruel, but most had simply been swept along by the current of the Empire, believing the world owed them deference because it always had.

Now the world was repaying its debts.

The Duke had seen the headlines. Governor-Generals dragged from their estates, their coats torn from their backs. Dukes and Viscounts placed in makeshift tribunals, their names read like a ledger of crimes. Some were given a day's trial, others none at all. Colonial governors who had enforced the Empire's policies with ruthless efficiency now stood before crowds demanding retribution. For the people who had suffered under the weight of those policies, justice was swift.

But justice, the Duke knew, was rarely clean. Not every name on those lists belonged to monsters. There were those who had served the Empire without cruelty, believing in its promise of order and stability.

They were guilty, perhaps, of complacency. Of cowardice. But was that enough to condemn them? The courts seemed to think so.

Some had fled in the chaos, their ships vanishing into the Atlantic under assumed names. Others never made it to the sea. The courts moved swiftly, the sentences growing harsher with each passing day. And for those who shared his name, the ones who had worn their titles like armor, there would be no mercy.

He could still hear his father's voice, etched into memory. "We are the stewards of civilization." It had been the King's most enduring belief, that without the firm hand of the monarchy, the world would crumble into chaos. Now that hand was severed, and the chaos his father feared was spilling across the map.

But what his father never understood was that the people weren't tearing the world apart for the sake of destruction. They were trying to rebuild it. The question was whether they would succeed before the weight of vengeance consumed them.

The Duke's stomach tightened. Some of those condemned had stood at his father's side, their loyalty unwavering. Others had been distant figures at endless banquets and parades, their laughter mixing with the clink of crystal glasses. And some had been friends.

That truth was the hardest to swallow. He had known the sons and daughters of colonial governors, the ones who hadn't wielded power themselves, but had benefited from it. He had dined with them, hunted with them, shared careless jokes about politics none of them truly understood. They had never questioned the Empire's foundations because they had never needed to. And now, stripped of their titles, they were learning the cost of ignorance.

He did not know if they deserved forgiveness. But he knew that the world was no longer offering it.

The Duke's hand curled into a fist, the pressure grounding him. His own survival had been a matter of circumstance. The rebellion did not see him as a threat, not yet. They wanted him to stand as a symbol, a transitional figure until the dust settled. But that did not mean he would be spared forever.

He thought of the courts. The hastily assembled tribunals. The accusations and condemnations. Collaboration. Complicity. Crimes of the Empire. Words that carried the weight of lifetimes. The Duke had no illusions. The moment his usefulness faded, the same judgment could fall upon him.

Vihaan would have known what to say. He would have reminded the Duke that survival was not the same as absolution. That this, the fragile peace, the tentative alliances, was the only way to honor the dead. The people weren't asking for a king. They were asking for time. Time to build something new. Time to ensure that when the fires finally died, the shadows they cast wouldn't claim what remained.

The Duke ran a hand through his hair, the weight of it all pressing down. They wanted him to wear the crown. Not as a king in power, but as a figurehead. A symbol to ease the transition and stave off further collapse. It was a burden he had sworn to reject, but now there was no one else.

He saw his father's face in the shadows. The clipped commands, the bitter sermons of duty and divine right. He remembered the cold judgment in the King's eyes when he had renounced his claim. Weakness. That's what his father had called it. To Charles, the monarchy was never a burden. It was a weapon. One to be wielded without hesitation.

But the Duke was not his father.

At the window, the distant city was still smoldering under the pale sky. The fires had burned out, but the smoke lingered, with the haze of construction, clinging to the ruins like a bitter memory. In the streets below, columns of vehicles moved through the rubble, armored personnel carriers repurposed for aid, supply convoys bearing the flags of India, Pakistan, and China. What had once been a city under imperial occupation was now the pulsing heart of an uncertain peace.

He watched the soldiers who guarded the perimeter, their uniforms bearing no single allegiance. The South Asian Union's green banners fluttered alongside the red of the Chinese peacekeeping forces. Pakistani and Indian troops, barely distinguishable in their fatigues, stood side by side. A year ago, they would have faced each other as possible enemies, both subjects of the Empire but still rivals of culture and history. Now, they patrolled together, weapons slung low, wary not of each other, but of the fragility of what they had won.

The Duke's jaw tightened. There had been no time for mourning. Even as Vihaan's body was carried from the palace, the machinery of victory had churned onward. India's declaration of independence had echoed through the shattered streets. Pakistan's followed, a swift and resolute proclamation that swept aside decades of distrust. Their leaders, bloodied but unbroken, had stood together before the world, pledging unity in the face of a shared past.

Vihaan had believed that moment would come. The Duke wished he could believe it would last.

A knock at the door broke the silence. One of the aides entered, bowing slightly. "Your Grace, the South Asian delegation has arrived."

The Duke nodded stiffly. The title still stung. Your Grace. It belonged to another man, to a family that had wielded it like a weapon. But that man was dead, and the family was shattered. What remained was only a name. A relic, held in place until the world no longer needed it.

"I'll be there shortly."

The aide hesitated. "And the press? They're expecting a statement."

He could already see it. The reporters, the cameras, the hollow questions. They would ask him about the future. About reconciliation. About justice. And the Duke would give them the answers they needed to hear.

But not yet.

He turned back to the window, the smoke still rising in the distance. Somewhere beyond that haze, India and Pakistan stood side by side. The Union they had built was no longer a dream. It was real, forged in defiance of the Empire's legacy.

And so must be the rest.

He straightened, his breath steadying. The weight remained, but now it felt different. No crown would lift it. No title would change it. The burden would stay with him until his task was done. Vihaan's memory demanded nothing less.

CHAPTER FORTY-FIVE

THE CAMERAS WERE READY. Their small red lights blinked patiently in the dim broadcast chamber, waiting for the signal. Beyond the fractured walls of the hastily restored studio, the world was watching. From the scarred cities of India and Pakistan to the uneasy chambers of European city halls, from the rebel-held streets of New York to the distant islands of the Pacific and the sub-continent of Africa, the Duke's words would reach them all.

The air inside the chamber was stifling, thick with the weight of anticipation. A makeshift flag of white linen, bearing no symbol, hung against the cracked wall behind him. There was no throne, no polished marble, no golden tapestries. Only the hollow remnants of what had once been the beating heart of the Empire. The shattered grandeur of the palace now served as a monument to what had been lost.

But this speech was not about loss.

A cracked desk stood in place of a podium, its surface scuffed and bare, lit only by the cold glare of the camera lights. The setting had not been chosen by accident. Every chipped edge, every shadow on the crumbling walls behind it, spoke of the cost of power. And no one understood the weight of that message more than Alexandra Baker.

She stood just beyond the frame, arms crossed, her sharp gaze locked on the Duke. The past few days had been relentless, the final battle not fought with guns and artillery, but with words. Draft after draft of the speech had passed through her hands, each syllable dissected and rebuilt. She wielded language like a weapon, with the precision of a strategist and the conviction of a revolutionary. The words Edward would speak were his to carry, but they were undeniably hers in spirit. Every phrase was sharpened to slice through the remnants of the Empire's illusion. Every pause was calculated to linger in the minds of those who still clung to the old world.

Alex had no delusions about the power of rhetoric. She knew the right words could move nations, stir rebellion, and topple monarchs. History had proven that. The pamphlets of Thomas Paine had ignited the fires of American independence. The declarations of men like Jefferson had shaped republics from the ruins of tyranny. Now, it was her turn. But where those men had called for freedom against distant crowns, she was speaking to the fractured heart of an Empire in its death throes. This was not just a statement of intent, it was the creation of a new reality.

There was no room for vanity in her work. Every sentence bore the weight of expectation. The rebels in the bombed-out remains of New York would hear Edward's voice and judge whether the revolution had truly won. The families of the fallen in India and Pakistan would listen for proof that their sacrifices were not in vain. In the Pacific, in Africa, in the Middle East, those who had endured under the Empire's boot would demand more than promises. They would demand acknowledgment, justice, and the assurance that the world would not simply trade one oppressor for another.

Alex had given Edward the words to deliver all of that. Words that would offer a path forward while making it impossible for the world to return to what it was. But words alone were not enough. She needed Edward to believe them. To embody them. For the speech to matter, it could not be spoken as a tired concession. It had to be a proclamation, the sound of a world breaking free.

A lesser man might falter beneath the burden. But Edward had agreed to stand before the world, to declare the end of his father's Empire. That, at least, she respected.

Off-camera, the red recording light blinked steadily. The time had come.

Alex's jaw tightened. Her arms uncrossed, fingers brushing against the cool fabric of her sleeve. There was nothing more she could do. The words were his now. But if they were enough, the Empire's last act would not be written in blood.

It would be written in truth.

He gripped the edges of the desk, the rough surface splintered beneath his palms. There would be no pomp. No gilded lectern. The chamber was stripped of all illusions, the ruined palace a monument to what had fallen. Even the air felt stale, thick with the bitter scent of ash and smoke.

But it was not the palace that mattered. It was the world that waited beyond it.

The technician gave a nod. The broadcast had begun.

To all the peoples of the former British Empire,

My name is Edward, Duke of Canada. Today, I stand before you not as a ruler, not as a conqueror, but as a witness. I have seen the ashes of the Empire. I have walked through cities shattered by war. I have heard the cries of those who lived beneath the weight of a crown that claimed dominion not by consent, but by force.

My father believed the Empire could endure forever. He believed that banners and battalions could hold together a world unwilling to be ruled. He was wrong.

The Empire has fallen.

King Charles is dead. The throne he clung to, the armies that fought in his name, the fleets that once darkened your shores, they are gone. There will be no restoration. No return to the old order. And yet I know that the end of the Empire does not erase the wounds it inflicted. The legacy of authoritarian rule is not only measured in the ruins left behind, but in the lives forever altered by its reach.

I will not ask you to forget that. I will not ask you to forgive it.

But I will ask you to decide what comes next.

Today, I accept the title of King. Not as a claim to power, but as a solemn responsibility. I do not stand before you to wield authority. I stand to relinquish it.

The right of self-determination now belongs to you. Every nation, every territory, every community that once stood beneath the Empire's banner will have the right to choose its own future. No foreign power will dictate your path. No monarch will hold sway over your decisions. The will of the people will be the only law that remains.

To that end, I call upon the people of each land to form councils of their own choosing. Let them be composed not of nobles, nor those who once claimed titles by birthright, but of those who have known the true weight of the Empire's rule. Teachers. Healers. Workers. Elders. The people who built your communities and endured their hardships will now decide how to govern them.

Their choices will stand. There will be no army sent to enforce the will of a distant throne. The soldiers who once fought under the Union Jack will not return as conquerors. They will return to rebuild what was destroyed.

To ensure this transition is carried out freely and without fear, peacekeepers from India, Pakistan, China, the American states, Canada, and France will stand as guardians. They come not to impose their rule, but to ensure that no tyrant rises from the ashes. These nations, once divided by the politics of Empire, now stand united in the pursuit of lasting peace. I will not allow one Empire to be replaced by another.

But I must speak directly to Russia. The world has witnessed your conquest of Germany, a betrayal that defied the very principles of justice and sovereignty that so many have fought to reclaim. The occupation of Germany must not stand. The German people, like all others, have the right to govern themselves. I call upon Russia to withdraw its forces and return Germany to its own people. Let them determine their future free from the shadow of foreign armies.

This is not the first time Russia has acted without honor. Throughout this war, Russia has been an unreliable actor, not a defender of peace, but an opportunist. While nations fought to liberate themselves from the grip of Empire, Russia waited, seeking the perfect moment to strike. They aided the

British Empire when it suited their ambitions, then turned on their so-called allies the moment they sensed weakness. And now, with Germany on its knees, Russia's true intent is laid bare.

The people of Germany did not ask for Russian salvation. They are not pawns to be claimed by the victor. The justifications Russia offers ring hollow. This is not a war for protection. It is a war for expansion. But the world has changed. The age of conquest, of nations seizing land by force and claiming dominion without consent, has come to an end. The people of every nation will decide their own fate, and Germany is no exception.

Russia now stands at a crossroads. The world is watching. Every nation that has fought to free itself from the chains of imperialism now looks upon them with distrust. Even those who once called Russia an ally question what loyalty means to them. The promises they made were as fragile as the treaties they broke. And while the weapons may grow silent, the memory of their betrayal will remain. Trust cannot be reclaimed with words alone.

But there is still a choice. Russia can abandon the path of conquest. They can withdraw their forces and allow the people of Germany to determine their future. It is not too late to prove that Russia can stand with the world, not against it. They can choose diplomacy over domination, cooperation over control.

If they refuse, they will find themselves isolated. The world will not stand idle. No empire will rise in the shadow of another. The people of Germany will not be forgotten, and the nations that have fought for their freedom will not turn away. Russia's claim will not stand unchallenged.

The path forward is clear. Return Germany to its people. Let their voices guide their future. The right of self-determination is not a favor to be granted, it is a right that no nation may deny.

Russia must decide. And the world will remember what choice they make.

Now I turn to those who have already claimed their freedom, your independence is yours. It will not be challenged. India and Pakistan stand as living proof that the bonds of imperial rule can be broken. They have reclaimed their sovereignty not only through struggle, but through unity. And though the wounds of the past remain, their leaders stand together, a testament to what can be built when old divisions are cast aside.

To the people of Africa, the Pacific, and the Americas, the Empire's hand has withdrawn. The choice is yours. Whether you stand as republics, unite in alliances, or forge entirely new paths, no monarch will stand in your way. There will be no crown demanding your fealty. There will be no distant parliament governing your lives.

And to the people of England, the fate of this nation is yours to determine. If you choose to cast aside the monarchy, I will not stand in your way. If you seek a republic, it will be your right. The titles and crowns that weighed so heavily on generations before you are no longer chains. They are relics. Symbols without power.

As for me, I make this promise, I will serve only as long as I am needed. The title of King means nothing if it is not willingly accepted. I will not remain a day longer than required to ensure the transition is complete. And when the world no longer needs a bridge between the old and the new, I will step aside.

I grieve for those we have lost. I grieve for Vihaan Chadra, whose name will forever be written among those who dared to stand against tyranny. I grieve for the innocent who died, not for crowns or banners, but because they stood in the path of ambition. No words can bring them back. But what we build now, the peace we forge, the justice we pursue, will be their legacy.

The Empire is gone.

But what comes next is yours to decide.

Choose wisely.

CHAPTER FORTY-SIX

The Kremlin, Russian Federation —Winter 2053

THE AIR IN THE KREMLIN'S war room was thick with the heat of old machinery and the stale breath of too many anxious men. Flickering light from the massive screen cast long shadows across the walls. On it, the Duke of Canada's voice echoed through the chamber. His words were clear and unyielding.

"The occupation of Germany must not stand," the Duke declared. "The German people, like all others, have the right to govern themselves."

The broadcast showed the Duke standing tall, bearing the crown reluctantly but with resolve. His condemnation of Russia was not tempered by diplomacy. Every word had been deliberate, sharpened to cut.

And beside him, Alexandra Baker, her red hair tied neatly in a bun.

She said nothing, but her presence alone spoke volumes. The slight tilt of her chin, the unwavering gaze, it all radiated the assured confidence of victory. She was no mere political figure. She was the voice of the rebellion, the woman whose words had ignited movements across continents. Even without speaking, she commanded the world's attention.

And behind her stood Andrew Greg. The man who had torn apart the Empire's armies, piece by piece. While Baker shaped the world's perception, Greg reshaped its battlefield. Together, the three of them projected the image of a new order. One that had no place for Russia's ambitions.

The screen went dark. The silence that followed was deafening.

President Boris Aslanov stood motionless, hands clasped tightly behind his back. The hollow echo of the Duke's final words still clung to the air. His pale eyes remained fixed on the empty screen as if daring it to flicker to life once more.

"He dares," Aslanov said at last. His voice was low, unhurried. The calm that came before a storm. "A pretender to a ruined throne, making demands of Russia."

The advisors surrounding him shifted uneasily. The war room, once a place of swift decisions and calculated strikes, now felt more like a tomb. The Russians had taken heavy losses to defend the Empire's last grasp of power in hopes of strategic advantage. Now, they had to salvage what was left of their conquest and convince themselves it was some form of victory—pyrrhic at best—self-delusion more likely.

"His words will carry weight," General Mikhailov said, the lines on his face deepened by the long months of conflict. "The world is watching. Germany's occupation was justified by our alliance with the Empire, but now that the Empire is gone..."

"Now we are the last villain standing," Aslanov interrupted, his lips curling in bitter amusement. "Let them watch."

A wiry advisor cleared his throat, adjusting his thin glasses. "Mr. President, the calls for sanctions are growing. France has already convened an emergency council. The Americans are emboldened. Even our allies in the East are distancing themselves. If we don't respond..."

"We will respond." Aslanov's voice cut through the tension, cold and precise. "But not with apologies."

No one dared to object.

"They believe that the Duke's words will turn the world against us," Aslanov continued. "But Russia has endured far worse than condemnation. The Germans have forgotten who broke their armies. The others—this disjointed alliance—believe our restraint is weakness. They underestimate what it means to challenge us."

General Mikhailov shifted. "The occupation cannot last forever. We cannot rebuild while constantly suppressing rebellion. The small insurgencies are already bleeding us. Something larger would be unmanageable."

"They will bleed more," Aslanov replied, his voice unwavering. "We will outlast them. And when the world grows tired of its righteous fury, Russia will remain, as it always has."

The men nodded, but the acceptance was hollow. They understood the cost of the President's resolve. Germany's streets burned with resistance. The occupation drained Russia's already stretched forces. Yet none dared suggest retreat.

There was one in the room who had not spoken.

The man known only as Yuri stood apart, a shadow against the wall. Unlike the generals and ministers, he wore no uniform. He bore no medals or ceremonial ribbons. Dark civilian clothes clung to him like a second skin, his presence carefully unassuming. And yet, for all his stillness, the weight of his presence unsettled the room.

He had not spoken. He never needed to.

But Aslanov knew he was there. He always did.

"You've been watching, I assume?" Aslanov finally said, turning just slightly in Yuri's direction. There was no warmth in his voice, no hint of pleasantries. Only the slow, deliberate cadence of a man laying the foundation of something inevitable.

Yuri's dark eyes met the President's, unreadable.

"The Duke," Aslanov continued, looking back to his generals. "He grows bold, believing their war is over."

The tension thickened. No one else dared speak. They all knew what Yuri was. What it meant when Aslanov spoke like this.

"The Duke... he thinks himself a peacemaker with his damned American friends. A king without a real kingdom. Yet kings who stand without real armies rarely stand for long."

There was no need for further elaboration. No command. No declaration. Only the weight of Aslanov's gaze, and the certainty that Yuri understood.

One life. One carefully timed act. And the illusion of peace would shatter.

"You are dismissed," Aslanov said to the room, glancing back at Yuri. "We will speak again when the world has had time to react."

The advisors rose swiftly, bowing their heads before slipping through the heavy wooden doors. Only Yuri lingered, the shadows clinging to him as if unwilling to release him.

Aslanov's voice dropped to a near whisper. "Ensure the world sees. Let them know who still holds the power."

Yuri gave the faintest nod.

And then, without another word, he turned and left. The door closed with a quiet, deliberate thud. Aslanov remained alone, his hands still clasped behind his back. The flickering light of the blank screen reflected faintly in his eyes. The world believed it had seen the end of war. Russia would remind them otherwise.

CHAPTER FORTY-SEVEN

Toronto, Independent Canada —Early 2054

THE GREAT HALL OF CANADA'S newly convened parliament bore little resemblance to the gilded chambers Edward had once known. There were no velvet thrones, no towering banners emblazoned with the emblems of a fractured Empire. Instead, sunlight streamed through tall windows framed by simple oak, illuminating rows of parliamentarians seated in a semicircle. The architecture was intentionally modest, dignified, but without the grandiosity that had so often masked the sins of the past. The air smelled of freshly polished wood and coffee, a far cry from the bergamot tea of the Imperial courts.

Edward stood at the head of the chamber. The room was heavy with expectation. Behind him, a plain wooden podium awaited, bearing no royal seal, only the maple leaf that now served as the nation's defining emblem. There was something striking in its simplicity, a deliberate rejection of excess. The grandeur of Empire was gone. In its place stood something unassuming, but determined.

The path that led him here had been neither swift nor certain. In the weeks since his father's death, the world had reshaped itself with astonishing speed. Territories that once bowed to the Empire had seized their own futures. The declarations of self-governance came in rapid waves, from Delhi to Lagos, from Buenos Aires to Sydney. Each with its own vision, its own promise of freedom. Leaders emerged from the shadows of occupation, their voices no longer tempered by fear. Streets once lined with Imperial flags were now filled with banners of liberation. Some movements were jubilant, others uncertain. But the march of self-determination was unstoppable.

And yet, even as the Empire's remnants crumbled, Canada had chosen something different. They had not severed every tie. They had summoned Edward. Not as a king to claim dominion, but as a man to answer their questions.

The Canadian parliament's decision to retain the monarchy, even in this radically altered form, had stirred debate across the world. Many questioned why the symbolic weight of a crown should linger when so many others had cast theirs aside. But for Canada, and for the people of England and Wales who had aligned themselves with this fledgling government, the answer was not so easily defined.

It was not nostalgia, nor reverence for royal blood. It was something far more practical. Stability. Continuity. A recognition that in the vacuum left by the Empire's collapse, the world was watching. To have a monarch without unchecked authority, one beholden to the will of the people, was a compromise that, for now, felt necessary.

Edward understood this. He had not wished for the throne, and certainly not in this form. But the people did not ask him to rule. They asked him to stand.

He shifted his weight, his hands clasped behind his back. He was dressed simply, in a black suit that bore no trace of embellishment. The crown, what remained of it, had been left behind. Even the title King seemed more like an echo than a truth. For now, he was Edward. No longer merely the Duke of Canada. No longer the son of a tyrant.

The Speaker of the Parliament, an older man with stooped shoulders and a face worn by years of service, stepped forward. His voice, though calm, carried the unmistakable weight of history.

"Your Majesty." The title was spoken with formality, though it carried none of the trembling reverence Edward had once known. It was an acknowledgment, nothing more. "You stand before this body not as a ruler by divine right, but as a custodian of trust. Today, we ask you to acknowledge the terms set forth by the elected representatives of Canada, Wales, and England. Do you understand the gravity of this moment?"

"I do," Edward replied, his voice steady.

He could feel the scrutiny of the parliamentary body before him. Some watched him with curiosity, others with skepticism. There were those who had openly opposed the decision to retain the monarchy, and others who had reluctantly conceded that a symbolic figurehead might prevent further chaos. Whatever their stance, none of them regarded Edward as infallible. That, at least, was a relief.

The Speaker's hands rested lightly on the oak podium. "The monarchy will not be restored as it was," he continued. "There will be no more claims of divine right. No heritable titles passed from father to son. You will serve at the will of the people, and the will of this parliament."

Edward gave a slight nod. He had read these words a dozen times before. He had rehearsed the proper responses, felt their weight settle into his bones. Still, hearing them aloud was different.

"The monarchy is now a conditional office," the Speaker went on. "You shall hold your position only so long as this parliament deems you worthy. It is not a crown of conquest, nor of right. It is a title of service. Should you fail that service, this body reserves the right to revoke your authority and appoint a successor of its choosing."

The words left no room for misinterpretation. The authority that had once been absolute was now fragile, deliberately so. There would be no royal decrees, no unchecked dominion. Whatever power Edward held would exist only by the people's consent.

"We understand that this is a departure from the traditions of the past," the Speaker said, his gaze steady. "But it is also a recognition of what was lost. The Empire ruled through force and fear. This parliament will not. We ask for your consent to these terms as a citizen among us entrusted with responsibility."

The chamber was silent. Edward could feel the weight of their expectation. He thought of the scorched ruins of Bombay, the shattered remains of New York, the bloodstained halls of Nashik. He thought of Vihaan, who had died believing in a world where no ruler held unchecked power. And he thought of Alex, whose voice had carried the rebellion's truth to the world.

There had been too many crowns. Too many kings.

"I accept," Edward said, finally. His voice was firm, but there was no triumph in it. "I stand before you not as the heir to my father's throne, but as a man who understands the cost of his failures. The people of this nation will decide my worth. And should the day come when I am no longer fit to serve, I will step aside without protest."

A few parliamentarians nodded. Others remained still, their judgments reserved. Edward could not blame them. Trust was not given; it was earned.

The Speaker gave a brief nod. "Then it is done."

A clerk approached with the formal agreement, its unadorned parchment a deliberate contrast to the Empire's once-glorious decrees. The words it bore were simple, but irreversible. Edward lowered the pen, the ink dark and resolute against the page. His name, once a symbol of inherited power, was now a mark of obligation.

When he lifted his gaze, the Speaker's voice rang clear.

"By the will of this parliament and with the consent of Edward, Duke of Canada, the office of the monarchy is reconstituted. It shall serve the people, not rule them."

There was no applause. This was not a coronation. It was a contract.

Edward inclined his head. He did not bow. The act would have felt hollow. Instead, he stood before the parliament as their servant, not their sovereign.

"Long may the people reign," the Speaker said.

The words echoed through the chamber. For the first time in his life, Edward believed them.

The storm had rolled in swiftly, thick clouds swallowing the last remnants of daylight. Rain lashed against the balcony railings, streaking down the stone facade of the old government building. Beyond the terrace, the city flickered with uneven lights, the wet streets below empty except for the occasional sweep of a security patrol. The distant hum of engines was muffled beneath the constant rumble of thunder.

Edward stood just inside the open balcony doors, the heavy curtains swaying in the breeze that carried the damp scent of rain. The dimly lit chamber behind him seemed smaller now, the shadows clinging to the walls like something alive. He had left the fire unlit, unwilling to bring warmth into a room that mirrored his own cold thoughts.

The storm fit the mood.

A single glass of whiskey rested on the small table beside him, untouched. He had poured it more out of habit than want. The amber liquid caught the faint light from the city, but it no longer held the same comfort it once had. Edward traced the rim with his fingers, lost in the rhythm of the rain.

The crown weighed heavily on him, though not in the way his father had described. There was no gilded grandeur here, no applause or reverent bows. The crown that Edward wore now was intangible, a burden of expectations and uncertain allegiances. He had agreed to the terms of parliament, vowed to serve rather than rule, but the weight remained.

From the balcony, the dark skyline of Ottawa seemed swallowed by mist. The Parliament building loomed in the distance, its faint silhouette barely visible through the downpour. This was his capital now. Not London, or New York, or Bombay. Not the sprawling courts of the Empire. Here, the halls of power were lined not with marble but with the memories of those who had fought to tear down the world his father had built.

But the world still had its ghosts. And Edward knew better than to think the war had ended.

He had felt it in the eyes of the parliamentarians. Even as they declared him king, their trust was conditional, a delicate truce. They did not see a monarch. They saw a temporary fixture, a relic given one final use before being discarded. And beyond Canada's borders, the eyes of the world watched. Some with curiosity. Others with suspicion.

And then there was Russia.

Edward exhaled slowly, his breath mingling with the chill air that drifted through the open doors. Aslanov's silence since the Duke's condemnation lingered like a threat unspoken. The occupation of Germany remained. The atrocities persisted. While the rest of the world turned toward rebuilding, Russia held its ground, daring anyone to challenge its claim.

The Duke's words during his address had been clear, a demand for the Russian withdrawal, a call for justice. And though Edward had not named himself a ruler of nations, his voice now carried weight. The question was how long it would be before Aslanov answered.

Lightning flashed across the sky, illuminating the city for a heartbeat. Edward's reflection flickered in the rain-streaked glass. His own face startled him. The weariness that had taken root in his eyes was no longer easy to ignore. He ran a hand through his damp hair, the strands clinging to his forehead.

A knock echoed from the far side of the chamber. He didn't turn. The guards had their orders, no interruptions unless necessary.

"Enter," he called, his voice low.

The door creaked open, and the sound of rain shifted as the wind stirred through the room. A young aide stepped inside, his uniform damp from the storm. He carried a pad, clutching it close to protect the contents.

"Your Majesty," the aide began, bowing slightly. "A dispatch from the foreign office. Updates on the latest security assessments."

Edward nodded but did not move from his place. The aide hesitated, then carefully set the glowing tablet on the desk. The dim light cast uneasy shadows across the edges. The man lingered for a moment, waiting perhaps for acknowledgment, but Edward offered none. He only returned his gaze to the storm.

The door closed softly behind the aide's departure.

The room was silent once more. Only the rain remained, its relentless drumming against the balcony rail echoing in Edward's thoughts. He knew the contents of the note without needing to read it. Russia's movements. Rumors of insurgencies in the German countryside. The tightening of Moscow's grip. The pattern was clear.

But it wasn't just the external threats that gnawed at him.

There were whispers. Not loud, not overt. Just murmurs at the edges of conversations. Men who spoke of unfinished business. Loyalists who still clung to the belief that the Empire could be reborn. And perhaps most unsettling, those who saw Edward's crown as a liability. A symbol that needed to be erased.

He had no illusions. The rebellion may have won the war, but the shadows remained. Even now, with the storm veiling the city, the unease gnawed at him. How many men like Yuri still moved in silence? How many had been given orders that no longer aligned with their fallen king? There were no certainties. Only the quiet understanding that power, once seized, was rarely abandoned without violence.

Edward's hand brushed against the edge of the whiskey glass. He considered it once more but left it untouched.

Outside, the storm rolled on. The wind tugged at the curtains, and the distant boom of thunder rattled the glass panes. He stepped closer to the balcony, the cool rain misting his face. There was no movement below. The guards remained in their posts, their silhouettes barely visible against the darkness.

He searched the shadows for something, a flicker of motion, a glint of steel. But there was nothing. Only the empty streets and the ceaseless rain. And yet, the feeling remained.

A presence. Not seen. Not heard. But felt.

Edward lingered a moment longer, the tension unbroken. He exhaled, the cold air filling his lungs. Then, with a deliberate motion, he reached for the balcony doors. The hinges creaked softly as he pulled them shut, sealing out the storm.

But the weight in his chest did not lift.

The lightning flashed again, illuminating the chamber for the briefest instant. And though Edward saw nothing but the reflection of his own face, the shadows behind him seemed somehow darker than before. He did not turn.

Chapter Forty-Eight

New York, New York —Early Spring 2054

THE AIR IN NEW YORK was heavy with the mingled scents of rain-slicked pavement and distant smoke. Though the city still bore the scars of war, shattered glass in forgotten alleys, the husks of burned-out vehicles lining the edges of the harbor, life had returned. Slowly, defiantly, the people of the city reclaimed what had been taken. Neon signs flickered once more. The hum of generators echoed down narrow streets. Laughter spilled from crowded bars and cafes.

At the *Hop and Pig*, the celebration had begun long before the first round of drinks was poured. The rebel stronghold had become a gathering place in the days since the ceasefire, its rough wooden tables cluttered with empty bottles and cigarette ash. A tattered Empire flag hung from the ceiling, its edges scorched and curling, not as a symbol of loyalty, but as a trophy. Someone had scrawled "Long Live the Rebellion" across it in red paint.

At the center of it all, Alexandra Baker and Andrew Greg sat side by side. The long months of war had etched lines into their faces, but the weight they carried had eased, if only for the night. Greg leaned back in his chair, his arm draped lazily over the backrest, while Alex nursed a glass of whiskey, her dark eyes gleaming beneath the low glow of the bar lights.

Across from them, Vinny Carcione lit a cigar, the smoke curling in lazy spirals above his head. He wore his victory like a second skin, the tension that had once hardened his features now softened by the warmth of celebration. Next to him, Bear tipped back a bottle of dark beer, the ever-present shadow of past battles dimming as laughter shook his broad frame. Bo, the enigmatic elder of the group, sat quietly at the edge of the table, the corners of his mouth twitching in amusement as the others swapped stories.

"Here's to the end of it," Vinny declared, raising his glass high. "To us. To the ones who made it."

"And the ones who didn't," Bear added, his voice low but resolute. The table fell silent for a moment, the weight of absent friends pressing down.

"To Vihaan," Alex said, her voice steady.

They echoed her, the name lingering in the air like a prayer. Vihaan had become a symbol, not just of victory, but of the cost it demanded. His face had been painted on walls across the city, alongside slogans of freedom. And though he was gone, his presence remained. Alex could feel it, even now.

The moment passed, and the hum of conversation returned.

Greg glanced over, and for once, the steel in his expression softened. "I told you we'd make it here."

Alex gave a half-smile. "We're not done yet."

"Maybe not." He paused. "But I'm not waiting forever."

"You know," Vinny said, a mischievous glint in his eyes, "I wasn't so sure about you two at first."

Greg arched a brow. "That so?"

"Oh yeah. First time I saw you, Greg, you looked like you hadn't slept in a month. And Alex, you had that whole 'I'll rip your throat out if you say the wrong thing' vibe. Charming, really."

Alex smirked, taking a slow sip of her drink. "And yet, here we are."

"Here we are," Vinny echoed. He leaned forward, jabbing the air with his cigar. "But don't think for a second I didn't notice how you two look at each other."

Greg shifted, clearing his throat. "We've been through a lot."

"Yeah, yeah," Vinny waved a hand. "Just saying. When you've spent as much time around people who lie for a living, you get pretty good at spotting the truth."

"Vinny's just mad he didn't get to spend more time with Alex," Bear rumbled, his grin wide.

Greg rolled his eyes, but Alex only smiled, the warmth of their friends' teasing filling the room. For all the pain they'd endured, moments like this reminded her why they had fought, for laughter, for friendship, for nights that didn't end in gunfire.

At the far end of the table, John shifted his chair closer. The man's face was still marred by a healing scar across his temple, but the gleam in his eyes showed no regret.

"So, what's next?" John asked, the question heavy with curiosity. "The Empire's done. The King's dead. The Duke's playing figurehead in Canada. But what about here? What about us?"

Alex's smile faded as the reality of the question settled over the table.

"The fighting's over," Greg said carefully. "But the rebuilding? That's only just begun."

"And it won't be easy," Alex added. "The scars aren't just in the streets. People still remember what it was like to live under the Empire's thumb. The fear doesn't vanish overnight."

Bo, who had remained quiet until now, spoke with the slow, deliberate cadence that always commanded attention. "But fear can be replaced. Not by another ruler. Not by a flag. But by choice."

Alex nodded. "We fought to give people that choice. To decide what comes next."

Greg's hand brushed lightly against Alex's as he shifted in his seat. Neither of them pulled away. The tension that had once stood between them had softened.

"We'll be in Philadelphia soon," Greg added, his voice steady. "The states are sending delegates. Every temporary leader, every community council, they'll all have a voice."

"They're going to try and make something lasting," Alex said. "The Canadians might have their system, but here? It's different. We have no idea what to do. The people, all of us, will decide."

Bear grunted, rubbing his chin. "You think they'll go for it? After everything?"

"Some won't," Greg admitted. "But most will. They don't want a power vacuum. People want stability. They want to know they're not just trading one master for another."

John nodded. "And you two? You're heading there to... what? Advise?"

"To help," Alex corrected. "To make sure the right voices are heard. The people who fought. The ones who lost everything. They're the ones who should decide."

Vinny raised his glass again, the edge of his grin returning. "To Philadelphia. And to you two."

"To Philadelphia," the others echoed, their glasses clinking together.

The celebration continued, but in the back of her mind, Alex knew the road ahead would be anything but easy. The war was over, but the future, the one they had fought so hard to make possible, was still unwritten.

Philadelphia, Pennsylvania —Spring 2054

The heavy oak doors of the Pennsylvania Government House stood open, letting in a sharp breath of spring air that carried the scent of wet brick and magnolia. Outside, Philadelphia hummed — not with celebration, but with the cautious energy of a nation trying to shape itself from the fragments of war. Inside, the grand chamber swelled with fatigue and friction. It had been weeks since the first delegates arrived. They were farmers, soldiers, philosophers, engineers, old governors, and upstart rebels — some barely out of their teens, others white-haired and wearied by revolution. Their flags hung unevenly across the gallery, many stitched by hand or scrawled on canvas.

Three factions had emerged.

The first, led by a contingent from New England and the upper Midwest, had pushed for full alignment with Canada. They argued that Edward, the Duke of Vancouver, had already proven his restraint and commitment to peace. He could be a stabilizing symbol. Let the states join the new Commonwealth, they said. Let Edward be crowned king — not of an Empire, but of something quieter, steadier. This group was orderly, pragmatic, suspicious of idealism.

The second rallied around Andrew Greg. He was a veteran, a strategist, a man forged in fire. His supporters argued that the new world required strength — not monarchy, not symbolism, but leadership from someone who had actually won the war. Greg had held the rebel coalition together when everything else threatened to break. But critics warned he lacked the finesse needed for diplomacy. As the weeks dragged on, his temper showed and in his impatience he lost some allies. His instincts, well suited for war, might falter in peace, they worried.

And then there was the third faction. Looser. Louder. More desperate in its unity. They didn't want a lifelong career warrior or a foreign crown. They wanted Alexandra Baker.

Her supporters were mostly volunteer soldiers, southern organizers, and citizen-delegates from the cities and they pointed to her ability to speak to common people, to make sense of chaos without retreating into cold rhetoric. She had stood in the fire and survived. But opponents raised a fair objection: she had never governed. Never brokered policy. Never faced down a chamber like this one. Was she ready for what came next? Over the weeks of debates, she had become a peacemaker among the factions. She listened and carried messages between disparate groups and the very large personalities that lead them. Initially, she had not been a contender for power at all and had been working to lobby for her husband. But the more the delegates got to know her, the more they came to a different conclusion.

Now, in the late afternoon light, all arguments had been exhausted. Rain had come and gone. Datapads and reams worth of paper scattered in the conference rooms where impassioned debates and quiet meetings had dominated until just hours ago. Parliamentarians rubbed sleep from their eyes and whispered their last misgivings.

Alex stood near the rear of the hall, tucked in shadow, her arms crossed. She didn't speak. She hadn't spoken during the final day of debate. Not even to Greg, who stood nearby, silent and watchful. They had not strategized that day. They had simply endured. It was agreed that the votes would be secret until tallied and read.

Evelyn Ward stepped forward, her gavel in hand, her voice measured and clear.

"We have reached the final vote," she said, the words rolling through the hall like thunder beneath a calm sky. "After weeks of deliberation, the structure has been chosen. A constitutional monarchy: conditional, restrained, and answerable to parliament. Modeled loosely after the Canadian solution, but subject to our own values and customs. A monarch may serve, not rule, and only so long as the parliament maintains its confidence."

There was no applause. Just silence, tight and expectant.

"This model was not adopted in the abstract," Evelyn continued, her eyes scanning the room. "It was adopted because no alternative garnered enough trust. The executive council fractured. The federal assembly plan collapsed under infighting. A republic with rotating leadership was voted down. We chose this, not because it was perfect, but because one name made it viable."

Greg turned to Alex, his brow furrowed. His expression said everything: *They're doing it.*

"Three names were considered," Evelyn said. "Edward of Vancouver. Andrew Greg. And Alexandra Baker."

There was a ripple in the room. Greg shifted, looking down. Alex inhaled slowly, her shoulders tense. She had asked for none of this.

"Edward," Evelyn said, "is already king to those who wish to remain in the Commonwealth. That door is open to them. It is not ours to walk through."

A few delegates clapped, polite, not celebratory.

"Andrew Greg," she continued, "has earned this nation's respect. His leadership is beyond question. But his own supporters have conceded he is a soldier first, and peace must now belong to civilians."

Greg didn't flinch. He gave no signal of approval or disappointment.

"And so," Evelyn said, her voice quieting, "we are left with the one figure who has transcended faction, if not criticism. Alexandra Baker."

There was no swell of applause. No thunder of consensus. But there was a stillness. A held breath. The sense of something inevitable crossing a line.

"She is not a politician. She is not a royal. She is a former reporter, an accomplished rebel battlefield commander in her own right. Importantly, she has earned the trust of the people who gave this country back to itself."

Alex stared at the floor awkwardly.

"She has been opposed," Evelyn added. "Some argue she lacks experience. That charisma is not governance. That symbolism is not structure. But in this chamber, in these weeks, no other name has crossed the aisle. No other name has turned skepticism into consensus."

Evelyn turned toward her. "Miss Baker. Do you accept this position, granted not by inheritance, but by the will of a people who believe in your voice?"

The room exhaled.

Greg's fingers brushed hers, gently. "You don't have to," he whispered.

Alex looked up. Slowly, deliberately, she stepped forward. Her boots echoed against the old floor. She passed the delegation from Texas. From New York. From the broken Gulf coast. All of them watching.

At the podium, she rested her hands on the worn wood. She didn't blink. Didn't look back.

"I never wanted this," she said, her voice level stripped bare. "Not the title. Not the power. I fought because the world we had was wrong."

She looked up, meeting the eyes of the doubters first.

"I am not a queen. I am not your ruler. I am not your savior. I am simply willing to hold this title so long as it means protecting what we've earned."

Her voice cracked slightly. But she pushed on.

"I accept this role. Not as a prize. But as a burden. And I swear I will lay it down the moment it serves itself instead of you."

Silence. And then, the faintest murmur of approval.

Evelyn stepped forward, lifting the plain circlet of steel that had been forged from a melted Imperial sword. She placed it lightly upon Alex's brow.

"In the name of the assembly and the free people of these United States, we recognize Alexandra Baker as the first Queen, servant and sentinel, of this new nation."

And this time, the applause did come. Not thunderous. Not joyful. But relieved. Grateful. Earned.

Greg watched her, his jaw tight with something like grief.

"Your Majesty," he said quietly. Alex rolled her eyes. And with that, it was done.

The clouds parted just before noon, letting sunlight spill across the city like a benediction. Rainwater steamed off cobblestones and rooftops, casting faint ribbons of mist into the warm spring air. Down on the square, the crowd pressed shoulder to shoulder. They had come not to cheer a coronation, but to witness a turning point. A compromise made flesh. A rebel made queen.

Greg stood with Bear, Vinny, and John near the edge of the platform—half honor guard, half silent warning. Though the speeches were over, the risk was not. The war might be over, but the danger never left. Not for her.

"She's late," Bear muttered.

"She's thinking," Greg said. "Wouldn't you be?"

He scanned the rooftops again, fingers tight around the comms. Layers of security were in place, sharp-eyed and silent. But instinct still crawled at the back of his neck.

From the shadowed hall behind them, the tall double doors creaked open.

And then she stepped out.

Alex wore a crisp white dress—not regal, not ceremonial, just a tailored dress simple enough to be worn again. A dark blue sash crossed her chest, the only nod to state. Her crown—steel and unadorned—rested light on her brow. The weight came from elsewhere.

She moved down the steps slowly, not grand but deliberate. Every camera turned. The crowd quieted, then surged in applause and relief. She nodded once to the mass of them—acknowledging their presence, not claiming it. Her face was solemn. Steady.

Greg's breath caught.

She reached the podium. Her hands braced the wood. For a moment, she just looked at them—this crowd of scarred survivors, of former subjects trying to remember how to be citizens again.

"I accepted this role today," she began, "not to rule—but to hold a place. A place no one else could hold without breaking what we've built."

Silence spread through the square, taut and reverent.

"I am not your monarch. I am not your destiny. I am only a voice who swore to never speak for you without consent, and a witness to what we suffered to reach this fragile peace."

Greg's hand twitched.

She looked out over the crowd, eyes scanning the faces, her voice still strong.

"I promise you this—"

And then, from somewhere beyond the rooftops, it came.

A sharp, singular crack.

Not the hollow echo from distant fireworks, but something more deliberate. More final.

A gunshot.

Alex's body jerked. Her hands released the podium as her legs buckled beneath her. The white of her dress bloomed red. She collapsed, crumpling against the stone steps, the force of the impact lost beneath the sudden, deafening screams.

Greg's world shattered.

"No!" His voice tore from his throat, but the word was drowned beneath the panic. He surged forward, his feet pounding against the pavement. Around him, chaos erupted. The crowd surged in every direction, some throwing themselves to the ground, others desperately pushing for cover. Security forces shouted orders, but the confusion swallowed them whole.

Bear was already moving, shoving past the crush of bodies. Vinny's gun was drawn, scanning the rooftops with the frantic desperation of a man too late. John's voice crackled over the comms, calling for medics, for guards, for anything that could undo what had just been done.

But Greg saw none of it. All he saw was Alex.

He reached her, dropping to his knees at her side. Blood pooled beneath her, staining the pale stone. Her chest rose and fell in shallow, labored gasps. Her eyes, wide and dark, searched the sky above as if trying to grasp the incomprehensible.

"Stay with me," Greg pleaded, his trembling hands pressing against the wound. The warmth of her blood seeped through his fingers. "Alex, stay with me."

She tried to speak, but the words came as only a faint whisper. Her lashes fluttered, the light in her eyes dimming.

Greg, she thought. *Don't let it break.*

Then she saw it—just for a moment. A torn banner fluttering in the wind. Her name, scrawled in bright red paint by a child's hand.

And the sun. Still shining.

"Help!" Greg's voice broke. "Somebody help!"

The medics were coming, their voices lost in the roar of sirens. But Greg knew. He saw it in the stillness creeping into her limbs, the awful, irrevocable stillness. The tears came, unchecked, as he cradled her against him.

High above, the cameras still hovered. The world was watching.

And far from the chaos, Yuri moved through the shadowed alleys, his rifle disassembled and stowed in a simple canvas bag. The panic that spread through the city served his purpose well. No one stopped him. No one saw him. He slipped through the crowds, his face unremarkable, his presence already forgotten.

There was no triumph in his step. No satisfaction. Only the cold certainty of a mission completed.

The Queen of the United States was dead.

And the world would never be the same.

CHAPTER FORTY-NINE

THE SKY OVER PHILADELPHIA HAD dimmed to a dull gray. Rain pattered against the slate rooftops, dripping in slow, steady rivulets down the stone facades. The streets, once so alive with celebration, were subdued. Banners still clung to broken lampposts, their edges fraying in the damp air. Wilted flowers lay in heaps where mourners had gathered, their petals darkened by the weather. A city that had been ready to embrace its future now stood in the heavy shadow of its loss.

The Queen was dead.

In the days that followed Alexandra's assassination, the nation's grief became a low and steady hum. Candlelit vigils lined the streets of New York, Chicago, and Atlanta. Crowds gathered in silence, faces etched with the weight of disbelief. Photographs of Alex, smiling, fierce, unrelenting, were plastered to walls and shop windows, their edges curling in the rain. Her name echoed through the airwaves, not as a fallen monarch, but as a symbol of what could have been.

In the halls of government, the void she left was suffocating. There were no precedents for this. No protocol to follow. The monarchy had barely begun, and now it was gone. There was no heir, no line of succession. Only questions, whispered in anxious tones.

In the echoing quiet of the government house, days after the assassination, advisors approached Greg in hushed urgency.

"The nation needs leadership," one said. "*Your leadership*. They'll offer you the crown."

Greg didn't answer right away. He stood before a hastily hung portrait of Alex in the corridor, the paint still drying in places. She looked out with the same steady, unsparing gaze she'd worn on the battlefield. Not regal. Not sanctified. Just resolute.

He remembered her voice: 'I will lay it down the moment it serves itself instead of you.' The crown had been a duty. Never a desire. Never a prize.

Taking it now would make her sacrifice a footnote. A failed detour before another general took power. No.

He would not build his rule on her grave. He would build the republic she deserved.

It was Andrew Greg who answered.

He stood before a room of the most powerful figures in the nation—governors, generals, civic leaders—their expressions grim, their voices subdued. The Chamber of Assembly, recently a place of argument and fractured loyalties, now sat in tense, unified, anticipation. This moment had brought factions together in unexpected ways.

Greg's face was hollowed with grief. His dark hair, streaked with gray, clung to his temples. The bruises beneath his eyes spoke of sleepless nights, of pacing empty corridors and wrestling with what came next.

"There will be no crown," he said, his voice low but firm.

The words cut through the stillness like a blade. Some had expected reluctant acceptance. Others believed he would simply rise to the obvious duty. But not this. Not the man who had stood at Alex's side, who had fought through blood and fire to see her vision realized.

"She was never meant to rule alone," Greg continued, his hands gripping the edges of the podium. "And now she will not rule at all. The monarchy died with Alex."

No one spoke. The rain thrummed softly against the chamber windows. Outside, the muted wail of distant church bells drifted through the air.

"We called her Queen because we believed in her ability to unify us," Greg went on, his voice trembling. "Not because of the title. Not because we wanted another throne. She stood for something greater. The right of every man, woman, and child to choose their own future. That choice was hers. And it must remain ours."

He swallowed, voice thick. "Her acceptance was conditional. Her reign—tragically brief. Her death proves the inherent danger, the unbearable weight we place upon one person, one title. We cannot honor her by seeking a successor to that fragile crown. We honor her by building the republic she truly fought for—governed by the many, not the few."

He paused, his chest rising and falling with the weight of it.

"The question before us is not who shall rule. It is whether we will allow grief to break what Alex fought to build. Whether we will cling to the shadows of the past or step forward and face what comes next."

The faces in the chamber shifted, some lowering their gaze in contemplation. Others sat rigid, unwilling or unable to accept the finality of Greg's words. But none spoke.

"No. I will not stand before you as a monarch. *No one will.* There is no one worthy of that crown. Least of all a soldier who has known the power of command in war. That power has no place at the head of a free nation."

His voice cracked, but he pressed on. "Instead, I propose that we do what our ancestors did in their own time of uncertainty. We gather. We deliberate. And we build something new."

A murmur rippled through the chamber.

"This assembly shall be a constitutional convention," Greg said, the words settling over the room like the first heavy drops of a storm. "We delegates from each of our states will decide now. Not merely as leaders, but as servants of the people. We decide how we shall govern ourselves."

He paused, his gaze sweeping across the room. The assembled leaders and representatives, hardened by the trials of war and rebellion, shocked to grief by Alex's assassination sat in tense silence. Some wore the colors of their respective states, while others bore no insignia at all, only the weight of what had brought them here. All wore the black armbands of mourning. These were the survivors. The architects of victory. And now, the stewards of what remained.

Greg's voice grew steadier, rising with conviction. "But to do this, we must stop what has already begun. The divisions. The power grabs. The ambitions that threaten to unravel everything we fought for. I have heard the whispers—of governors considering declaring themselves sovereign rulers, of generals who see an opportunity to claim what was denied to them on the battlefield."

He shook his head. "This is not why we bled. Not why we burned the Empire to the ground. The promise of this rebellion was not merely to end a monarchy. It was to end the belief that a nation must be ruled by the whims of the few."

Greg's words struck like hammer blows. He saw the shifting discomfort on the faces before him. Some lowered their gazes. Others bristled. But he did not falter.

"Look to France," he continued. "A nation that broke its own chains not with the rise of a single ruler, but with the strength of its people. They cast aside the crown not to crown another, but to stand as citizens, equal in voice and in purpose."

He stepped forward, hands braced against the podium. The weight of Alex's absence was heavy in the air, but her memory seemed to steady him.

"We cannot let her death become a justification for tyranny. We cannot allow her name to be twisted into a banner for the very oppression she died fighting against. If we are to honor her, we must do so with the courage to stand for the principles she lived by."

Greg's gaze locked with each delegate in the front row, in turn. "I am calling on every leader in this room. Every governor, every commander, every councilman who believes they have earned the right to shape this nation's future. Lay down your claims. Step back from your ambitions. Seek no power as rulers, but as servants of the people."

A murmur rippled through the chamber. The tension was palpable. Greg saw the flashes of doubt, the stubborn refusal on some faces. But he also saw the spark—the glint of something long buried beneath fear and pride. The hope that maybe, just maybe, there was another way.

"This convention will be the beginning," Greg declared. "A gathering of voices from across the states. They will write the laws, shape the institutions, and elect a government that serves their needs."

He let the words settle, then delivered the final blow.

"We will elect a president."

The chamber erupted. Some delegates slammed their hands on the wooden tables, their protests drowning the air with overlapping voices. Others whispered fiercely among themselves, calculating the implications.

Greg held firm, waiting as the roar subsided.

"Do we cling to the ashes of what was? Or do we build something worthy of her memory?"

The words hung like a challenge.

Slowly, the murmurs faded. Some nodded, though uncertainty remained. Others crossed their arms, their expressions hardened. But the seed had been planted. The question lingered, demanding an answer.

Greg stepped back from the podium. He did not wait for applause. There would be none. This was not a victory speech. It was a reckoning.

As the room settled into restless quiet, Evelyn rose to her feet. The interim Speaker of the Assembly, her silver hair pulled tightly back, commanded the room with a simple glance. She rapped the gavel against the table, the sharp sound bringing order.

"We have heard the call," she said firmly. "Let it be known that this shall be a constitutional convention. And the future of these United States of America shall be forged here by the hands of these servants."

The words, though simple, marked the turning of an age.

But there was a path. And for now, that was enough.

Philadelphia's streets, still slick from the storm, gleamed under the pale morning light. Carriages rolled through the narrow avenues, their wheels splashing through shallow puddles. Crowds gathered in small knots along the sidewalks, some holding banners of remembrance, others watching in silent curiosity.

The hall, once chosen for Alex's coronation speech, now stood as the birthplace of something uncertain. Its stone pillars bore no banners. No crimson carpets lined the stairs. Only the pale façade, weathered and bare, awaited those who would decide the nation's fate.

Inside, rows of chairs filled the chamber, their polished wood gleaming beneath the soft glow of hanging lanterns. Nameplates marked the seats of the delegates, representatives from every corner of the fractured land. New York and California. Texas and Virginia. The Carolinas, now united in their mourning. Even the still-unstable Midwest had sent their voices, unwilling to be absent when history was made.

Greg stood near the entrance, his hand resting lightly against the worn marble frame. He had not slept. His thoughts lingered too often on the past. On Alex. On the promises they had made to one another.

He felt her absence like a phantom. The way she would have stood beside him, her steady presence keeping the fear at bay. The way her words would have filled this hall, fierce and unrelenting. She had been the voice that silenced doubts. Now, all that remained was the echo.

A hand touched his shoulder. Bear and Vinny stood at his side, his cigar gone but the ghost of it lingering on his jacket.

"It's time," he said simply.

Greg nodded.

One by one, the delegates entered, their footsteps muted against the stone floor. Some nodded to old allies. Others walked alone, faces set in quiet resolve. The chamber held no ceremony—only the weight of what they had come to do. No voices rose above a whisper. No eyes lingered on the empty seat where she would have sat.

Evelyn stepped to the front of the hall, her presence commanding despite the lines of exhaustion etched into her face. She raised her gavel, and the room stilled.

"We convene," she said, her voice steady. "For the purpose of forming the government."

Greg exhaled, his fingers curling tightly at his sides. He placed a firm hand on Bear's shoulder—a silent gesture of gratitude and resolve—then turned and walked out into the sunlight.

And so a new nation was truly born.

Epilogue

The Appalachian Mountains —Months Later

THE MOUNTAIN AIR WAS STILL. The last light of the day painted the ridgeline in muted gold, the distant hum of the wind threading through skeletal branches. From his cabin, Yuri could see the peaks folding into the horizon, their jagged silhouettes softened by the fading sun. The woods were quiet, save for the occasional rustle of unseen animals. It was a silence he had earned.

Inside the cabin, the fire burned low, casting flickering shadows against the bare wooden walls. The room was sparse, no photographs, no mementos, only the essentials. A narrow bed, a table worn from years of use, a single chair. Tools lined the walls, meticulously arranged. In the center of it all, Yuri sat, his hands steady, his focus absolute.

The block of wood in his grip had begun to take shape. A heron, wings outstretched, emerging from the grain. Each delicate feather was slowly coaxed from the fibers, his carving knife gliding with precision. He had been working on it for days, the process as much an act of discipline as it was creation. There was satisfaction in the slowness. The heron had always been within the wood; it was simply a matter of revealing it.

The old radio on the shelf crackled with distant static. Yuri never turned it off. He had heard the news. The chaos that followed the assassination. Protests in the streets. Governments teetering. And now, a constitutional convention in Philadelphia. The queen was dead, but her vision, her voice, had ignited something even the most calculated bullet could not extinguish.

Still, the world moved on. And so did he.

The rhythmic scrape of the knife filled the cabin, each motion deliberate. He did not dwell on the past. The mission had been completed. The target was gone. What came after was not his concern. He was a tool, one sharpened, used, and discarded when the job was done. That was the nature of his existence. He had no regrets.

But even the most honed blade dulled with time.

Yuri paused, the heron's eye now fully formed. He studied it carefully, his own reflection caught in the smooth curve of the polished wood. For a moment, something stirred, the faintest flicker of thought. Regret, perhaps. Or curiosity. Would her death change anything at all? Would the world remember Alexandra Baker, or would her ideals be swallowed by the same shadows that consumed all who dared to stand against power?

He set the carving aside. The questions didn't matter. He had done his part.

Yuri rose from the chair, his movements fluid despite the ache that lingered in his joints. Age had crept into his bones, but discipline kept it at bay. He poured water into the metal kettle, setting it on the stove. The evening routine, methodical, predictable, brought a certain comfort. The kind only a man like Yuri could understand.

But outside, the shadows had shifted.

He didn't notice at first. The distant mountains remained as they were, silent and unmoved. The woods still whispered with the wind. But beneath that soft hum, something else lingered. A presence. Subtle. Patient.

Yuri's eyes flicked to the window. The light had dimmed, the last traces of the sun slipping below the horizon. The trees stood like sentinels, unmoving. He scanned the darkness. Nothing.

Still, he knew.

He moved without hesitation. The kettle remained on the stove, forgotten. His hand slipped to the drawer beneath the table, where the weight of the cold metal pistol greeted him. The smoothness of it, the reassurance of readiness, steadied his breath. The world could crumble, the governments could rise and fall, but this, this was familiar.

The cabin door creaked open. The cool night air seeped inside, carrying with it the earthy scent of damp leaves. Yuri stepped onto the narrow porch, his gaze sweeping the tree line. The shadows pooled thickly beneath the pines, and the wind whispered as though conspiring.

And then he saw him.

Luciano.

He stood at the edge of the clearing, barely visible in the darkness. Dressed in black, he seemed a figure carved from the night itself. But the gleam of his eyes was unmistakable, a predator's gaze, sharp and unyielding.

Yuri did not raise his weapon.

There was no point.

"You should have just let it go," Yuri said, his voice low.

Luciano didn't answer. The silence between them was taut, stretching like a wire ready to snap. He took a slow step forward, the shadows shifting with him.

"I thought you would be smarter than this," Yuri continued. "It's over. The girl is dead. You can't change that."

Luciano's voice, when it came, was quiet, far quieter than the weight of his presence. "No. But I can finish what she started."

There was no more time.

Yuri moved, the pistol rising in one swift motion. But even as his finger curled around the trigger, he knew. Luciano was faster. The flash of steel. The sharp crack of suppressed gunfire. Pain bloomed in Yuri's chest, white-hot and absolute.

He staggered.

The pistol fell from his grasp, landing with a dull thud on the wooden planks. His breath came ragged, but no sound escaped his lips. Luciano advanced, his face impassive. There was no triumph. Only purpose.

Yuri's knees buckled. The world tilted. He collapsed to the ground, the scent of earth and pine mingling with the copper tang of blood.

Luciano knelt beside him. No words were exchanged. There was nothing left to say.

The assassin's hand lingered for a moment, as if confirming the finality of what had been done. Then, without ceremony, he stood.

The shadows welcomed him as he disappeared into the night.

And Yuri, the man who had lived without regret, was left alone beneath the darkened sky. The stars blinked faintly overhead, bearing witness. The wind carried no lament. Only the empty hum of a world that had already begun to forget him.

The heron, still perched upon the table inside, remained unfinished.